In Dangerous Paths.

CHAPTER I.

THE QUESTION ASKED.

"WHO is she?"

"Who is 'she'?" languidly replied the person addressed, a young man of fashion, who with several companions was standing up in the stalls to criticise the arrivals in the boxes.

It was a Nilsson night at Her Majesty's, and the theatre was rapidly filling.

"Why, of course that girl over there in the first tier box on your right," replied his companion, elevating a lorgnette that he might better bring to bear on the "new beauty" the fine connoisseurship of which he was so proud. "The face is new to me, and I thought I knew everyone in society."

"It is possible she is not 'in society,' dear boy."

"She looks an awful swell, and is really a beauty, 'pon my word; everyone is staring at her!"

So they were; but the scrutiny of "everyone" seemed to disconcert the young lady under discussion not at all.

She had just entered a box, and had dropped her rich mantle from her shoulders as she took a seat well in view of the house.

She was accompanied by a gentleman, who might probably be her father, and who exchanged nods with several men in the stalls.

NOTICE.—With this Number is Given Away a Coloured Picture for binding with the Work.

The young lady also bowed and gave a smile to some of these favoured ones; but a shrewd youth remarked that her acquaintance did not apparently extend beyond a circle of men.

"Mamma," whispered pretty Alise Mainwaring to her mother as the two ladies settled themselves in their box with much flutter of wraps and patting of gowns, "do you see those two over in the box nearly opposite? That exquisite girl, who can she be?"

Mamma put up her lorgnette.

"A beautiful creature," said she; "a face new to me; the gentleman also I do not know—some distinguished foreigner, perhaps. He looks rather foreign, and there is something not altogether English-looking about her."

"Oh, I must know," exclaimed Alise, who was an enthusiastic young lady, and also a curious one, and must know everything from A to Z. "Where is someone to tell me? Where is Devereux? He ought to be here."

She leant over the box, in order to scan the stalls, and turned her bright eyes in all directions in search of the missing Devereux, but apparently without success.

"My love," remonstrated mamma, "pray do not be seen staring at the stalls in that way; people will certainly say you are looking for Devereux."

"Which is exactly what I am doing, mamma," rejoined the young lady. "Tiresome fellow! why doesn't he come? Oh, there is the overture commencing, and there's no hope of getting him to speak while the music is going on, even if he were here. See, mamma, how many men we know are bowing to the beauty! How funny we never saw or heard of her before!"

"I don't know, my dear," returned Mrs. Mainwaring with a slight smile. "Do you suppose we are acquainted with everyone whom your cousins know?"

"Ah, now, mamma, you are censorious; that girl is in society, of our world, I am sure. One sees it directly."

Mrs. Mainwaring held her peace; she was not a censorious, or a very stiff British matron, but she had observed the limits of the girl's acquaintance, and that the only lady to whom she had bowed was a pretty little woman who was "in society," but generally called by her male friends, "Kate Cranleigh," her proper style and title being Lady Cranleigh.

It is not too much to say that the much-talked of occupant of the box won a good deal more attention from the audience than Nilsson that night; at any rate, during the first act of "Faust."

Those who did not know her wondered who she was, and seemed never weary of studying the soft lines of the face, the curve of the cheek, which rested on one slender shapely hand, the magnificent dark eyes which did not stray from their fixed yet dreamy look on to the stage.

Was it only the music that was claiming her attention, or the strange power of that story which never grows old, attracting all her thoughts?

Was she pondering over the problem of the "world well lost for love," or wondering in a vague way if some day a "Faust" might enter into her life?

No one below in the stalls could tell, of course, what were her thoughts, but they took note of every gesture or movement, and one remarked that "the *diva* was quite absorbed."

He seemed to know who she was.

"Oh, mamma," cried Alise, as soon as the curtain was down and the usual exodus between the acts set in, "there is Jack in the beauty's box, and she has given him her hand, and looks too, too charming! Oh, what would I not give to get an introduction."

"My dear Alise, how can you be so silly! you know absolutely nothing about her," said her mother with amused vexation. "Of course, if they are anyone we can know we are sure to meet them in society; perhaps after all, she is only an actress or a singer."

"Well, we could know her then, said Miss Alise stoutly; "we know a great many singers. Old Lady Woodly declares our set is much, much too wide!"

"One can't be so very tight in the present day," remarked her mother; of course, in my younger days, there was no debatable land where one met indiscriminately actresses and ladies of position, and artists and heaven knows who, all bundled together and associating on equal terms."

"I think I like my young days better then, mamma," said Alise, with her opera-glass up. "I can't imagine why Devereux doesn't come."

"Poor Devereux! is he quite out of your favour then, fair lady?" said a soft, sweet-toned voice almost at her side, and Alise turned with a start and a bright flush, and a pleased light in her pretty eyes to welcome the new comer, her handsome cousin, Viscount Devereux.

"At last!" said she, giving him her hand. "I have wanted you for the last hour!"

"That is very flattering, dear coz," said the young man, smiling and taking the vacant seat at her side; "it is quite a soothing feeling to be 'wanted' in that sense, you know."

"As if you would be ever wanted in any other sense! But I wanted you particularly to-night to tell me who is that exquisite creature in the box over there."

"There's a tumble for my vanity! So you only wanted me for what you could get out of me, like the rest of your sex," said the viscount; he lifted his eyes—large brilliant grey eyes they were, heavily fringed with long lashes, that despite their at times dreamy look, yet suffered very few things to escape without observation. He had seen the girl, of whom everyone was talking—when, indeed, did a beautiful face and form escape Viscount Devereux's notice!—and had already made up his mind that whoever she might be, he would get to know her.

"Well," said Alise with some impatience, when her cousin had gazed for a minute steadily at the girl, "who is she?"

"I am sorry to be obliged to disappoint you, my dear child," returned the viscount coolly, "for I don't know the young lady."

"Nonsense, Devereux!"

"A fact, Alise! the face is unknown to me; nothing strange, as I have only lately returned from California."

"And you haven't even heard of her? What are you good for?" said his cousin, striking his shoulder playfully with her fan.

"Well, not much "—there might have been a shade of bitterness in the light tone, but Alise could not observe it; "so you see I am a broken reed."

"You can ask! Ah, do be a dear boy. There is Jack Crawford in the stalls; he has just been up to her box," said Alise, clasping her hands ecstatically.

Devereux laughed.

"What an enthusiastic little person it is," said he, looking quizzically at his cousin; "you are amazingly disinterested. What a commotion for one fair lady to make over the appearance of another!"

"Don't talk nonsense! that's one of those ridiculous cynical masculine axioms which you don't believe in more than I do," retorted Miss Mainwaring. "Now go quickly, and get all the information you can."

"To hear is to obey," answered Devereux, who was always vastly amused by his cousin's pretty way of ordering him about.

He made his way down to the stalls, caught Jack Crawford, and asked him who the young lady was.

Jack stared.

"You don't know?" began he, but suddenly recollected. "Ah, of course, been away, dear boy; she is too splendid for anything."

"Yes, I see that; but it does not tell me who she is," suggested Devereux.

"Well, her name's Temple; that's her father. They live in Bruton Street; got a splendid house. She drives a vic., and rides an Arab mare, and all the rest of it, and is simply bewildering."

"The *menage* or the girl? Who is she, then?"

He had asked the question before, but of course, to say that Miss Temple was Miss Temple was not to define her status in the world.

"Who is she?"

Jack laughed.

"You wait for me under the colonnade to-night, and I'll take you there—then you'll see. I don't know any harm in her," he added quickly.

Devereux, whose eyes had been drooping, lifted them quickly a moment and scanned again the face of this mysterious *diva*.

"In society?" said he briefly.

It was a sort of pain to be trying to define the position which this girl was to hold in the world. Yet he had seen her for the first time this evening.

Jack laughed again.

"Society has very wide borders now-a-days," said he; "Kate Cranleigh's in society, and the Princess Glinka is in society, and the one runs about the country playing in public-private theatricals, and the other lets in the dawn on her card-tables four nights out of six!"

"Ah, thanks; I'll wait for you," was the viscount's reply. "Adieu, so long; the curtain's going up."

"She is a Miss Temple, and her father lives in Bruton Street," said he to Alise, leaning over her chair, and with his eyes looking over to Miss Temple's box. "Hush! now the music begins."

But, of course, to say that the *diva's* name was Temple, and that she lived with her father in a fashionable street, was not to say who she was.

CHAPTER II.

THE QUESTION ANSWERED.

R. BERKELEY TEMPLE occupied a large and splendid house in the fashionable quarter of the town; it was furnished *en prince* from top to bottom—that is, the only "top to bottom" with which the world and himself could be concerned—the depths below, and the heights above, were nobody's business.

The reception-rooms were marvels of artistic taste—æsthetic, as far as modern æsthetics are true art, but stopping short of all extravagance and exaggeration of sound principles.

The wide hall was tesselated, so was the staircase, and there was no carpet upon it, so that none of the wonders of ceramic art might be lost; and in hall and staircase, in the recess at the top of the first flight, which had been made into a conservatory, was a profusion of flowers, from which white statues gleamed, graceful nymphs holding flower-baskets or slender pitchers.

None were suffered in this house to be the shapely vehicle of the gas-pipe, and the taste was not offended by that clash of ideas afforded in the spectacle of a classically-attired female, holding aloft a lamp, from which springs a gas-jet!

At such a sight Vera Temple would have shivered; so would Berkeley Temple, unless it was in someone else's house. There was a soft glow of light on hall and staircase, and in the drawing-rooms above—for all light came tempered through exquisitely-tinted glass. In the large drawing-room now thrown open, as well as the two smaller apartments which were *en suite*, a bright fire added its soft glow to the effect produced by rich but subdued tints, and the atmosphere, if the expression may be allowed, of dead-gold, which seemed to pervade the rooms; it was yet early in April, and in an English spring one cannot afford to bid adieu to fires.

The inner rooms were only divided from the principal saloon by heavy velvet *portieres*, now looped back, giving a vista of beauty where neither shape nor colour offended the eye, but charmed by their perfect harmony.

On the other hand, certain card-tables set out in these rooms might have offended some eyes.

The tall, slender girl who stood alone in the large drawing-room seemed to harmonise exactly with her surroundings—they formed a perfect background for the picturesque beauty that had charmed the Opera House to-night. She had that combination of hazel eyes in which seems at times to lurk a kind of golden light, with bronze-gold hair, which produces such a picture-like effect.

She wore her hair short in clustering rings that fell carelessly over the broad forehead, imparting a dreamy look to the eyes when in repose—a look of which one still saw the possibilities even when her face lighted up in conversation. It was, indeed, a face capable of a hundred expressions, capable, perhaps, also of wearing an expression not at all prompted by the inward feeling which might be supposed its author.

There lay the indications of many and varied powers in that young face, powers which in her strange and ever-changing life were not unlikely to be put one day to the test.

The eyes were at once brilliant and soft, far removed from boldness in habitual expression, yet one received no impression that they would droop with a young girl's instinctive modesty or shyness before a man's gaze; they looked fearless and frank, as did the whole face, and not as if they could be disturbed by a girl's half-sweet, half-troubled confusion.

Perhaps she had been too accustomed to receive looks and words that meant homage to be moved by them. Perhaps the secret lay in this—that all homage of whatever sort had been given to her—she had given none.

She stood on the hearth to-night watching the rippling blaze that laughed up into her eyes, one foot resting on the silver bar of the fender, her hands clasped lightly before her, her head a little back—a fair sight, to make a man's heart throb, and a mother's heart ache.

She did not look up as she heard a step crossing the floor—it was only her father.

He came up to her side—a fine tall man, whose hair and moustache were but lightly streaked with grey, and in whose countenance one saw the faint reflex of his daughter's beauty, though none of a certain nobility of expression that lent hers much of its charm.

"What, all alone yet, *ma chere?*" said he, smiling.

His voice, though well modulated and refined, would have produced on a very sensitive ear a not entirely agreeable impression.

The voice that answered was like perfect music, having perfect music's own attribute—a certain pathetic ring which dwells on the ear and haunts the memory.

"You see I am; it is very pleasant."

"A pleasantness that, alas! cannot last," said her father, shrugging his shoulders; "but I suppose its charm lies in the fact of its rarity!"

"Probably. Are many coming to-night?"

"How can I tell, my child? You know when one loves to keep open house, anyone may drop in with a friend. What an impression you created to-night, Vera."

"I always do, don't I?" said the girl quite coolly.

"*Ah, ça!* of course; it would be strange if you did not," said Berkeley Temple, laughing softly. "Did you see Viscount Devereux in the stalls?"

"I think so"—she had seen him, but some quite undefined, almost unconscious, feeling made her willing to affect uncertainty on the point; "a handsome man, young, was he not?"

"Why, yes, Vera; I wonder you did not notice him more particularly—all the women have eyes for this Apollo; we must get him here."

"I suppose he'll come if he has got money he wants to be rid of, or if he has no money, to get it," said Vera dryly.

Her father laughed.

"What a caustic tongue you have," said he, patting her shoulder, a course which seemed to afford her neither pleasure nor the reverse.

"Viscount Devereux has plenty of money; I am told, however, that he manages to spend it all, and a little besides."

"Who is he?" asked Vera, the same question which had been asked about her.

"The Earl of Evringham is his father. Did you see also that pretty little girl in the box nearly opposite ours? She is his cousin—young Devereux's—and an heiress, and they say that he is to marry her; they have been half-engaged for a long time."

"Since he was in knickerbockers, and she in pinafores," said Miss Temple, "since a long time must bring her back to that period of her life."

Berkeley laughed.

"She is older than you, my love," said he.

"But then I never had a pinafore period," returned Vera. "That preserves one's youth, you know, wonderfully."

"She looks older than you, despite your maturity of character. You have a beauty that will preserve your youth when you are past thirty."

An almost imperceptible shiver ran lightly through the girl's limbs, there was an involuntary knitting of the straight, dark brows, but she only laughed by way of answer, and the desultory conversation was put an end to by the arrival of a guest, who entered unannounced, as did most of Mr. Temple's guests.

He was a handsome man, with very clear finely-cut features, and very keen grey eyes, but the eyes were both too small and to cold, and the lips too thin to make an entirely pleasant impression. He was evidently a welcome guest here, however, for Berkeley greeted him with a warm hand shake, and if Vera did not return the pressure of Lucius Linwood's hand, she gave him a smile and a few bright words.

"First again to-night, Mr. Linwood," she said, sinking into a low high-backed chair near, and taking up a hand-screen of peacock's feathers to shield her from the heat of the fire. "You don't spend much time over gossip and absinthe at the clubs."

"I find a greater attraction here," said Linwood, bowing low.

"That is the regulation thing to say; I suppose I must believe you for lack of any other reason."

"Do you think I should say anything but the truth to you?" said Linwood, bending a little towards her, and laying the slightest stress on the last pronoun.

"My dear Mr. Linwood, of course not; everyone says the truth to me—that I know—and I believe them," said Vera, laying her head against the chair-back, and looking at him from under her long lashes.

"By the way, thanks for the pretty present you sent me this morning; but I have sent it back."

Linwood started, and a transient flush passed over his usually colourless cheek.

"I had thought," he said in a voice studiedly controlled to suavity, "that at least such a gift—poor as it was—would find favour in your eyes."

"So it did; as far as his pugship went, he is the dearest, funniest little thing I have seen for a long while. I was sorry to pack him up again," said Vera quite thoughtfully, "but you know I told you I didn't want a dog."

"Ah, but—but perhaps you don't like pugs?" said Linwood, looking down on her as he stood close by, leaning one arm on the mantle-piece and smiling— Berkeley had left the two together.

"Yes, I think them immensely droll," returned Vera, "but I won't accept this one."

"You will allow me then to send you another? I have a beauty, a young Irish setter; you would like him, I know, you are so fond of dogs," urged Linwood.

But Vera shook her head and laughed.

"No, no, you cannot tempt me, I shall not accept any dog."

"But it is such a strange whim," said Linwood, gnawing his lip.

"Isn't it? But I am a creature of whims, and enjoy an immunity from conducting myself like other folks," returned Vera. "Come, don't be angry. There is Kate Cranleigh and with her the Princess Glinka—two such charming women ought to put you in a good humour again."

"You mistake me, Vera; I am wounded, not angry," said Linwood in a quick, low tone. "Do you think I cannot see that it is from me you refuse to accept a dog? I can read your mind; nor do I forget what you said once."

"What a memory you have! What did I say?" asked Vera, lazily fanning herself, and still looking at him with laughter in her eyes.

"That you would like a dog to have some associations with the giver."

"Oh, then I suppose the pug was a—a sort of a test," remarked Vera, stroking the feathery ends of her screen with dainty touch. "How could you expect me to have any 'associations' with you after a few week's acquaintance?"

Linwood made no answer; though inwardly deeply angry at the cool return of his present, his vanity bitterly wounded at the rebuff he had received, he did not wish Vera to see what power lay in her hands.

Notwithstanding, Vera knew perfectly well the power she possessed, and knew exactly how far to use it, and how to use it, with each one of the men who looked upon her as a *diva,* whether a corruptible *diva* or not depended on their own discernment to determine.

The Princess Glinka at this moment coming up, saved Linwood the necessity of replying to Vera.

He turned to her, with an added homage in look and bow that Vera read perfectly well, and regarded with as perfect an indifference. She did not value Mr. Linwood's homage.

The Princess Glinko, said to be the most beautiful foreigner and the most inveterate card-player in London, gave a hand to Linwood to touch with his lips, tapped Vera lightly with her jewelled fan, with a gay "Ah, *ma chere,* so we meet once again!" and sank into a low chair which Linwood brought forward for her.

GELLERT, AS IF IN ANSWER, PUSHED HIS NOSE INTO VERA'S HAND. . . SHE SAT DOWN BEFORE THE TOILETTE-GLASS.

"I have been to one dinner—one of your long dreadful English dinners—and three assemblies to-night," said the princess; "and I come to the only house—yes, positively the only house in London—in England, where one is at one's ease, where one is happy, where one meets society the most charming, and," putting her pretty hand before her mouth, and in a whisper, "where one can play baccarat."

"You overwhelm me with pleasure, madame," said Vera, "we are so rejoiced to find our poor society so highly treasured. Mr. Linwood, you owe the princess her revenge at that same inadmissible game, don't you?"

"If *madame la princesse* will honour me," said Linwood, bowing to the lady.

"But you are a dreadful man," said the princess, showing all her beautiful white teeth as she smiled upon the "dreadful man." "To have one's revenge with you is but to lose again. I shall be quite ruined, M. Linwood—quite!"

"You should not play, princess," observed Vera gravely.

"Not play, *ma chere* Vera! I live only on the excitement of play!" cried the princess, flashing her bright eyes like a couple of diamonds, as she turned them from one to the other; "without it life were a desert, truly. How you can play so coolly, you who are not stolid like the English, I do not comprehend."

"I can't get up much excitement on cards," returned Vera, rising. "You will excuse me, dear princess? You and Mr. Linwood are dying, I know, to see who shall play the other's pockets empty. The rooms are filling."

She bowed gracefully, and passed on, mingling with the other guests, many more of whom had arrived, all men but Kate Cranleigh, who held a little court around her, entertained with her lively sallies.

Coffee was being handed round, served in delicate porcelain cups, and therewith, for those who liked, cognac and costly liqueurs in tiny decanters, and tiny glasses richly cut.

The princess took cognac with her coffee without scruple.

Kate Cranleigh made a pretty *moue*, but was persuaded to accept a thimbleful of Benedictine—a kind of compromise, like half the things she did.

She whispered to Vera that it cleared the head, and Vera laughed and shrugged her shoulders.

The room was pretty full by this time, and a move was made by some to the card-tables.

It was understood that at these late receptions of Berkeley Temple's the chief business of the evening was play.

He had other receptions, perhaps as brilliant, where music and recitations took the lead, and where only a moderate game of whist or *ecarte* was supposed to be *en regle;* and most visitors of the latter receptions did not attend the former, nor did those frequenting the first-named assemblies gossip much, if at all, about these late affairs, when, not seldom, the host's beautiful daughter was the only lady present.

"For this is quite a field-day," said Vera to young Lord Charleston, a very fashionable youth, who adored in about equal parts cards and Vera Temple, and passed his life between a state of losing money at play, and borrowing money wherewith to discharge his debts of honour; "it is seldom that you have three ladies to talk to."

"We don't want it when you are the only lady," said the young man gallantly.

He was thrown into a state of the greatest delight when Vera spoke to him, for his chief occupation, outside of play and his numerous engagements at Tattersall's, was writing despairing sonnets to the object of his adoration, which found their way invariably into the waste-basket.

And he had remained constant to this idol for four whole weeks, probably because his sonnets were thrown into the waste-basket.

"Very pretty," said Vera, smiling, "but not quite true. You want change, you know—different styles—so forth."

"How can you say so, Miss Temple?" remonstrated Lord Charleston pathetically. "Do I want a change? Don't I live in the hope that one day——"

"Exactly," interrupted Vera good-humouredly. "Hope keeps the flame alive—such as it is."

"You don't give me much to feed hope on," said he, disconsolately.

He thought she meant her last words to apply to the hope, but wasn't sure.

"Well, you see, the flame isn't much," returned Vera, by way of reassurance, and to put him out of his doubt; "it would die down to nothing if hope was turned to certainty."

"'Pon my honour, you're mistaken," cried the young man, as eagerly as he could, not to be heard by a group of men not far from them. "If you would only try——"

"'Twould be trying a foregone conclusion, dear boy," answered Vera lightly. "Now I'll give you a piece of advice, if you will take it, and it will do you much more good than getting any number of sweet answers to your sonnets: Don't play so much with Linwood."

The young man flushed slightly; he did not like the implication that Linwood's play was superior to his.

"Why not?" he said.

"Because you will lose everything to him; you know you can't approach his play, and you really will be ruined; your long-suffering papa will 'turn rusty,' as you would say."

"But—er—really, Miss Temple——" began the young man, whose self-love was inclined to be offended directly he was the recipient of good advice.

Vera laughed her soft laugh, that was so silvery, and could be so mocking.

"Yes, yes, you propose to manage your own affairs, etc., *n'est ce pas?*" said she; "and instead of being very grateful to me for taking enough interest in you to advise you, you begin to be angry—so is the world. Ta-ta; I must talk to Mr. Talbot, who I see over there."

"Our *chere* Vera," murmured the Princess Glinka softly, to Lucius Linwood, who still talked persistently with her, perhaps to show Vera there were other women in the world beside herself, "is in one of her mocking moods to-night. But she is quite charming!"

Lucius bowed; if this was a lead for compliment, he did not feel inclined to take it up.

"And she will have much money?" presumed the princess, in a sort of purring way, nestling like a graceful kitten among her cushions.

"I have heard so," replied Lucius indifferently.

"Ah, *fi donc, mon cher;* that is something you should be assured of if you propose to marry her."

"Who said that I proposed to marry her, madame?" asked Linwood rather coldly.

"At least you are in love with her," said madame; "and in your odd country, when one is in love, one marries."

"Does one?" said Linwood dryly. "Allow it for the sake of argument. I have not said I am in love with our fair Vera."

"No; but one sees it."

"Madame has wonderful eyes, said Lucius with a bow and a smile, and the princess laughed.

"Oh yes, I see very much. And now you must not let Viscount Devereux carry away your prize. Aha!" and the princess held up a slender finger and began to laugh; "you see I was right. You are jealous, and when one loves one is jealous. But I fear, *mon cher,* it is too late! See there, at the door stands Mr. Crawford, and with him your handsome Count with the *beaux yeux.* Throw up your cards, M. Linwood, he will trump them all."

As she swept off, laughing wickedly, to greet the new comers, Lucius Linwood gnawed his nether-lip and looked darkly at the new guest.

"But perhaps I hold a card that will take the trick," he muttered savagely.

CHAPTER III.

DIAMOND CUT DIAMOND.

"VERA, *ma chere*," said the soft voice of Berkeley Temple at his daughter's side, "let me present to you Viscount Devereux."

The girl, who had just been making some laughing rejoinder to a remark of her companion, turned and bowed with a bright smile, and a curious feeling at her heart that was half pleasure and half vexation. But the frank gaze of the hazel eyes that met the grey ones, in which lay an involuntary look of admiration, did not show anything of the opposite feelings that stirred her.

"I think myself so fortunate," said Devereux, smiling, "to have obtained the favour of an introduction to you almost the first night of my return to England. Crawford undertook to be my sponsor, hazarding the assurance that any friend of his would be welcome."

"He did not count too much on his powers," answered Vera. "Have you been long away 'doing' the States, as it is the fashion now for young Englishmen, as it is the fashion for young America 'to do' Europe?"

"But I have not been 'doing' the States in that sense," said Devereux, laughing; "I have been a year away, and am just come from California."

"Ah, you have been to San Francisco?"

"I spent two months there and in the neighbourhood; you seem to know it—yet the journey is not one generally made by young ladies."

"Oh," said Vera coolly, "you will soon find out that I generally do what young ladies don't, and *vice versa*. I know 'Frisco very well, also a good many places in California. How did you like it?"

"The climate and the scenery should make it a paradise."

"But they don't; one can't fancy poker and euchre in paradise; did you learn those mysteries, by-the-bye?"

"I had that honour"—how familiar she seems with the names of those games, thought Devereux—"if it may be called so, to add another gambling game to one's list."

"Certainly, I think it may," said Vera with gravity; "knowledge is power, you know, even if it only enables you to transfer a hundred or two from somebody's pocket to your own. Poker does that, doesn't it?"

"Do you speak from experience, Miss Temple?" asked Devereux. He spoke jestingly, with a smile on his lips; it did not occur to him seriously that this young girl, so witching, so fair, could possibly be acquainted with anything so unfeminine as poker.

If there was the hundredth part of a second's hesitation on Vera's part before she answered, it was scarcely to be felt.

And yet afterwards he fancied that her next words had not followed his question immediately.

"Do I look like an individual who plays poker, Lord Devereux?" said she with an arch upward look, and he answered impulsively:

"Certainly not; I could not connect the thought of you with anything——"

"Take care, take care," interrupted the girl, raising her hand, and laughing; "don't commit yourself to anything rash. Perhaps I have a passion for gambling—perhaps especially for poker, which reminds me of San Francisco. Why should men have a monopoly of the gambling spirit?"

"Unfortunately they do not have it," said Devereux, glancing over to a table where Lady Cranleigh was playing eagerly with a man belonging to his club; "but I would fain hope that the spirit had left you at least untainted."

Vera looked up into the handsome face of the man beside her—a face that had more than the beauty of form and feature to lend to it power of attraction—a loyal and noble face, if passionate and proud, and perhaps reckless. A shade fell on her own, a strange, unaccountable feeling compelled her; she would like to have said she had been jesting, she would like not to have fallen short of his conclusion that she had been jesting.

"Untainted?" she said, and there came an unconscious wistfulness into her tones. "Who is to be the judge? Why is a woman 'tainted' more than a man?"

"She is by nature a more delicate plant, she is easier hurt; a touch will brush the bloom off a peach, or taint the purity of a lily."

"Oh, ah," said Vera with a sort of dry and half-impatient bitterness, "that lily theory again. Do you suppose all women are pure like lilies?"

"I should think all true women would be so," answered Devereux quietly, inexpressibly pained by her way.

He had, naturally enough, a man's, and especially a young man's, very lofty and, perhaps, impossible ideal of a "true woman."

Men are apt to draw such a sharp line between the good and pure and their frailer sisters; that "true women" may have their temptations does not enter into their calculations.

"Ah, poor women, that is the intolerance of you men," returned Vera, in the same half-bitter way; "but what is a 'true woman,' and where is she to be found? Is poor little Kate Cranleigh less a true woman because she gambles and flirts almost to the verge of scandal?"

"Ah, now you bring it down to personalities," said Devereux, smiling. "I don't want to judge anyone, and I have never said that a lily's beauty is destroyed because it has a speck, or a peach's flavour is ruined because the bloom is off the skin."

Involuntarily the girl drew a silent breath; it was as though a certain load that had pressed unconsciously on her heart was taken off, and why should that be?

Vera soon shook off, however, the more serious feeling that seemed to oppress her, and turned the current of the conversation with a jesting answer, with her own bright manner again, free from bitterness.

"Ah, so you will allow that much? But what a very serious conversation we have been drifting into, and in a *salon* where everyone has come with the object of playing cards! Everyone is moving off to the tables, Lord Devereux; won't you be a votary also?"

"I had rather be a votary at beauty's shrine," answered Devereux, bowing.

Vera laughed.

"That is very pretty, and if true you are not a born gambler. I don't think a galaxy of beauties would keep Mr. Linwood, for instance, from the tables. You know him? See, he plays baccarat with Princess Glinka."

She gave him a covert glance as she mentioned the game; if he felt any surprise he did not show it, but looked over to where the two sat.

"I know him," he answered, "although our acquaintance is rather slight. The princess I have met also, once in Paris, and once in St. Petersburg. She is very beautiful."

"Is she not? and very charming, and very rich."

"Three golden pass-keys to success," said Devereux; "but she will fade before she is eight-and-twenty, as these Russian beauties do."

"She was married at sixteen," said Vera. "I was one of her bridesmaids. Her husband is sixty, and lives on his Livonian estates, while *madame la princesse* is here, there, and everywhere. I suppose we have met in every capital in Europe."

"You have travelled a great deal, I believe?"

"I? Oh, enormously," answered the girl. "This is the third time only that we have been in London since I was quite a little child, and," added she gravely, but with a half-wicked look in the great, dark eyes, "I remember then my first appearance in society, perched up on a high chair by papa, and playing cards with Prince R——, whom you may remember as a very clever player!"

"And I suppose you won a great deal of applause as the 'baby player?'" said Devereux rather dryly.

"Of course, I carried off no end of charming *bon-bonnieres*, and I have no doubt ate too many chocolate-creams. But I am shocking you dreadfully, my lord," said the girl, laughing; "confess!"

He paused a second before he answered her, his eyes meeting her fearless gaze with a look that seemed to wish to probe the depths of her heart.

"No," he said then, quite gently, "I'm not shocked —only pained."

The colour sprang to the girl's cheek; for one brief moment a perfect tumult of conflicting emotions had possession of her spirit, then she laughed lightly and half moved away.

"Pained! Nonsense. What for? Come, don't be pained or shocked if I challenge you to play poker with me."

She swept his hand lightly with her slender fingers as she spoke, and he must smile back into the dark eyes that were lifted to his with such a witching look—half appeal—half command. And so, after all this fragile, beautiful creature could sit down to play poker!

There was some curiosity manifested among the assembly, when these two sat down to play a game that is so little known out of America; probably, besides Viscount Devereux and his fair antagonist, not one was acquainted with its intricacies, except perhaps Vera's father, and there was soon a little group round the table where the two sat.

Linwood and the princess came to look on, the princess considerably in the gentleman's debt again; and Linwood watched with darkened brow.

Their play was in amusing contrast to that of the others. Neither had the least eagerness of manner or played as though the affair had any more moment than a child's game for nuts and oranges; neither was absorbed, but seemed able to keep their faculties alert for the game, as well as to exchange a word or laugh with the onlookers.

"You are like two dreadful Americans," said Kate, pretending to be shocked, "introducing that poker— what an outrageous name!—into a London drawing-

room! Vera, my dear, are you not ashamed of yourself?"

There must be a great attraction in the game," said
Lucius Linwood's deep level tones, "to draw Miss Vera
into the whirl of play."

"Do you generally eschew play?" asked Devereux,
in a quick, low tone, looking up as he laid down a
card.

"I am not a card-devotee," answered Vera, evasively,
but without embarrassment; "there, my lord," smiling,
"I think the unknown quantity will be mine."

"What!" cried Jack Crawford, "you have won, Miss
Temple? Bravo! happy Devereux!"

Devereux thought so himself. He knew in his heart
it would be an exquisite pleasure that she should receive
something from his hands.

"What are the stakes?" asked Berkeley Temple,
smiling, and looking over to his daughter.

Was it Devereux's fancy that in Vera's voice he
seemed to detect the ring of defiance, though she
laughed as she made answer:

"Nothing very appalling—a cigar-case against anything Lord Devereux may choose."

"Capital, my love," returned Mr. Temple, nodding
approvingly and rubbing his hands softly. "Capital!
but, my lord, you'll have your revenge."

"I am at your service," said Vera; "will you try
conclusions?"

"With pleasure."

It was a pleasure that Ernest Devereux did not
choose to deny himself, although all the time something
was chafing on the fine sense of the lines outside which
a young girl should not step—something was in continual clash with a certain lofty ideal he had always set
up as to the kind of woman he should——

But when his thoughts, if they could be called
distinct thoughts, got so far, he pulled himself up with
a mental start—what perfect nonsense it all was!

"What are the stakes to be this time?" enquired
Vera's father, leaning over his daughter's chair, and
resting his hand lightly on her shoulder.

"Anything your daughter wishes," said Devereux, bowing; "I am happy in her hands."

"You may win this time, Lord Devereux," said the girl, laughing.

She dropped her fan at the moment, and stooped to pick it up, though Linwood stepped forward to render her the service.

"I won't choose; somebody shall make choice, and we'll pledge ourselves to abide by it; do you agree, my lord? Of course you do, only not for money; I'm not in a humour to play for money."

"Allow me to suggest," said Linwood, as he leant to her to return her fan, and he smiled as he looked at Vera, but the smile was on the lip, not in the eyes, "that jewelled heart you wear against—a dog."

His words could not be heard by the rest of the group around them.

Devereux only caught the last word, and the tone struck him.

But Vera's eyes met Linwood's without a change of colour.

"Famous!" she exclaimed. "Mr. Linwood makes a capital suggestion, my lord. I shall stake my locket here, against a dog. I want one. I had one given me to-day, but I sent him back."

"I shall do my best to play carelessly," said Devereux, "in order to have the happiness of presenting you with one."

"But," remarked Linwood, smoothly, though he gnawed his lip, and his brow was black, "Vera has, I believe, a peculiar fancy about such things. She will not accept a dog from anyone she has not known some time—till she can form some estimate of what their character is—isn't that it?"

"Oh dear no; you have quite mistaken me," returned Vera in her frank way, that could cover a wide field of meaning. "I won't have a dog from anyone I don't like. I am sure you will understand my feeling, Lord Devereux," turning with a smile to him, "but remember, if you lose, I don't pledge myself to receive your dog!"

IN DANGEROUS PATHS.

"I shall dare to hope," answered Devereux, "that my offering may not be unacceptable, at least, if only for its own sake."

"But you are going to win," laughed Vera, gaily. "Now, gentlemen, you must please maintain a rigid silence; the stakes are high, and we need our wits about us."

"Hearts to win," murmured Kate, through her white teeth, "eh, Mr. Linwood?"

The sharp eyes and sharp wits had comprehended that there was some under-current to the chaff about the dog, and was delighted to see Linwood "taken down"; not that she had any particular dislike to him, but no special liking, and she made it a matter of principle to rejoice when her own sex triumphed.

"'Love me, love my dog,'" returned Lucius, sarcastically. "I wonder our fair friend liked to take up in public what I proposed in pure jest."

"Oh, nonsense!" said little Kate briskly. "Vera can do what she likes, it's only fun. Talk! what does that matter; we all talk each other's heads off, and no one is the worse that I can find out. Come and play *écarte*—I feel one ought to set an example after poker."

"There seems an extraordinary interest in that game," observed Linwood rather superciliously; he was bitterly angry, and had not sufficient control entirely to hide his feelings.

"The interest is in the players, not the game, *mon cher*," said Kate, who dearly loved to stick her little sharp penknife under people's ears. "Vera is too exquisite, and Devereux is her match."

"I know all you ladies rave over him. He is everyone's favourite!"

"Dear me! the game is over," putting up an eyeglass to look across the room, "there is quite a stir— "who has won, Jack? Come and tell me," to Crawford, who detached himself from the group and came towards Kate.

"Miss Vera again—don't know whether Devereux let her—he takes his two defeats as though he liked 'em. By Jove! wouldn't I—if I had the chance."

"Poor Jack! she says you play too badly," said Kate sweetly.

"I hardly know," said Devereux when he was taking leave of Vera, "whether to be most glad or sorry that I lost."

"Oh, be most glad," returned the girl, laughing; "they say it's more blessed to give than to receive."

"But it is also blessed to receive—and to accept," said Devereux with a bow and look that was an appeal, and not immediately dropping the hand he held.

"Perhaps it is," sweeping him a low bow. "Good night, Lord Devereux."

Some minutes after the rooms were deserted, and Berkeley Temple coming back from seeing his last guest to the door, met his daughter just as she was going upstairs to her chamber.

"My dear," he said, "going already? I had wanted to talk to you."

"Good things will always keep, papa," responded Vera, nodding him good night over the balusters. "I'm too tired—talk to me to-morrow!"

The dawn was breaking over the eastern sky as the girl entered her room—a luxuriously-furnished chamber, where still a bright fire burned, and where wax tapers shed their pale soft light, doing battle now with the cold grey of the early morning.

The girl went straight to the window and drew up the blinds, and stood, leaning her forehead against the glass, looking out, her eyes uplifted to the blue sky.

And the young face had changed, and this seemed only a shadow of the Vera who, downstairs to-night, had exchanged jest and repartee with the men who came to her father's house—of the Vera who had charmed, and fascinated, and pained, and repelled Ernest Devereux all at once.

For now the wistfulness that lay latent in the beautiful eyes was predominant in every line of the face—an unexpressed yearning that was infinitely pathetic.

What had brought such yearnings to her, who had lived her life in the hot-house of *salons* of Paris, Vienna, St. Petersburg, whose earliest recollections were of princely gamblers, and whose nearest friend was a woman for ever hovering on the borderland that divides society? What was she musing on, what were the soft lips murmuring:

"He said a speck would not destroy the lily—a true woman; what a terribly lofty ideal he must set. I wonder——"

She broke off abruptly, and turned away, sitting down before the toilet glass, and leaning her arms on the table, pushing her hands through the thickness of the rich soft hair, looking deliberately and long into the rare beauty of the face that looked back to her. She shook her head gently, slowly.

"No, he must not come here; he was startled and shocked to-night by the contrast between what I am and what I look; he must not ruin his life and that young girl's.

"You are so beautiful," she said wistfully to that other self in the glass. "He is not like the others—not like them. And I—no one has tempted me with love; they have tempted me with gold and jewels, and some with state and position, and that was nothing, I could pass them by, but love——"

She dropped her head down on her arm and the lips half parted in a smile, soft, bright, infinitely sad. "What might not one do for love? the world well lost —but, ah, is it the world only?—the soul well lost for love!

"Oh, no, no!" the girl shivered strongly and bent her head lower yet, and the smile died on her lips. "Oh, God! for me love means only temptation! And how shall I stand—the lily has lost its whiteness, the bloom is off the peach!"

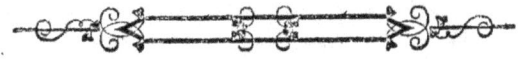

CHAPTER IV.

BEHIND THE SCENES.

R. TEMPLE'S study was as well and appropriately furnished as the rest of the house, and looked particularly comfortable and business-like with its carved oak writing-table, possessing drawers and pigeon-holes innumerable, and its despatch-boxes, and even an iron safe or two.

Everything was good and solid and possessed even elegance, but is was business elegance, there was no gimcrackery. It was said that Berkeley Temple was a man who had some business Citywards, that vague term which may mean anything from a hardworking underpaid clerk to the important personage who takes the chair at shareholders' meetings, gets up companies, and "dabbles in stocks." Something of the kind Mr. Temple must be, for what does a private gentleman want with such formidable-looking premises?

He sat, the morning after the late reception, writing at his table, perfectly dressed, although the hour was but nine; he was rarely to be seen in dressing-gown and slippers, and used to hold himself up as a pattern to the young men of his acquaintance who indulged in these articles and late breakfasts.

He looked so neat, and so gentlemanly, and so kind, and well-to-do, you might have taken him for the secretary of a society for the rescue of young men in the world, or something with an equally benevolent intention.

Hearing a light step on the stairs, he looked up, his hand pausing from its writing; then he rose and went to the door, opening it a little way.

"Vera, my love," he called gently, and the girl who was stepping across the hall paused and came towards him.

She had looked exquisite in the rich evening dress, she looked no less so in the simple black gown of the morning, her only ornament the ruby locket she had pledged herself the night before to play away to Lord Devereux.

"You want me?" she said.

"Yes, *ma chere;* come in a moment if you have time."

He held the door open for her, and closed it after her, resuming his seat.

She went and stood by the fireplace, where a bright fire burned, and leaned one arm lightly on the mantel-shelf.

"Do you know, Vera," said her father, taking up a pencil as he spoke, and beginning to point it very finely, "that you surprised me very much last night?"

"Indeed."

"Yes, really; I wondered at you, with your talents, actually—well, I may say, condescending to"—here he paused to blow some fine pencil dust off his finger—"yes, to play for such trumpery stakes as young ladies play for in country houses. And you had the field absolutely before you."

"So I had," answered Vera, thoughtfully. "It really was a pity, now I come to think of it. How much money do you suppose he had about him?"

"Tut, my dear Vera! now you are in one of your strange mocking humours, and I only wish to talk seriously and point out to you that you must not commit such mistakes. Do you think Lord Devereux only plays up to the amount he has in his pocket at the moment?"

"Oh, I dare say he plays much over what he has at his bankers!" returned the girl. "But, my dearest papa, you are short-sighted, after all, and judge all men after the same pattern. Don't you see that very likely Lord Devereux would never have come here again if I had started with money stakes—that is your own point of view, mind."

"What is yours then, my love?" asked Mr. Temple, holding his pencil up to the light and examining the point critically.

"We will talk first of yours, please," replied Vera.

"Very well. Why do you imagine Lord Devereux to be more sensitive on this point than anyone else?"

"My woman's sharper wits, I suppose, lead me to guess it—it may strike a man of rather fastidious taste, you know, to see a young and handsome girl staking her tens and twenties quite coolly; it's a little incongruous, you will allow."

"I don't wish to argue, Vera, but you know as well as I do that Lord Devereux is not very likely to be shocked away from your side; and, in short, you may do anything you like with him, as you may with them all."

"Perhaps, I might——"

"And," said Berkeley Temple, now trying the sharp point of the pencil on a piece of paper, and looking closely at it to see the effect, "of course you will do it, my love."

Just a second's pause, a droop of the dark eyes, not the meek casting down of a submissive spirit, but the droop which should hide a flash she did not care to let him see, then Vera said lightly:

"You take so many things as a matter of course, *cher papa;* of course I shall do as I like, as I always have done."

"But I cannot understand this whim all of a sudden about this especial nobleman," said her father, not apparently ruffled by the cool assertion of complete independence.

"You know I always object to play for money."

"Very ridiculous, but you do it sometimes. I hope we are not going to have any absurd fancies, my dear child," said Berkeley Temple, looking at his daughter with a smile. Vera did not even change colour.

"It isn't the first time," said she; "you know I always refuse to play with little Charleston because he's too stupid ever to win, and with Jack Crawford because he only pays by dipping into that concern of yours," pointing to the iron safe, "or nearly ruining his mother."

Berkeley Temple turned right round in his chair and looked at his daughter.

"Upon my word," said he, slowly, after a rather long pause, "you are developing a very pretty mood of sentiment! What a wonderful thing is the feminine mind—or heart, perhaps, I should say! after all these years—seventeen years!"

"Fifteen, papa," corrected Vera, smiling; "you know even I didn't play cards in the cradle."

"So, on account of this young man's mother you are melted to pity," pursued Mr. Temple, not heeding, and leaning back, and fitting the fingers of one hand with great nicety against those of the other; "is it then a mother or a sister, or, possibly a sweetheart, who moves your heart so amiably in the case of Lord Devereux?"

"Oh, I don't think he has mother or sister," returned Vera, moving away a little as if to go. "Is that all you wanted to say?"

"No, not quite. Listen to me, my love; whether you play for money or not with the viscount, remember that I will have him encouraged in every way; he is likely to pay you great attentions, you must not repel them—do you understand?"

He was watching her closely as he spoke, and she knew it; a flash of colour on her cheek, a quiver of her lip, a droop of her eye, would tell him, acute as he was, and on the *qui vive* already, that something had awoken in her which could make her give a sign that his words stabbed her.

She broke into a soft amused laugh as she made him a half-mocking bow.

"This poor viscount," said she, "what traps you lay for his unwary feet. Is he so very rich. Is it likely I shall be very rude to such a splendid gentleman, papa? And he is going to give me a dog, too, this very day perhaps. *Au revoir!* I must really go. I promised to drive with Mrs. Morley, and she has quite a good position in society, and mustn't be offended on any account."

CHAPTER V.

IN WHICH LORD DEVEREUX PAYS A DEBT OF HONOUR.

 "AH," Vera murmured, half bitterly, when she reached her own room, "if some of the people who come here could see behind the scenes! What a strange dual life it is! But I suppose I oughtn't to feel amused at it, but I can't help it."

She rang the bell, and in answer to her summons her own maid appeared, a woman who had been about Vera from the time she was quite a child, and who had but one article of faith in her creed, and this was her blind faith in her young mistress.

She would do anything for her, and was thoroughly trustworthy, not only in will but in fact.

She knew how to keep her own counsel, and not only could guard the citadel, but also defend the outworks.

And such a person was needful in Vera's strange and perilous life.

"How late you came up last night, Miss Vera," said Janet Benfield, coming in quickly, and proceeding to lay out her mistress's driving dress. "I heard you, and I don't believe you went to bed at once, neither."

"You are a lynx-eyed duenna," laughed Vera. "Supposing I didn't go to bed at once, I am none the worse for it this morning."

Janet pursed up her lips and shook her head.

"It's an unnatural life you lead," Miss Vera, said she; "you don't feel it while you're young, but——"

"Perhaps, I never shall be old," interrupted Vera. "You dear old croaker! I'm used to turning night into day; I couldn't sleep before 4 a.m. if I tried."

"Wasn't there a new gentleman came last night?" asked the attendant, as she handed Vera the large graceful hat, which the young lady poised on with scarcely an appeal to the mirror.

"Viscount Devereux? Yes, Mr. Crawford brought him," answered the girl, drawing on her gloves. "I dare say he'll come this afternoon."

"He's a wild one, Miss Vera."

"That's nothing to me, Jannie; we are used to the species," said her mistress, not the least offended at the kind of warning felt in the tone of her faithful attendant. "That must be Mrs. Morley's carriage that has just driven up. I must go, Janet."

On coming back from her drive, Vera was informed that Lord Devereux was in the morning-room, Vera's own domain.

"I showed him in there, Miss Vera," said old Jeffreys, grunting—he was the man-servant, and was contemporary with Janet Benfield in the Temple service —"because you see he had a great dog as big as an elephant with him, and he wouldn't go in the drawing-room."

Vera half smiled at the mention of the dog, and went across the hall without first removing her outdoor attire.

There was a singular pleasure of anticipation in meeting again her last night's antagonist, and as she laid her hand on the door, she did not for the moment remember that "he must not come here."

Devereux rose as she entered, from a seat near the table, where he had been skimming the last week's "Societies," and Vera held out her hand with a bright smile.

"Ah, Lord Devereux, how do you do?" she said. "What a careful guardian of a lady's drawing-room you are. Jeffreys told me you refused to introduce your comrade to the sacred precincts."

"I could not dare without permission," answered Devereux, "especially as Jeffreys looked rather askance at the four-footed intruder. You see I come betimes to pay my debt of honour."

"You assume that I shall accept the payment?" said Vera archly.

"Why, naturally," returned Devereux with smiling audacity. "I am certain Miss Temple is too generous to refuse me the pleasure of satisfying a debt of honour, and also, I will dare hope, of giving her pleasure."

"But what a splendid brute, Lord Devereux," said the girl, not directly answering his words but bending over the dog, which, having received no command to rise, had lain expectant but quiescent stretched upon the floor, his magnificent head lifted, an attentive listener apparently to the conversation.

He was a St. Bernard of great size and beauty, about ten months old, and evidently had received perfect training.

He responded to Vera's overtures by flapping his bushy tail on the floor, and trying to lick her hand, gazing the while in her face as though he were what is called "taking stock" of her.

"Here, Gellert," said Devereux, addressing the animal, "get up and show yourself," which Gellert proceeded to do.   "He is in capital training; you won't have any trouble with him, and his temper is perfect.   He has been brought up hitherto at Evringham, but I had him in town this season to give him society manners."

"He is too splendid," said Vera, shaking her head; I must not deprive you of him."

"You will give me infinite happiness by parting me from him," returned Ernest—it must be admitted a little hypocritically—but he meant it. "The woman who hesitates—you know, Miss Vera, and so," he smiled, "you must indeed accept. Besides which," added my lord with that assurance which in some men is all-persuasive, and in others is only impertinence, "you see your name is already engraved on his collar, and so——"

"So you quite reckoned on my acceptance," said Vera, laughing. "Really, Lord Devereux, I ought to be very angry."

"Ah, but you cannot, and if you were—still you will retain Gellert."

"Now I see you are one of those who never give up a point," said Vera. "Well, I will accept Gellert, and thank you very much. I think, my lord, you pay your debts with interest," she added with one of those sunny, sweet smiles that played like light in the depths of the large eyes, and was surely reward enough for Ernest Devereux.

"If Gellert pleases you, that is enough," he said simply, "and Gellert will be happy in being your companion."

"I hope so. But you are not going, Lord Devereux? You will stay to luncheon, of course; my father will be delighted," said Vera, and of course Ernest accepted, and passed the next hour in a kind of paradise.

And Vera was brilliant and playful to-day, and not mocking and bitter. She was not consciously trying to avoid bringing her ideas and thoughts into clash with his—but she involuntarily sheered off from those subjects which must show him the difference between what she was and what she looked.

"Now Gellert," said Devereux when he was taking leave, "remember I give you your new mistress in charge. She is to be loved and obeyed, and served to the most of all your powers."

And Gellert looked wise, and grave, and understanding, and as if in answer shoved his nose into Vera's hand.

Nor did he forget, when she had need of him, Ernest Devereux's parting charge.

And neither of them dreamt of a dark and terrible future in which the dumb brute's powers should serve both the giver and the recipient.

CHAPTER VI.

INGENUE, OR COQUETTE.

I'T was a strange and, in many ways, a most anomalous position, which Vera Temple and her father occupied in the world of London, a position perhaps only possible in the present day, when there are so many people to some extent "in society" whose credentials will never pass them to the inner sanctuary, but with whom newly-moneyed people like to mix, and whom also that large class of persons who form the tail of the aristocracy accept without scruple, because their ways agree, and their morals are not too strained.

In this kind of aristocratic Bohemia are many whose reputation is perfectly sound, but who are said to be "fast," and some stray in who are not even "fast," but who, skimming the surface life of the set, find the society very lively, taking, and far pleasanter than that of their own more immediate world.

Of such Mr. Temple and his daughter knew a good many, and though many things were said about him and the beautiful girl who reigned in his house, this undeniably respectable portion of their circle was pointed to as convincing proof that all was right, and Mr. Temple was obviously only a gentleman of means, who employed his leisure in some City way, who kept a good house, gave charming little dinners and music parties, and, for those who liked them, card parties.

He made himself very agreeable to all the world, and paid the most courteous attentions to ladies, and of course, amongst men, Vera was the rage.

The women were much divided on this point.

Berkeley Temple had come to London alone in the February of this year, knowing already a host of people, English and foreign, whom he had met abroad ; he had

had no difficulty, therefore, in establishing his footing in society, and many people desired to be introduced to him, and visited at his house, solely from curiosity, because there was no man in London, perhaps, so much talked over as the quiet tenant of No. —, Bruton Street.

And, of course, when Vera joined him from Vienna, where it was understood she had been staying with an archduke and his wife, the talk grew faster and louder, and she became the fashion as she had been in every capital in Europe, from the time she could take her part in the world.

And this time had occurred very early in Vera Temple's life; of childhood, as we mostly understand that brightest period of human existence, she knew nothing—her playthings had been cards, her amusements receptions, theatricals, society, precisely as they were now, the only difference being that whereas now she put on a long gown for some " swell " affair, then she wore a short one.

The slim dark-eyed child, whose wondrous beauty was the talk of many circles, had been petted and complimented, and had been the favourite of princes and nobles from the time she made her *debut*, as she had related to Viscount Devereux, playing cards with Prince R——.

She had exchanged bright repartees with men, and summoned one and discarded another, when she ought to have been dressing her doll; and had recited and played Chopin and Liszt before a roomful of company when she should have been fast asleep in bed.

She had lived always in the glare of publicity, had been used from a child to be the attraction of her father's *salon*, become inured to the talk and the admiration of men before she was able, by reason of her extreme youth, to fully understand how she might be harmed thereby.

And when she fully knew, she had experienced no shock—how should she? It was simply a fact that she must be able to steer her course clearly between rocks and shoals innumerable.

It gave her sometimes indeed a sort of amusement this dangerous play in which she knew exactly when and where to give and take—a bitter half-cynical amusement it was—and she often wished with a wild, and in some moods, despairing wish, that she could feel horror at the often doubtful homage rendered her.

But it was no use, and what was the good of fruitless wishing that made one old before one's time? And what was she when her youth and beauty were gone?

She had grown, not only used to her brilliant garish life, but in some sort to like it—that is, she would have missed its constant change and excitement, and could never have settled herself down to a humdrum existence.

No one had yet found a way to tame the heart that was so full of passionate feeling, that could have lavished a wealth of love and counted nothing lost, nothing sacrificed, for that love's sake.

Perhaps it was well for her that none had.

Vera had had many offers of marriage from men high in rank and position; some who had truly loved the beautiful girl who exercised such singular fascination over men without exerting herself for the purpose of captivating; who would have run counter to the wishes of their family, the commands of parent or guardian, cheerfully for their sake. And for such Vera was bitterly sorry and pained.

"I thank you from my heart," she had said to the young Viennese, Baron Bergstadt. "You have done me an honour that others, professing to love me, have not offered. But I cannot be your wife; you can give me nothing that I have not now—rather I should lose, because so many in your exclusive world would resent my introduction to it."

"And does my love, my devotion, count for nothing?" cried the young man in despair.

"But I?" said the girl. "Why should I sacrifice so much, when I do not love?"

"You would learn to love me. In a new and safer life you would grow to——"

"No," Vera had answered gently; "I should not appreciate, perhaps as you would like your wife to do,

the advantages of this 'safer life'—not as your sisters
do—you would be disappointed. I do not think," she
added, with a smile, half sad, half bright, "that I shall
ever love. I have seen so many, I have liked so many;
I like you, but liking is not love!"

And yet even then she must have felt within her the
capability of loving, must have, perhaps, known there
lay in her nature possibilities that had never yet been
called forth.

In these days, when she did not merely give herself
up to the delight of living from day to day, with the
vague golden hope that each day held for her, she was
asking herself if this very delight which existed for her,
and which had no need of past or future to make its
glory, was because she loved one man out of all those
who visited at her father's *salon.*

The question was asked, but never was answered in
so many words. She pushed off the thought, she
shrank with an ineffable dread from standing face to
face with the fact.

She would not even try to analyse why one voice was
sweetest music to her, why she looked for one face in a
crowd, why or how something had seemed to come into
her life that made her go to rest at night with a sort of
vague sense of hope for the morrow, that had tinted all
the mists with a golden light, soft as the dawn of a new
day.

After that first night on which Ernest Devereux had
come to Bruton Street he did not suffer the acquaintance
to drop, and she had no real wish that it should drop,
although she had told herself that he ought not to
come.

He came to their receptions, and met Vera at various
places besides. He never paused to ask himself if he
were wise—what would be the end of all this? but
gave himself up recklessly to the fascinations that lay
in the mere presence of Vera.

He was moved with a passionate pity for her in this
strange position, which seemed to have left her with so
little taint; he wondered, indeed, how it were possible
that she could occupy such a position without losing all

the charm of womanhood; for, of course, he, as other men, gauged pretty accurately the true position and living of Mr. Berkeley Temple, and knew that Vera was simply a beautiful decoy to catch the suffrages of the gilded youth who patronised his *salon*.

His pretty cousin Alise attacked him more than once on the score of his friendship with the Temples.

She was wild to know Vera, this beautiful, fascinating Vera, who was turning all the men's heads.

"Yours among the number," said Miss Alise archly, looking at her cousin over her fan.

There had been a small dinner at Mrs. Mainwaring's, and Devereux, according to his custom, had joined the ladies very soon after their withdrawal.

"Oh yes, you cannot deny it. I have heard all about the St. Bernard."

Devereux laughed.

He was not the least disconcerted at his cousin's charges; they were no new things of which he was accused.

"Of course you have," he answered; "everybody hears of everything now-a-days. Do you grudge Vera Gellert?"

"That is an unkind cut! You know I don't care if you gave her your own stag-hound. I am not so fond of dogs. But is it true, Ernest, that she won Gellert of you at cards?"

"Quite true, fair coz. I hope you are not horrified?"

"Oh n—no," rather dubiously.

"But a little, eh? Vera, you see, has passed most of her life on the Continent, and a good deal in Russia, where ladies are not so shocked at the sight of cards as some of ours are."

"Besides, I suppose it was in jest?"

"In jest, of course."

"I wish I knew her," said Alise enthusiastically. "I do wish, Devereux, you would introduce us in some way, I'm certain you could."

"Shall I chaperon you to an evening in Bruton Street?" asked Devereux mischievously.

"But you are so tiresome, you always turn it off in some way," said Alise almost pettishly, "one would think you imagine they weren't good form."

If Alise had some idea of making this a leading assertion, in order to find an answer to some vague rumours she had heard, she gained no enlightenment either in look or manner from Devereux—the unconscious egoism of his cousin's phrase struck him as so exquisitely ludicrous, that he burst out laughing.

"Forgive me, dear coz," said he. "I really couldn't help it," but he didn't say what had amused him. "But don't you see that they move in such a different set— you never come across each other—you have no mutual friends."

"Except you," persisted Alise.

"I? But then I'm not the sort of steady-going respectable head of a family style of fellow to be standing for everyone all around. All the same if you come across each other somewhere, I'll be happy to effect an introduction."

"There's a dear boy—do tell me something about her," said Alise, who had an eager curiosity to get acquainted with the personality of a girl who was so much talked about, as well as a real desire to know one so brilliant and beautiful.

"You know all I can tell you," answered Devereux, smiling. He was not eager to discuss Vera and tell little anecdotes about her, just as if he were a writer of notes in "Verity." And in saying this he put some of Alise's notions rather at a non-plus, for if he was in love with Vera would he not be only too ready to talk about her," argued this young lady. "You know, in fact, more than I can tell you, because you see the Societies."

"But that's all make-up. Is it true that she plays and—and all that?" concluded the young lady vaguely.

"She plays divinely," returned Devereux gravely, and Alise flicked him with her fan and declared there was nothing to be got out of him.

At this same time, Mr. Linwood was standing in Vera's drawing-room, looking gloomily down on the recumbent form of the dog Gellert. Gellert lay with his nose between his paws, but his eyes were not shut, they were fixed with an upward watchful gaze on the face that in turn watched him. The dog had manifested no particular welcome to Linwood, he seemed rather indifferent to him, or was, perhaps, conning over in his doggish mind whether this visitor was worthy of his regard and trust.

Lucius was something more than indifferent to Gellert, however; he very distinctly hated the animal, for the giver's sake.

"Isn't he a beauty?" said Vera, coming over to the mantelpiece by which Lucius stood.

Vera had the coolest way of ignoring any past unpleasantness when she chose.

"So you've got your pet," Lucius returned rather roughly.

"You see I have; is he not charming?"

"I don't pretend to be a judge of dogs; if you are pleased with him and his late master, that's all that need be said."

"Of course, and I am pleased with both," returned Vera, kneeling down by her favourite, and laying her soft cheek against his head; "it's a great pity you don't like dogs."

Lucius turned away with a gesture of impatience.

"I wonder," he said with some bitterness, "how much of your worship is given to Gellert himself—how much to the giver through Gellert."

It was a bold speech to make, and one that Vera might have chosen to resent. Lucius would never have made it to any other girl "in society," and Vera was aware of this, but she was not insulted as one of these would have been, and felt more amused than angry at Linwood's vexation.

"How would it do, Mr. Linwood," said she, looking up archly, "if I were to ask you how much your dislike to Gellert is due to him personally—if I may use the term—and how much to the giver?"

"It was a piece of confounded insolence," Lucius broke out with sudden fierceness; "this haughty Devereux who has never known defeat where he chose to trouble himself to win, who has grown insolent because he always triumphs where women are concerned, he thinks that he has only to look to put aside all other claimants. Would any other man have presumed to go so far on the strength of one evening's acquaintance?"

Vera, whose clear cheek had slightly flushed at this unexpected outbreak from Linwood, rose and stood erect, but even now if she was angry she did not show it.

"You are taking a very great deal on yourself," she said quietly and coolly. "Who made you a censor over Lord Devereux's actions or over mine? The giving of a dog, bah! what is that? Haven't scores of men sent me richer presents than that on an acquaintance as slight. You are absurd, *mon cher* Linwood, and if you give vent to such sentiments in public, you will become ridiculous."

"But you madden one, Vera," Lucius muttered.

He gave a sort of flickering glance up into her face, as if uncertain how she would take that "Vera," but she took no overt notice of the venture.

She let it pass, making allowance perhaps for his agitation.

"You madden yourself, you mean," she answered carelessly. "What dreadful heroics you have been treating me to, and all over a dog!"

"Why will you so wilfully misunderstand?" said Linwood; "why will you not be more approachable?"

"Why are you so inconsistent? Just now you thought me too 'approachable,' whatever you may mean by that," said Vera, pulling a spray of roses from a bowl near, and laying it against her cheek.

"I have known you so long, yet you denied me a pleasure that was granted at once to an hour's friend," said Linwood.

He had come a step nearer, and put out his hand to take hers—gently enough, but both hers then were busy settling her roses in the bosom of her dress.

"You have worn that complaint quite threadbare," she said rather abstractedly, intent on her adornment; it's more like young Charleston to harp for ever on one string than a man of your experience. There! how do you like the effect against the dark dress—pretty, isn't it?"

She might have been the veriest *ingenue* playing with fire without knowing it as she lifted her eyes and asked with them as innocently as with her lips that innocent question; or she might have been the veriest coquette that ever played with fire, quite well knowing how much she might let it run on her garments, knowing these fire-proof.

Linwood fell back a step, he gnawed his moustache savagely after his way, and his cheek flushed darkly— was there no way of forcing this girl to listen to him?

Yet he felt a sort of fear of her; she seemed armed at all points against him, and he had no golden key to unlock the close-shut door of her heart.

"Everything you wear looks well," was all he could find to say grimly, when she made him a curtsey.

"Thank you; if that had been better said it wasn't so bad, but the manner spoilt it; you really might take a lesson from Devereux."

This time Linwood made the step forward again, and this time found her hands unoccupied with her roses.

He grasped one fiercely, and bent down close to her.

"Vera, have you no heart?" he whispered hoarsely; "is it only women who can torture with so refined a cruelty as you torture me? Are you not afraid to trifle with my love as you do?"

"I never was afraid of any man yet," said Vera.

She was smiling; she did not say the words defiantly, but quite cheerfully, stating a fact; and though his clasp was both close and heavy on her wrist, she did not tell him so, or seek to remove it.

"And you really should not get up all these tragics over two things which do not exist."

"What are those?" he asked rapidly, as she paused —to make him ask.

"My heart and—your love."

He almost flung her hand from him with a short laugh.

"The first I believe," he said.

He controlled himself with difficulty. His passionate and overbearing temper, over which he habitually could keep an iron hand, was all but mastering him. He could not brook opposition or rivalry, and here he had both, for he chose to erect Lord Devereux into a rival.

But he knew perfectly well that Vera was not to be overborne by an imperious temper. She must be won, if possible; if not, then there remained, perhaps, coercion.

He had already let his passion carry him too far, and sought to repair his mistake; but the struggle was visible, and he knew that Vera watched it with quizzical eyes, not with sympathetic ones.

He turned away, and went a few steps from her, then came back, and his brow was clearer and his voice gentler when he spoke.

"Forgive me," he said quite humbly, "believe that it is only my love for you that makes me forget what is due to you. I will hope that one day you will learn to think kindly of me, and so, at least acknowledge that my love is faithful and sincere. You are not angry with me?"

"Angry? oh, no; on the contrary, I am amused. You can't think," said Vera seriously, "how droll it is to see you men taking such odd ways of recommending yourselves to our notice; it's a metaphysical study. And all quarrelling over the bone, and, you know, only one can have the bone."

Linwood paused a moment, and then said, with a half smile curling his lips, and a cruel gleam in his eyes:

"Only one, fair Vera—and that one will be he who has most power."

Vera nodded, smiling too.

"Oh, of course; he who has most power, if anyone ever has the bone at all. Are you going?"

"Yes."

"Good-night, then."

"Good-night."

"What would he say," muttered the girl, when alone, with a bitter smile, "if he saw me—heard me with Linwood? Oh, why cannot I cut this bondage and live a different life?"—she caught her breath suddenly, and put her hand to her forehead—"since when have I found this a bondage?" she said slowly.

And the answer came only too clear through the silence of the great dim room:

"Since I have known Ernest Devereux."

CHAPTER VII.

A WARNING AND AN OFFER.

O one looking, at any rate superficially, on Vera's life at this time would have thought it a bondage; it seemed as brilliant, as dazzling as the beautiful spring days that came in with April, and cheated the people into believing that we were going to have a real summer this year.

There was a rush back to town after the Easter holidays, and a rush it remained till the middle of July, and as Vera was in the rush—in the very thick of the onward current, her life was an extremely brilliant one, and no doubt an extremely enviable one.

Money was never lacking in Bruton-street, and Vera could have what she chose, and having been brought up in very lavish ways, and accustomed to a great deal of splendour, she did very often choose.

She was a great deal photographed, both alone and with Gellert, and many a time Lord Devereux bit his lip and set his teeth when he passed the shop-windows where Vera's rare beauty was the attraction which gathered crowds around to stare and speculate, and speak carelessly of the girl who trod her dangerous path so lightly and so surely.

"But why do you allow it," he said to her.

It hurt him that this girl, before whom, for good or for evil, he had laid down his life, should seem willing to be public property.

"Why do you assume that I care one way or the other?" answered the girl.

The words and the tone were careless, yet there was underlying them a trembling anxiety.

"No," he said gloomily, turning half aside; "I don't see exactly why you should care."

"I am glad you have come to such a satisfactory conclusion," remarked Vera dryly.

Yet the answer gave her the cold chill of disappointment, and it must have been this which prompted the restless desire to justify herself in some measure to him, for she added, with a sort of hurried bitterness:

"Why should I care? What difference does it make? Am I not always before the public, and have I not always been? People stare at me in the street; at the Academy I am mobbed, though you call the mob a well-bred one. Hadn't they better stare at me in the shops, when I am not there to see and hear them? It is the penalty one pays, I suppose, for being beautiful and famous, if one calls this ephemeral notoriety fame."

He was more deeply pained than he chose to show, for he knew that if he spoke the words which rose to his lips he should say more than was wise, and more than he had indeed any right to say in their relative positions.

But it was a bitter thraldom to him to have to hold his peace, and he chafed under it, and chafed under the many bands which held his imperious will and his most ardent wishes in subjection; he felt that he should break through them soon, somehow.

There was to be one of Berkeley Temple's delightful and informal little dinners this evening, and later many more guests would come, and there would be play of course—high play, as there always was.

But to dinner were coming only Lord Devereux and Lucius Linwood.

Berkeley had asked them only that morning, meeting one at the "Regina," and one in the park, and he had smiled to himself when both accepted.

"They are an excellent foil, the one to the other," said Berkeley, lighting a cigar. "It won't do to give one an innings over the other. My dear Vera must be careful, she is too inclined to make favourites. Both these men are dangerous; Linwood because he wants her money, Devereux because he is fool enough to retain an old-world predilection for honour."

"WHAT, IN THE DARK STILL? MUSIC AND TWILIGHT—HOW AWFULLY ROMANTIC."

No. 3.

NOTICE.—With this Number is Given Away a Coloured Picture for binding with the Work.

He came into the drawing-room with Linwood about five minutes before dinner was announced, and the latter greeted Devereux with a somewhat marked coldness; Devereux on his side meeting the other with his usual easy grace of manner.

He did not care for Linwood, but he had no especial enmity towards him, he was not afraid of his rivalry.

The dinner was such a *recherche* repast as Berkeley Temple understood how to give.

He had a French cook whose performances Mr. Linwood, who was by no means indifferent to the value of such a person in a household, was accustomed to extol at the club; the wines were choice, and the service was prompt and silent.

And Vera was a hostess who would have made most men even forget whether they were eating boiled beef or the wing of an ortolan; perhaps Linwood's admiration for her did not go so far as this, but she made an excellent addition to an excellent table, and he appreciated every good thing which was offered him.

The conversation was as sparkling as the champagne, and flowed as readily, and if Devereux and Vera were the principal starters of topics, the other two more or less following their lead, Linwood had the lead with the wine, and Berkeley was satisfied.

When Vera rose to go up stairs, Devereux, who was seated nearest the door, was naturally though quite quietly before Linwood in opening the door for her, and as she passed out, he said, bending down a little:

"May I not be allowed to enjoy a half-hour's paradise of music before they come up?"

Vera smiled, and said "Yes," and went out, but Berkeley called out to Devereux:

"What! are you going to desert us already, you unnatural young man? Has wine no attractions for you?"

"None at all. But music has, and Mademoiselle Vera has promised me a rich treat," answered Devereux, smiling as he closed the door, and bounded up stairs like a bird let free, while Linwood muttered a curse under his breath.

And in this delicious half-hour, Vera gave herself up to the dreamy, dangerous happiness, and played Chopin's exquisite nocturnes, and sang songs of Schumann and Schubert to Ernest Devereux in the gathering twilight.

And he sat near and watched the wondrous beauty of the face that the soft spell of love left only strangely tender, and forgot the outside world, forgot that an outside world even existed, and that there lay a gulf wide and deep as the ocean between Ernest, Lord Devereux, future Earl of Evringham, and Vera, the dazzling beauty, known in the great cities of the old and new world.

But we all it is only fitful glimpses of paradise we get on this lower earth, and theirs came to an end with the opening of the drawing-room door, the broad rush of light that came in therewith, and the forms of the host and Lucius, who advanced, saying with a veiled sneer:

"What in the dark still? Music and twilight—how awfully romantic."

"Isn't it," said Vera, looking round and laughing.

Away went the dream-world, up came the tinsel and the gilt, and the masked puppets, that dance, and talk, and whirl, and laugh the hours through.

And Devereux rose, and as he passed her, bent low, and whispered:

"You have given me heaven; now the golden gate is shut again."

And the words made her tremble and be glad of the darkness that hid her face.

The servant came in and lit the lamps, and Linwood, perhaps not to be outdone by Devereux, begged Vera for some music.

"I hope you won't regard me as a sort of ogre breaking up such a delightful musical *tete-a-tete*," said he, coming over to the piano, "I assure you I feel an intruder.

"I shall not try to persuade you out of such a nice suitable frame of mind then," returned Vera, laughing. "I consider it too rare in a man to feel that he can intrude. But you are a stranger in the land of Chopin and Schumann, and I will sing you rather——"

She did not finish her phrase, but dashed off at once into a sparkling French *chanson*, and found when she had finished it that her audience had increased by the advent of Jack Crawford and two other men. She rose, nodding slightly to Linwood in acknowledgment of his thanks, and crossing over to Jack shook hands and began talking to him.

"You owe me my revenge, Devereux," said Linwood, touching the Viscount on the arm.

"Yes; shall we fight it out now, then?" Devereux answered. "I am at your service."

He fancied that at his answer Vera's face changed ever so slightly.

Play lasted deep into the night, and seemed to absorb the players, brain and soul.

Devereux, who played always coolly, and often carelessly, was habitually a lucky hand; but his luck seemed strangely to desert him to-night. Perhaps it was that his thoughts were not at all with the cards, but with the fair girl who sometimes looked on, sometimes would touch a few cords on the piano, and then get up again with a kind of suppressed restlessness.

He would much rather have been with her, but could not break up the party; and so, feeling chafed and impatient, in reckless mood went on doubling and trebling the stakes, winning sometimes, but more generally losing, until he rose, laughing, as was his way over his losses, and declared himself "ruined."

He was in Linwood's debt, and more deeply in Berkeley's, and was more vexed than he chose to show because he was obliged to let his debts stand over until the following day, a thing which he hated to do.

It was not often that he played so high but that either the cash he had about him or a cheque would settle the amount, but just now he was not at all clear that all the cash at his bankers would be sufficient to meet his debts.

He supposed, with a mental shrug of the shoulders, that he must ask his father for a cheque, and that he hated to do, for not only would it bring down a lecture on his head, the worse to hear in that the viscount knew that the lecture was deserved, but also would entail a quantity of excellent advice as to the desirability of marrying his cousin Alise, and settling down into respectability.

"No, I'll try no more to-night," said he, smiling, not the least excited or angry through his misfortune; "my hand is out of its usual luck, and so I shall retire from the contest. Mr. Temple, you carry all before you. I will, with your permission, devote myself to Mdlle. Vera."

And he came across to Vera, who was in the large drawing-room.

"Tired of your faithless Mistress?" said she, looking up with a smile as he drew near.

"She has deserted me; she has gone over to the enemy in the person of——"

"My father," Vera put in quickly.

"I have had the pleasure to lose to your father," said Devereux, bowing and laying a light stress on the last pronoun; but Vera did not smile, her face was grave rather, and indeed almost stern, the delicate brows drawn together.

"And to Mr. Linwood, too," she said; then with a fleeting, upward glance: "Why do you play so much? Surely—surely you do not care for it so very much?"

The red colour flushed for a moment to his brow; his eyes drooped; there was a half-expressed disappointment, and a sort of appeal in her tone which stung him with pain. But he answered, recovering himself at once:

"You have put me a hard metaphysical question, Mdlle. Vera. I don't think I can analyse on the moment why I play—*pour passer le temps,* for one thing, I suppose."

"That is very well for Jack and men of his calibre; but you——"

"The distinction is flattering," said Devereux, amused and fascinated by her frankness. "Well, I suppose I must give up that theory as untenable. Because it is a sort of habit, because others do it, and I dare say, when one once begins, there is a kind of interest in going on."

"You played so recklessly to-night," said Vera, not directly answering his words.

She paused half a second; her colour came and went fitfully; it seemed as though she forced herself to say the next words, and she said them rather hurriedly, bending a she did so over Gellert to arrange his collar, which did not require it.

"You are a very clever player, Lord Devereux, but you are not so clever as my father."

Then she looked up laughing, and what she said now effaced, at any rate for the time, the vague impression conveyed in her former words. "So, you see, you ought not to play for such high stakes. It is dreadfully imprudent!"

"Shall I tell you," said Ernest, bending towards her, "why I was reckless to-night? I was impatient—wild because I was chained to that wretched table, and I would fain have been with you."

If inwardly the girl's heart throbbed with something that was half joy, half fear, she never lost her self-possession.

"Am I to take that as a compliment or not?" she said, smiling archly, and taking up a fan, which she waved idly backwards and forwards—fans are useful adjuncts in civilised life. "You tell me that I, in fact, have made you lose a lot of money."

"And is not that the most severe test of a man's devotion?" said Devereux, with a touch of irony.

"Not of yours," Vera answered directly, "because you don't reckon money at much—do you? They are breaking up over there——"

"I am sorry," said Devereux; "it means that I too must go, and cut short the few minutes of happiness I have had to-night."

"That was your own fault," observed Vera, laughing
—she was bent on not being serious to-night apparently.
"You could have enjoyed my society long ago— What,
Mr. Linwood!" turning to that gentleman as he came
up, "you are really going? Have you won enough to
pay for your gloves?"

"A good deal more," answered Linwood, with a
covert glance at Devereux, who looked quite unconcerned. "Fortune has smiled on me to-night, and
frowned on Devereux."

"Ah, what she takes with one hand, she gives with
the other, *mon cher!*" said the viscount, smiling, and
Linwood bit his lip, and made his adieu rather abruptly,
accompanied by Crawford.

Ernest also took leave, but just outside Mr. Temple's
study-door his host touched him on the shoulder, and
drew him inside the room.

Devereux, a little surprised, followed him.

"You will forgive me, I am sure," Berkeley said,
"if I perhaps seem to intrude on your private affairs
when I have really no right to do so. You have lost
heavily to-night, and to a man who, believe me, if not
at once paid, can make himself an enemy."

"You are very kind," said Devereux, perhaps a little
haughtily; but instantly remembering that it was Vera's
father who addressed him he softened his tone quite
naturally. "I have no intention of letting this
debt of honour run—not the least—neither his nor
yours."

"Oh, my own—that is nothing," said Berkeley,
smiling; "take your own convenience. I know you
young men get through a lot of money, and can't always
lay your hand on the cash at once. What I wanted to
say to you is only this, pray make use of me if you
should want a few hundreds for a few days; I assure
you it would be a pleasure to me to serve you in any
way."

"Again I can only thank you for your kindness,"
returned the viscount, "but I could not put myself
further in your debt—certainly not unless I were indeed
more hard pressed than I am; nevertheless, I thank you."

Berkeley Temple said no more—only disclaimed any need for thanks, and said as he accompanied his guest to the hall-door:

"Still, I hope if you should have need of my small services you will not hesitate to apply to me. I would not, for a great deal, have any young man in whom I was interested in the power of Lucius Linwood. Good-night."

Berkeley smiled as he came upstairs, slowly and softly rubbing his hands.

"If not now, later," said he to himself; then raising his voice a little, "Vera, my love, I want to speak to you."

CHAPTER VIII.

FATHERLY COUNSEL.

ERA lifted her eyes as her father came in, closing the door carefully behind him.

"I am here," she said briefly, "and ready to listen to you."

But Berkeley Temple did not immediately speak; he took a few turns up and down the room before he paused opposite his daughter, who was seated in a low chair, and glanced sharply from under his brows at the graceful girl who might yet destroy all his plans with her "fancies," and of whose strong will he was rather afraid. Vera was always something like a half-tamed filly—he never felt exactly sure of her.

"Yes," he said, as though answering some mental proposition, "I want to speak seriously to you, Vera; for I am vexed with you—you have not acted with your usual prudence."

"What have I done, or left undone?" was the answer.

She never moved or showed that she was paying any attention, and yet inwardly every faculty of attention was keenly awake.

"You have allowed an admirer to become an aspirant for your hand. Lucius Linwood has asked me this evening for your hand in marriage, and of course in any case marriage is out of the question."

The girl drew a long and silent breath; she knew he was watching her, and that she must not let one line, one look, one quiver, betray her.

"Mr. Linwood would have done better to come to me first," she said, in the same nonchalant manner; "we don't live in the Middle Ages, nor am I a French girl. Well, what did you say?"

"I was very much vexed inwardly, Vera, that you had allowed affairs to get such lengths, but I did not allow him to see that, naturally. I answered only that I was much flattered and the usual things, but that I should never force or even influence your choice, and I could only refer him to you, that I thought you too young, etc., etc. It is for you of course to temporise, and so forth—you women understand that sort of thing."

"I shall tell him," said Vera quietly, "that I cannot marry him—now, or at any time. I am not going to temporise with Lucius Linwood."

"Why not, in Heaven's name?"

"People don't come here to marry me," said Vera, smiling; "they come to lose money, or to gain it occasionally, and to see me and flirt with me—Mr. Linwood must understand that. He only wants my money, you know, papa."

"I believe, on my soul," said Berkeley emphatically, "that the man is in love with you."

"That may be, after his fashion," resumed Vera with a curl of her lip; "but as I am not the least bit in love with him he will have to get over his affection, as he has done in many other cases!"

"Love, Vera, has nothing to do with the question," said Berkeley Temple, and tone and words alike sent a cold thrill through the girl's veins; "if anyone wished to marry you, with whom you were, as the saying is, in love, marriage for you would be equally impossible; I hope you will understand that."

"We needn't discuss the question," said Vera carelessly; "it isn't often I am honoured with offers of marriage, and shouldn't be in this case only that Mr. Linwood happens to know that on my marriage a large sum of money becomes mine, bequeathed by my mother."

"I am not concerned to enquire into his motives, my dear; I am only concerned to keep well with Linwood. He can and will be a dangerous enemy; you must know that if you will only be reasonable, and not *farouche*; he could circulate more rumours about you and me, in London, than either of us would care to meet."

"It must come sooner or later," said Vera, shrugging her shoulders. "We live on a volcano, and it will burst some day; why not now?"

"You are talking like a child," said her father with contemptuous anger. "Are you getting high-flown notions from your friend, Lord Devereux?"

"Oh no—only I am in a sort of philosophical fatalist mood to-night, and it amuses me to think what a bubble it would be to burst right in the middle of the season. The poor dear ladies, who find me 'just a little eccentric,' perhaps a 'little fast, but so charming, so original'—a mere decoy duck for a card-sharper's dupes!"

"Vera!" cried her father sharply, "are you in your senses?"

"Oh, quite, papa!" answered Vera seriously, sitting up now. "Shall I tell Mr. Linwood I am not going to marry him because I am the attraction here, and you can't spare your dear daughter Vera?"

"You will tell Linwood nothing of the sort," said Berkeley, controlling his anger and speaking more quietly, for he felt it was worse than useless to try and subdue Vera by commanding obedience. "You have lived long enough to know that it does not pay always to come out with the downright truth at once. Keep Linwood on; don't give an exact answer now, because you know well enough how to keep two balls up at one time. Linwood is set on this marriage, and will be easily persuaded to hope for a final answer agreeable to his wishes. That is the part you must follow, Vera."

"That is the part I shall not follow!" said the girl.

She spoke—without heat or anger—deliberately and quietly.

She looked straight at her father—frankly—with her great hazel eyes, that seemed as though they could never know the flicker of fear.

But Berkeley Temple knew it was with no bravado that she spoke, and knew also that on certain points Vera was absolutely immovable.

"You are becoming quite a saint, my dear," he observed dryly, after a short pause. "Is your refusal to help me—for that is what it comes to—to maintain

our position, based on moral and religious grounds?
And is this also part of my lord viscount's teaching?"

"My lord viscount is not what one calls a saint," said
Vera coolly—she alone knew at what cost she maintained this appearance of unbroken indifference at the
sneers which cut her like a knife; "and I am not
aware how he looks on such affairs as the one under
discussion. You needn't be afraid; Lucius Linwood
will not be frightened away from your card tables on
account of my refusal."

"See that he is not," said Berkeley harshly, and he
made a step towards her, laying his hand heavily on
her arm, for the girl had risen from her seat, and stood
opposite to him. "Listen to me, Vera, and be warned.
You have defied me this time, and your defiance may
cost us both dear, or it may not. It is your fault,
because you ought never to have allowed flirtation, or
whatever you like to call it, to go so far as an offer of
marriage. Marriage is not for you. You are necessary
to me. I have clothed, and fed, and trained you from
a baby, and I expect to receive some compensation for
the money spent on you. I never interfere with your
expenditure. You have what you like, and you keep
your presents when you like. You owe me some
gratitude, at least. You refuse to marry Linwood, and
that is right—he has nothing to give you that you don't
now enjoy. But"—he spoke with a slow cruelty of
intonation that made Vera inwardly flinch, and that
sent every drop of blood from her cheek—"there is
another man who may ask the same gift of me or of
you; and will you refuse it to him? Aha! have I found
now where to stab you? Is my cold Vera cold no more
when my lord viscount whispers in her ears and looks
into her eyes?"

He laughed softly, and paused as though to give the
girl time to speak, but she said no word. Every faculty
was bent to hide and keep down the fierce agony and
passion that held her. Her father tapped his fingers
gently on her arm.

"I have no objection, my love," said he, "Oh," none
whatever. My Lord Devereux may whisper what he

"This lady is the prisoner's wife," replied Mr. Ray, with a ring of triumph in his voice.

likes to you, and you may listen; but there must be no talk of marriage, and you must not leave my house—we must be respectable before all things."

"If you dare say one word more of such insult," Vera said, through her set teeth, "I will leave your house this night, this hour—your house where you have degraded me, and made me what I am. It is not your fault that I have not long ago flung away the last remnant of a woman's honour. God knows it is but the remnant I keep!"

She turned away, and without waiting for anything more her father might have to say, went swiftly across the room, upstairs to her own chamber, and shut herself in.

She paced up and down, clasping and unclasping her hands in a passionate agony that swept over her like a whirlwind—and all the while she knew that this new sensitiveness to such wounds as Berkeley Temple had dealt her, was born of something that had till now left her soul untroubled.

For it was not the first time that he had told her she might do as she liked, only keep clear of scandal and marriage, and the words had not hurt her as they did now.

"Ah, child," her friend the Princess Glinka had once said to her, half playfully, half bitterly, "you will bear your life, and be tolerably happy as things go, only don't let yourself love anyone; I haven't and I am happy and merry always. For if ever you love, Vera, as of course you will, notwithstanding my excellent advice, it will be something that will make or wreck your life."

And the princess was both wise and kind, although she played half the night, and was not a woman whom a mother might choose for the friend of her daughter.

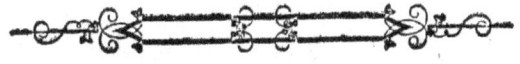

CHAPTER IX.

"IT IS A VERY OLD STORY."

VISCOUNT DEVEREUX occupied chambers in Piccadilly, which overlooked the Green Park, and were models of luxury and comfort, although not merely luxurious. The furnishing and appurtenances thereof gave ample evidence of a fine and correct taste in both literature and art; and a Broadwood grand occupied one portion of the sitting-room, to the serious crowding of some articles of furniture which most men would have considered far more important. But Devereux, who was a proficient in music, always said if he had only ten feet square of room, his piano must take up the lion's share of it. His father, the Earl of Evringham, did not live in town, although there was a splendid town house on Carlton House-terrace.

He preferred the country, he said, and only ran up to town occasionally from a place he had just above Henley, to dine at the Carlton, and vote in the Lords on some important question.

It had not occurred to him that he might perhaps have made a home for his son in London, and in many ways have been a check on the reckless expenditure which he was constantly deploring, and which was the occasion of not a few quarrels between him and Ernest. For Ernest had a deep affection for his father, notwithstanding the jars, and was very susceptible to the influence which is dictated by affection; but, somehow, their lives flowed apart, and the earl did not understand his son, and perhaps the son had too little inward toleration of the father's views.

And so people said, "they did not get on together."

Lately the earl had taken up with great fervour the idea that Ernest and his cousin Alise were made for each other, and was inclined to make his marriage with her a *sine quâ non* to every cheque he drew for Ernest.

It is needless to say that Ernest did not himself take this view, nor, in her heart, did pretty Alise, who found Jack Crawford "too delightful," and much more on her level; but who would, all the same, have taken Viscount Devereux, future Earl of Evringham, had he asked her, though secretly glad that he did not, and apparently was not going to.

The morning after the dinner in Bruton Street Devereux sat alone, looking through his letters, of which he had a great many, and at least half of which he threw on one side without looking farther than the address.

It was yet early, according to some men's reckoning of that word, the hands of the clock pointing to eleven; but Devereux was always up, and had breakfasted and generally ridden out before most of his friends had "opened their eyes to the sun."

But, after glancing through several and throwing aside several, Devereux paused suddenly in his work and pushed aside the little pile, with a half-impatient movement and a quick short sigh, and leaned back, shading his forehead with his hand.

"It is no use," he half muttered; "I cannot attend to these things now. It is her eyes I see looking up into mine from these pages—her voice I hear—the touch of her hand in mine! And what can come of it all?"

He bent his head down lower on his hands and set his teeth, and a shiver passed over him—the shiver of that deathly chill which alone answers the heart's cry, that would fain make an impossible vision its own dear reality.

It was to be the old battle fought out again and again —lost, who knows how many times, to honour—how many times to pride!—love in the lists against honour and pride.

He was the last of a line of noble men and peerless women; she the love of his life—of gentle birth, true, but that gentle birth marred—the daughter of a mere money-lender and professional gambler—disguised though his calling might be.

"She is not responsible for her father's sins," the inward voice cried out passionately, fighting those hard facts that would not be crushed out of the way. "She is pure as the sunlight from heaven! No man or woman dare point at the wife of Devereux, or breathe a word of suspicion against her! The proudest blood is not contaminated by mating with a woman who has breathed such an atmosphere, and yet remained what she is."

Should he who loved her be the first to tempt her from that noble purity which was her crown?

Could he force himself to see her no more—to leave England, to avoid her always, to put seas and continents between them?

He knew he had no strength for that. At first it had been perhaps possible, but then he had been reckless, and driven away the thought of what must follow. For love with some natures is not the growth of months, the slow building up of deeper feelings on a foundation of esteem for good and noble qualities, and his had been no such "learning to love." Some swift subtle sympathy, coming straight from soul to soul, had possessed him from the first night he saw Vera. Then it was too late.

And yet to link his name with one so placed; to sink his pride of birth and honour, and to burst all those bands which social life lays around its children; to break with his father, who looked to this his only son to redeem all the hopes that had been garlanded around his very cradle; to keep the glory of the old name; to make alliance with some name not as old—as stainless!

Could he do this?

Could he bear to hear it asked, "Who was Devereux's wife?" and the answer, "Oh, don't you know that old card-sharper's daughter, the *diva* of Paris, and New York, and every city under the sun?"

The very thought was madness.

Yet Vera's was not the fault or the sin.

The world was really beginning to wake when Devereux at last roused himself from the thoughts that had held him in subjection, and was no nearer victory, one side or the other, than he was since he had allowed himself to think definitely at all.

He drew some letters towards him, and began mechanically to turn them over, when a knock came to the door, and Devereux drew his brows together.

"Some chattering fool!" he muttered impatiently. "I am in no humour for that sort of thing. Come in," and the door opened, admitting Jack Crawford.

"Thought I should find you in. How do, old fellow?" said the young man, coming up to Devereux and throwing himself into a chair. They were friends enough to dispense with the formal salutations of meeting. "Confoundedly hot. You look cool enough, though."

"I don't find it hot," answered Devereux, smiling. "Have a cigar, Jack?" pushing over his cigar-case."

"Thanks; and a S. and B. if you love me."

"Not I, Jack; you've probably had two or three already. I shall hold myself guilty of slow poisoning if I let you have any more."

"It's all very well for you," grumbled Jack. "Everyone isn't such a fellow as you, who can turn night into morning, and then get up ever so early and go riding. Never saw such energy!"

"If you did the same, dear boy, when you felt your seediest," remarked Devereux, lighting a cigarette, "you would have twice the energy. But 'tis no use preaching."

"Preach away; I'll listen."

"I haven't the least doubt. Everyone listens; that's the easiest part," said the viscount, laughing. "What brought you out so early?"

"Don't be sarcastic, Dev. I've been down to the club already; and, tell you the truth now," said Jack, sitting up and propping his elbow on his knew, "it's what I heard there that made me come on to you."

"Ah, What's the 'Regina' concerning herself about me for?" asked Devereux rather lazily.

"Well, it's not the Regina exactly, but one of its members returned Jack; "it's that sneak, Linwood, whom I detest. Can't think how he ever got in. You were at Berkeley's late last night, weren't you? I left early, you know."

"Yes; what then?" the same quiet half-lazy manner, but his pulses had quickened a little.

"Linwood came in this morning and began chaffing me for going off so early, and then asking, apparently in joke still, but any fool could see with intention, if you had quarrelled with your father, or with the 'last lady of your choice'—that he hoped not the first, at any rate, for you had lost ever so much to him, and had asked him to let it stand over. 'Singular thing for Devereux to do—eh?' he said, with that kind of sneer he intends to do duty for a laugh. I said it was nothing singular for a man not to be able at once to lay his hand on a couple of thousands; and, hotly enough, you may believe, if he wanted to say anything against you, he'd better say it out, in Heaven's name!"

Devereux laughed.

"The man is a blackguard," he said quietly, knocking the ashes off his cigar, "and not worth anyone's while to quarrel with. I was a fool to play with him, a greater fool to lose to him."

"Your luck quite deserted you last night?"

"There's no mistress so fickle as this same 'lucky hand,'" said Devereux. "Mr. Linwood need be, however, under no apprehensions. I told him it would stand until to-day, and it will be no longer, whatever I have to do for it," he added through his set teeth.

"Cleaned out?" said Jack succinctly; adding almost immediately with a sigh of envy: "But your governor's such a trump, he'll always come down with the ready. Wish my mater would do the same."

"Oh, yes; no doubt," answered Devereux, a little absently. "I am going down to Beechmore to-day."

"I wish you all success, but, of course, you will have it, lucky dog! Wish I was flush, you wouldn't have to be bothered—'tis generally t'other way about," added poor Jack, ruefully; "I should feel queer paying you up."

"My dear Jack, we needn't talk about that," said Devereux. "While I've a guinea you're welcome to half of it."

"I know it, Dev. Heigho! If I could listen to and practise all the grim lectures I get from the *diva* on my extravagance! Queer quarter that for such advice to come from, but it's a fact. She positively wont play with me."

"Very good for you, *mon cher*," said Devereux, rather shortly.

It hurt him beyond measure to hear Vera spoken of in connection with play.

"Why, yes, because, you see, she's such a clever hand. Father's clever, too. What an odd position it is for that girl! Glorious creature she is!"

Devereux glanced at Jack covertly from under his long lashes.

"Are you dangerously hit, Jack?" said he, with a smile.

"I? Lord no! She's miles above me," returned Jack. "Besides, what's the good? You see, of course, one couldn't marry a girl in such an equivocal position——"

"And the man who would dare to offer her less," said Devereux, deliberately, "would deserve to be kicked out of every club in London."

Jack opened his eyes.

"Oh, of course," he said, rather hastily; "Miss Vera's above anything of that kind. Besides," he added, as if glad to be away from that subject, and propping both elbows on his knees, and his head on his hands, "you know very well, Dev, I'm hard hit in another quarter; but it's no use!" And he sighed profoundly.

"My cousin, Alise, you mean," said the viscount: "doesn't the young lady smile on you?"

"She's awfully kind," Jack answered, with enthusiasm dashed by melancholy. "She's just an angel! I have fancied sometimes that she does care for me; but what could she or any of them say to a poor devil like me? Besides——"

"Well?" as Jack paused, with the air of a man who was about to step over a precipice.

"You see, all the world knows that your governor and mater want to make up a match between the heiress and you, and, of course, I am not such a fool as to think I could cut you out, even if I would."

"My dear Jack," Devereux said, bending forward a little, "you can put me quite out of court. I haven't the least intention of becoming a suitor for my cousin's hand, nor have I the least idea that she cares for me in any other way but a sisterly, cousinly fashion. And I am very sure that my affection for her is no more than a brotherly, cousinly one."

"Your governor will be awfully disappointed," said Jack, visibly brightening up; "but still, what you say don't alter the fact of my being almost as poor as the church mouse of fable, and she has loads of tin."

"She isn't mercenary," said Devereux; "and you have expectations—that is, if you haven't forestalled them all; so you need not be so doleful, Jack. If I can help you I will do it gladly. And I should think the chief objection to you would lie, not in your want of money—my aunt is not ambitious—but in your present way of life. You see, a man can afford to racket when he's rich; it's another thing when he's poor."

"What a cynic you are, Dev!"

"Not at all—it is quite true. I would not like to say that even Mrs. Mainwaring, though not Alise, would not be unconsciously influenced to forgive in me all memory of delinquencies to which she would not shut her eyes in you. But now," he added, rising, "I must interrupt you, for I must be off if I am to catch the train to Beechmore."

"You haven't too much time now," said Jack, rising also. "Well, good-bye, Devereux, all luck to you, and thanks for your information. You've lightened me of a load, although, of course, I daren't hope much."

"'Faint heart,' &c.," laughed the viscount. "Go in and win, and I'll give you my blessing, if only because then it will be impossible for me to be 'in the running.'"

Jack laughed and departed, and in a few minutes more Lord Devereux was being driven at a good pace down to Paddington Station.

CHAPTER X.

"THE FIRST THREAD IN THE WEB."

"IT'S a large sum to ask for, Ernest, and I don't at all see my way to paying this debt of yours, which ought never to have been incurred."

The Earl of Evringham said this with some testiness, as he paced rapidly up and down the library at Beechmore; his son stood in one of the deep embrasured windows, with folded arms and drooping eyes, and close set lips; he had made no concealment about this debt, but had asked straight for the money, telling the earl he had "played and lost," and it galled him bitterly to let a "debt of honour" stand even for twenty-four hours.

He had said all this quietly and in few words, adding no promises for the future, and what seemed to him only straightforward and without useless "palaver" struck his father as decidedly "cool."

"You come and ask me for money," said he, "and never say a word about the future, or make the vaguest hint at a promise that you will not do the like again."

"Promises are easy to make when you want a favour," answered Devereux, shortly; "you would not believe me if I made twenty vows."

"I am not prepared to say that I should," said the earl dryly; "but it would show that you at least were sensible that some reform was needed in your life."

"Pardon, father; it would simply show to you that I wanted money and hoped to 'come round you,' as the phrase is, with pretty promises that I never meant to keep."

The earl paused in his walk and looked at his son.

"London life must have spoiled you indeed, Ernest," he said, "if that is your true character."

"I was painting myself as you see me," Devereux answered, speaking the last words with an evident effort.

His father misjudged him, he knew, but he was both too proud and too sensitive to protest this when he knew he should not be believed.

There was no confidence between them, he felt bitterly enough.

The earl made no direct reply to his son's words, but paced up and down for a few moments in silence.

"You are dreadfully extravagant, Ernest," he said at length; "you get through more money in a year than I did at your age."

Devereux half smiled.

"You always lived in the country, father," he said, gently; "but I am not justifying myself; you have been always very generous to me, and I would not have worried you now with my affairs if this had not been so pressing."

"That is not the question. I must say I don't like throwing money into the sea, for that is about what these gambling debts come to; but I would not grudge you even that now, if," said the earl, impressively, "I could think that this would be the last occasion of such an application—if I could have some guarantee that in future you will not lead such a very reckless life."

Devereux could have smiled at the term. He wondered what his good father would say to the really very reckless lives, in comparison to which his, indeed, was quite puritanic.

"It's coming now," he murmured under his moustache—"the usual panacea for all scapegraces." Aloud he said, a little ironically: "I will certainly promise you never to bring my debts under your notice again. I think I have never broken my word to you."

"That is not much to promise," returned the earl, rather sharply. "No; I suppose you will go to the Jews, like the other young men of your set—an easy road to ruin! I can't understand why you won't marry and be respectable; it is high time."

"I am afraid a wife would not help the case, sir," said Devereux, smiling, "for there would be two to spend money instead of one."

"I don't mean any of your modern flimsy girls," said the earl, angrily, "who spend all their own and their husband's and other women's husbands' money on dress and nonsense, but a sensible well-brought-up young woman, with a good fortune and a pretty face—a nice well-bred girl like—like your cousin Alise, for instance."

Devereux was obliged to smooth away a smile at what the earl considered his diplomatic way of introducing the cousin, before he answered:

"Alise is all that you say. She is a good little soul, pretty, and her fortune would keep her when I am in the Bankruptcy Court."

"What in Heaven's name are you talking about?" cried the earl. "I wish you would be serious. It is the dearest wish I have that you two should marry. The Mainwaring estate just joins ours, too—everything fits exactly!"

"Except one thing," said Devereux.

"Well, what is that? Her mother would be delighted! We have talked this over years ago."

"Why, you see," answered Ernest, "I may be a very modern young man as you say, and do a hundred things I ought not to do, but I have one old-world prejudice. I think when a man marries he should love the woman he will make his wife."

"Love! Pooh!—faugh!—nonsense!" said the earl, testily. "Now you are talking like a romantic school-girl! Of course you will love her; that comes, of course. A young man can love any woman when he likes," said the old gentleman, dogmatically.

"I am afraid I must be rather a singular specimen then," said Devereux, gravely, "for I have never been able to fall in love with Alise, much as I like her."

"You like her? Very well; what more is needed? Liking grows to love when you are married."

"Unfortunately, my dear father," answered the viscount, dryly, "experience often proves the reverse.

Some men and some women can live so, and not suffer much; most men, and some women, console themselves elsewhere; but though I am a modern, that I could not do; my faith—my allegiance—must belong to the woman who bears my name. At least, that is my code of honour. Who knows whether I should act up to it if I married where I had no love to give!"

"Well, my dear boy, of course that is very right, and I am not saying a loveless marriage is a good thing; but where is the difficulty? Surely Alise is very lovable?"

"Yes, father; but I do not love her."

The earl uttered an impatient exclamation, and turned away, and Devereux added:

"Besides, in our arrangements we have quite left out an important factor. I have no idea that Alise cares for me enough to become my wife if I asked her."

"Oh, as to that," said the earl, who considered that a young lady was always actuated by a desire to do her duty, and that in consequence duty became inclination, "Alise can have no very violent predilections at her age, and ought not to have—very unwomanly indeed. A good girl will do as her elders wish; and you could make any girl love you, Ernest, if you chose."

"Without disputing that point, on which I am naturally not fitted to judge, in this instance I don't choose," said Devereux, quietly.

"You mean to say," said his father, stopping and leaning one hand heavily on the table, "that you absolutely refuse to think of marrying your cousin?"

"Certainly—now, or at any time."

"Are you mad, Ernest, or are you caught in some wretched entanglement? I cannot conceive else why you will not follow the wishes of your whole family. If you will please me in this and also benefit yourself, I will pay every shilling you owe, whether this debt be all or not; but I tell you candidly that without such conditions I must refuse the request you have made. Don't expect me to help you in your headlong course any more from this time."

"I'M AFRAID WE CAN'T MAKE YOUNG PEOPLE SEE WHAT IS BEST FOR THEM," SAID SHE.

No. 4.

If the earl intended to bend his haughty son to his wishes, he had grievously misunderstood the nature which, open to all influences of love, was unyielding as iron to all coercion.

The young man had flushed slightly, and then grown pale to the lips as his father spoke; now he quitted his previous rather careless attitude, and his voice was suppressed and low as he spoke.

"So be it," he said, briefly; under such conditions I will accept nothing; I shall not trouble you again. There is nothing more to be said—good morning!"

He turned, strode quickly across the room, and was gone before the earl could even call his name, dismayed in the moment that his son took him at his word, yet angry at what he termed his "obstinacy."

"Some woman is at the bottom of this," he muttered, fiercely. "Well, let him go his own way—to the devil if he likes! He'll come back to me one day."

*   *   *   *   *

That evening a letter was put into Lucius Linwood's hands as he was going into the club to dine. He opened it and drew out a cheque signed in the viscount's clear hand.

Linwood clenched his teeth, and his brow grew black; an unusual thing for a man to be angry at receiving money.

"Where the deuce did he get it from?" he muttered savagely. "His father, I suppose. The old fool's as soft as butter, and Devereux can twist him round his finger. Or——"

He paused, and his eyes gleamed as a thought struck him.

"I wonder—hem! I must find out if so. Once get him into that net, and I can pull the string easily, and then I will sweep him out of my path as a man may brush a troublesome fly from his hand."

"The first thread is spun," murmured Berkeley Temple, softly rubbing his hands after his manner, as he entered his lighted drawing-rooms this evening; "the rest is quite easy; but I must be wary, or my lord will shy back. He is not a fool like these others."

And while this spider was trying deftly to weave his web about what he took for a rather sharp-witted fly, he was so eager that he absolutely never gave a thought to such a possibility as a broom coming his way and knocking down spider and web with one blow.

CHAPTER XI.

PLAYING WITH FIRE.

R. LUCIUS LINWOOD dined alone at his club that evening, and, contrary to the usual way of things, his meal was not sweetened by the thought that he had two thousand pounds in his pocket-book as the money seemed to burden him rather for some reason, and the waiter who attended to his rather numerous wants got the full benefit of Mr. Linwood's ill-temper, so much so that the individual in question informed a brother waiter afterwards that he never did see such an uncertain gent; he wasn't to be satisfied that day.

"Where in Heaven's name did Devereux get the money?" muttered Linwood, with frowning brow. "From his father? Surely not. I heard that the last time he paid my noble friend's debts, he swore it should be for the last time. Yet he went down to Beechmore to-day, I know. Or was it borrowed? And if so," a flash of triumph lighted up the close-set grey eyes, "was it our Bruton Street friend who was accommodating? If so—by Heaven! all plays into my hands—I will ruin him yet, for it is he who stands between me and Vera—and her money."

He rose as he finished his murmured soliloquy, glancing round to satisfy himself that he was alone, and then took his way from the club to Bruton Street.

Vera had said she would see him this evening; she had sent a message by her father that afternoon, and Linwood had asked him how the girl took his proposal.

"My dear sir," he replied, "she is, as perhaps you know, what one calls *difficile*—she is, perhaps, coy, or what not. Can one ever fathom the ways of women? She laughs and turns things off, declares she will not marry —will not desert her father——"

"Nonsense!" said Linwood roughly; "such whims are not for girls who should be glad for any man to marry them."

Berkeley drew himself up with his haughtiest air.

"Mr. Linwood," he said, "you will recollect, if you please, that we are speaking of my daughter."

"A fact which I have not forgotten," returned Linwood, with a veiled sneer; "but you know and I know, my dear Berkeley, that these heroics of yours are all very well, but—— Well, I will say no more—I don't want to do you any harm, naturally."

"Why, no," said Berkeley, smiling; "since you count on my favour with our adorable Vera to push your suit."

"You give me your consent, then, and influence?" asked Lucius, quickly.

Berkeley shrugged his shoulders.

"Of course, as far as I can," he said. "You know I told you how pleased I should be to see my Vera happily settled in life, but I cannot force her inclinations. You, after all, must recommend yourself to her as a lover."

"Do you think she will say yes?"

"How can I tell? She might say 'No' to-day and 'Yes' to-morrow—women are so. And you must remember that Vera wants a great deal of management; one must not treat her as one would many girls; she is peculiar."

"She is splendid!" said Linwood. "To tame such a woman is worth a man's while."

Berkeley, who was seated during this colloquy in Linwood's chambers, leaned back, half closing his eyes, a peculiar smile hovering on his lips.

"Ah," he said meditatively, "yes; to tame her would indeed be a worthy task, but a difficult one, *mon cher*."

"Difficult or not, I will do it," said Linwood, frowning.

"Then you must make her love you," said Berkeley, quietly.

"Why the devil shouldn't she love me?" asked Linwood, starting up, and beginning to pace the room. "Love—bah! What women want is power, or the semblance of it, and jewels, and balls, and such trumpery."

"Vera is peculiar," remarked Berkeley, with a sigh —"very. She has everything the wishes for in that line now."

"Except position," sneered Linwood.

"The position is good, and abroad even higher than here," resumed Berkeley, passing by the sneer. "I assure you she has been offered a coronet before now."

Linwood glanced sharply at Vera's father and flushed.

"And she may be again, you would say," he said; "but take care how you give any countenance to such an idea. I brook no rival."

Berkeley laughed.

"What fiery creatures you lovers are!" said he. "Fancy half a dozen fellows going mad over one girl's face! But I suppose I was as foolish in my young day."

Linwood had been much disquieted by the hint which he felt Berkeley had purposely thrown out. Would he play him (Linwood) false?

"We shall see," thought Lucius, grimly, as he took his way to Bruton Street, meditating of these things. "If so, let him beware!"

But he smoothed the dark frown from his brow as he went up the stairs to meet Vera. He must come, at least, with the semblance of a lover who pleads and does not command; he must sheathe the claws, like the tiger, in soft wrappings of flesh.

The drawing-rooms were lighted up brilliantly, as if for an assembly, when Lucius entered, and that fact surprised and angered him not a little. Did Vera mean to have it in her power to put an end to the interview at any point by pleading the arrival of guests?

She was there, looking radiantly beautiful in white satin, embroidered with raised flowers of gold, with ruby necklace flashing on her breast.

Had Vera thought better of her defiance to her father? Did she intend to fascinate, and bewilder, and dazzle this lover of hers, so that he should be submissive to her will, whatever that might be?

She was turning over an album as Linwood approached her, and half turned, stretching out her left hand with a careless, "Ah, how do you do, Mr. Linwood? Please look at this photograph and tell me how you like it."

"Did you send for me to look at photographs?" returned Linwood, gnawing his lip; his overbearing temper would support but little strain.

"Did I send for you?" said Vera, blowing away an infinitesimal speck of dust which had settled on the lovely face gazing back to her from the picture.

"Did you send for me?" repeated Lucius, compelling himself to tender reproach. "You cannot have forgotten your words, nor the purpose with which I came, the hope which I have dared to cherish; and, coming so at your bidding, I find you here, waiting to receive guests. Is this time or place, Vera, for a man to plead his cause?"

"That depends so much on what you have got to say," said Vera archly. "And as I think I know by heart the usual gamut that is sounded, we may shorten matters by taking it as read."

"Yes? And your answer?" said Linwood eagerly, bending forwards.

"Can't you take that as read too?"

"But you are playing with me," cried Linwood impatiently. "Oh, forgive me, my love, for you make me unreasonable—you keep me in suspense! Answer me. I love you, Vera; I lay my life at your feet. Cannot my devotion move you to be kind?"

"You will love me—half a year," said Vera, smiling; and the mockery that was so witching from her stung him to further protestations.

"My life long," he said, speaking quickly and with the same eager manner, "you shall command me. I will be your slave. You shall make of me what you will!"

Vera lifted her hand, still smiling. She did not seem touched by his words, but she did not send him away.

From this he gathered hope, yet half feared she only played with him, a jealous anger gaining every minute fresh force in his heart against Devereux.

"Now, 'methinks you do protest too much,'" said the girl. "You are nearly as romantic as the young Italian count, who told me he would lie at my feet and I might walk over him! Strange idea. One doesn't want to walk over one's husband—at least, not physically!"

Linwood fell back a pace, his face flushed, his teeth set.

"Vera," he said, under his breath, "you are trying to play with me, and to put me off. One bears a great deal from the woman one loves, and all girls must coquette, I suppose; but take care how you try me too far!"

"What will you do?" asked the girl unmoved apparently, still with the same smiling archness. "Make me a scene? We don't do such things nowadays. Just now, too, when anyone may come in at any moment; and it's one of our respectable evenings, you know."

"I know one thing," said Linwood, and almost roughly seizing her wrist, and with difficulty commanding himself to speak with some measure of restraint, "that I will have an answer to-night. You shall make sport of me no longer. You enslave men with your beauty and your witchery, and, woman-like, when they yield to your power you play with them as a cat does with a mouse."

"A very bad simile, Mr. Linwood," interrupted Vera with smiling gravity; "for pussy eats the mouse in the end, and I am not a cannibal, you know!"

"Bah! you shall not so turn it off. You will learn that I am not so easily turned from my purpose. You think, perhaps, to keep me in your court waiting on you until my Lord Devereux has made up his mind whether to fling the handkerchief. Think you I will play lacquey to him?"

"Now you are becoming passionate and ungentlemanly," said Vera quietly. "Be pleased to let go my hand. What have I said or done to make you so angry? Girls must always coquette, you know."

"But there must be a truce to coquetting," returned Linwood, scarce knowing how to take Vera's words—as mockery or as a sort of yielding. "I am in earnest—stern enough earnest, for my life's happiness is at stake, and I will never yield you up—remember that. I offer you my name and position, knowing what I know of you, and the way all this splendour," with a gesture of his hand, "is kept up. Do you think the proud Devereux will offer you as much? For, if he does not know as much as I do, he yet knows enough to be sure that Vera Temple is not his equal. And, if you will not yield to my love, you shall yield to my power. I can destroy you with a few words whispered in club and drawing-room; I can make you come yet a step lower in the social scale, and be glad to choose your companions from the ranks of the *demi-monde*."

Only the paramount necessity of preventing, if possible, a complete rupture with this man; only her own heart's wild fear lest the man in whose eyes she would fain remain at least such as he knew her, should learn all from this bitter enemy; kept Vera from putting an end to the interview at once—from forbidding him ever again to enter her presence.

She dared not follow the impulse; she dared only step back with a certain haughty defiance.

"You take a strange way now," she said, "to recommend your suit to me. You have insulted me, although you offer me the honour of your name—an insult which it will be difficult to forget or pass by; you cannot expect more from me this evening, Mr. Linwood, after what you have said, and I hear the first arrival."

She bent her head slightly, and with only a glance at his face passed by him to the door, where she took her stand to receive her guests.

But she had given him no answer after all.

CHAPTER XII.

A NEW FRIENDSHIP.

"OU are not quite yourself, dearest Vera," said the Princess Glinka.

Vera stood, buttoning her glove, in the dining-room dressed ready for riding, while her friend, who had come in for a few minutes on her way to Regent Street to do some shopping, sat in the capacious armchair considered to be the special seat of the master of the house.

Vera glanced quickly up for a second as she heard this charge.

She was indeed conscious of a change in herself, of a great weariness, and of a new sweet joy in her life; but she had not thought that this could have been discovered even by the sharp eyes of the princess, who added to natural female acumen the sharpness of sympathy and affection; for there existed between her and Vera an affection which dated from the early childhood of the girl, and indeed the Russian princess was the only woman for whom Vera had felt any of the ties of friendship.

"In what am I different?" asked the girl, bending a little over a troublesome button, preserving her ordinary manner of speaking, though startled internally. "You have sharper eyes than most, but they have played you false this time."

"I think not anything of the sort, *chere*, returned the princess, shaking her head. "I see much, and I saw last night, as I entered, that there had been something between you and Mr. Linwood."

"Oh," said Vera, laughing, and relieved, "he is very tiresome, and, indeed, last night was quite rude. I confess I was angry—I am not often—and, of course, I can't dismiss him altogether."

"He will marry you?   But he has, then, a dangerous rival."

"A great many, for aught I know," returned Vera.

"I do not know about that," said the princess.   I speak of one—Viscount Devereux."

"Now you talk nonsense," said Vera coolly. "Viscount Devereux will, of course, marry in his own rank —is, in fact, I believe, engaged to his cousin, Miss Mainwaring."

"Now, I think, chere, it is you who talk nonsense, or, at least, what you do not believe, for Jack told me that he is distractedly in love with the pretty Miss Alise, and that Devereux would do all he can to help him. So does not a man who is in love," concluded the princess, nodding her head, and sitting up to emphasise her remarks.

"It is all nothing to me," said Vera with a touch of impatience. "Why do you tell me these things as if they could have any bearing on my life? That will go on the same, I suppose. Why should there be any change?"

Perhaps there was a certain bitterness, or hopelessness, or weariness in the girl's words or tone of which she herself was not conscious.

The princess caught, at any rate, the evidence of some new phase of existence which was making itself felt in the girl's soul.

She paused for a moment before she made any answer, then said softly and half sadly:

"Oh, my Vera, you have not taken my advice after all; did I not say if you will love you will then find yourself unhappy?"

For one brief second the girl was silent—startled with a strange terror passing swiftly through all her being; for that second she had it almost on her lips to answer to the sympathy and softness that the princess showed, for she had at times such a great longing for some such sympathy, for none of us, be we what we may, can live entirely to ourselves.

But the moment passed by, the impulse was overcome almost unconsciously by the indomitable habit of repression of her inner life. And Vera turned smiling to the princess and said, half lightly, half seriously:

"But I have not said I was unhappy. Only you must know, too, that one has moments of depression, when everything about one seems mean and sordid. And yet I could not live any other life, I suppose. How late they are with my horse this morning! Ah, Gellert," stooping to pat the dog's head, "you are impatient, too. Come, we will see if Andrew is in sight."

"And I must certainly go," said the Princess Glinka; "I shall never get through my shopping; and I must lunch with Mdlle. Devinet afterwards. The new tenor is to be there also. Adieu, my dearest; we shall meet again to-night."

"Oh, I suppose so," returned Vera, accompanying her friend to the hall door, without which stood the pretty little victoria.

But the princess paused on the step a moment, saying while she settled the flounce in her dress:

"Ah, by-the-bye, child, have you, perhaps, heard that Devereux has had a—what does one say?—a quarrel or a breach with his father?"

"No—no one has said anything to me," answered the girl, undisturbed apparently by the news. "How did you get to hear it?"

"How did I get to hear it? Let me see," said the princess, reflecting. "I scarcely know. I think in some way through the servants; one hears these things so—servants are so indiscreet. But it is, perhaps, not true; the old man will have him marry the cousin, and so——"

And she shrugged up her pretty shoulders, smiled, nodded, and, stepping into her carriage, drove off.

Vera set her lips together, and, almost unconsciously, her hand rested on Gellert's noble head.

But her thoughts were scattered at a sound which smote suddenly on her ears—the sharp swift clatter of horses' hoofs, the rattle of wheels, and a woman's cry for help.

A pair of ponies, drawing a victoria, came tearing down the street from the square, and the occupant of the carriage was alone—there was no driver on the box —and had evidently failed to catch the reins, for they were half hanging down, threatening every instant to become entangled in the horses' feet.

Vera saw, from the little distance that intervened between her and the carriage, a white terrified face, which she scarcely recognised, for sight and action were one with her.

She never paused to think whether she were risking her own life for the chance of saving another from injury, but sprang forward into the roadway and caught the horses' heads, holding the reins, with a nervous grasp, as they swerved and half paused, startled by the suddenness of the check.

And in the same moment several servants rushed excitedly from houses near, occupants appeared at doors and windows, and there was immediately a small crowd gathered round the trembling ponies and the heroic girl whose prompt bravery had prevented, at all events, a serious accident.

Of course half-a-dozen grooms seized the ponies' heads, and half-a-dozen more men took the reins, while Vera went to the side of the carriage and assisted the bewildered occupant to the ground; and Vera knew at once, with a feeling that was half shocked and half joyful, that it was Alise Mainwaring to whom she had done this great service. For was not Alise Devereux's cousin, and was it not a double joy to serve any friend of his?

"You had better come into my house," said Vera gently, for the poor girl stood trembling and dazed with the shock she had sustained, and seemed scarcely aware of her surroundings. "Some of my people will take care of the horses, and neither you nor they are fit yet to drive home."

"You are very kind," Alise answered faintly, though with a strong effort to rally. "I seem to know you, but——"

"But you must not talk just yet," said Vera, soothingly.

She gave some directions to her own groom, who was one of the helpers, and then, amid admiring remarks,

and more than one "Bravo!" from the crowd, she led
Alise into the house. The door was shut to, and though
there remained a group about the carriage, and a knot
of idlers before the door, who watched with interest the
outside of the house which sheltered "the young lady
what was a brick," the people gradually dropped off,
and left only those concerned with the horses to disturb
the quiet of Bruton Street.

Vera took Alise into the library, where, she said, no
one would come, rang for wine, and tended the girl with
such gentle and quiet sympathy as charmed the
recipient thereof, and she very soon recovered, and
forthwith congratulated herself on attaining to an introduction with Miss Vera, albeit under undesirable
circumstances.

"How good you are to me!" she said gratefully, and
regarding the beautiful face of the girl before her with
deep and unconsciously-expressed admiration. "How
shall I thank you for your noble courage, for indeed you
have saved my life?"

Vera smiled, yielding her hand with a new strange
pleasure to the warm clasp of this young girl who was
so pure—so little like those she called her friends.

"You must not speak of that," she said, gently; "anyone would have done the same who had that instinctive
feeling which possessed me of capability to accomplish
the act."

"It was terrible," said Alise, shuddering. "I was
quite alone, for I had sent Charles with a message, that
I had previously forgotten, and waited for him in the
square. You know the ponies are so quiet, but they
got frightened by one of those horrid bagpipe men
suddenly striking up close by, and ran off before I could
get hold of the reins. "I don't know what would have
become of me but for you, Miss Vera; for, you see,"
smiling and colouring a little, "I know your name——"

"And I yours," answered Vera; "a mutual introduction, without any formalities."

"Oh, you can't think," said Alise eagerly, "how I
have longed to know you, and how I have teased
Devereux to introduce me, but, somehow we never met

at any mutual friend's; and so—— But now its managed beautifully!" clapping her hands, regaining all her liveliness once more.

"We were not likely to meet anywhere," said Vera, with a certain ring of irony in her tone, not caught by Alise; "we live in such a different set."

"Oh, but I want, above all things," cried Alise, "to meet some people—like that, you know—nice, free, Bohemian sort of people."

Vera laughed.

"Bohemia, as you call it, seems to have such a strange attraction for everyone over the borders," said she; "it is very curious——"

"Well, but isn't it delightful?" questioned Alise.

"Anything is delightful as long as it is new," returned Vera, answering in generalities; "and as nothing is new long, it follows that 'anything' soon loses it charm."

"What a wise, sententious, dreadfully cynical thing to say!" laughed Alise; "and you are so young—younger than I am. Oh, forgive me, I am such a rattle-pate—Devereux says so."

"And what he says must be true," said Vera, half mischievously, yet with a pain, too, at her heart.

"Oh no—not always, by any means," returned Alise. shaking her head; "but then he is so clever, and likes women who can talk up to his level and do all sorts of things. Have you heard him play?"

Vera answered "Yes," smiling at the little lady's prattle, and not ill-pleased to hear these praises of Ernest Devereux.

"Isn't it splendid? And he says you play so beautifully, Miss Vera; some day you must let me hear you, because, you know," said Miss Alise with a kind of implied defiance at somebody, "I don't mean to be a stranger any more to you—that is, if you will condescend to me; you are so grand with everyone at your feet."

"It would give me the deepest pleasure to be allowed to call you friend," said Vera, with an impulsive quickness for which she caught herself up the next instant;

adding quietly, almost coldly: "We may meet some-where in the world, Miss Mainwaring; anything more than that is scarcely likely, because, you must know, of course, that many people consider there is a great difference between Miss Mainwaring, of Highmere, and the daughter of Berkeley Temple."

Alise looked first disappointed, then vexed, colouring deeply.

"I know—I have heard," she said, tracing invisible lines on the floor with her sunshade; "but, of course, it is nonsense—people are so ridiculous and starched up!"

"The cry is that they are too lax nowadays," returned Vera, with a smile, "or perhaps they are too concerned about the outside of the cup and platter! However, we will not quarrel with the starched ones, and I will only say that"—she paused a moment, then added in a low voice, as though half unwillingly, yet impelled to the confession by some feeling too strong to be controlled—"your friendship would be very sweet to me."

She turned away directly she had said it, as if she wished to pass by the subject, and Alise, struck by the girl's tone and manner, said no more, but only took Vera's hand in hers, saying, smilingly:

"What a strong hand you must have to have held those horses so firmly! I could never have done it."

"I have been so used to horses all my life, and have always ridden spirited animals that took a firm hand," answered Vera. "What, you are not going?" as Alise rose, looking at her watch.

"I am afraid I must," she said, "though I don't want to. I could sit here and talk with you for ever; but mamma will get anxious, and I am so afraid she may hear something about the accident, and be frightened. Besides, you are going to ride—I have kept you."

"I am glad to have been so detained, though not of the cause of that detention," returned Vera. "Well, I must not try to keep you."

The girls parted with many fervent wishes on the part of Alise for a speedy meeting—wishes met by Vera with a pleased but inwardly half-doubting assent.

And as she watched Alise drive away, Vera smiled to herself :

"If she only knew," she murmured, a little bitterly, "how very frail is the position she calls 'so grand,' and that 'everyone' is limited to members of one sex only! How sweet she is! how unsullied she seems! I should like to know her very well. I wonder if I ever had a friend of my own age and sex! Not a girl such as she is, certainly! Come, Gellert, we will not be disappointed of our ride—come!"

CHAPTER XIII.

A LITTLE NOTE.

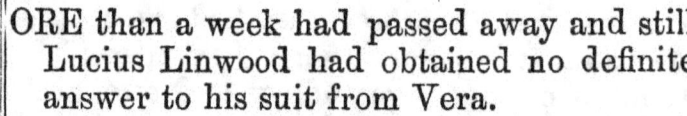ORE than a week had passed away and still Lucius Linwood had obtained no definite answer to his suit from Vera.

She showed herself now indulgent and gracious in her own unapproachable way, now impatient and a little haughty; at times she bewildered and dazzled and yet angered him with a shower of raillery which he had neither the wit to answer nor the even temper to endure with a good grace; at other times she would be cold and short, barely vouchsafe him a word or a look; nor did she ever give him another opportunity of finding her alone.

He tried to persuade himself that this variable demeanour was due to the fact that she loved him, but, like a true woman, must coquette a little first with him before surrendering her life finally to his keeping.

If he could only have seen the girl when all the miserable hours of the day were over—how in a very passion of self-contempt, of loathing for the part she was playing, of wild longings for a better, purer, truer life, of anguish which was yet in part so sweet, for that which had awakened those new longings within her— how, then, when once alone, the girl would pace her room for hours, too unhappy and restless to sleep; how, then, her heart was filled with one image—how willingly she could have surrendered her life to the keeping of the only man for whom such self-surrender had been no sacrifice—how easily she had tamed her wild heart to his loving hand, and meekly for his sake tried to learn a new code and so become worthy of his love, for if he loved her now, so always was the tenour of her thought, it must be only to his own despair, and she had rather, ten thousand times, suffer her life long than that he should know this same suffering—and yet, all the time, deep in her heart, lay the knowledge that he loved her, and that with this knowledge, even though they must be parted, life would not be that poor, dull passage of time to which it seemed to be narrowing down.

Would Lucius Linwood have dared flatter himself then that Vera loved him?

But none ever saw a trace of those many night-hours on the brilliant beauty of the season.

Alise Mainwaring, her new friend, who had kept her resolve of becoming something more than a mere bowing acquaintance, thought her life one of cloudless happiness, and made Vera her model in all things, admiring her with all the enthusiasm of a young, generous soul, and with that peculiar adoration which is — if sometimes rather ridiculous, yet a touching trait in girl friendship—exalting Vera's very faults into virtues.

But Ernest Devereux could not be so blinded. He looked at Vera with different eyes from the rest of the world, and could see that she was not the Vera he had known even a month ago.

There was no alteration in her manner or mode of thought or speech, save to him. The eyes that met all other men's with that fearless frankness of hers, which was yet not boldness, drooped sometimes before his.

There was a subtle, and, to herself, wholly unconscious, change at times in face, and voice, and manner when he spoke with her.

Was it for his sake, then, that there had come this shadow over her life?

"I will know!" he said, setting his teeth. "I will brave all; and if she loves me as I love her, I will forget all but love and honour!"

And yet Viscount Devereux's position at this time was far from that state of security and wealth in which a man may easily and with a light heart defy a phalanx of outraged relatives and a world to whose usages he has hitherto adapted his life, and after whose precepts he has always thought—at least, to some extent—to shape his career.

His father had not relented in his resolve to make a marriage with Alise the condition of all future help, and Devereux was also as far as ever from yielding to this command. His very pride would have prevented him, if there had been no other reason; and it was his pride now that made him utterly reckless in money affairs.

Debts were settled in other ways, and more than one bit of Devereux's "paper" reposed in the strong-box of Berkeley Temple.

"I am afraid," said the latter one day to Vera, as he glanced over the morning paper, and covertly watched her the while, "that it is quite true about Devereux and the old earl, who is an exceedingly worthy but obstinate old gentleman."

Vera scarcely lifted her eyes from the task on which she was engaged—namely, that of balancing a piece of sugar on Gellert's nose. She said rather absently:

"What do you mean? Oh! about some quarrel. Who was it asked me? The princess, I think."

"Very possibly. I want to know for certain, and I think you can help me. He will tell you anything."

"I don't know about that," answered the girl. "Steady, Gellert! Keep your nose down, sir—so! Men, you know, papa, are not so ready to talk of their money affairs to ladies. But why do you think there has been a quarrel?"

"I? Oh! I have many ways of telling," returned Berkeley, smiling, meaning her to understand exactly what she did—that the viscount had transactions with her father, for he desired above all things to erect as many barriers as possible between her and Devereux.

"Well, his affairs have nothing to do with me," said Vera, indifferently. "I suppose you have lent him money, and so assume that the earl has stopped supplies. No, you needn't answer. I know you can't chatter about your clients. Do you know I have a card for Mrs. Mainwaring's ball on Thursday? She gives it at The Rosery—that pretty place at Twicken-ham."

"So—that is very good; that was a fortunate accident of Miss Mainwaring's."

"Oh, very!" returned Vera, dryly; "some people will be rather astonished to see me at the Main-warings, however. Now you may go, Gellert," added she, rising, and caressing the animal's head as he looked up to her, evidently expecting some reward for his patience, and Berkeley, seeing the girl's action, said half to himself, with a smile that was almost a sneer:

"'Love me, love my dog'—eh, Vera?"

But the girl had passed from the room, and gained her own.

Then she went straight to her desk, and drawing forth paper and pen, wrote steadily, but without allowing herself a moment's thought which might shake her resolve:

"DEAR LORD DEVEREUX,—You will be at the ball on Thursday; manage it so that I can have ten minutes alone with you. I have something to ask you.—Yours,   VERA."

The little note went on its way, and was treasured by Ernest Devereux as though it had been a letter pages long; and, indeed, what sweeter thing could she have written to him, than that she "asked something of him," and what was there that he would not grant to her?

CHAPTER XIV.

"THE OLD HEADS PROPOSE."

RS. MAINWARING'S ball was always considered to be the most delightful "thing" of the season; she herself was the best of hostesses, got together the best of people, had a charming daughter —who was an heiress—and last, but not least, a charming ballroom, opening on to grounds which offered many a shaded walk or secluded harbour for flirtations, serious or ephemeral.

Everything to outward seeming was delightful, and the hostess, as she stood receiving her guests, looked as if anxiety or worry never came or could come near her.

And yet her heart was by no means thoroughly at ease, for there were one or two elements that might prove "tiresome" at her ball this year.

First, she was rather doubtful about the expediency of having asked the Temples, against whom in several quarters existed a certain prejudice, moral mothers shrugging their shoulders at mention of the acquaintance. She herself was as much taken with Vera as anyone could be, but to mammas with pretty daughters many considerations arise with which persons not so situated are unconcerned.

Viscount Devereux was said to be much in Bruton Street, and he was sure, she surmised, to prefer Vera to Alise; then, to her annoyance, the Earl of Evringham had taken it into his head to come up for her ball, to see how "the land lay," he said, between his disobedient son and the heiress—if possible to bring things to a crisis.

And he, she knew, would not be best pleased to see Vera the queen of the evening, and Devereux, perhaps, the courtier-in-chief. Then there was Linwood, who was said to be paying court to Vera, and there was Jack Crawford, who was in love with Alise, and whom, she greatly feared, Alise, alas! favoured more than she did her handsome cousin.

From all which it will be seen that Mrs. Mainwaring's smiles covered a somewhat anxious heart.

The rooms were brilliant with the throng of well-dressed and distinguished guests when Vera, leaning on her father's arm, entered. A little stir about the doorway, a sudden turning, as if every eye had been a needle attracted to a magnet, towards the point of entry, would have announced the advent of some sensation.

"There she is!" said the men, with an involuntary movement doorwards. "In gloss of satin," with diamonds and rubies that gleamed like liquid fire, but more radiant than all her jewels, the beauty that subdued, for the moment, all feelings, save those of admiration, the girl stood there, the very centre of observation.

Yet as perfectly unembarrassed thereby as though she had been alone, for it was not this homage which made her heart beat a little faster, that sent the light flashing quicker from the ruby heart lying on her breast.

"How good of you to come so early!" said Alise, greeting her friend with *empressement;* but she was not able then to have Vera to herself, that young lady being in far too great a demand, and Alise was obliged to give her attention to other guests, among whom she noted, with bright eyes and heightened colour, Jack Crawford, who, after the first greetings, made haste to secure from her as many dances as he could with any face ask for.

"You mustn't be encroaching, sir," said she, with the prettiest coquetry, "you see I have many duty dances to do, and of course Devereux, as my cousin, will claim some, and——"

"Oh, Devereux!" blundered Jack, eagerly, "he'll give over a dance to me, I know, any day. Oh, I beg your pardon," as Alise began to laugh, though

pretending to look haughty; "I didn't mean, you
know, but you know——" and Jack here floundered
helplessly, looking very penitent and rather foolish.

"Well, of course, that you must settle with Devereux,"
said Alise, with a fine assumption of indifference, "but
as I never said I preferred to dance with you——"

"Oh, but you do—don't you?" said poor Jack,
blankly; "I thought——"

"Very well, think so still, if you like," returned the
girl, merrily; "now go away, because the duke is
coming for the first dance, and one has duties to a
duke."

Jack assented with a rather rebellious air to this
axiom, and went off, as directed, to find a partner.

"I am sorry, Mr. Linwood," Vera was at this time
saying to Lucius, "this dance is already given. No;
and that, too, and the last before supper."

"To Devereux!" muttered Linwood, biting his lip;
"you have kept none for me!"

"He who asks obtains," laughed Vera; "you did
not make sure of any dance beforehand."

"I did not think you would give them all away,"
returned Linwood. "But you will let me have this
lancers and a waltz, at least?"

"If I stay so late," answered the girl, mentally
resolving that she would leave before the waltz in
question, "now are you satisfied? Ah, Lord Devereux,
is this yours?"

She turned with an inward relief to the viscount, and
put her hand on his arm, as he came up, bowing slightly
to Linwood.

"Forgive me," he said, as he led her away; "don't
hold me a laggard knight. I could not come before; I
am not quite a free agent as the 'nephew' of the house;
and my father kept me also. Did you know he was
here?"

"No," Vera answered, with an involuntary half-
startled glance round the room.

But she controlled herself directly, angry with herself
for the feeling to which she had allowed expression,
and that surely Devereux must read aright.

"AND DO YOU SUPPOSE," SAID LINWOOD, "I SHALL TAKE AS FINAL THE REFUSAL OF A GIRL OF SEVENTEEN?"

No. 5.

Whether he did so or not, Devereux appeared not to have remarked anything, and said :

"He came up to-day. He is standing there by Aunt Mainwaring, looking at my fair coz and the Duke of Alton, as though he could not make up his mind to be pleased or not that the duke isn't the viscount."

"But of course you must give way to the higher rank," said Vera, demurely.

"I am content. High rank has its penalties !" said Devereux, serenely.

"For shame, my lord ! Do you call it a penalty to dance with Alise, you who are supposed to be the very essence of courtesy ?"

To which reproach the delinquent made no answer but to put his arm around the girl, and glide with light graceful step into the dance.

And the Earl of Evringham, standing beside his hostess, put up his eyeglass and bent his old brows together, trying his best to harden his heart against that beauty which had even in its wondrous charm a certain pathos which could not but touch a nature not really hard.

"So that is the new beauty !" he said. "Well, niece, I can't say I think you were prudent to invite her here ; with all partiality for our pretty Alise, I must say that the beauty eclipses your daughter."

"She is a different style," returned the mother quietly. "Vera is very beautiful !"

"And Devereux is very handsome," said the old earl grimly.

Mrs. Mainwaring flushed and glanced into his face, and then uttered a little sigh.

"I'm afraid we can't make young people see what is best, in a worldly point of view, for them," said she. "It is very provoking !"

"Tut ! the boy will come round to his duty," said the earl, who was very sore at the prospect of having his favourite plan thwarted. "A fancy—young men rave over every new face that comes up nowadays ; they weren't so volatile in my time," added he with that somewhat aggravating conviction that "the old times were better," in which old men are wont to indulge. "Marian was the only woman I ever cared for."

"I fear," said Mrs. Mainwaring, rather sadly, "that Vera is the only woman for whom Devereux will ever care."

The earl turned to her sharply.

"Nonsense!" said he, almost roughly; "that girl whom nobody knows, about whom one hears hints—a regular professional beauty. That fellow Lin—Linwood, yes—said something to me in the club to-day."

"Yet I am told," said Mrs. Mainwaring a little dryly, "That he wants to marry her."

"Very well—let him," rejoined the earl, petulantly. "Linwood—Linwood, a very decent north-country name; let him chose a wife from where he likes. But my son! Good Heavens, Ellinor! and here is a sweet, innocent child just made for him!"

"Hush, dear uncle—pray don't raise your voice so!" said Mrs. Mainwaring soothingly, though she felt greatly inclined to laugh at her relation's little outburst. "Though we are standing apart, still you may be heard. I beg you not to credit all the foolish gossip which flies about over a girl of Miss Vera's beauty. I own I am very fond of her, and then she saved my Alise's life!"

"Well, well, a sweep might have done the same," said the earl, a little mollified by this recollection; "but still you would not invite him to your ball."

"But, dear uncle——" began Mrs. Mainwaring, laughing.

"Yes, yes— all very well, niece," said her uncle, nodding his head, highly pleased with his own remorseless logic. "Women are never logical—always let their feelings run away with them. However, we won't talk any more about it now. But I must speak seriously to Devereux again, and you to Alise."

"Alise can't do anything, dear uncle," said his niece, smiling.

Alise whirled by at that moment with Jack Crawford. She was talking and smiling to him, and as she passed flung her mother such a happy smile and bright look that made the mother's heart rejoice and quake in one moment.

"Everything is going wrong," she sighed inwardly, and hoped her uncle had not observed that this was Jack's second dance.

"'Man proposes and God disposes,'" said Mrs. Mainwaring with a certain trust in the better management of the Higher Power.

Bnt the earl grumbled:

"A more ridiculous axiom I never heard. It means that young men's and young women's fancies dispose. Thank Heaven this eternal waltz is over, and now perhaps Devereux will have the kindness to do his duty!"

Meanwhile Ernest Devereux's idea of doing his duty was to lead Vera out into the gardens, where many dancers were promenading. He had the usual perverted ideas of youth on this subject.

CHAPTER XV.

THE YOUNG HEART'S DISPOSE.

HILE the older heads were planning, and the older hands were weaving, Fate stepped in as usual, and maliciously, so it seemed, struck a thread right across this deft weaving of theirs. To be sure, the thread was brightest gold, but all the same it spoiled the pattern, and looked thoroughly out of place.

"Shall we sit out this dance," said Devereux in a low voice, when he came to claim Vera later in the evening.

He had not till now in the most distant way alluded to her request, which though it had perhaps puzzled him a little, he had not in the least misunderstood, as she feared he might have done.

She made no answer in words, only bent her head slightly, and avoided his glance, doing, in that silent second or two, her utmost to control the tremor that seized her.

What would he think? Oh, what could he think? was her mental cry; and what right had she to intervene in his affairs? Poor Vera! she had not been used to trouble herself with what men thought of her.

Devereux folded her wrap about her with a gentleness from which he studiously strove to banish all that was lover-like.

She had been compelled, for some good reason, of course, to step down, if ever so little, from her woman's pedestal of pride. She should not be embarrassed by a thought that he would take advantage of the movement.

There were women in his own world, he knew, who for some frivolous excuse would not have hesitated to ask such an interview, but though Vera had lived a life that could not but rob her of much that is prized in woman, she was not one of those.

And Vera thanked him in her heart, with a swift flash of pride, too, for him, for this noble chivalry.

And her woman's perception told her that it were best to take the whole thing in the most business-like way; yet how difficult, she said to herself in despair, as they paced slowly side-by-side, her hand on his arm, under the deep shade of the lime-grove, only flicks of moonlight here and there falling athwart the pathway.

She had done before some such things as this, had had no fear of seeming to take too much interest in the welfare of the man she had warned; but then she had not loved, and in such things a woman who loves is a coward.

And Devereux, while he spoke quietly of indifferent things to her, divining something of her feeling, was suppressing the impulse that told him, in the throbbing of heart and pulses, with a sort of triumph, that the hour was his, that here, in these brief moments too quickly flying, she was his, and he might tell her all his heart.

But had she not put herself in his power, and trusted him who might so easily have misunderstood her?

It was hard, all the same, for he loved her so, and the most noble, the most chivalrous, is but man, after all.

The girl paused after a while, with a sudden resolution, and drew her hand from his arm. It was easier to say what she had to say when they stood apart.

There was no tremor in her voice, rather was it cold from the very desire to keep from it the ring of even legitimate interest.

"You must have thought it strange," she said, "that I asked to speak to you so, and you may think it a great impertinence in me to intervene in your affairs at all——"

"I should only think it a kindness for which I am grateful," Devereux interrupted gently.

"Thank you." Vera smiled a little, regaining something of her own strangely-lost confidence. "I am sure you will forgive me, at least. My father told me," and now she breathed rather hurriedly, and her hands were clasped together under her lace scarf, " that you had, to some extend, broken with the earl; that you were in difficulties; he hinted that you were deeply in his debt. Oh, forgive me!" she said, and her voice sank and almost broke. "Oh, if you could know what it is to me to say this!"

For at the first words, that showed him the purport of Vera's request, Devereux had involuntarily stepped back with a deep flush.

Who had dared? Had her father, then, committed this breach of faith, and talked to her about his affairs?

But he recovered himself in a second, and his own pain was forgotten in the girl's; yet he would not come nearer to her, and checked the almost involuntary movement to lay his hand on hers.

"I was only startled," he said in a low voice, yet speaking without a visible effort. "Forgive me, and do not misinterpret my movement. Your question—I will confess it—took me by surpise, not because I had any thought in my mind that it was unfitting for you to ask it, but——" He paused and bit his lip; he could not say to the girl, already suffering the worst pain of shame for one who should be, but is not, honoured: "Because it is an unpardonable breach of faith for your father to have spoken of my business with him."

But Vera finished quietly:

" You would say because you considered it dishonourable in my father to have told me as much? Do not fear to pain me. I think," she said with a sort of hopeless bitterness that cut him to the heart, " that no one can give me much more pain than I have now in knowing myself his child. But that is nothing; I did not come to complain, or to ask sympathy or pity. I wanted only to warn you—as I have done others.

She added the last words almost as though they had been an after thought.

Did she want him to believe that it was only for the sake of abstract right that she so warned him?

"Warn me?" Devereux repeated slowly; "against what, and against whom?"

"I will tell you," said Vera in a low sweet voice. She spoke quickly, with a passion in her voice that was only suppressed, though she had striven hard to banish it. "Against falling deeper and deeper into my father's debt, and into his power. You may or may not know entirely all that he is; you will form, perhaps, a mistaken estimate of him; but I have seen so much—so much! and have so often been powerless to save—till I have almost grown callous, and thought cynically that if men like to go to him they may. But you are not like others—you are neither weak nor vicious; you are reckless because you choose to be, and, perhaps, blinded because—you have been a guest and friend in our house. Tell me frankly, do you hold him to be anything different from those of whom men generally borrow money?"

"Yes," Devereux said through his set teeth; "he is your father. Could I think other of him?"

She shrank a moment, but did not lose her self-control.

"My father!" she said again bitterly; "and am I so pure, so guileless, that you should deem it an impossibility that my father should be a friend who stings while he presses your hand? He lives in a fine house, and keeps a dainty table, and one meets good society sometimes in his *salon*. And that is all the difference between him and the Jew money-lender who lives on the folly and the vice of men. Therefore, I warn you to be on your guard, for——" She stopped abruptly, and added quickly: "I have said enough to show you that it would be reckless folly to allow yourself to be in his power——"

Devereux lifted his eyes with a sort of flash, and made a step forwards.

"That is not what you would have said," he cried; "why should he single me out above all men to hunt down to ruin? Is it not his interest to keep silence. He knows that I am heir to estates that are entailed?"

"Yes, he knows that," Vera answered, but there was a subtle change in her voice as though she were forced now to speak and would fain be silent; "yet men before now have been led on, unthinking, unknowing, until they woke to the fact that it will pledge their income for years to come to pay off the debts of their youth. I do not say you would let things go so far, but if you have once begun, you cannot say where you will stop; you must have money, and Berkeley Temple is only too ready to let you have thousands that he may hereafter either make an irreparable breach between you and your father, or hold you in his power for years. In either case you would be ruined, and you have a noble name and a noble heritage; you have something worth making a sacrifice for, and you will do it, I know—you will bend your pride a little, and be reconciled with your father."

She spoke with an accent half of assertion, half of entreaty, but Devereux said, still always putting that control on his impulses which made his voice sound cold in its quietness:

"Be reconciled to my father in order that he may pay my debts! Is that keeping a noble name?"

"No, no," the girl cried out with a sudden passion; "not for that; this shall not be your motive. Oh, you think because I am his daughter, because I have not the crystal purity of some women in your world, that I have lost all power to judge how you should preserve a noble name. But forgive me——" She stopped abruptly with a half-caught breath; "the reproach was not just from me, and I did not mean it; it was my own pain; you must not think of it any more." She was speaking a little hurriedly, falteringly, now, and made a half move as if to go. "Now I have said all, and you will not think me very impertinent? I will— we will go back."

"God!" muttered Devereux under his breath, "I cannot keep silence!"

He put out his right hand with a gesture of detention, and it fell on hers, and with that touch fell away the last barrier of his self-restraint.

He forgot all but that she had put her soul under the harrow of pain for his sake.

"Vera," he whispered passionately, and bent his head to hers, "you must not go so—without one word— my heart, my life, my love!"

A tremor shook the girl a moment from head to foot.

His touch, his clasp, thrilled every chord of her being.

She gave one swift wild glance upward into the eyes which she could no more meet with her fearless gaze, and, swift even as her glance, across all the dazzling joy those words of his brought to her, came the thought that she must not yield herself to this sweet joy—for his sake.

She strove to gather herself together, to collect the scattered forces of her old archness—the laughing coquetry that had so often turned aside serious word and intent.

"Nay, nay," she said, smiling; "you have forgotten. Between you and me, my lord, there must be no speech of love. To-morrow you will have forgotten your words, and I will forget them too."

"Vera, Vera," Devereux interrupted, "will you try to put me off with the light jests you might use to others? It is life and death to me. I have dared to hope—to think that it was—it could be so to you. To-morrow—a year hence—a lifetime—I shall remember, and you will remember. Look me straight in the eyes, laying aside all remembrance of difference in the world's thought, and tell me truly if you love me."

She could not—it lay beyond her strength to tamper, even for his sake, with such terrible earnestness as this.

How could she meet truth with pretty fencing, bringing the light armament of arch words against the strength of his love?

She bent her face down on the hand that held hers.

"Oh, why will you make me say what can only be your misery?" she said with a half sigh.

"Not my misery—my joy, my life! and yours, my Vera! Ah, say that your thought is only for my misery—and you?"

He paused, waiting with trembling eagerness her answer. And Vera drew a long breath and said softly:

"For me? Ah, I think it would be almost enough to know only that you loved me."

He drew her to his breast, holding her in a clasp that seemed like the promise of shelter against the whole world, and his lips met hers in close long pressure—the seal of a troth that should never be broken. And Vera suffered him so to hold her, and it was a sweet and most exquisite joy. And just for those first moments no thought of the future—no definite thought at all dimmed the golden light that for her had shone out so brightly.

She heard her lover murmur a hundred soft and tender words to her; knew that he sheltered her—that she was his because he loved, and that was all.

But do men give love only to part? What was she, Vera, the queen of a gambler's *salon*, to be to Viscount Devereux, heir to all the broad lands of Evringham?

It came to her suddenly, like a sharp swift pain, that thought, which pierced her heart like a knife.

He loved her! How could he, loving her, ask of her aught that should be dishonour? Did she doubt him?

Yet why not? He was a man, after all, and he loved as men can love, and the world stood between him and love with honour for Vera. And what was she, and why should he think her better and purer than her own outward life had made her?

She lifted her head with a sudden half-wild movement from him.

"I must go," she said with hurried incoherent words, "No, no, you must not keep me; we must part; I can be nothing to you."

But Devereux did not release her; he held her hands, still looking down into her troubled eyes?

"Nothing or all, Vera," he said quietly.

He felt her shrink and tremble, and added with tender gravity:

"Could you think, my Vera, that I wooed you as less than my wife?"

"Forgive—forgive," the girl said, bowing her head, while the crimson rushed over cheek and brow. "What am I—what can you think me that—— But that must not be! How can I bring shame on you?"

"Shame! How could you bring shame to me, who would be my crown and honour?" said Devereux with passionate vehemence, forgetting for the moment that all the world was not Vera's lover.

"The world—your world—would think I had, Ernest," said Vera, half-sadly; "and would it not be true? Nay, hear me—because I speak reason and am wiser here than you," with a half smile. "You have a great name—and the traditions of a great name to keep pure and entire; your father looks to you to wed with some woman whose name and fame are above and beyond suspicion."

"Vera, in God's name forbear!" Devereux cried with passionate pain.

"I cannot, Ernest," answered the girl, crushing back her own bitter pain for his sake; "I would die for you to save you a moment's sorrow, but I may not take your heart and break it, or your life only to make it an eternal sacrifice to me. You know what I am, how men speak of me, and with justice, perhaps," she said, and her voice sank almost to a whisper. "I have been reckless, and cared little to keep my life, so that men shall have no cause to speak lightly of me."

"No man dares utter a word against you," said Devereux through his teeth.

"No man can bring proof of aught against me," answered Vera in the same gentle way that uttered so little of the agony it cost her to cast herself—if that were possible—from her place in his honour; but do they not shrug their shoulders when my name is before them? Do they not canvas whether I am—just on the right side of the borderland? Do they not know what my father's position is? Ernest, is this how they shall speak of your wife?

"No one who knows you, Vera, but bows his soul in honour before you, because in countless temptations you are yet untainted."

"Ah!" the girl said with a fleeting smile of indescribable pain, "is that all that shall be said of Devereux's wife—that she just managed to keep herself from actual sin? Ernest, you told me once that when the spot was on the lily, the perfect radiance of its beauty was spoiled. Well, you think no more of the spot now, but the world will."

There was a moment's silence.

It was all so true—so bitterly true; and Devereux felt with an almost savage wrath how utterly impotent he was.

He longed to take his darling from the life she must lead as long as she was under her father's roof. But how was it possible?

To present Vera to the world as his wife meant a complete rupture with his father and his kin. Setting apart any feelings of affection for his father, such a rupture would have the practical consequence of obliging Viscount Devereux to keep a wife on next to nothing, or to live on borrowed money until such time as the estates came to him, for though, of course, he could not be disinherited, the estates being entailed, he was dependent for present needs almost entirely on the allowance made him by the earl, and that in the event of a marriage so displeasing to the old man, would be withdrawn.

"Vera!" he said presently, and stopped; and the girl looked up and met his eyes and smiled.

"Is it very hard what I say?" she said, half wistfully.

Devereux made no immediate answer, but put back with tender touch the soft rings of hair from her forehead, still looking down into the dark eyes that were lifted to his.

"The very first thing that I ask of your love will be a sacrifice," he said at length, unsteadily.

"Well? What then? But for you there is no sacrifice."

"A true woman's answer, my Vera," said Devereux, softly. "Do men ever make such, I wonder."

"I don't know—perhaps," answered Vera. She spoke a little wearily, and dropped her head again on his breast, closing her eyes.

"Ah! why will you speak now of the future? I am so happy—oh, so happy, only just to know that you love me! It is like some beautiful dream that one fears will all melt to shadows with a breath."

"It is no dream, Vera, that will melt away," said Devereux, low and passionately. "My darling, it breaks my heart to hear you speak so, as if love, that should have been your daily bread, was so strange to you. I must speak of the future; it shall be bright for you, brighter than your life has ever been; your future is mine, Vera, and mine is yours: there can be none apart for either of us. Oh, it is bitter—bitter," he said, bending his forehead down till it rested on her bright hair; "bitter that I cannot lead my wife openly by the hand before all the world, that I must ask the woman I love and honour to bear my name in secret."

He felt her start and make a half movement as if she would free herself.

"Ernest!" she said under her breath.

"That is the sacrifice I ask of you, Vera," he went on in the same low pleading way. "Do I ask too much? Is the sacrifice too great?"

"Hush; Oh, no, no!" the girl said half wildly, putting her hand to her head. "For you—for your sake —I must not. It would be just the same now or later; sooner or later the world must know."

He pleaded passionately with the force that only love can make so powerful—the old, old story that every man who asks a woman to give up her woman's pride for his sake, tells again and again.

When once she was his wife, the earl would never hold out against his only son—would never tacitly say to the world that that son's marriage was a disgrace.

And the future!

So many things might happen. The present was theirs. He wanted only the right to protect her—to take her from that life she led, if it became more than she could bear.

And the picture was all too beautiful to the girl who had lived her life without that gentle protection which love wields so lightly.

She shrank with a dread horror from the thought of an eternal parting, for he was more to her even than the man to whom she had given heart and soul; he was the sheet-anchor to which she clung, that should steady her in the purer, better life she would lead.

He was the first and only being who had awakened in her those longings which had slumbered, but which even her garish life had not been able to kill. At his touch they had risen to life; his hand only could lead her, and if he went and she was left alone in that dreary gilded life of hers!

"Oh, Ernest!" she said, with a half sob, and her fingers clung round his hand as a child clings frightened in the dark to a mother's; "I cannot—I cannot; I don't know what is right! I am asking that who never stopped to think what was right or wrong; you plead so, and I am so weak to you. But to be alone again, to feel myself going back body and soul to that life!"

He soothed her tenderly with loving words and touch, and every word and every caress was a chain that drew her surely to him, to bind her life with his.

"It is for my sake you hesitate, dearest," he said, softly. "Well, let that reason have no more weight; for my sake then, for my happiness, consent to this step. I cannot give you up, Vera—no, I know what you would say—neither can I wait indefinitely. I said before, and I say it again, the present is ours, but the future, who can foretell. If," he said, after a slight pause, "misfortune or death overtook me, why then your future would be assured—nothing could prevent that."

Vera started and shivered and lifted her head quickly, looking round with a sort of nervous terror.

"Don't talk so," she said, under her breath; "what could overtake you like that? Oh, Ernest, if when it is too late you should find out that I am not all you deem me now! I am not like the women you have always honoured. I am not good as they are."

"I have no fear, my Vera. These eyes could not look at me as yours do if they did not mirror a soul as pure as that of any of the women you say I have always honoured. Will you not trust me, my heart?"

"I cannot strive with you more, Ernest," Vera said, and dropped her head on the hands that clasped hers. "You can make me do as you will—I am yours."

And Devereux strained the trembling form yet closer to his heart, and kissed the soft lips again and again.

"God help me," he said, in a low voice, "to be true to this dear life and trust that you have given me, my Vera!"

CHAPTER XVI.

AFTER THE BALL.

HERE is Devereux?" asked the earl, with some uneasiness, of Alise, who found herself near him in the course of the evening. "Why is he not dancing with you? I never knew him a laggard in such things before."

"Oh, he finds 'metal more attractive,'" laughed Alise, not in the least put out or jealous because her cousin had not devoted himself particularly to her. "You see, when such a beauty as Vera comes on the scene——"

"It seems everyone's head is turned by this new beauty. And who is she? That's what I want to know! What is their county?—who are their people? —where is their place? These are the questions people used to ask in my day before society opened its arms."

"Yes; but, you see, dear uncle, Vera is so very nice! She is her own credential," said Alise, whose eyes were wandering round the rooms in search of someone. "Oh, there he is—Devereux, I mean; he has just given Vera to the duke, and is coming to ask me to dance. "Oh, dear!" sighed the young lady, as the earl moved away a few steps to talk to another "fogey," as the young men irreverently styled them. "Why doesn't Jack come!"

As if in answer to this appeal, Jack came up at this opportune moment, and evidently preferred his request to Lord Devereux with so many arguments in favour of himself that the young man retired with a half-smile on his handsome mouth, and probably nothing loth, went to see if Vera were disengaged.

When Vera and her father were leaving, Lord Devereux was there to put her wraps about her, and to have a last farewell.

"It has been a charming ball, has it not?" said Berkeley, as he shook hands with Devereux, "especially to you young people who dance and flirt—we old ones have the pleasure of looking on."

"Secure and happy in the thought that all your troubles are over," laughed Devereux. "*Au revoir,* Vera; I shall see you to-morrow, of course. You promised to allow me the privilege of riding with you."

"At ten, then," returned Vera, giving him her hand, which he held longer than was absolutely necessary for politeness sake.

And so the carriage drove away through the dawn, back to London.

Vera leaned back, closing her eyes as though she were weary, and her father's eyes scanned the unrevealing features with a keen scrutiny, which failed to read anything of what was passing in her mind.

"You found it a pleasant ball?" he said, after a short time, "and you were certainly the belle, *ma chere.* That alone ought to make a woman happy."

"Oh yes, it does; we women don't want much to set us in the seventh heaven," answered Vera, lifting her white lids for a second, and settling her head more comfortably against the cushions. "It was a charming ball. Did you notice how much attention the duke paid me?"

"I thought Devereux paid you more," said Berkeley with deliberate bluntness.

"So he did. Do you know, papa," said Vera, with a little animation and a half-laugh, "I have been thinking I should not mind being a duchess."

"My dear Vera, that is something new."

"Yes, I know; but I was thinking this evening, when the duke was with me—he isn't bad at all, very amusing, and has so much money—that the position would be splendid."

Berkeley looked at his daughter for a moment in silence.

He was astonished at this new notion of hers; she had hitherto thrown back any idea of marriage at all.

"You see, papa," continued Vera, "it would be good for you also, because look at the position it gives you! People could never talk."

"Hem!" said he, "this is rather a sudden idea of yours, Vera. Has the duke asked permission to call?"

"Yes; and was exceedingly earnest over it. Of course I only thought of it to-night when I saw what a very great personage his wife would be."

"And what," said Berkeley, with some irony, "is to become of my *salon* if you put your excellent scheme into execution?"

"Oh, you could go abroad and do as you like. Nobody would know anything about you; but," she added, closing her eyes as though weary, "we need not discuss it any more to-night. There's no hurry."

And no more was said on the subject during the remainder of the drive home.

CHAPTER XVII.

"I WILL BE HAPPY."

EVEREUX called early the next morning before anyone was likely to come, and was shown into Vera's own morning-room, to which general visitors had, of course, no *entree*.

Vera was already there, and came forward to meet him with a soft glad light in her eyes, and he took her hands in his and kissed her.

"My privilege," he said, half smiling. "Am I too early, Vera?"

"Oh no, that could not be," answered the girl, adding a little wistfully: "The time seems long when you are not with me."

"My darling, how I wish I could be with you always! Ah, Vera, I wonder if I am doing right?"

"I am so happy, Ernest. It is you who make me so; there can be no wrong to me—but to you. Ah, Ernest, if you would wait!"

"But to wait, dearest, would be of no avail," answered Devereux, smoothing back the girl's sunny hair from her forehead, "and then I cannot wait. How could I when you say you are so happy with me?"

"Ah, Ernest, you are using my own words as weapons against me," said Vera, smiling; "is that fair?"

"'All's fair in love and war,' you know, sweetheart," Devereux answered. "But now to be serious; have you any person about you whom you can trust?"

"Yes; my own maid, who has been with me from my birth. She is as true as gold."

"Very well; when you say she is true, I know that you mean she is also discreet. I asked because it is better that you should have someone with you. You shrink now and tremble, dearest. You will not draw back?"

"No, Ernest; you have my promise."

"A willing one, Vera?"

The girl smiled, and only nestled closer within his arm.

"There is nothing I would not do for you," she said, simply.

"And it is nothing very dreadful I will ask you to do," said Devereux, "only to meet me one day next week at Greenleaf—it is a little village in Wiltshire; you can easily make some excuse for being absent the whole day."

"I can spend the day with Princess Glinka," said Vera, with a half smile.

"So now, sweetheart, I will make all necessary arrangements and let you know when I shall expect you."

He paused a moment, and added softly:

"You trust me perfectly, Vera?"

"Why, of course, Ernest."

"Yet there are many who will tell you that Ernest Devereux is not a man to whom a woman may lightly trust her happiness, Vera."

The girl glanced up with a smile.

"Ah, now you are trying me," she said. "Do you, man-like, want many protestations of trust?"

"Nay, darling, your eyes are a bond for all," answered Devereux. "You have no need to make further protestation."

"Then I will make none. But in return for your forbearance, I will make you a confession," said Vera. "Mr. Linwood has honoured me with an offer of marriage."

"Linwood!" said Devereux, with a flush and contraction of the brows. "He has dared?"

"But I suppose," said Vera, archly, "the poor man had the same privilege as you, at least, to ask?"

And then Devereux laughed at his own impetuosity, and cleared his brow.

"My father," continued Vera, "would not have me marry at all—you can easily divine the reason—but as he also did not wish to make a quarrel with Mr. Linwood, I was compelled to temporise with him. It was not right, perhaps," she said, with drooping eyes, "but I have not learned to look at these things as you would see them, Ernest, and it was hard to me because it seemed a disloyalty to you in my heart."

"But now, Vera," Devereux said, gently, "you will give him a definite answer?"

The girl made no immediate reply, but stood with her face still hidden from him. Then she said:

"He can and will be a deadly enemy to you and me, Ernest."

"We need not fear him," said Devereux, a little haughtily.

Vera shivered and drew a long breath.

"You!" she said. "But I? Has he not already taunted me with refusing him for your sake? He looks upon you as a rival."

She paused a moment, then added in a low voice:

"He knows more of my father than any man in London, and he would do all that lay in him for revenge. Oh, Ernest," and now she spoke passionately, lifting her eyes to his face, and clasping her fingers closer round his hand, "if you would but draw back now while it is yet time! If, afterwards, you should find, when all too late, that the world looks with scorn on your wife, that would break my heart!"

He held her close to his breast, and answered her with gentle tenderness:

"My darling, I thought we had argued that out last night. My resolve is quite set, and no considerations of that sort will change it. For Linwood—— Well, let him look to it that he utter no word against my wife. I shall know how to guard her name, and, after all, what can he do? For he will know nothing, so let your heart rest, dearest."

"I will try, Ernest," she said, "but I have so strongly on my spirit that sense of coming evil that haunts one at times. I suppose it is because I am so happy. It cannot last for me."

"Have you never known any happiness, my Vera," said Devereux, with a deeper pain at his heart than he cared to let her see, "that you have such a gloomy foreboding? Why, you seem made only for happiness."

She shook her head, smiling half sadly.

"I am foolish," she said then. "I am not wont to be 'nervous,' and I will not be so now. Forgive me!"

"The offence is not past forgiveness," returned Devereux, smiling. "Now I will leave you for the present. There is much to do, and you will hear from me to-morrow."

He bent and kissed her softly, and went out.

Vera remained standing motionless for many minutes after he had left her, her hands clasped, her large eyes looking out straight before her.

Was it, as she had said, that the burden of this great happiness lay heavy on her, or was it the doubt, the perplexity, as to whether she was doing right, that gave her this dim foreboding when she thought of the future?

"Am I right—am I right," was her constant inward cry, "to let him bind himself to me? I have striven, but he will not listen. And how can I give him up? How could I bear to part from him now?"

She covered her face with her hands, and shivered at the mere thought.

"At first I was so brave, and deemed I could suffer even that. But now—— To go back to that life, without one ray of light ever to shine across it!"

She moved quickly, as if by movement to dispel that vision which her own words had conjured up. The die was cast, and she would not harass herself with useless and perplexing questions of right and wrong.

"I cannot help it now," she said, with that sense of relief in the fact that this something about which we have some doubt is gone out of our hands. "I will not weary myself. I will accept happiness. But Linwood——" she mused, pausing with her hand on the lock of the door. "Well, well, what can he do?" She swept the hair from off her forehead, and laughed, opening the door and stepping into the hall. "I was going to be happy, was I not? Going to be? No; I am happy! Gellert, Gellert!" she called, and the St. Bernard came bounding towards her. "Ah, my Gellert, we shall be very happy—you and I—shall we not?"

CHAPTER XVIII.

"FAR FROM THE MADDING CROWD."

UIETLY, in a little village church, quite out of the beaten track of tourists—far away from the curious eyes of friend or acquaintance—Ernest Viscount Devereux, was married to Vera.

There was no train of bridesmaids, no crowd of admiring friends. The bride's dress was not such as would have been thought worthy of a chronicle in the *Court Journal*, for it was only a simple morning gown of white serge, and the bride's only attendant was her old and faithful servant, Janet; altogether not such a wedding as the world expected that of Viscount Devereux to be. However, there was, at this marriage, what is sometimes lacking at many grander weddings, and neither Devereux nor his young bride missed the grandeur which ought to have attended the marriage of the heir of Evringham.

"I cannot realise it all yet," said Vera half dreamily, as they stood on the platform later, waiting for the train which was to take Vera and her attendant back to London. Devereux himself would go across country to another station. "Can it be really I who am standing here with you, and I belong to myself no longer? I feel almost afraid, Ernest, standing so on the threshold of a new life."

"There is no room for fear, heart's dearest," said Devereux softly; "shall I not be henceforth ever at hand to help you? And, Vera, come what may, I shall not leave you long under your father's roof."

If either of those two could have seen in what manner Vera Devereux would quit her father's roof! Vera's undefined presentiment gave her no prescience of that which should fall on both in the days to come.

"VERA CLUNG TO HIM IN THE SILENCE OF A PASSIONATE JOY, CONSCIOUS NOW ONLY THAT HE WAS WITH HER."

No. 6.

Vera had told her father that she was going to visit her friend, the Princess Glinka, who often, in the summer, occupied, for a few days, her Villa at Richmond; she had also taken the precaution to write to the princess and tell her that she was supposed to be visiting at Richmond. The princess, she knew, would ask no questions.

Vera reached home in time to dress for dinner, and though she seemed to herself to be moving and talking in a dream, she put force on herself that there might be no change observable in her manner.

She found Linwood and Jack Crawford of the party to-day, and though she would rather have dispensed with the company of Linwood, she was not sorry to have Jack; she had dreaded somewhat the ordeal of a *tete-a-tete* dinner with her father. With Jack she talked and laughed, was brilliant and witty as ever, and gave far more attention to him than to Linwood.

That little ceremony of this morning, how slight a change it made in her apparently, and yet what a gulf lay between the Vera of yesterday and the Vera of to-day!

Vera could almost have smiled at the contrast that was between her inward life and that which she now seemed to be leading.

When she rose to quit the room Linwood opened the door for her, and followed her out into the hall.

"A like privilege," he said, "was once accorded to another. I dare to presume to claim the same indulgence."

"I will not say you nay," answered Vera carelessly, "only I cannot promise you a like amusement."

She added smilingly, as they entered the drawing-room:

"You would not care to hear me play Chopin and Schumann?"

"I should care to hear you play anything," returned Linwood with suppressed force; "but I had hoped to hear something from you yet sweeter than any music."

Vera had reached the middle of the room as he said these words. She turned now and stood still, facing him; there was no mocking light in her eyes, no smile, half mocking, half arch, on her lips; she met his gaze with grave eyes, and her voice as she spoke had only a serious earnestness in its tones.

"I am afraid, Mr. Linwood," she said, "that I have nothing so agreeable to say to you, for of course I know with what intention you have followed me here. It is to renew the proposal you made me a few weeks ago—the honour I must decline."

Linwood fell back a step, looking at her for a moment without speaking, the blood coming slowly to his cheek. Then he said hoarsely:

"And you have kept me all these weeks waiting your answer only to tell me at last that you refuse me?"

"I never gave you any leave to hope, Mr. Linwood," said Vera quietly. "You insisted on refusing to take my answer as final. It is not my fault if the hope you have determined to cherish is disappointed."

"A hope," said Linwood almost fiercely, "that you yourself encouraged by your manner towards me!"

Vera shrugged her shoulders and smiled.

"That is my manner to everyone," she said. "If you chose to take assurance of hope from that, can I help it? Mr. Crawford might just as well say that he had claims from my manner to him. It is very unfortunate, but you see I cannot help being friendly with people."

"And do you suppose," said Linwood slowly, "that I shall take as final the refusal of a girl of seventeen who does not know her own mind for two days together? You have trifled with me, Vera, and I am not one to be played with so lightly, and I know for whose sake it is that you have so trifled with me. But I swear before heaven that he shall never wed with you. Let him know a tenth part of all that I could reveal, and your high hopes of becoming Viscountess Devereux will fall to the ground."

He had spoken with growing passion, and seemed only now to pause because his parched lips refused him their service; in truth Vera's final answer, from which he knew there could be no appeal by fair means, meant something very serious to him. He was deeply in debt, and had reckoned on Vera's money to relieve him of his embarrassments.

Vera was perfectly aware of all this, and the knowledge took away, naturally, all pity for his disappointment.

There could be no question of a wounded heart here. She surveyed him with a quiet, half-amused glance, and shook her head gently.

"You go into such heroics, Mr. Linwood," she said, smiling. "I do not know that I should wed with Lord Devereux as you put it, if he did me the honour to ask me—and you have really no ground for your jealousy of him; however, you must be aware that I am at liberty to do just as I please in these matters, and, therefore, it is no use saying any more—is it? We may as well put an end to an interview which cannot but be painful to both. If you still like to be friends, I shall be always pleased to see you here, but you must distinctly recognise that it is only as a friend that I receive you."

He turned, and began pacing the room, Vera watching him covertly, an almost deadly suspense in her heart, although no one would have thought it to judge by her half-careless mien.

It was an intense relief to her when Linwood turned and came back to where she stood. He felt that it was his best policy to appear, at least, to acquiesce in Vera's decree.

"Friends then," he said in a low voice, into which he introduced a quiver that did not in the least deceive the girl, "So let it be, Vera."

He took her hand and touched it with his lips, and the touch had almost made her shiver. But she made no sign, and only experienced a sensation of relief when at that minute the door opened, and her father and Jack came in.

CHAPTER XIX.

A FATEFUL PROMISE.

INWOOD was not himself to-night," said Berkeley Temple to his daughter when their guests had taken their departure. "Have you been snubbing him very much?"

"A final snub," returned Vera; "he asked me again this evening to be his wife, and I refused."

"Vera, are you mad?" said her father with anger. "Do you not see that you have made an enemy of Linwood?"

"I cannot help it, papa; you are mistaken if you think a man will remain for an indefinite time in suspense; and although one knows Linwood only wants my money, still that does not make suspense any easier to bear. We parted friends."

"Friends!" said Berkeley, pacing the room in much agitation. "You know as well as I do what the friendship of a man is worth when he considers himself unfairly treated by the woman he wants to marry. Could you not have kept it up at least till the end of the season?"

"Impossible," answered Vera, moving to go. "Besides, I was tired of him and his importunities, and so I have put an end to them."

With that she said good-night and left the room, for she was weary, and for once felt herself unable to sustain her usual part; she longed to be alone—to feel herself able to drop the mask, and relax the tension to which every nerve had been to-day so terribly strained.

She wanted to try and think out her position and be able to realise the step she had taken; to measure to some extent the forces against her, and the strength of those forces with which she must meet the enemy.

For she realised thoroughly that Lucius Linwood was now a bitter enemy, and an enemy who could work dire evil to the one who was dearer to her far than her own life or soul; through her Linwood could reach Devereux, and wound him where he had no shield with which to guard.

Vera's life had been indeed ever blameless, but not one in a hundred would believe that she had been so sinless, if the way of her life were revealed.

Passing from city to city, without settled home, without any female society, save that of women of at least doubtful reputation, the heroine of a gambling-saloon—who, indeed, but the most charitable or the most fervent upholders of the purity of human nature, could believe that a girl, so young and so beautiful, flung into every sort of temptation, should have passed through these with comparatively so little harm?

And she was now Devereux's wife. It was of Devereux's wife that these things would be said; it was Devereux's honour that would be wounded—it was his name that would receive a stain.

"Why—oh, why," murmured the girl passionately, "was I so weak—so selfish? Oh, I who can do so little for the man I love—I could have saved him from linking his name with one that can be so dishonoured! Now it is too late!"

She could do nothing, indeed! The die was cast, for good or for evil. Alas, for Vera, was the one love of her life to bring her still, even with its exquisite joy, such bitter pain!

It was long before the girl slept that night; and when she did at last sleep, her dreams were troubled, and only carried on the dim forebodings of her waking thoughts. She woke gladly from such dreams, even though it was to the strain of a new day, and then— would not the new day bring again Devereux to her side?

It was in the Park, however, that they first met. Vera was riding with her father, and Lord Devereux, also mounted, met them near Apsley Gate, lifting his hat to Vera, and giving her his hand with a smile, in which she alone read the meaning hidden from all other eyes.

"We are well met, my lord," said Berkeley with his most genial manner. "A charming morning, and the most charming society to be met with in the world here."

"A very Paradise," said Devereux, with a smile and a glance at Vera.

"Only," she interrupted archly, "there are here so many Eves."

"I see only one," answered Devereux, bowing, "looking at it from an egotistical point of view."

"Ah, you mean, of course, the Eve for the time being," laughed Vera; "and while she reigns of course poor Adam is blind."

"Till he eats of the apple the woman gives him," said Devereux mischievously, "and gets driven out of Paradise, and then finds that his Eve is no more the Eve of his dreams."

"He goes and straightway fetches him another," returned Vera, nothing daunted; and Berkeley struck in, smiling:

"My daughter, you see, is no believer in man's constancy. Vera, my dear, is that our friend Mrs. Mainwaring and her charming daughter over there by the railings? And is that not Linwood with them?"

"Yes," Vera answered; "let us go and talk to them, shall we? And there," she added in a low voice to Devereux, bending to pat her horse's neck, "is poor Jack Crawford, who now is in Paradise, but is it a fool's paradise?"

"I think not, if it depend on my fair cousin," answered Devereux. "But many things, as we know, enter into the making of a fashionable marriage, besides the old-world ingredient of love."

They had turned their horses' heads towards the railings, where the group they sought was gathered, and each side greeted the other with expressions of pleasure.

"We were just talking of you, Miss Vera," said Mrs. Mainwaring to Vera—"wondering whether you will be at this costume ball?"

"What! Kate Cranleigh's? Oh, certainly," answered Vera, forgetting for the moment that this mode of indicating the lady might shock Mrs. Mainwaring. "I suppose everyone will be there?"

"Everyone who is anyone," said Linwood, with a scarcely veiled sneer to Vera, but she made him no answer, turning to Alise instead, and asking her how she intended to go.

"I haven't thought yet," she answered laughing. "I suppose my cousin Devereux will decide for me, as usual; won't you, Dev?"

"With the greatest pleasure in life, coz," said Devereux; but he added, in a low voice and with a wicked smile: "Unless you can find somebody before-hand who can interpret your wishes better!"

"For shame, Dev!" said the girl, colouring and laughing; "how dare you, sir, hint that there is anyone who can do that better than you?"

"You see I was not vain enough for that assumption," said Devereux.

"You mean," retorted Alise shrewdly, "that you don't care enough about it; men are vain enough to assume anything."

Devereux laughed.

"Well done, little coz," said he; "you are getting quite *au fait* to all the weaknesses of our sex. Whence comes so much astonishing knowledge?"

"What a tease you are, Dev! What character shall you take at the ball?"

"I haven't decided yet," answered her cousin.

"Oh," cried Alise eagerly and vaguely, "take something Greek or Roman, and wear that curious old dagger of yours."

"Brutus, *par exemple?*" said Devereux gravely. "Only I think a twelfth-century dagger would look rather out of place as worn by a Roman?"

"Oh, well, I suppose it would to an antiquary, or somebody of that kind," returned Alise; "but I don't suppose anyone else would be much the wiser."

"What's that about a dagger?" asked Vera, turning from Linwood, with whom she had exchanged a few words, to join in the conversation, "and Brutus? Lord Devereux are you cherishing dire intentions towards some unconscious Cæsar?"

"It is one of the many daggers in the collection at Evringham," Devereux answered her. "I had it sent up to town; it is very curiously wrought."

"I should like to see it," said Linwood, joining, for the first time, in the general talk. "I am very much interested in old and curious weapons."

"Bring it with you one evening," said Vera. "I should like to see it also. You are both coming to our evening?"

"Of course," assented Linwood, while the viscount merely bowed. "I hope your friend the princess will be there; she was not at the last reception."

"Ah, my poor friend!" laughed Vera. "She is in despair. Yesterday there came a telegram from her husband; he is very ill, and she must go at once back to Livonia. She went this morning."

"Poor thing!" said Devereux gravely; "that must be a great trial for her."

"Very sad," assented Mrs. Mainwaring sympathizingly, while Alise looked at her cousin in a rather puzzled way; "how dreadful to be so far from him! But, Alise, my love, we really must be thinking of returning home. What has become of Mr. Crawford?"

"Here, as ever your devoted servant," Jack's voice replied as he himself came from the background, where he had been talking to a friend, "willing to escort you all to the moon if necessary."

"Not quite so far as that," answered the lady smiling, "We will stop short at Eaton-square. Adieu, Miss Vera!"

She shook hands with the girl and her father, nodded to Devereux, and after allowing a reasonable time for the adieux of her daughter, departed under convoy of Jack Crawford.

Linwood would fain have detained Vera, but the riders gave no indication of wishing to remain by the railings, and he was therefore obliged to forego the pleasure, and substitute that of seeing Vera ride away with Lord Devereux by her side.

"My time will come," he said to himself with a sour smile, watching them as they mingled with the crowd of equestrians. "I can wait."

CHAPTER XX.

HONOUR BEFORE ALL.

FEW weeks passed away, to all appearance quietly enough. There was no change in the *menage* in Bruton-street.

Vera still remained the queen of the gambling-saloon and the *diva* of the gamblers. Linwood came just the same as usual, as did Lord Devereux also.

He was now never absent on the reception evenings; he chafed bitterly under the necessity of this concealment.

It was a torture to him to see his wife—the woman he loved, the woman he had sworn to protect—the heroine of such a life as this; he longed to snatch her from this contamination, to set her as a queen in the kingdom to which she was of right born.

If he had followed his impulse he would have gone straight to his father and told him all and abided the consequences; would have proclaimed to the world that the *diva* of Bruton-street was his wife, to be honoured by the world even as he honoured her.

"I cannot—I will not suffer it much longer," he said to Vera one day; "come what may, I will not leave you here in this house." He paused a moment beside her as she sat in a low chair, and laid his hand with tender touch on her head, meeting her wistful upward look. "You look at me so pleadingly, darling," he said, and half turned away with a short bitter sigh. "It is a stain on one's honour, Vera. I reproach myself every minute that I allow you to pass to the world as Vera Temple. I will throw everything to the winds, and give you the rights that are your due."

The girl rose from her seat and laid her hand gently on his arm.

"Don't you think, Ernest," she said with a great wistfulness, "that I am happy only to bear anything for your sake. And what do I bear? I am used to all this that you find so dreadful. And have I not your love? Have I not the knowledge that I am yours?"

"Mine!" repeated Devereux passionately—"mine! —mine by the bare letter of the law! Not mine even in name to the world. What joy can that give you? What does my love do for you? Has it taken you from a life that is a weariness to you? Has it lifted you to the only place Devereux's wife can occupy? Vera, do not seek to persuade me any more. I will keep up this wretched mask no longer. It were to sink my own honour in the dust."

The girl was silent for a moment; but there was a half smile of infinite pride and tenderness on her lips.

"His honour!" When he pleaded that! What is there that one can set in the balance against honour? And would she willingly have had him suffer less? For this suffering was noble!

She came to his side, clasping her hands on his arm, and looking up into his face still with that proud smile in her eyes.

"You have put a powerful plea in the way of anything I can plead," she said then. "But, Ernest, let me say one thing. Do you think I could know a moment's happiness if I brought disunion into your family—if I was the cause of your ruin?"

"Must we always set happiness above honour, Vera? I think you are only trying to combat me with a plea that you know is most powerful with me—are you not? For I know that you understand me, and could not love so well if I were quite content to leave my wife unacknowledged to the world."

"I do understand you perfectly, Ernest," said the girl. She paused a moment as though struggling for self-control, then suddenly bent her head down on his breast, with a deep-drawn, quivering breath. "Oh, for God's sake, don't give me the self-reproach that my love has brought you—not joy, but sorrow!"

"Vera, my darling," said Devereux, startled, "you must never have such a thought. I took upon me freely —gladly—all possible consequences. I made this step deliberately. My only bitter regret now is that I persuaded you to my wish. You have no cause for self-reproach."

"Ah yes; you do not know," Vera said, still in the same low passionate tone. "When you first came—I may tell you now—I might have prevented you being with us so often. A woman has a thousand ways; I tried—oh, Ernest, I did strive—to shut my heart to you, but I could not. I said to myself—for, remember, Ernest, I had lived in the world so much, and I knew that I was beautiful and that all men were attracted to me— that I would try to shock you at every point, that you might be repelled, rather than drawn towards me, for love with you would be no mere transient passion. You could spoil your whole life for a woman; but I could not crush my heart so cruelly—I who had never known what love was, how should I have the courage to cast it from me when it was laid at my feet?"

To some, perhaps to most men, the low-spoken confession of their power to bend a woman's heart to love against her will would have given more pleasure than pain.

To Devereux no such sweet triumph was possible, for to him was only ever present the knowledge of the bitter struggle through which the girl had passed; the agony which had swept over this young soul as she felt her strength failing before the mightiest power which sways man to good or evil. How deep, how pure was this love of hers that had striven even to crush itself rather than bring an hour's pain to him.

"Vera, my heart," he said, and clasped her yet closer to him, "how could you strive to shut your heart so cruelly? Why—why seek such suffering? Lives there the man who is worthy of your love? For all that a man gives a woman, believe me, Vera, a woman gives tenfold."

The girl looked up, half startled by the almost vehement earnestness with which he spoke, and shook her head.

"You exalt women too much, Ernest," she said sadly.

"That is not possible when one speaks of such women as you."

"Such women as I!" echoed Vera half bitterly. "I don't think, Ernest, that I am so nobly endowed with all noble qualities."

"Need you be so very good, then," answered Devereux in a lighter tone, "to be quite above me? But that we need not discuss; and we need not also discuss what I am about to say," and now he spoke more gravely. "It neither beseems your honour nor mine that you should longer remain in the false position you now occupy. Nay—hush, my Vera! On this question I allow no argument, from this decision there is no appeal. So it is no use to look at me with those beseeching eyes. I am strong enough to resist them when it is a question of right or wrong to you."

The girl looked at him a moment as though she would fain measure her strength against his. There was a smile on his lip, indeed, but that in the eyes which met hers which showed her that prayers would be unheeded.

"You assert authority very soon," she said a little archly, and then a sparkle of mischief came into her eyes. "What if I will not leave my father's house?"

"You have promised to obey me, dear Lady Independence."

"Obey! Ah, so I have! Well," said Vera, with a sigh that was strangely contented for so independent a young lady, "it is not so difficult to obey you. Only, Ernest, I will exact a promise from you."

"A thousand, sweetheart."

"It is only that the next time our wills clash, you shall obey me."

"That would be to reverse the order of things," said Devereux, smiling; "and, then, I could not consent to make such a promise in the dark. Who knows?—we might differ on some very serious question."

"And then," answered Vera archly, "I am quite sure I should be in the right."

"Women always are in the right," laughed Devereux. "All the same, I object to making promises in the dark."

He paused a moment, then added in another tone:

"Now that this question is settled, I am of a lighter heart. You look so grave, dear, as though I had announced my determination to spring over a cliff—or perhaps you deem the one step equivalent to the other?"

An almost involuntary shiver went through the girl's frame.

"Do not speak so lightly," she said earnestly. "I do not know—I cannot tell——"

She broke off abruptly, and swept her hand over her forehead, as though by the action to clear away the "cobwebs" from her brain.

"Never mind me," she said, moving away from him a little. "You know people say all women have fancies of some sort, and though I didn't know till now that I had any, I suppose I am no exception to the rule."

Devereux was silent, watching his young wife as she moved across the room.

In truth, he was not without anxiety with regard to the step he intended to take. It would, he knew, make, if not an irreparable, at least a very wide breach between him and his father, and he could not contemplate the prospect of such breach without the deepest pain. But for the especial fear which Vera entertained, he had the haughtiest contempt—Lucius Linwood might do his worst. Devereux came again to Vera's side as she stood by the window, and said softly, passing his arm about her.

"You must not let these fears trouble you, my darling. Be very sure that no word man or woman should say against you would gain a second's credence from me. Nothing could dim my love for you, and for the rest"— he shrugged his shoulders and smiled—"you may be sure, sweetheart, that Viscountess Devereux will soon live down all adverse criticisms."

Vera looked up with a bright smile.

"It seems so strange," she said, not making any direct answer to what he had said; "I cannot realise it in the least. It seems to make so little difference in one's outer life. The inner "—she drew a long breath and closed her eyes, leaning against him—"that is so changed."

"And so, Vera, it only remains to put the outer life in harmony with the inner," said Devereux. "Now, that being granted, we had perhaps better remember that it is twelve o'clock, and that we are going to ride, Kate Cranleigh being forthcoming as chaperon."

"I think she has just ridden up," said Vera, turning and glancing out of the window. "Yes; so I must go and dress, and you can flirt with her, my lord, in the meanwhile."

CHAPTER XXI.

THE LAST EVENING IN BRUTON-STREET.

GROUP of men sat in the smaller of the drawing-rooms, devoted in Berkeley Temple's house to play.

It was a silent group, for all were intent on the chances of the game, and no one had a thought to spare from *vingt-et-un*. Even Vera retired into the background of men's thoughts when the god play was set up to worship.

This did not, however, trouble the girl. She would rather be without the worship some of them gave her.

She stood to-night leaning lightly on the back of Jack Crawford's chair, watching the progress of the game, just as able as any of them to say what card it was best to play, but, of course, taking no part.

Perhaps half the time her thoughts were not at all with the play or the players, but were wandering away to some pleasanter field than any in which cards had a part.

Linwood, watching her covertly from time to time, could not discover that she seemed to listen for knock or ring which should announce the advent of Lord Devereux, for Lord Devereux was expected to-night, he having said at the club that he should probably look in.

This evening somehow sent Vera's recollections back to that first time when Lord Devereux had been expected. There were many points of dissimilarity, of course: not nearly all the guests who had then been present were present now. There was no ladies to-night except herself.

The Princess Glinka, her only friend, was far away. A telegram had that morning informed Vera that she was ill of the same fever which had struck her husband down.

Everything was changed—she herself most of all. And what further changes would the future bring forth?

One, the most striking of all, would pass over her perhaps before many days, or even hours were gone, for Devereux had told her that it might be he should speak to Berkeley that night.

He had wished for several days to find an opportunity of seeing him, but Berkeley had appeared to avoid him.

Either he thought that Devereux wished to ask for Vera's hand, and he did not like the task of refusing or putting him off, or he surmised that he wished to settle his debts, which also did not suit Berkeley.

Devereux, however, did not intend to be put off any longer, therefore he asked Vera to give him a latch-key, with which he could come into the house when it suited him. Moreover, he did not desire all the frequenters of the salon to know that he had private business with the master of the house.

About eleven o'clock came a ring at the door-bell, distinctly heard in the silence of the room.

Gellert, who was lying on his own favourite tiger skin, pricked up his ears, and lifted his head. He knew as well as Vera who this late comer was.

Linwood again glanced from under his brows at Vera, to see if she changed countenance at all, but her face gave no sign of the gladness within her, and Lucius was baffled.

"That must be Devereux," said Jack, breaking the silence.

And Berkeley answered, "Yes," quietly, and the next minute declared a "natural," and swept up the stakes, adding with a smile as he rose:

"We have just concluded in time, gentlemen, for I think Lord Devereux loves to talk rather than to play, and here he comes."

"Just in time to save me from despair," whispered Jack tragically to Vera; "I am nearly cleaned out."

"I think," answered Vera with a glance at Linwood, who was looking like a thunder-cloud, "that Mr. Linwood is quite cleaned out."

Then she turned to Devereux, who had been exchanging greetings with her father and the other men.

"How late you are!" she said, giving him her hand; "you have just missed a most exciting struggle. I assure you there was a most death-like silence reigning for the space of many half hours."

"Ah, well," returned Devereux, laughing, "you know cards never excite me up to a very furious pitch. I do not regret the time lost from them but from you."

"Thanks, my lord; but what have you there? Something that looks very warlike."

"I have brought the dagger I promised to show you," answered Devereux, and as he spoke he drew the weapon from its jewelled sheath and laid it in Uera's hands. "Thus, fair lady, do I yield you up my sword."

"It is splendidly tempered steel," said Berkeley, coming forward to look. "A wonderful knack those old armourers had."

"And see how curiously wrought on the hilt!" said Vera; "the crest and motto are here also."

The dagger was passed about from hand to hand, and tried in various ways, and stood every test.

"As the dagger of a Devereux would," said Vera, laughing.

"And in what character are you going to wear that most *recherche* affair?" asked Linwood, speaking for the first time, although he had examined the dagger with great interest.

"I scarcely know even yet," answered Devereux; "the ball is far enough off to allow one a little latitude in the matter of a choice."

"It will be a most brilliant affair," observed Lord Dalston.

"Yes," said Vera. "It is only such a pity that the Princess Glinka will not be there; she is always the life of any such affair; Kate was lamenting to-day her absence."

"We are all lamenting it," said Jack dolefully. "She always helped one so with her notions about the dresses."

"It is very sad," said Berkeley sympathetically; "but Vera, my love, are we not getting on to rather melancholy subjects for our guests? Here comes Armand with wine; that always exercises a cheering influence."

All but Devereux appeared to agree with this sentiment, for they spared not the wine which the servant just then brought in and placed on a table, retiring then with the injunction from his master "not to sit up any longer, that he would let out his guests."

But the men assembled to-night could not long remain away from the gaming-tables. They were for the most part what Berkeley called the *elite* of the gambling world, and found their chief, if not their only happiness, in the touch of cards.

Devereux would fain have talked to Vera, rather than play, but submitted with a shrug to the public voice, which declared that he must play.

"I will try conclusions, then, with our fair hostess," he said; "that is, if she will so far honour me?"

"What?" cried Jack, laughing. "You two will try your skill with 'poker' again, as you did the first night you came, Dev, and kept all the room round your table in a state of excitement?"

"Is it to be 'poker,' Lord Devereux?" asked Vera, with a spark of mischief in the glance of her dark eyes.

"That is for you to decide," answered the viscount, bowing.

"And what are the stakes to be this time, Miss Vera?" said Linwood with a half sneer. "Lord Devereux is perhaps tired by this time of playing dogs against hearts, since mademoiselle's skill is always greater than his; and to give all and take nothing becomes tiresome."

"I suppose you have found it so," returned Devereux with an air of polite deference. "I have no experience of that unenviable condition."

"'I came, I saw, I conquered,'" said Linwood with a smile that was bitter. "A haughty motto, but I presume you are not without justification—in some cases, at any rate."

"If any man likes to dispute the motto with me," answered Devereux with apparent carelessness, but with a certain deliberateness of tone, "he can do so; I am willing to throw down the glove on it."

Devereux said the words as he was passing to go to the tables, and Linwood paused the space of a second, perhaps, before he made answer; then he said slowly, and in a low voice:

"I take up your challenge, my lord, but not here, and not now. I can afford to wait."

"As long as you please; it is all one to me," answered Devereux, laughing and shrugging his shoulders. "You are wonderfully melodramatic to-night, Mr. Linwood. Miss Vera, I am entirely at your service."

Vera came up, glancing from under her long lashes at the two men.

She had not heard the little by-play between them, for she had turned away to say something to Lord Dalston.

But she would have known from the look on Linwood's face that these few words had been of a not altogether amicable character, and a cold chill shot through her.

Were her fears so soon to be realised?

But she did not appear to notice anything, saying only, smiling, to Devereux, "that she was quite ready to accept his challenge."

And this time Linwood said nothing about the stakes.

It was near twelve when Lord Devereux rose.

"A winner," Vera said, laughing.

She would settle her debts to-morrow.

"If you come about ten," she said, "you will find me at home. But you are surely not going so early?" she added, as he glanced at his watch.

"I fear I must," answered Devereux, "if you will allow me. It is stern duty alone that takes me away. I have promised to meet a friend who has come up from the country, at the club. He wants, of course, all sorts of advice about things in general, and has fixed on me for the purpose.

"Unfortunate individual!" said Vera. "Well, under the circumstances, we will hold you excused."

They were standing by the mantelpiece, apart from the others, who were all intent on cards.

Devereux stooped to caress the dog lying at his feet, and said in a low voice :

"And you? You will not remain here? You look tired too; you want rest."

"I will not stay if you wish me to leave," answered Vera. "I have no wish to do so, and I am not wanted here; the men are too deeply absorbed in gambling to think even of me."

"So much the better," said Devereux, drawing his brows together; he did not know what jealousy meant with regard to Vera, but this was not the homage he wished for her.

"What, are you going?" cried Jack Crawford, and the question was echoed by the other men, and by the ever-polite host. "Why such an early bird, Dev? Pooh! you're not half a gambler."

"I must own the impeachment," answered Devereux, gravely; "duty, however, takes me to the Regina at 12.15, and I must obey the call."

"The plea is allowed," said Berkeley, smiling graciously; "don't forget your dagger, though. I would not like to have that costly toy in my charge all night."

"Toy!" laughed the viscount, taking up the dagger and looking critically at the fine edge of the blade. "This would prove no mere toy if it were struck well home!"

Linwood looked up rather sharply.

"I should not advise you to carry such a dangerous weapon," said he dryly.

"Thanks for the advice," answered Devereux carelessly; "but have no fear, Mr. Linwood; it is far too melodramatic a weapon to use when you and I come to try those conclusions of which you spoke. Good night, gentlemen;" he bowed to them, and turning to Vera, took her hand and lifted it to his lips.

"Adieu," he said softly; it was all he could say there, where every word would be heard and misinterpreted, yet the simple word enclosed all that love could wish for her; and so he took his departure, only pausing in the hall to put the dagger in the pocket of his overcoat, which garment he threw over his arm, as the night was warm and sultry.

Outside, away from curious eyes and Vera's keen glances, his face changed; his lip lost the half-tender smile that had curved it as he had said his farewell to his young wife, his brows were bent and his lips closed together.

"By Heaven!" he said, through his teeth, "it shall be the last time; I will see Berkeley this night; and it will be the last night Vera shall rest under his roof, come what may."

"Come what may."

So we speak, moving the whilst through the dark, not able to see one step before us, or able to lift for one second the veil that hangs between us and that which the next hour shall bring forth.

CHAPTER XXII.

A FATAL MEETING.

T was not long after Lord Devereux's departure that Vera intimated her intention of retiring; she was weary, she said, and she withstood the remonstrances of the guests and the look which her father gave her, and accordingly retired.

It had been no mere polite fiction serving as an excuse when Vera declared she was tired; she felt truly intensely weary, and only longed to forget herself and everything in sleep; nor was it long to-night before sleep came to her call.

She heard her father let the men out—heard their voices as they lingered a moment on the step to light up cigars, and heard Berkeley's step across the hall to his study, and the closing of the study .door; then all sounds became faint, and finally mingled with her dreams.

She was all unconscious that perhaps half an hour afterwards the very man of whom she was dreaming was putting a latch-key into the lock and entering the house.

When his guests left him, Berkeley Temple turned back and went into his study, closing the door carefully, and waving away with some impatience Vera's dog, who always wandered loose about the house at night, and who doubtless felt it rather lonely in the small hours by himself. He thought Berkeley's company was better than none, for he had no affection for the master, and was, in his doggish way, at no pains to hide his indifference—an indifference which was quite reciprocal.

"That tiresome dog!" muttered Berkeley as the dog retired with a look that was almost human in its reproach. "I wish Vera would keep him in his proper place. I hate dogs all over the house!"

And yet, poor repulsed Gellert would have done good service to Berkeley if he had not shut his heart to that wistful look.

Berkeley closed the door, adjusted the light of the lamp, which burned on the table, to his requirements, and seated himself at his desk, leaning his head on his hand thoughtfully.

"Things are working to a crisis," he mused—"a crisis I cannot avert either. Linwood is clamouring for some action on my part with regard to Vera, and he will not be put off much longer. Then there is Devereux—*peste* on the men! Why can't they be content to look at a beauty only, or, at any rate, to leave her to be still the queen of my house? But my proud daughter flashes scorn at me if I only hint at such a road out of the wood. I can't imagine," said the father with a sigh, "where she gets such ideas from. I am very much afraid that Devereux also will not be put off, and he is even more dangerous to deal with than Linwood. To be sure he owes me a good deal of money; but that doesn't seem to make a great difference with these fiery sort of men like my noble friend."

He rose and began walking thoughtfully up and down.

"I think I might frighten him away with pressing for that money; the worst of it is, that heirs to entailed estates can always get an advance to any tune they want. Who's that?"

He uttered the exclamation sharply, and stopped in the middle of the room, listening as he heard the sound of a light footfall in the hall without; but his anxiety was relieved to a certain extent when the door was quietly opened, as though the incomer had the most perfect right there, and Viscount Devereux entered.

Berkeley's stare of surprise was almost amusing.

"Lord Devereux," he said, half bewildered, half haughtily.

"Don't be alarmed, Mr. Temple," said the viscount, laughing, and quietly putting his overcoat down on a chair near; "I am neither come to steal nor to borrow money, and I entered the house in a perfectly legitimate manner—that is, I did not break open the door."

"BUT YOU TALK ALL THE TIME TO YOUR KITTEN," SAID LINWOOD REPROACHFULLY.

"You have taken me very much by surprise, Lord Devereux," said Berkeley unbendingly, "and I am at a loss to think what can have brought you to my house at this time of night when the whole day stands open to you. Pardon me, but I cannot but regard it as an unwarrantable intrusion."

"I crave ten thousand pardons," returned Devereux, with a slight bend of his head, "and will only remind you of the fact that great needs sanction extraordinary measures."

"And may I ask how you got in?" said Berkeley coldly.

He had neither asked his unwelcome visitor to be seated, nor had he himself taken a chair.

"A very pertinent question," answered Devereux, "but one which I will postpone answering until I have told you that which indeed I came here only to communicate to you. I must tell you first, however, in apology for my entrance to your house, that I was under the impression that you have avoided giving me an interview which I have for the last few days sought Being under this impression, I felt compelled to take you unawares. A circumstance which happened to-night determined me to see you at once, and, knowing that you often sat up reading, or what not, I came, and fortunately found you."

"And your business after this elaborate apology?" said Berkeley. "It must be extremely important."

"It is," returned Devereux, speaking now in an altered tone; "it concerns the happiness of your daughter, and therefore mine also——"

"You need not explain further, Lord Devereux," interrupted Berkeley, lifting his hand. "I know what you would say, and so I may as well save you the disappointment of pleading your cause with all the eloquence of which you are master, only to be refused. My daughter is too young to entertain any such proposals as you would make."

Devereux suffered Berkeley to conclude his somewhat formal speech without interruption, though his lip gave, and he felt more inclined to laugh than to look grave at the assumption to which he must deal such a cruel blow.

"Pardon me," he said; "I come to make no proposals. I do not think you have an idea what I would say, and it is quite beyond your power to inflict any disappointment on me so far as Vera is concerned. As she has already honoured me by becoming my wife, you will see that all objections are too late. I thought it was time you knew this, as I have no intention of allowing my wife to remain here. Family reasons prevented me from claiming her earlier before the world, but I have now decided to regard these no longer."

The countenance of Berkeley Temple while Lord Devereux was speaking, and ere he mastered himself sufficiently to conceal his feelings, was a study; incredulity, amazement, anger, were all blended, the first, however, predominating, as he recovered his self-command, and rapidly decided that it were best to treat the statement as a fiction, indulged in by the viscount for some purpose of his own.

In pursuance, therefore, of this *role*, Berkeley turned his eyes full on Devereux, with a slightly sarcastic smile curling his thin lips.

"And do you really expect me to credit all this, Lord Devereux?" he said quietly.

A haughty flush rose to the young man's cheek; the hinted meaning of Berkeley's question was not lost upon him, and his impetuous spirit was fired directly. He checked, however, the words which rose to his lips, and answered calmly, and even carelessly:

"It is quite immaterial whether you credit me or not; a marriage lawfully performed is of all things easiest to prove, and as I am prepared to produce every proof, it will be impossible for you to doubt any longer, if indeed, pardon me, you do so in truth now."

"Produce me, then, your proofs," said Berkeley with a half sneer; "it would require indeed chapter and verse to make me believe that you would raise one you consider so far beneath you to the dignity of your name; your scheme to make me yield my daughter up to you is too transparent. When Vera leaves me it will be to go in honour, not——"

Devereux made a step forward, and laid his hand with a grasp of steel on the other's arm, and Berkeley shrank and grew pale at the passion which blazed in his eyes.

"By heaven!" he said, his voice low with the very force of the control he was putting on himself, "dare not to utter one word more that does such foul dishonour to her and to me. You would have no right to give reproach to her or to me, if I had offered and she had taken less than the gift of my name. Not to you does she owe the purity of her soul; you have flung her into the very hotbed of temptation, and never asked or cared whether she passes scatheless through it or not. You would give her to me now, if all I asked stopped short of taking her from under your roof—if you might still retain her services to be a kind of decoy for the brainless fools who circle round her, and pour money into your coffers; but that is all over for her. I, her husband, claim my wife, and the law makes my claim good against yours; Vera will leave this house to-morrow."

He dropped his hand as he said the last words, and turned as if to go, but Berkeley's voice arrested him.

"Stay!" he said, and glanced furtively at Devereux from under his brows, "stay!"

Devereux paused with a sudden haughty impatience in look and mein.

"There is nothing more to say," he said; "why prolong a useless interview."

"Wait and see," returned Berkeley, apparently unmoved. He had recovered his balance. "You are very impetuous, my dear lord—very much in love, I suppose, and ready to go through fire and water for the goddess installed for the time being; but this, like every other process in the present day, requires money, and that, my Lord Devereux, is, in your case, the 'one thing needful.' You see I have not quite forgotten my Scripture, though I have no honour left. You are, of course, prepared to quarrel irreparably with the earl, since he will not take this step of yours quite so easily as you have done it."

"That is entirely my concern," said Devereux.

"Not so, my lord; it is not entirely yours. I have a right, for one thing, to know how my daughter is to be maintained, for you know, I presume, that the money Vera inherits from her mother is only conditionally hers on her marrying with my consent, and as my consent has never been asked, she will, of course, come to you penniless, with the exception of the jewellery and presents she has received from others beside yourself. Pray hear me patiently a moment. You cannot have forgotten that you owe me a large sum of money, which I do not in the least feel inclined to forgive to my noble son-in-law. Your nerves are well under control—that did not make you wince. How and when is my debt to be paid?"

"Have no fear either about your ducats or your daughter. Lady Devereux will not want for every luxury she has enjoyed here, plus that of an honoured home; for your debt—that will be paid you in two days."

"That means to say that you will borrow the money at usurious interest, and that you will also live on money-lenders' gold till your father leaves you in possession of the estate. I offer you a way out of these difficulties which will benefit you and me at the same time; if you will consent to leave me Vera, not claiming her as your wife, for the rest of this season and the winter in Paris, I undertake to cancel your debt to me, and help you on easy terms in the future."

Berkeley Temple must have been a bold man, or else long years of moral obliquity had rendered his knowledge of the estimation in which most men held dishonourable transactions exceedingly superficial, otherwise he would never have made such a proposition to Devereux; and he was not prepared for the fierce passion with which Devereux turned to him—a passion that seemed to shake the man to the very centre of his being.

"God in heaven!" he said through his teeth. "If any man but Vera's father had said such words to me, it had gone hard with him.   You are safe, and you may thank God that I can still remember this!"

He turned away without one word more and strode from the room across the hall, not so much as seeing Gellert on the mat, and flung open the hall-door.

As he stepped outside, a dark figure almost brushed against him, and then drew back quickly, muttering half to himself, for it is doubtful if Devereux more than just saw that someone was on the step:

"Devereux—by Jove! Forgotten my overcoat. Stupid of me!"

But Devereux was already out in the street, striding quickly away, and Lucius Linwood went into the house to fetch his overcoat as he had said.

CHAPTER XXIII.

FOR HIS DEAR SAKE.

ERA, always an early riser, woke the next morning earlier than usual—woke almost with a start, an unaccountable feeling of dread and anxiety oppresssing her.

She rose immediately and dressed quickly, trying all the while to account for this anxious feeling, and remembering that of course she was anxious. Had not Devereux said that he might possibly see her father last night?

She came downstairs as far as the drawing-room, and went to her piano to practise, as was often her custom, till breakfast-time, wondering a little that Gellert did did not come as he usually did to greet her, and lie under the piano while she played.

It was about half-past eight when Janet entered the the drawing-room and came up to her young mistress.

"Miss Vera," she said, "will you have breakfast? Your father is not yet down?"

Vera paused in her playing, her hands resting on the keys.

"He is very late," she said; "are you sure he is not in the study, Janet?"

"The door is still locked, Miss Vera, though the key is in the lock; he must have forgotten to take it up-stairs with him. I did not dare go in, you know, Miss Vera; he is always so angry if any of the servants enter without leave; and Gellert is on the mat, and don't seem inclined to let me disobey orders either."

"Gellert!" said Vera, lifting her brows. "What a strange freak for him to take! He is not so much in love with papa generally," she said, as she spoke and crossed the room. "I will come down," she said.

She went quickly down, Janet following and passing on to the kitchen staircase.

As Vera reached the hall her eyes fell on the dog, who was lying right before the study door, his nose between his paws, nor did he, according to his custom, as soon as he saw his mistress, jump up and spring forward to receive her caresses, but remained at his post—for in such light he evidently regarded his position, only lifting his head and moving the extreme tip of his tail.

But Vera saw at once that the dog was not himself for whatever reason; his ears were laid down, and his manner altogether strange and cowed, as unlike his somewhat boisterous and free-and-easy manner as it was possible to be.

The girl's heart beat faster as she came up to Gellert. There was a strange fear on her spirit—a fear of she knew not what; yet, strangely enough, she never connected Gellert's most unusual demeanour with herself, although the first words she spoke to him seemed to point to such a supposition.

"Gellert," she said, and knelt down beside him, laying her hand on his his head, "what is it? Why are you lying here?"

Vera always spoke to her dog as though he had been a human being, and quite understood every word she said to him, as no doubt he did; he certainly answered her as plainly now as if he had comprehended.

He rose up and put his nose under the door, and then looked back at her, now waving his tail with growing excitement and agitation, and uttered a low, short bark.

The girl paused a moment, putting her hand to her forehead; she knew not what wild intangible fears flashed like lightning through her mind. She laid her other hand slowly, and with a half hesitating touch, unlike her usual decided movements, on the lock of the door. Only for a moment this shrinking, this great dread of the unknown something she should see beyond the door; then she turned the key and pushed it, going in quickly, Gellert creeping close to her side, with drooping tail and ears. She made two steps into the room, and stopped suddenly with a thrill of horror turning every drop of blood in her veins to ice.

The apartment was in disorder; papers were scattered about the writing table as though they had been tossed here and there by someone under the pressure of haste, and a side drawer stood open.

But it was not these things which first arrested the girl's attention; it was not these things which sent that chill of horror into every limb; there almost at her feet where she had stopped, her father lay, still and lifeless, a dark stream flowing slowly on to the floor, and dyeing the oaken boards red.

It was but the space of a second that Vera paused, almost as motionless as the dead form at her feet. That first shock passed, the girl was now, as ever, prompt and swift to act; she could never have analysed the strange sort of feeling that made her first close the door, that no servant passing might look in and so make it impossible to keep the matter in her own hands.

Then she knelt down and laid her hand over the heart that was so still; the hands were quite cold too; there could be no hope of restoring life here, the girl saw at once with a sickening feeling of her utter impotency, and a chilling dread and fear of all that must follow. Who was his murderer, and why had he been sacrificed?

These questions came, of course, naturally to Vera. Robbery would seem to have been the motive, judging from the open drawer and scattered papers; yet surely in that case Gellert would have given the alarm. And now, for the first time, Vera, lifting her eyes in the natural following out of her thought, saw that which made her spring to her feet, locking her hands together in a strained tension that forced the blood back from the finger nails—her eyes fixed with that burning stare of horror on the one spot where lay only a piece of glittering steel, jewel-hilted, and stained with the life-blood of the man who was her father.

"Oh, God!" she whispered under her breath, and clasped her hands before her eyes; "his dagger! No, no; it cannot be—it cannot be!"

Then with a feverish haste the girl went forwards and bent down, looking closer at the weapon. There could be no mistake about the fact of it being the same dagger which Lord Devereux had shown only the evening before to her father's guests.

Devereux must have left it there, of course, when he went away last night, not caring to take it to the club with him; no other solution of the mystery was possible to Vera—but to others, who would not have her faith in him?

No one must see it. The thought flashed rapidly through her mind, and co-existent with the thought the impulse to spring to the door and lock it.

Too late!

Even as she reached it the handle was turned, and Vera fell back a step with a smothered cry.

The very last man she would willingly see at this crisis, Lucius Linwood, stood before her.

There was a moment's death-like silence. Linwood had almost instinctively closed the door, and stood looking with horrified gaze at the prostrate form, and from this to Vera.

But the silence was first broken not by either Linwood or Vera. A low, fierce growl from Gellert, whom Linwood had not at first noticed, made him start, a yet deeper pallor than had been there spreading over his cheeks.

"Call that dog of yours off!" he said, with a touch of roughness engendered by fear. "He does not know friends from foes."

"Lie down, Gellert," Vera moved her lips to say, and laid her hand on the animal's head.

She remembered that Gellert had never growled or shown his teeth at sight of Linwood before.

Then, with a supreme effort, she mastered herself, stepping aside, as if inadvertently, so that her dress fell over the dagger.

She had small hope that Linwood had not seen it; and though he appeared not to have observed her action, she was sure that he had done so.

"This is dreadful!" Linwood said at last, as if only now could he find voice to speak. "I am more shocked than I can say! How did it happen?" he bent, as he spoke, over the dead man, and, as Vera had done, laid his hand on his heart. "There is no life," he said, quietly. "Are you the first to have found him?"

"Yes," the girl answered. Now, as once before, she was measuring her strength against his, and this time she knew she was playing the losing game. "He was so late this morning that I came to see if he was perhaps ill. When I came in I found him, lying as you see him, the desk broken open, and the papers scattered about. Clearly robbery has been the motive."

"Clearly," said Linwood, gravely.

He did not speak for a moment, but stood quite still. His face was very grave, even stern, and there was a sort of pained perplexity, too, visible.

"It is very strange," he murmured, half aloud. "I scarcely know what to do—what I ought to do."

Vera drew a long, silent breath, and waited.

"Whose coat is that?" said Linwood, suddenly raising his eyes.

The girl followed the direction of his glance. But she made no answer as Linwood stepped to the place where the garment lay on the floor, and took it up.

"It is Lord Devereux's!" he said, under his breath. "Great Heaven! it is, then, as I thought!"

"What is as you thought?" said Vera.

"How comes Devereux's coat here?" Linwood said, making no direct answer to her. "He left apparently last night before we broke up."

"I suppose he left his overcoat here, that is all; there is nothing strange in that, is there?"

"He must have left the dagger with it, then," said Linwood. "It is too remarkable a weapon not to be easily identified. I think," he said, laying his hand lightly on the girl's shoulder, "that if you kindly move we shall find the weapon with which the deed was done, and which your dress at present not very successfully hides."

Vera moved without a word, but stooped quickly to take up the dagger. Linwood, however, with a swift movement, laid his foot on it.

"Not so, Miss Vera," he said with a cold, cruel smile; "the ends of justice must not be defeated for such a small price."

He lifted the dagger and examined it carefully.

"It is evident to me," he said, "that this is the work of no common robber; indeed, as far as I can see, there is no sign whatever of burglars having broken in. This is the dagger which Lord Devereux was showing to us last night. It remains for him to explain how it came to be here, close to the dead body of your father, with blood-stains fresh on the blade."

"No doubt he can explain it," said Vera directly. "Of course he must have left both coat and dagger in this room when he went away. He did not return to the house; why should he?"

"You are very sure he did not return to the house?" said Lucius, slowly. "What his business was I could not tell at the time. Now it comes plainly before me he did return to the house. I was passing, on my way back to my chambers, having accompanied Crawford part of his road, and Lord Devereux came out of this house, evidently very much agitated. He scarcely seemed to notice me, though I am sure he saw me. He was in his evening dress, just as he left us. But he had no overcoat with him. He did not pause a minute, but strode quickly away. I was very much astonished, and I will own not a little, in a vague sort of way, suspicious. It was this vague feeling of uneasiness which made me come so early to see if all was right. I am glad that I did so come."

While he spoke Vera stood perfectly still; she was white to the very lips; only her eyes glowed and burned with a strange fire.

"You see yourself," Linwood added, "how strong the evidence is against him. Ask a motive? He owed your father money—a large sum. What was Devereux doing here after everyone else had gone?"

"It rests only on your word that he was here," Vera said, quietly.

Linwood smiled a bitter smile.

"Devereux will not himself deny it," he answered her. What he will deny is, that the old man came by his death through him—will account in some way for the damning fact that it is his dagger and his coat that are found beside the murdered man, and that he was seen coming out of the house at an hour when, on the face of it, he had no possible business there. These are ugly facts, which cannot well be explained away."

"Nevertheless, he is not guilty of this deed," said Vera; "and you know he is not."

Linwood went a shade paler, and did not meet the steadfast gaze of those clear eyes that seemed to read him through.

"It is natural, I suppose," he said, "that you should not believe it, although your judgment must be at war with your heart. But how I should know that Lord Devereux is not guilty, I am at loss to divine. Fortunately, that will not be for you or me to decide; a more impartial judge must be found than you."

He half moved then as if to step towards the door, then, for the first time, Vera moved—she seemed to start suddenly, awake to all the terrible issues at stake.

Then she seemed first to realise the power Linwood held over the man she loved.

Quick as thought, following the impulse of the moment, the girl sprang forwards, between him and the door, forgetting all her pride, her haughty contempt for him—forgetting all but that he held the life of the man she loved in his hand.

"You will not?" she half whispered, lifting her eyes to his in passionate entreaty. "You will not?"

The man's eyes rested on her and kindled; the lips drew slowly back over the teeth in a smile.

The moment was exquisite to him—it was a keen enjoyment to see this proud Vera, who had always held him in scorn, who had been contemptuous alike of his claims and his pleadings, suing him for favour.

The coarser nature triumphed—as coarse natures always do—in the knowledge of the torture it must be to the finer soul, thus to abase itself where it had ever commanded.

So, for the space perhaps of a moment, they stood; and then Linwood, glancing aside, let his eye fall on the dog, who approached him slowly, growling deeply, and showing his teeth.

"Take that dog out of the room," he said.

And a fine ear could have detected the accent of a vulgar triumph even in the ordinary words.

It was sweet to him to command in so small a thing.

Vera laid her hand on Gellert's head, and he was mute.

"He will do you no harm," she said.

"Perhaps not; nevertheless, he is unpleasant," answered Linwood. "I have something to say to you, and the dog may interrupt me."

Without one word more, Vera led Gellert to the door, and gently bade him wait on the mat outside; and he stretched himself down in obedience to her order, keeping vigilant watch, however, on the closed door.

Vera came back and took up her old position facing Linwood; she shivered as in doing so she passed close to the dead man.

But now was no time to give way to softer feelings— the moment held too stern issues for the living.

There was a pause, broken first by Linwood.

"I will not profess," he said, "any very profound sorrow about this unfortunate affair, for I suppose you would not believe me, and there is, besides, no time for anything of the sort; we must come quickly to some decision—the servants will be wondering what is wrong, and once set the servants on the scent and it is all up with concealment. I am not averse to tampering with justice—for a price."

"I will give you any sum you name," said the girl directly.

"Money is not my price," Linwood said slowly, watching her the while; "I require something more precious than money—yourself."

The girl sprang back a step, putting out her hands, the hot blood rushing to her brow, and then receding, leaving her pale as the dead.

"No—no!" she almost gasped; "not that—not that —ask me anything but that. I will give you all I have; money, jewels — they are worth a king's ransom."

"I will have nothing," cried Linwood fiercely, stung hy the horror she had evinced. "It is I now who dictate terms, I who am master and lord of your fate; you, proud as you are, who must submit and ask mercy of me, if you will save your accursed lover's life!"

He caught himself up sharply, and bit his lip till the blood came, and went on in a softened tone.

"Vera, why will you always shrink from me so, as if my very words could be a pollution to you? Why will you never believe that I love you truly? I would make you happy; every wish of yours should be gratified."

"Cease—cease," said the girl passionately; "these are the promises men make to a mistress, to be broken as soon as their frail passion shall have spent itself. Strip your offer of all flimsy ornament and it means a sordid bargain. Is it only money bargains that can be sordid? But you overrate your power; Lord Devereux's life is not in your hands."

"I do not think," said Linwood, "that I do overrate my power. Listen quietly while I recapitulate the evidence that is before us, and your own good sense will tell you that a jury will not be 'in love' with Viscount Devereux.

"Lord Devereux is seen, by a reliable witness, to come out of a house, between two and three in the morning, plainly in such a state of agitation that he does not even greet his acquaintance. The next morning the master of the house is found stabbed to the heart, and the dagger of Lord Devereux is lying beside him; the wound corresponds with such a cut as the weapon would make; the dagger is easily identified; so is the overcoat, also the property of Lord Devereux which is likewise found in the study of the murdered man. Devereux is known to have owed his victim a large sum of money, larger than he could settle out of his own resources, and he was also known to have quarrelled with his father.

"If no one had seen him near this house the case would have been different; he might have got up an alibi, but someone did see him, and that someone was myself, and I will keep silence on my own terms, or I will go out this minute and have Viscount Devereux arrested on a charge of murder.

"A jury will give him the benefit of a verdict for manslaughter, or possibly, as he is an earl's son, he might get off legally, but no one will have the slightest moral doubt of his guilt, and his life will be simply blighted. Now you see it all clearly, and it lies with you to save him or not as you think fit; women always love to sacrifice themselves, they say; here is the road open for you."

He ceased, and for many moments Vera remained silent.

Yes, she knew all the terrible truth, and knew, too, that she had to deal with a man who was utterly unscrupulous as to the means he used in order to gain his ends. He had stated the case fairly enough against Devereux. It would have been useless, he knew, to do otherwise, as Vera could see clearly the weight of evidence, and how much appearances were against her lover.

She stood pressing her hands over her heart, striving to still its painful throbbing—trying to force her mind to think—trying for a few moments in vain. Only the one overwhelming sense of impending calamity, and the one way, so it seemed, by which she could avert this calamity from the man she would have died to save, was present with her.

Time was flying. Every minute lessened the chances of keeping the matter quiet; and what could she do?

"I must have time," she said at last, desperately. "I can give no promise until I have seen Devereux, and he has told me with his own lips that he was here last night."

"We have but a few more minutes," Linwood answered her. Her agony did not touch him. It was to him only a gratification. "It will be difficult enough to provide some reason for our remaining so long here. There could be no object in your seeing Devereux first. He will not deny that he was here. You can ask him anything you like when you are my promised wife. Three minutes you can take."

He leant back against the door and waited.

Vera turned away, and went over to the window. With a powerful effort, evolving thought out of chaos, one wild and almost desperate scheme came to her—a scheme so daring that she almost shrank from venturing to put it into execution.

If Devereux would consent!

Rapidly she ran over all the possibilities and impossibilities—if, indeed, to her daring spirit these could be said to exist.

She had, in truth, a desperate game to play, and barely time to do more than resolve on the merest outline of the moves she intended to make.

One thing she quickly decided—Devereux must know nothing till it was too late, and for the rest she must trust to her wits to arrange details.

Now, as ever, she must act a part.

She turned at length, just as Linwood moved from his position, and faced him once more. A kind of stony despair was in the dark eyes she lifted to his. Surely the look on that young beautiful face might have touched him.

"I will give you the promise you ask," she said in a clear measured voice, "that is, I will be your wife on conditions."

Linwood's cheek flushed.

"I should hardly have thought you in a position to make conditions," he said.

"You will see that I am," returned the girl in the same measured accents, but there was a sudden glitter in her eyes, "for I may as well say at once, that if you refuse my conditions, I throw up everything, and you must do as you will. And these are my conditions: The marriage must be before a registrar—you have no religious scruples—and must be secret. We must part for one year; I go my way and you go yours. You will not see me, for I shall pass the time in complete retirement; and, lastly, you will undertake never, by word, or look, or deed, to exercise any power over Lord Devereux for any purpose whatever—never to let him know that you have such power for a year. Should you fail me in this last condition, the bargain will be cancelled, and though I shall be your wife according to the law, I will never bear your name or live under your roof."

There was that in the girl's face and mien which told Linwood that the limits of his power were reached. His countenance was livid, and the veins stood out on his brow like cords as he listened to these daring stipulations from a girl whom he had thought to bend completely to his will.

He strode a step forwards and laid his hand with an almost savage grasp on her wrist.

"You dare!" he said, through his teeth, "to try and foil me so—to make conditions! I am your master—do you understand? It is my turn now, and, by Heaven, you shall feel my power! Yours shall be a complete surrender!"

"So help me Heaven!" the girl made answer, facing him without the quiver of an eyelid, "it shall not! Take my conditions, or go out and denounce Devereux as a murderer."

Lucius fell back a step, then turned, and with one stride he reached the door.

He laid his hand on the lock and turned the key; Vera held her breath; her very life in that dread moment seemed to have stopped.

Would he really go, or was it only a last trial to see if she would fail?

But, ah, to her failure was not possible. She could give up no more!

With a fierce oath Linwood dropped his hand, and came back.

"I accept your conditions," he said; "see that you keep your part of the bargain. Remember that I hold your lover's life in my hands."

"I shall not forget," Vera said bitterly; "you wield your power unsparingly enough. Now we understand each other, it will be well to discover that my father has been murdered. Come into the breakfast-room—the servants do not know yet that we are in here—then I will go as if to call my father."

Linwood stooped and picked up the dagger, and slipped it into the pocket of Devereux's overcoat, which he flung over his arm.

"No one will know it is not mine," he said with a half sneer. I will keep them safely, Vera—have no fear."

She made him no answer, and controlled the involuntary shiver that almost shook her when Lucius Linwood took up the dagger—that fatal weapon.

But she turned, and in silence followed Linwood from the room, closing and locking the door again.

No one was about the hall or in the breakfast-room, and, uttering some commonplace remark as they went, Vera opened the street door, and Linwood hailed a passing hansom.

"Good-bye," she said to him in her usual tone; and he answered her in the same manner, jumped into the cab, and was driven off.

Then Vera turned and went into the dining-room, standing for a moment perfectly still with her hands close pressed over her eyes.

"Have I saved him?" was the cry of her heart. "Will it avail? Oh, God, help me, for his dear sake!"

CHAPTER XXIV.

THE MURDER IN BRUTON STREET.

HROUGHOUT the terrible task she had set herself, Vera never faltered or shrank. Every faculty was braced up to meet the needs of the hour—needs which would endure long after this first day of unutterable misery had passed away.

Every look—every tone must be studied, and more than all must she guard herself against betraying to Devereux the promise she had given to Linwood.

On leaving Linwood, Vera went a few steps across the hall, and then paused, looking at her watch.

She shook her head and glanced towards the study door, as if a little uncertain what to do, and finally stepped quickly to it, and, for the second time that morning, entered the chamber which held for her a horror beyond that of again seeing the dead man.

Nevertheless she entered without faltering.

The next moment a sharp cry of pain and horror rang through the silent house.

Janet, her own woman, heard it as she was just ascending the stairs, and started forward with an exclamation.

"Good Heavens!" she said; "something has happened." And she ran swiftly up, and in another minute stood in the room.

"Miss Vera," she gasped—"oh, what has happened? My poor master!"

Vera lifted a deathlike face as she knelt beside the corpse.

"There has been murder done here," she said in a voice that plainly showed the difficulty of maintaining her self-control. "Go, Janet—or stay—no; send Andrew for a doctor; bid him be quick for his life."

She stopped, pressing her hand to her brow. "Oh, Janet, Janet!" she said, bowing her head down with a half sob, that indeed was not all acting, "it is too late! See here, this terrible wound!"

Janet bent over the prostrate form, and then laid her hand tenderly on the girl's shoulder.

"Vera, my dear," she said gently, "no doctor could do him any good now; he has been dead for hours. We must, of course, send for the doctor, but there is nothing to be done."

She paused, as though hesitating whether she should add something, then said:

"And, Miss Vera, dear, you know, perhaps, that we must send for a constable at once, before your father is moved?"

Vera shivered a little, but made no opposition; and Janet left the room to seek Andrew, the old manservant.

Then, swift as lightning, the girl sprang to her feet, and went to the bureau, searching quickly through the drawer which had been broken open, and in which her father, she knew, had been accustomed to keep money just received, or which he did not wish to transfer to his bank account.

A bundle of notes which she had seen him put there only the day previous was gone.

A second she stopped, and then, all the while acutely listening, opened with a spring only known to her, a tiny draw just above, and took out of it a book, in which was inscribed the number of all the notes her father received. This Vera transferred to her pocket, until she could put it in a safer place.

And just as she had done this, Janet returned, saying she had sent off Andrew for doctor and constable.

"My father has been robbed," Vera said; "notes he received yesterday have been stolen. It has no doubt, been a plant; and my father, resisting, has been struck down. Singular, though, that Gellert allowed anyone to pass."

"That was it, then," exclaimed Janet; "I thought it strange at the time. When cook came down this morning she found Gellert shut behind the door at the top of the kitchen stairs; he was whining and scratching at the door.   The thieves must have lured him there.

"Of course," assented Vera.   "Ah, if we had only heard him!" she said wearily, dropping her head on her hands as she sat by the table.

"Miss Vera, dear, is there anyone you will like sent for?" said Janet, after a moment's hesitation.   "Lord Devereux, perhaps?"

"He was coming about eleven," answered the girl quietly, not a tone betraying how she was dreading yet longing to here the next knock at the door, lest it should be he.   "Mr. Linwood was here this morning, and we sat talking in the breakfast room, never dreaming of this."

Nothing further was said by either until the arrival of the doctor, who was accompanied by an inspector of police.   Dr. Hunter, after a brief examination, announced that Berkeley Temple must have been dead at least four or five hours, adding that the weapon used had been probably a long very sharp dagger; there must, of course, be an inquest.

The inspector examined the state of the room; and asked a great number of questions, all of which Vera answered simply; her evidence, of course, would be required at the inquest.   He was of opinion that the thief must have been in collusion with someone in the house, as there were no marks of a forcible entrance anywhere about, as far as he could at present see.

"The thief," suggested Vera, "might have managed to get in unperceived, and conceal himself.   I can answer for our servants; they have all of them been with us for years."

The inspector admitted that it was possible, but the official mind dearly loves to suspect somebody, and servants who have been years in a family had before now proved themselves unworthy the confidence reposed in them; however, all would come out at the inquest.

When the inspector had taken his departure, and while the servants were performing the last offices for the dead man, the doctor lingered, not quite knowing what to make of Vera or her position.

"Pardon me," he said, with some hesitation, "have you any relative whom you would like sent for? Pray do not think me impertinent or interfering, but you ought to have some male relative to manage things for you."

"I do not think you at all interfering, Dr. Hunter," returned the girl with a fleeting smile and upward look; "on the contrary, I am very grateful to you for your kindness. But I have no relations to whom I could send, and I can undertake all that is necessary; I am quite used to acting independently."

The doctor bowed.

"You look rather young," he said, "to be here all alone; however, if you should want any help, pray make use of me."

"Thank you, doctor, I will."

"It is very singular," muttered the doctor to himself, as he went out; "queer position—never a creature to be with her at such a time, and she seems not the least dismayed; all this crowd outside too."

For of course there was already a throng of curious and excited people without, which a policeman was, in vain, endeavouring to disperse. The news had travelled like wildfire, as such news always does, and as there appears to be some very great attraction for the average mind in viewing the outside of a house where a murder has been committed, all these people had collected, and would not be sent away; and the doctor as he came out of the house was the object of much eager questioning, to all which he made reply, with impatience, that they would know everything there was to know on the inquest, and pushed his way through them and walked rapidly away.

That morning, while all these things which were to affect his life so closely were passing in Bruton Street, Lord Devereux sat in his rooms, where he had sat ever since his return from that fatal interview with Berkeley Temple.

He had scarcely moved once, nor had he even sought sleep. Thoughts, many and anxious, crowded on his brain this day, and would have effectually banished sleep. But more even than anxiety for the future **was** the deep joy that now he had claimed Vera, had thrown aside the fetters which had bound him; he felt like a man who has regained his freedom and rejoiced in it; there was a kind of exultation in the very thought, which made his heart throb, and his eyes flash with a new glad light.

And yet he could not shut his eyes to all the consequences of the step he was about to take. It would certainly cost him at least for a time, the friendship, already so severely strained, of his father. And Mrs. Mainwaring, who was the only one of his relations whose good wishes he really valued, would not, he felt sure, look upon this marriage, much as she might like Vera personally, with great favour.

But what, after all, mattered it? Vera was his; if she loved him and was willing to face a little coldness for his sake, why then need he trouble himself about others?

"I will take her abroad," said Devereux; and there was a half smile on the curved lips. "People will not be inclined long to look askance at Viscountess Devereux, and even my father cannot, I think, long stand out against Vera."

Just then his servant entered with chocolate, and the morning papers, and letters. Devereux looked up a little surprised.

"Is it so late then?" he said.

"Eight has just gone, my lord," answered the man. He laid the papers beside his master, set down the tray, and so evidently lingered, pretending to move a book or arrange something that did not need his good offices, that Devereux, with an amused smile, asked him if there was something momentous on his conscience? He was always free and easy in his bearing towards his servants, and did not consider it an offence past forgiveness for a domestic to volunteer a remark that did not strictly concern his duties.

"I've heard, my lord," said the man rather hesitatingly, "that there's been a murder somewhere in Mayfair this morning."

"THE DOOR WAS THROWN OPEN, AND THE SERVANT ANNOUNCED "LORD DEVEREUX."

"A murder in Mayfair? Well, that is not a usual place for murders; we don't commit crimes in polite society."

"No, my lord," the man answered, and glanced rather nervously up into his master's face, adding, "I hear there is a great crowd there, my lord, and that it's a gentleman; leastways, your lordship's groom came round from the stables and said he thought it was some-one in Bruton-street."

Devereux looked up with a quick flush and a vivid enough interest now.

"What did you say?" he said with an abruptness unusual with him, and the man repeated the information given him by the groom.

Devereux sprang to his feet. He knew not with what dark foreboding.

"Get me a hansom at once!" he said.

The order came by habit to his lips, but he did not wait for its fulfilment; instead he sprang past the man, and had reached the street almost before his servant had recovered his astonishment, and flung himself into a passing hansom.

"Drive like the wind to Bruton-street," he said.

Cabby looked a trifle surprised, seeing that Bruton-street was barely a quarter of a mile distant; but he nevertheless obeyed as literally as was possible under the conditions of London streets; and in another moment or two a hansom dashed into Bruton-street, and the man pulled up on the very edge of the crowd, scattering some of the people, and Devereux was out even before it had stopped.

"Heavens!" he muttered under his breath. "As I thought. Vera, Vera!"

He gave the man the first coin that came to hand—it happened to be half-a-sovereign—and went up to the door, where a policeman stood on guard.

He moved aside as Devereux knocked, and looked at him half curiously, but the door was almost immediately answered by Janet, who uttered a low cry of gladness as she saw who it was.

Devereux stepped in and the door was once more closed.

"Vera!" was all he said then, and laid his hand with a grasp like steel on the woman's arm.

"She is safe, my lord," Janet answered. "She expects you."

"Where is she?"

"In her own room."

Devereux waited for no more. But Vera's own room was upstairs, and thither he went at once. He knocked softly, and then opened the door, and closed it.

And without a word or a cry Vera came to him, and his arms enfolded her, and her head was bowed down on his breast, but the agony that shook her now was none that he could divine—and the tender pressure of his lips on hers, his murmured words, were so many sharpest stabs to her.

CHAPTER XXV.

HIS SACRIFICE.

EVEREUX held the girl silently to his heart and did not seek to check the long-drawn quivering sobs that shook her from head to foot, but waited quietly until she should be able to speak.

It was not long. She grew after a time calmer. That giving way had been but an inevitable reaction from the terrible strain she had been obliged to put on herself all this morning.

"I could not help it, Ernest," she whispered tremulously; "it has been so hard——" She broke off abruptly and lifted her head. "Have you heard anything?" she said.

"I only heard from my man that something terrible had occurred in Bruton-street," answered Devereux gently. "I came here at once, of course, but only stopped to know if you were well, my darling. Would that I had been with you!"

"Don't say that," the girl said hurriedly; "I thank God you were not. My father was found stabbed to the heart this morning. Ernest, tell me one thing—were you with him last night after all the other men had left?"

"Yes; I returned after leaving the club."

Vera drew a long breath.

"Then it was true what he said," she murmured half to herself, and Devereux started slightly.

"What do you mean, Vera?" he said quickly, and the girl lifted her clear eyes to his face for a moment.

"Tell me," she said then, "if you saw anyone as you left the house?"

"I certainly passed somebody as I got into the street, but who it was I could not exactly swear to. My impression was that it was Linwood."

"It was Linwood," Vera said in a low voice; "he it was who saw you leave this house."

"What then?" answered Devereux directly, but stopped short with a quick-caught breath. "Ah, I remember!" he said, and put his hand to his brow and so stood for a space.

The shock smote him with all the force of the unexpected. He had forgotten about the dagger, and had only vaguely remembered, until Vera recalled it to him, that anyone had passed him on the steps.

He saw at once the terrible significance which could, and, indeed, must, be given to the fact of the discovery of his coat and dagger in the study.

It was so easy to say he had forgotten these—alas! so difficult to prove! For there was nothing really he could deny, except that his hand had dealt the fatal blow.

"How was it?" he said, after a moment, in a suppressed voice; his hand closed round Vera's with a yet closer clasp, as though he would fain gather strength from the very touch of her fingers, and the girl's heart leapt up with quick glad pride. He had not even asked whether she had had the faintest doubt of him.

In answer she told him simply all the events of that morning down to the time when Linwood came.

Then she paused. It was harder than she had deemed it to deceive Devereux, though it was for his own sake.

"My poor child!" Devereux said tenderly, thinking she shrank from again going over the events that were so full of pain. "Tell me no more now—later."

But the girl interrupted him with feverish haste.

"No, no," she said; "now—now—! There is no time to lose. You must know all. Only, Ernest"—now she spoke with a change of tone, and laid her hands with all the force of entreaty on his breast—"promise me—ah, as you love me!—promise that you will not be angry with me?"

"What, with you?" said Devereux, half smiling even in this moment.

"You might—you will be," answered Vera in a low voice, and bent her head a little. "But it is for your sake, and for mine." Again she paused; then, with an effort gathering herself, as it were, together, went on steadily: "You might be angry because I have bound you to silence, for a price, and the price I will pay; I alone can pay it."

Devereux drew back a step, the dark flush rising to his brow.

"What have you done, Vera?" he said; and his eyes sought hers with a scrutiny she dared hardly meet. "As I understand the matter, Linwood's evidence would show conclusively that I was in this house at an early hour in the morning. He will not be slow to speak, when by speaking he can blight my life."

"Yes; he will be silent, because"—the girl spoke with difficulty, and turned aside her face—"I have made him promise to be silent. He will do it for my sake."

"For your sake!" interrupted Devereux, with an almost fierce passion. "Vera, you are trying me too far; I will be no partaker of the forbearance that is exercised. 'For your sake!' It is an insult to you."

She laid her hand with a touch light as a feather on his arm, yet with a force that drew him again to her side.

"Listen," she said, "and I will tell you what I have done: it is nothing that can be any dishonour to you, and it is only for a time. I have bound Linwood to silence for one year, on condition that I pay certain debts of his which are embarrassing him; in that year, Ernest, I mean to discover the real criminal."

There was a minute's silence; the girl had paused, perhaps to try and gauge the effect her words would have on him, or to discover whether her suspicions were also his. But he was still silent, and Vera continued rather hurriedly:

"I shall have money from my father—more than I want, and I have money of my own too, as you know, that will be all mine without conditions now. Ernest, I know it is much, very much to ask of you, but it is inevitable."

Again she stopped as he did not speak, only stood silent, holding her hands in his, his lips set **and very** pale.

"Ernest," the girl whispered tremulously with a sort of agony in her voice, "speak to me. Have I been so wrong? Why are you still silent?"

Then Devereux drew a long deep breath and put one hand over his eyes.

"Speak!" he said in a suppressed voice. "What shall I say? Oh, God! What shall I say?"

He turned aside, covering his face. It was a torture that seemed to grind his very soul in the dust. This demanded passiveness under a wrong that he had no power to prove a wrong; this alternative between a name irrevocably stained and saving that ancient name by a stain he deemed hardly less deep.

"I cannot—I cannot!" he said; "better to take all chances, all risks than that."

The blow had come to him so suddenly as it were. Only last night he had been rejoicing in the thought that now he could acknowledge his darling before all the world; now everything was changed. He it was who was under a cloud, who could ask no woman to share his name until it was cleared from the stain which would rest upon it, if, indeed, such clearing was possible; for, in this first shock, he had seemed to have no time to think of, much less to closely examine, all that could be said for or against the theory of his guilt.

He lifted his head once more after a few moments and said half wearily:

"Was Linwood in your father's debt?"

"I think it likely, but I do not know it; Linwood would have kept such matters a profound secret; but there is money gone—notes; I have the numbers of them. While I was for a minute alone, before the inspector came, I secured the book in which my father used to take down the numbers of all notes received; whoever the murderer is, he has wished to give the impression that robbery was the motive of the crime, and that the thief was disturbed."

"What is your idea, Vera?"

"That Linwood is guilty," said the girl directly; "that when he met you he was going in to demand money of my father, that probably hot words passed between them, and Linwood caught up the dagger lying so ready to his hand; afterwards he would think how easy and how profitable it was to fasten the deed on you."

She had said all this in a steady matter-of fact sort of way, that to a casual observer would have given little indication of the terrible anguish of suspense that was in her heart; she did not dare to let a tinge of feeling so much as enter into her voice; that rigidly-maintained calm of manner was her only chance, nor did Devereux misread her.

"What grounds have you for this suspicion of yours?" he said.

The girl drew her delicate brows together.

"You will say, perhaps, that they are a woman's grounds," she answered, "and that my own strong feeling against the man has influenced me; but I do not think that is so. It is a small thing, very likely, but Gellert's demeanour was strange towards Linwood; hitherto he has always regarded him with indifference, but scarcely aversion; to-day he growled and showed his teeth—I think he would have sprung if I had not held him back, and then this has been no mere burglar's work—there are no signs of forcible entrance, the drawers are broken open in a clumsey manner, and some valuable things close to hand are not touched."

"And what," said Devereux, with an evident effort, "is your plan for bringing the crime home to him, granting this year's reprieve?"

The girl flushed now from cheek to brow, but the crimson died away directly, leaving her deathly pale; she lifted her eyes a second to his, and then dropped them, and bent her head down on his breast. In the action there was only a half-conscious reckoning of the effect it would have on the man who loved her; only a half consciousness that such an appeal is a woman's winning card.

"Will you not trust me, Ernest?" she whispered tremulously.

He pressed his lips in silence to her forehead, then said:

"I don't know how to trust you, my darling, where I am concerned; you would do and dare all for my sake."

It was enough, it was the last touch that broke the the hardly-held control which had been strained to the utmost tension.

The thought of that last sacrifice, that she, with all her love for him, had not been able to give; all the slender hopes and chances on which she was setting her life now—for him; the more than probability of failure, and all that must fall on him then—these thoughts rushed over her like a tide let loose from the barriers that bound it, and with a choking sob the girl fell down before him, speaking passionate words that moved him to the very depths of his heart.

"You must—you must!" She clasped with an almost frantic passion the hands he stretched towards her, as if to raise her. "You must—you will let me do this for you; you have done so much for me—you do not know, your love is my salvation; for my sake, when not for your own——"

Her voice failed her, she broke into convulsive weeping, that at first could not yield even to his power to soothe; he lifted her and held her close to his heart, bitterly grieved for her—bitterly perplexed whether he ought to give way to her prayers. He had willingly yielded all and everything only to be able to bring the smile once more to her lips, and he said so much, without exactly counting the cost of what he bound himself to.

"You shall do as you will, my own Vera," he whispered. "See, for your dear sake I will try and rival you in self-devotion, only do not weep so terribly—that is hardest of all to bear."

When she grew more quiet, he led her to the sofa and sat down beside her, still keeping her hands clasped in his; and then as she dropped her head on his breast like a grief-worn child, it came on Devereux with something like a shock, that he had given up his will and his control over her, and had surrendered all for her sake, as she had surrendered for his.

"It is hard—it is bitterly hard!" he muttered, sweeping his hand over his forehead. "Vera, Vera, what have you made me do?"

His young wife lifted herself.

"I know it is hard," she said softly. "That is more noble in you to give up to me. Afterwards you will not regret it; and you will forgive me," she went on wistfully, "that I was so foolish, and—and spoke such wild things? Ah, my poor Ernest, I think I have brought you only misery yet!"

He laid his hand lightly over her soft lips.

"Never speak so," he said gently and gravely; "that pains me above all things you could think. Now," he continued in the same grave and steadfast manner, "I have promised to give myself into your hands for this year, and have surrendered my right, to some extent, to control your actions. For this one year I do not claim you as my wife—you are free; only your love for me and the duty that love imposes can set the bounds of that liberty, for I have promised, and I cannot go back from my word."

He paused a minute, knitting his brows, as though the thought was pain, and Vera said: "It is best, Ernest; when you can think it out you will see that."

"I may, dear one, but——Well, well, we will say no more of that; only remember this, Vera: that I am always near you; and if," he said with a smile that was half bitter, half sad, "you are not under obedience to me, you are still under my protection."

"Dear Ernest," Vera whispered, deeply touched, her heart wrung, too, with a passionate gratitude for this self-abnegation, in men so rare; for she divined thoroughly all that the sacrifice was to him, and that it was made for her sake, "I am so grateful to you for your trust. You will be near me, and you will help me?"

"To the very utmost," answered Devereux strongly.

The girl rose, pushing the hair back from her forehead. She was very pale, and there were dark rings under her eyes; but the young beautiful face was set as with an impenetrable resolve.

"I think," she said, "that we ought to part now; any moment Linwood might come, and we must not seem to have any communication together, other than that of Viscount Devereux and the *diva*. And there is so much to be done and thought of : there is the inquest to go through. Of course, you will not be called, as you left the house before the others."

Devereux winced visibly, but only said :

"Shall you remain in this house, Vera?"

"No; I shall go into complete retirement," answered the girl, with a singular smile. "You will not be able to see me."

"You have some scheme already in that busy brain of yours," he said.

And Vera answered :

"Yes; you will know it, but not now. Hark! do I hear someone?"

There was a knock at the door, and in answer to Vera's "come in," Janet appeared.

"Miss Mainwaring, Miss Vera," she said, "has just come, and begged to see you. She was quite overcome; she had only just heard the dreadful news, and came away in a hansom—nothing should stop her, she said."

"I will come, Janet," Vera answered. "Dear child, how kind it is of her to hasten to me directly! You will come too, Ernest?"

"Surely—and will take Alise home," said Devereux, and they both went downstairs to the drawing-room, into which apartment Alise had been shown.

CHAPTER XXVI.

THE END OF THE HOUSE IN BRUTON-STREET.

HE terrible murder in Mayfair was the engrossing subject of conversation in every drawing-room within the sacred precincts for many days; murders in such quarters, one must allow, are not of frequent occurrence, and this one was of a sufficiently startling character, and closely affected at least a considerable portion of the male sex belonging to the polite world.

When the first natural shock at the crime was passed, some of these young men remembered with dismay that now the *salon* in Bruton-street must be, perforce, closed, for it was a perfect impossibility that Vera should continue alone those delightful card-parties that were so famous among the gilded youth.

"It's all over there," said Lord Dalton dismally, over the morning cigars at the Regina. "Of course Miss Temple will give up that house; wonder what she'll do?"

"It's a terrible thing for a girl to be left so utterly alone as she seems to be," said Jack Crawford strongly; "she don't appear to have a relation in the world, and is quite alone in that dismal house—only servants with her."

"Oh, she'll marry, or go on the stage, or something," put in a third.

"She need not do anything," remarked Dalton. "The old fellow must have left heaps of money, I should think; he got a lot out of us," he added with a laugh, "so there ought to be a sackful somewhere."

"But a girl can't live alone—a beauty, too."

"Well, she needn't if she don't like," rejoined Lord Dalton philosophically. "There are plenty who wouldn't think it *infra dig.* to offer their name to Vera Temple."

"Linwood, to wit," said Rorke, laughing.

"Linwood!" Jack said sharply. "She wouldn't have him, and he isn't worth such a prize."

"Hallo, Jack, my boy!" cried Dalton; "you seem to know a lot about the *diva's* predilections. Hard hit in that quarter—eh?"

"Hang it all," said Jack rather gruffly, "can't a fellow say a girl's too good for some confounded sneak or other, without being suspected of the tender passion?"

"All right, old man; I go with you every inch about our friend Lin. Tell you who I shouldn't wonder to see enter for the stakes, and that's Dev. I am willing to bet on it," concluded his lordship, who, indeed, was willing to bet on most things.

"What—Devereux?" cried young Rorke—"The proudest of men! Do you think he'd marry anyone who couldn't show who knows how many quarterings? Besides, he's going to marry his cousin."

"Pray where do you get your information?" asked Jack with elaborate politeness, and feeling an intense desire to take the young gentleman by the shoulders and put him out.

"Oh, dear boy, I heard it on very good authority. It'll be in all the 'societies' next week."

"The devil it will!" said Jack with some heat, "and I think the lady's name had better be left out of the conversation."

"Dear boy," interposed Lord Dalton gently and sweetly, while Charley laughed and shrugged his shoulders, "don't let Devereux hear you draw all that distinction between the *diva* and even his fair cousin. He was on to Ffolkes the other night at the R——, for talking over Miss Vera. The fellow said it didn't matter; the *diva* was anybody's property in that sense. Dev. went as pale as a sheet, as he does, you know, when he's in a devil of a rage, and for a moment, 'pon my word, I thought he was going to throw Ffolkes out of window or something of the kind; but he controlled himself in time—it wouldn't have done the *diva* much good to be championed by him, you see—and only just declined to play with Ffolkes any more."

"What has become of Devereux by the way?" put in Charley rather quickly, anxious to get the talk out of unpleasant channels. He hasn't been here for a day or two—not since the murder in fact."

"I met him at the Mainwarings' yesterday in the morning," said Jack, not averse to letting Charlie see that he was allowed the privilege of morning visiting at that house.

"Will he be called at the inquest?"

"Should think not—no. He wasn't there last, you know. I'm subpœnaed," said Dalton. "I was the last to leave, with one or two others, so I was the last who actually saw the old man alive."

"When is the inquest to be held?" asked Charlie. "I haven't seen."

"To-morrow; but I don't believe the police have an idea in their heads as to who was the murderer; there will probably be an ajournment after the formal business is got through, which just allows poor Berkeley to be buried."

"I don't fancy," remarked Charlie, "that the fair Vera will weep her heart out over her loss; it's rather what the good old ladies call a happy release for her."

"It was a queer *menage*, decidedly," acquiesced Lord Dalton; "but they seemed always to be good friends. I wonder what some of the ladies of our acquaintance would have said if they had known exactly what the *raison d'etre* of that house was."

"A few did draw off after a time," said Jack, knocking the ash off his cigar. "One lady told me one never met anybody there but foreign countesses, and that sort of person, you know. I think the poor Princess Glinka was her special aversion."

"Where is she now, by the way?"

"I saw a report of her death in the papers the other day," answered Jack. "Don't know whether it's true or not; she was very handsome—a good deal in Miss Vera's style."

So the ball rolled on, touching lightly one thing and another, never stopping long in one place; and meanwhile, for the subject of all these surmises, there was plenty for her to think about—plenty for her to do.

She firmly but gently refused all help; from Linwood she would have none; from Devereux she could have none, because she could make no distinctions.

Mrs. Mainwaring, following the prompting of her own kind heart as well as the entreaties of her daughter, begged the girl to come to Eaton Square, at least until after the inquest; but Vera thanked her gratefully, but said she could not possibly be absent.

No change could have been more complete than that which had passed over the house in Bruton-street and the manner of Vera's life in these days: from a perpetual coming and going to an almost deathly stillness—from light and laughter and gaiety to darkened rooms and that atmosphere of gloom inseparable from the house wherein death has made him his home.

Vera affected no grief which was unreal; she could not, in fact, mourn the loss of a father so much as feel a sense of freedom to which she had always been a stranger.

How, indeed, should it be otherwise? In these latter days, since Vera had known Devereux, there had been a distinct recoil from the life she was obliged to lead.

She had come even to hate the homage that night after night she must listen to. Now that was over, or if she must stilll for a time live in the hot-house atmosphere, still listen and smile, and respond to the adulation that was often of doubtful worth, the whole ground was shifted, the cause for which she worked would make all holy in her eyes.

She even reproached herself that she was not able to feel grief at the lost of her father. She knew it was more the manner of his death, than the death itself that gave her even a shock. But yet she was conscious all the time that she was not truly to blame.

How was it possible she should have any love for a father who had never looked upon her, save in the light of an attractive ornament to his entertainments, and a draw for bringing clients to his doors?

Something of all these thoughts was passing through Vera's mind as she sat, the day following the inquest and the funeral, in that room which had been her father's study.

Going through some of his papers—she had not, indeed, begun her task, but sat with her head resting on one hand—she had allowed herself to fall into thought, a luxury denied her in all these last busy days. Now there was a lull, at least for a time, and perhaps the painfulness of the task she must go through made her willing to allow this straying from activity, for bitterly painful the duty necessarily was; although not for that reason which usually makes looking over the papers of those dear ones who are gone such an anguish.

For Berkeley Temple's daughter the pain lay in the coming face to face with the record of so many transactions which must send the glow of shame to her cheek. And so she sat alone in her sombre mourning-robes in that silent study.

Well, one danger was past. At the inquest, which had been held, not in the house, but in the —— Hall, besides the medical evidence, only she, and Linwood, and Lord Dalton had been called.

The latter spoke to having parted from the deceased the night before, when he seemed in good spirits, and under no apprehension, evidently, of the terrible occurrence. Linwood's testimony was to the same effect, only with the addition of his relation with regard to the finding of the body. Asked whether there was any trace of a weapon found, with which the deed might have been done, he answered: " No ; he saw nothing, nor trace of anything."

And Vera drew a long breath, and a weight seemed taken off her breast.

When Vera was called—she had been, of course, the first witness—there was a visible stir in the hall, which was crowded to excess with people whose faces were well known in the fashionable world.

The girl stated briefly and clearly the circumstances under which she had found her father. She had heard no sounds in the night—had not heard her dog bark or whine. She was a light sleeper; but her bedroom was on the second floor, and it was not likely she could hear anyone go in or out. So little idea had she that anything had happened that she went to the piano to practise instead of going downstairs. There was nothing to show how the wound had been inflicted.

In the result the verdict returned was " Wilful murder against some person or persons unknown."

The funeral was strictly private. Vera alone followed her father to the grave. She would not hear of being accompanied by anyone save her faithful servant, Janet; and so it was.

So all the formalities were over, and the girl felt she had leisure to breathe. That morning her father's lawyer had been with her, bringing the dead man's will. Every penny he possessed and all debts due to him were left absolutely and unconditionally to Vera. No trustees were appointed, but Mr. Chard was left sole executor; and now Vera was going through her father's papers to see what they held.

One thing she had determined—that she would receive no money which was owed on gambling debts.

She had said as much to Mr. Chard, and he had shaken his head and smiled.

" I am afraid, my dear young lady," he said, " that we shall not be able to help it. You know, or at least I will tell you, that I, as executor under your father's will, am bound to call in all existing debts and hand them over to you within a certain time. I have no choice, and it is not in your power to give me dispensation."

" Not if there are certain debts that I don't wish called in ? "

" It would be a breach of duty on my part. I am bound to claim all money of which there are legal proofs."

And Vera determined that of one debt, at least, there should exist no " legal proof."

Her search among her father's papers, however, revealed to her the fact that Lucius Linwood was deeply involved—much more so than she had any knowledge of, and all papers relating to his affairs she put aside. That which concerned Lord Devereux she quietly burned. It would never do to allow a claim to be made on Linwood; it would equally never do to allow such important proofs to go out of her hands. She might be acting illegally, she thought with a half-smile, but since nobody was concerned except herself it did not at all signify, and surely Mr. Chard had meant to give her a hint in saying that he could only act on what he saw.

She knew that without these outstanding debts there would be plenty of money for the future life she must lead in the next year. Money, she knew, must flow like water.

CHAPTER XXVII.

ON THE WING.

HE polite world was already on the wing; all the talk was of this or that shooting-box, or invitation to some country house; some plan for a Continental trip or expedition to a remote quarter of the globe, in the hope of finding out some new experience—this hunt for something new, which is going on more or less the whole of our lives.

Lord Devereux, of course, as a universal favourite, was always loaded with invitations, the half of which it would have been quite impossible for him to fulfil.

This year, however, he had no intention of putting many miles between himself and Vera; he must first ascertain what were her plans for the autumn.

"Devereux," said his cousin to him one day when he came to Eaton-square, and the young lady looked the incarnation of archness, "do you know that I have asked Vera to come to us at the Court? Of course, sir, you must come, too."

"I take it for granted that your logic is unanswerable," returned Devereux with a smile. "Ladies' logic always is. But are you so sure that Vera is going to accept your invitation?"

"Oh, she must!" cried Alise, pouting. "What can she do all by herself? She would be wretched. Do persuade her, Dev, there's a darling!"

And Alise put both her hands on his arm and looked with the most coaxing of smiles into his face.

If the Earl of Evringham could have seen them just at this moment, he would certainly have thought that a tender scene was going forward, and that all his dearest hopes were about to be realised.

Nothing was farther from the thoughts of either of them, however. They had always looked on themselves as privileged persons from the time they had played as children together. Devereux knew that his cousin's affections were engaged, and Alise had never imagined that Devereux was in love with her.

And now Miss Alise had a pretty shrewd idea that her cousin was no longer the heart-whole personage he always used to pose as.

"Do you think, then, pretty one," he said, "that my influence is all powerful with Vera?"

"Oh, how can I tell?" answered Alise, laughing and colouring a little. "That you know best. We shall be very quiet, so that she need have no fear."

"I doubt if she will come, Alise. And for myself, I think I am going abroad."

"Abroad? Oh, what a shame! Where?"

"Can't tell yet."

"What a provoking creature you are, Devereux! You ought to know your own mind."

"So I do, pretty one, but my own mind just now is not to know my own mind. Who is coming to the Court?"

"Oh, two or three people, if Vera won't come; and —and Ja—Mr. Crawford," said Alise, catching herself up short, and suddenly finding out that the roses in the stand near wanted some dead leaves pulled off.

Devereux smiled and came over to inspect the process.

"Ja—Mr. Crawford," said he rather wickedly. "That's a curious sort of name, coz, isn't it?"

Alise did not as usual give him a laughing glance back and call him a tease; instead, she bent her head yet lower, and Devereux saw that her lip was trembling, and that the eyes she kept so studiously averted were full of tears.

"What, tears, dear!" he said gently, and drew both her hands into his. "Forgive me; I had no thought to pain you."

Alise struggled in vain against the tears that her cousin's gentle sympathy made more hard to conquer.

She was fain to lay her pretty head against his shoulder and let them have way.

So sorrows were touching this bright young life, too, Devereux thought bitterly, the pain cutting deep into his heart.

To him, too, it seemed such needless suffering, and when there is so much that is real and inevitable, why lay useless burdens on the lives of men and women?

"It is so stupid of me," Alise whispered. "I know men hate to see a woman cry, but oh, poor Jack, he is so unhappy!"

"And you, Alise—are you not unhappy also?" said Devereux softly, putting back the straying hair from the pretty flushed face. "You true woman, Alise! The burthen of your grief is, 'He is so unhappy!'"

"It does not matter for me so much," answered the girl tremulously. "Women can bear things better than men. We are more patient. But, oh, Dev—dear Dev!" with a burst of despair: "can't you do something for us? Everyone listens to you; and Jack loves me so!"

"And you, Alise? Forgive me, dear!"

"I can never be so happy without him," Alise whispered. "He spoke to me two days ago, Ernest, and—and then he saw mamma."

Alise lifted her head now and spoke more collectedly.

"Mamma told me afterwards that she liked Jack so much, and was pleased at his talking so frankly to her. He acknowledged that he had spent too much money, and all that, though I daresay he made himself out worse than he was," said Alise at which supposition Devereux smiled. "He said it was hard for him to have to ask for me. Few people would believe he was disinterested, but he did not care. He knows I don't think that, nor does mamma; you don't, Dev, do you?"

"Jack is the simplest-hearted fellow alive in those matters," answered Devereux; "and, confidence for confidence, little one, he has told me that he felt a great difficulty in speaking to your mother lest he should be misjudged."

"Mamma did not," said Alise eagerly. "She is so kind, and in fact has asked Jack down to the Court,

only she says Uncle Evringham will be very angry and
never hear of anything, because I am an heiress, and—
and he has other views," concluded Alise a little hastily.

Devereux smiled.

"I know he has," he said quietly, "but you and I
understand each other, Alise, and I told my father long
ago that we could neither of us meet his views."

"I know," returned Alise. "Oh, there was quite a
scene between mamma and him; he said you were un-
dutiful, and he was bitterly disappointed in his only son,
and a great deal more besides; but I don't see that the
heads of families have a right to arrange things for
their children, and then be very angry because the
children can't see their plans in the same light—it is
unjust; and as for me—well, I wish I was as poor as a
housemaid, Devereux—I do indeed!" The heiress
uttered this wish with so much fervour that Devereux
was obliged to laugh.

"I don't know that that would mend matters much,"
he said, "for Jack is not too rich, Alise, as I suppose
you are aware, and even his expectations are not worth
very much. But don't lose heart, dear; if mamma is
on your side it is only a question of time, and it will do
Jack no harm to serve an apprenticeship for you."

"Couldn't you speak to Uncle Evringham, Dev?"
said Alise coaxingly, and at the question a shade came
over the young man's brow.

"I fear, little one," he said, after a moment's pause,
"that my influence with my father, and especially on
that subject, is not very great. I will talk to Aunt
Mainwaring if you like; she it is who must really decide,
not my father."

"Poor mamma!" Alise said, the smiles beginning to
dimple again about her mouth. "She is so perplexed
between her love for me and her duty to the head of
the family: and what is the use? Because," said she,
laughing and looking saucy, "you won't have me."

"And you won't have me, coz," answered Devereux,
lightly kissing her forehead, glad to see her own merry
spirit come back to her; "we are contented to be
brother and sister."

"The dearest of brothers you are," said Alise earnestly; "but dear me," she added gaily, "what pretty compliments we are paying each other. But you have lightened my heart tremendously, Dev. How good you are! I wish——" She stopped and coloured crimson.

"What is it you wish?" asked Devereux. "Are you afraid of me, Alise?"

"A little, sometimes; you might be angry." She paused again, and then said in a low voice and with averted face: "I wish so you could be happy, too," and then waited trembling. Had she gone too far? For Devereux with all his apparent frankness of manner, was one of the most reserved of men with regard to his inner life; but he was neither vexed nor angry, only deeply touched by the girl's tender solicitude.

"Why do you think I am anything else, little one?" he said gently.

"I think you cannot be, dear Ernest," said the girl with more courage. "Because—ah, forgive me—there are—I suppose there must be—obstacles between you and the woman you love."

Devereux drew a silent breath, then he said:

"Perhaps the obstacles are not quite insurmountable, Alise."

She started and looked up with a bright flush, and Devereux only said gently:

"We will not talk of this, dear; forgive me—I cannot tell you how precious your love and sympathy are to me, but I cannot speak of these things that lie so near the heart; and promise me never to breathe word or hint of anything you may imagine—not even to Jack," he added with a smile. "One day, it may be, the clouds will clear away; there is a great deal in the Latin adage, *Omnia vincit amor.*"

And Vera whispered the words, "Love conquers all things," as she knelt in the moonlight and smiled, strong in the faith of that mighty power. Fear and jealousy would bring their power, too, to fight against her. Is love alone strong enough to conquer?

CHAPTER XXVIII.

THE PRINCESS GLINKA.

"HAVE you seen that note in the *Universe?*" said a club-lounger to another of the same species one day in the beginning of November; town was filling after the long dead season, and things were looking brighter, both in society and out of it.

The other club-lounger, who happened to be Lord Dalton, answered rather lazily:

"No, dear boy; what note? It can be nothing about our *diva*, I suppose, as she seems quite to have vanished, and there's nothing worth reading about else."

"Well, I don't know, it's something about a friend of hers, and that, I take it, is better than nothing."

"A friend of hers," said Lord Dalton, waking up; "let's see."

He took the paper and ran his eye quickly over the paragraph his friend pointed out.

"Rumour," said the *Universe*, "has again been proved to be 'a lying jade.' She very calmly killed off a charming lady whom we are all glad to have once more in our midst. I have authority for saying, however, that the Princess Glinka will pass the remainder of her widowhood in the strictest retirement; her house will not be opened at all this winter."

"The deuce!" said Lord Dalton; "I call that a shame. Why, there isn't a single place worth going to this winter, now Bruton-street is gone."

"What! you can't get over that yet, and it is quite three months ago that the *diva* disappeared?"

"That makes no difference, she was not a personality one easily forgets; but this is singular about the Princess Glinka. I wonder if it is true, or only just a bid for sensation on the part of the *Universe.*"

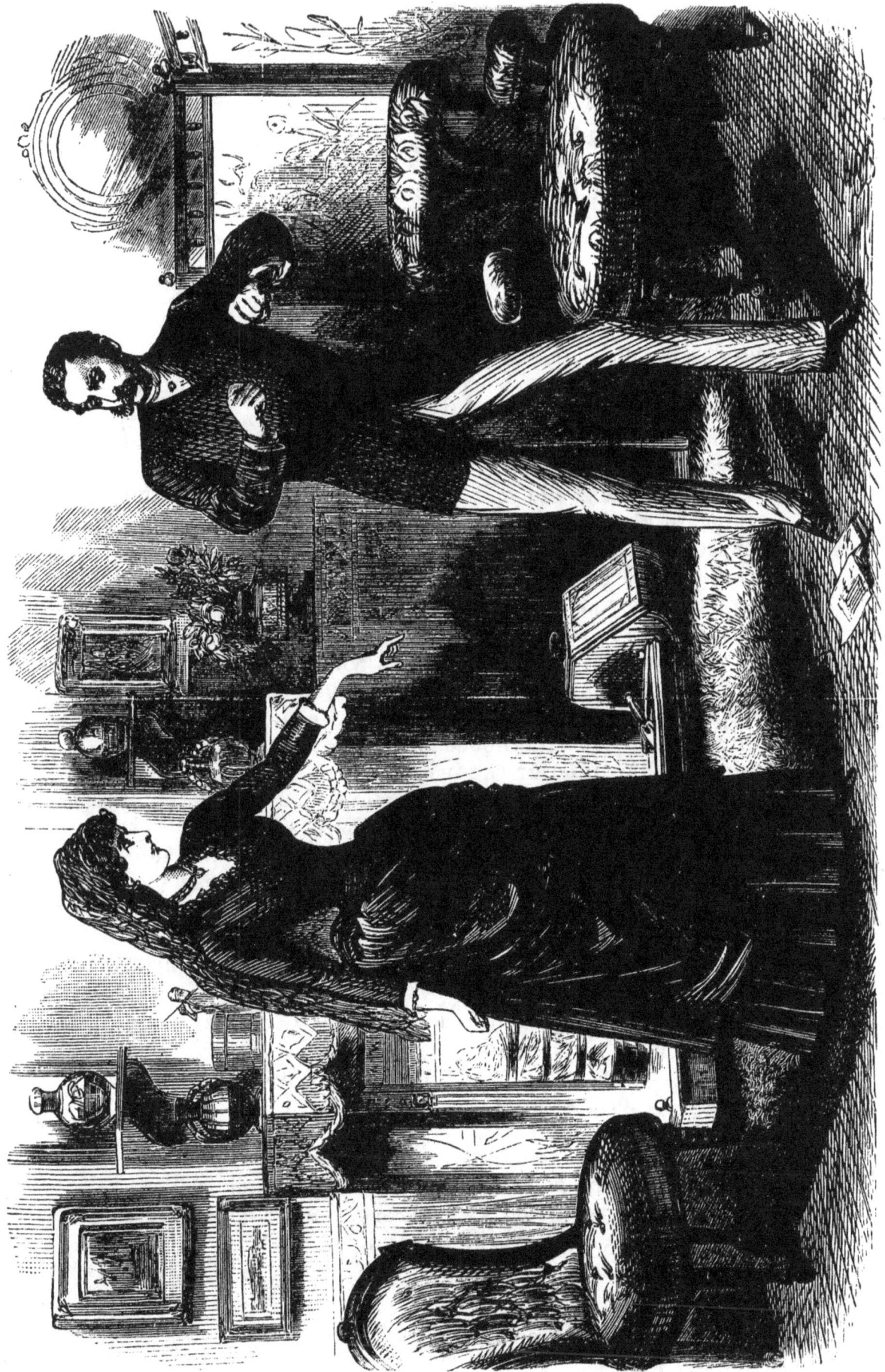

No. 9.

SHE SNATCHED FROM HER DRESS A LETTER, AND FLUNG IT DOWN BEFORE HIM.

But the announcement of the *Universe* was no mere bid for sensation; the Princess Glinka, in defiance of rumour, had seen fit to survive her husband instead of dying from fever or grief, and had actually come to London to pass in retirement the remainder of her first year of widowhood.

Many surmises were set on foot by those who knew of her advent, and who thought they knew everything; besides, people decided that the charming princess had come over to make a rich marriage, or by marriage to better her social status, which, as we know, had been previously regarded by some severe critics as open to improvement. However that might be, it was evident that the princess did not mean to open the husband campaign at present, for she neither went into society nor received at home, with the exception of certain privileged persons. But that was later; at this time she had received no one yet.

The house in which the Princess Glinka had installed herself was one of those pretty villas in Brompton, which the march of stucco semi-detached has not yet swept away; it was surrounded by a large garden, which entirely hid the house from view, so that it was here quite possible for the princess to enjoy that privacy which her bereaved condition demanded.

The early dusk of a short November day was falling, a light frost was in the air, giving to it a pleasant crispness, and rousing wild hopes in the breasts of skaters, but at the same time rendering particularly agreeable the warm glow of the fire, the drawn curtains, and all other snugnesses which we associate with winter.

In the drawing-room of the Princess Glinka's house the waning daylight was already shut out; a subdued— very subdued glow from fire and shaded lamp, for the princess abhorred gas—diffused a soft effulgence over the room.

In and out of the shadows and the firelight passed a tall slender form, robed in soft clinging black velvet; and often as she passed the mirrors, she looked in them at the face reflected there, and smiled a little.

Why should the princess smile at her own fair reflexion? She saw there a true enough reproduction of herself; a little altered, looking a little older perhaps, notwithstanding the artistic use of paint and powder to smooth away a line here and there. The dark hair, curling quite low over her forehead, gave to the eyes a soft langour that was still further enhanced by the black lace veil which she wore gracefully disposed about her head and shoulders, throwing a kind of shade over the face. The princess had always clung to this eminently becoming head-dress of her country.

She paused in her walk now, and again surveyed herself with a long and earnest gaze in the tall mirror.

"So," she said to herself, "I wonder if I shall do? I think so. I wonder will he know me? In this dim light it will be a severe test. And if I do not prove successful in this case, that will not be fatal, for I think," with a soft smile, "that he would know me anywhere."

Even as she turned from the glass there was a ring at the door-bell.

The girl paused with throbbing heart and a quick vivid flush, and a bright light in her eyes chased the langour from them, but with swift recollection she drew herself together, as it were. In another moment the door opened, and her Russian servant entered and announced "Lord Devereux."

In the dim shaded light Devereux saw only a woman's form, tall and slender, advance towards him with outstretched hands. And it was the princess's own well-remembered voice, her very manner, as she said to him in French, the language, by adoption, of every Russian:

"Ah, Lord Devereux, I am charmed to see you! How long is it since we met?"

For just half a second Devereux paused, then stepped forward, and not only the princess's hands were clasped in his, but he drew the slender form into his arms, and in the first moment of this meeting, unexpected though it was, forgot to ask why this disguise was assumed; and Vera clung to him in the silence of a passionate joy, conscious now only that he was with her—she was no more alone.

But Devereux first broke the silence, holding the girl a little away from him, and looking into the beautiful face that was uplifted to his with a searching and keen gaze, loving, grave, questioning.

Her lip trembled, and her eyes fell.

"You are surprised to see me so disguised?" she said a little hurriedly. "Forgive me, Ernest, that I hid my plans from you, even for this short time, but I wanted a strong test as to the efficacy of my disguise; and I think"—and now she smiled with something of her old archness—"I have succeeded, for you were just a little bewildered at first, were you not?"

"In the dim light I hardly saw your features," Devereux answered. But he spoke without a smile, and if tenderly, still very gravely. "But Vera, my Vera, are you keeping your promise with me? Why this disguise? or rather I hardly need to ask that, for I can divine, at least in part, your motive."

"I could see no other way, Ernest," said the girl, troubled, but evidently not prepared to yield her ground. "Do you think I would have put myself in a position where I must daily act as if I were disloyal to you, if it were possible to do otherwise—not only to receive and encourage, but to draw attentions that will be hateful? But there is too much at stake for me to shrink back from any ordeal, save one. For your sake nothing is too hard."

"Aye," said Devereux bitterly; "there it is. 'For my sake' you must not—shall not——"

"It is too late to draw back," said the girl; "and I would not if I could. I have set the one purpose before me as the aim of my life. I shall succeed—I have a strong faith that I shall succeed, and that only through the man himself is discovery of the criminal possible. In my own character I could not attain my object, but the fascinating Princess Glinka, with whom Linwood was always half in love in his way, can twist him round her fingers."

"And if you fail, Vera?"

"I shall not! I never think of failure as a possibility," answered the girl steadily. "My disguise is good, is it not?" she added in a lighter tone; I look a little bit like a Russian, don't I?"

"In this dim light, Vera, you will pass to those who know you most intimately, but in the broad glare of daylight I doubt your being able to tone down your beauty to the level of the princess."

"No one will ever see me under the full glare of any light," answered Vera smiling. "I live in retirement; for though I never was with the lamented prince a month in the year, still"—she shrugged her shoulders —"*les convenances*, you know; and I only receive a very privileged few—that is, you and Mr. Linwood, and that in the late afternoon. Besides, my eyes are weak, perhaps with much weeping for my late husband, and I cannot bear a strong light."

She said all this with such inimitable archness and humour that Devereux was obliged to laugh.

"Besides," added the girl, "all ladies, as I daresay you know, dare not submit themselves to the trying ordeal of a strong light; and I am no longer quite young."

"You could bear any light," said Devereux; "and I think for many years to come you will still be quite young." As he spoke he drew her to the sofa and seated himself beside her, taking her hands in his. "Tell me," he said, "a little more of what you are going to do. You can be, at least, my own Vera for an evening."

The girl leant her head against him and closed her eyes. Yes, just for this hour she might drop the mask and loosen the strain of a continual watch on herself— at the commencement of her difficult campaign she might allow herself this sweet relaxation.

"Afterwards," she said, half as though continuing her thoughts aloud, "I dare not, even in private, be myself, lest I, perchance, should lose my guard when I most want to keep it."

"Must even I see only the Princess Glinka, Vera?"

"It is safer, Ernest, is it not? You will not see me often—only enough to make Linwood a little jealous— not enough to make you a distinct rival."

"Was this what you meant to do when we parted in London a few months ago? Ah," he said half bitterly, and rising to pace the floor restlessly, "you did well not to tell me the scheme you had in your brain, Vera, for I think I could never have given my consent to it."

"Now it is too late," said the girl under her breath; she said it without defiance, without triumph, without regret; but her head drooped and her fingers were clasped more tightly on her knee. "I knew that you would scarcely consent to my playing this part; was I wrong to withhold it from you until it was too late to make any change?"

It smote him bitterly that he should have seemed even to imply any reproach to her; he turned quickly and knelt beside her with passionate words:

"Forgive me—forgive, my darling; I meant no reproach. Is it not enough that you are playing this hateful part for my sake? Could I find it in my heart to say one word of reproach? But it is bitter—bitter, Vera." He bowed his head on her knee, and she felt how the hands that held hers trembled.

"I know," Vera said softly; "I can understand so perfectly how you must feel."

And he knew that she did so understand him; that she said the words not merely to give comfort, but because there was a true and perfect sympathy with the man's pride as well as with the man's love, that made the forced position such a torture to him.

She said no more than those few words; they were enough; and after a moment Devereux lifted his head and kissed the hand that lay in his.

"And now, sweet wife," he said steadfastly, and for a second the bright smile that came more rarely now to his lips, flashed up like sunshine, "you shall never hear one bitter word more from me. Rather will I strive with every power I have to lighten your life—not to make it harder with adding suffering, because you think I suffer."

"You must suffer," the girl said sadly. "Could I love you so well if you did not?"

"I will at least show, then," said Ernest half playfully, "how much of the woman there is in me by suffering silently."

Vera smiled.

"There is a great deal of the woman in every true man," she said.

"Then I have to prove first that I am true man by being true woman? But, my Vera, to be true woman takes some kind of essence that lies not in man's composition—we cannot attain to it."

"Most men cannot—you can and do. You can lay aside even your man's pride—and that is the last thing that can be put down—because you love me," Vera said softly.

There was silence for many moments between them after that, then Vera said:

"I have sent for Linwood to come to me to-morrow about this time. He believes that I, Vera, am living retired for a time on the Continent."

"There was always a certain likeness between you and poor Olga," said Devereux; "though she could never approach you in beauty."

"Flatterer," said Vera, smiling, "you must not pay compliments to your own wife."

"They are not compliments, but sober truths," answered Devereux.

Vera laughed.

"Well," she said, "I have only painted Olga up a little. And now, Ernest, do you know, I think I must send you away, for it is getting late."

"It seems but a few minutes that I have been with you, my darling," said Devereux, but he made no resistance to the fiat, and only took the girl in his arms and kissed her.

"God keep you," darling!" he said softly and earnestly. "It is much that I can at least see you, and be ever at your call when you want me."

And so he left her, and Vera's new and strange life was begun.

CHAPTER XXIX.

THE PRINCESS GLINKA "AT HOME."

UCIUS LINWOOD sat alone in his chambers, over a late breakfast, the paper, and his letters. But though he held the *Times* in his hand he was not reading it, but staring moodily before him, with a brow like a thunder-cloud.

He was plainly in a bad humour, and, being alone, was therefore at no pains to conceal it.

He was, it may be said, at this time, in a chronic state of general wrath, for notwithstanding that all his schemes had seemed to succeed, still, in their very fulfilment, he somehow appeared to have come off second best.

Vera had baffled him, if only for a time; still she had managed to outwit him for that time. She had consented to a marriage with him, but had coupled with that promise a condition that filled him with impotent anger, for, as he elegantly expressed it, "women were the devil to pay," and as Vera was out of his reach, away from his immediate control, no one could trust her or premise what she would do. She was still abroad, and had expressed her intention of remaining there till the stipulated year was up.

He received letters from her, enclosing money, "according to conditions," she wrote, dated now from one place, now from another, but in almost every letter gave him pretty clearly to understand that if he tried to overstep the conditions of their bond she would throw the whole thing up; and this he knew she meant and would hold to. He felt clearly enough that there was a point beyond which it was of no use to try and drive the girl he held in his power.

His servant entering, gave him a note and retired. One of those thick cream-hued envelopes, faintly perfumed, and with crest and monogram, that not infrequently came to Mr. Linwood, but the handwriting of this was unfamiliar to him.

He did not, however, waste much time in looking at the outside, but tore open the covering and ran his eye down the lines, his brow visibly clearing as he did so; and indeed, the wording of this little note was calculated to soothe the ruffled feelings and compensate him for the absence of wife or mistress.

It ran:

MY DEAR FRIEND—for I think indeed I used to be able to count you one of my friends—will you, if you have nothing better to do, come and take pity on my loneliness, and charm a half hour away? I am at home and alone from five this evening.

Yours, OLGA GLINKA.

"The Glinka, by Jove! Then it was true what the *Universe* said," said Linwood with a brightening face.

He had always been one of the princess's train in the old days, and the terms in which her letter was worded pleased him.

A flirtation never came amiss to Lucius Linwood, and one was particularly welcome just now. Vera should see that he could console himself when she chose to withdraw herself from him.

"It is the greatest piece of good fortune that could happen to a fellow," Linwood said to himself, and he rose with alacrity from the table, as though by some movement to give expression to his enlivened feelings. "I'll go this very evening, and show my proud Vera, how well I can supply her place. These women think they may do what they like with us."

In which these women are not far wrong, for a clever woman can more often than not twist a man round her finger.

Linwood looked in at the club about luncheon-time, and found several men there. He nodded to them and sat down, taking up a paper, but he did not read for long. Throwing down the sheet he rose and crossed to the fire-place.

"Any news going?" said he to Jack Crawford.

"The Glinka's in town," rejoined that gentleman briefly. He did not affect Linwood.

"I know that, my son," said Linwood in the manner of one to whom nothing is news. "I suppose in the absence of the fallen star we shall make a *diva* of her?"

"We sha'n't get the chance," returned Jack rather grimly, "for they say she's not going into society—wants to create an artificial interest, I imagine. That's her game, depend upon it. Then we shall all talk about her, and all the world will canvass what her motive is. Pooh! One knows the whole gamut of these society beauties."

"You're awfully hard on the Glinka," remarked Charlie Wemyss, laughing. "Looks as if you'd come off badly in the lists at some period or other."

"Not I," said Jack; "she never was 'fair for me.'"

"Dev is going to be the favoured one," struck in a third; "just as he was with the *diva*."

Linwood hardly prevented himself from uttering a quick exclamation; as it was, he started almost perceptibly. Commanding himself, however, he only lorked up and said:

"Why?"

"He called there the other day," answered the last speaker; "that's all I know. My man saw him and told me. She don't receive the general world."

"It does'nt follow that Lord Devereux was admitted," Linwood said, gnawing his lip.

The club gossip had unconsciously played into Vera's hands by stimulating Linwood's jealousy of a possible rival.

Was Devereux always to be crossing his path?

"There aren't many places where Devereux calls that he has to wait on the steps," said Jack dryly.

Linwood having no reply ready, merely shrugged his shoulders and turned away.

But if he had ever had any doubt as to whether he should call on the princess, he had none now. Devereux should have no clean walk-over here.

The dusk of the short November day was deepening when Linwood presented himself at the gate of the Brompton villa.

He was rather curious, for many reasons, to see the princess again. He was by no means averse to renewing a certain flirtation which had used to exist between him and the fair Russian. More than that, he was very decidedly wishful to do so—more than ever, now that he had heard Lord Devereux had been received.

He was shown, not into the larger drawing-room, but into a smaller apartment, separated from it only by a heavy *portiere* of velvet. It was a luxurious little room, lighted only with the uncertain flicker of the fire, which burned on logs set far back on the tiled hearth; a lamp with a deep shade stood on a table, but did not add greatly to the illumination; but coming out of the mist and fog to the warmth and comfort of this bijou room, Linwood thought the dim light only served to heighten the effect, and to deepen the delicious sense of repose that pervaded the apartment.

And as if nothing should be wanting to the very *beau-ideal* of luxurious costliness, a tiny ball of white fur, which Linwood supposed must be a kitten, lay curled up on the fluffy sheepskin before the fire. He stooped to touch the soft fur, but the small sybarite resented the intrusion on her repose, and only lifted her head to open her mouth with a decided hiss, and Linwood prudently withdrew his hand.

"Spiteful little brutes, those Persians," he muttered with a frown. "What can women find to admire in those creatures, I wonder?"

"Ah, Mr. Linwood, this is indeed a pleasure!" said a voice at his side, and Linwood turned with a start, for he had heard no footfall, nor rustle of a dress, yet there before him stood the Princess Glinka, in the dim and flickering light, he thought, looking just the same as in the old days—lovely and charming always.

"Princess," Mr. Linwood said, taking her outstretched hand and lifting it to his lips, "you do me indeed an honour in allowing me the privilege to call. I had not dared to hope for so much."

"And unexpected pleasures are always the best—not," said the princess with her little soft, charming laugh, and her pretty foreign way of speaking; but Linwood noticed that she spoke, not exactly hoarsely, but with that sort of *voile* voice which people use when they are recovering from an attack of hoarseness. "But it is so kind of you to take pity on my loneliness."

"Surely, princess, you of all people need never be alone," said Linwood with a slight stress on the pronoun, "you who were a queen of society."

"And you think I can be a queen again? But no; I was but a princess when our charming Vera was there. You see," with a frank smile and a shrug of her shoulders, "I am frank, and I am jealous not at all." She coughed a little, and drew the soft black lace she wore closer round her throat. "Besides, I do not want to be a queen just now; an old friend who will be kind, that is all I want now."

She sighed, and a half-sad look flitted like a shadow over her face.

Was it possible that she was, after all, mourning the late prince?

If so, flashed rapidly through Linwood's thoughts, what pleasanter task could there be on these dull winter evenings than that of consoling a creature so fair and so charming?

For whether it were that absence had refreshed the somewhat jaded devotion Linwood in previous days had given the princess, or that she had indeed grown more fascinating, he knew not, but he found her certainly more charming than ever; perhaps she profited from the absence of comparison also.

"But," she said, with a change of manner, and she drew forward a chair, seating herself a little out of the glare of the fire, "now that you have come I will no longer be melancholy. Sit down, my friend, and let me forget for a while that there is sorrow and trouble in the world."

"That is easy to forget when one is with you," said Linwood, taking the seat she had indicated; "but surely," he added, bending forward a little, "you have been ill? You have suffered?"

"I? Oh yes; I have been at death's door. The same horrible fever that took from me my husband; and," with a smile, "some of your journals did me also the honour to kill me. I was quite amused."

"Heaven be thanked it was not true!" said Linwood earnestly.

"Ah yes, Heaven is certainly to be thanked, because, you see, life is pleasant, and when one is young one has not the wish to die. But I have been ill—very ill, and the doctors have told me I shall be yet very careful—you hear how hoarse I am."

"And you come to this climate, dear princess! Surely that is imprudent?"

"It does not matter, I could not keep away," said the princess.

She spoke a little hurriedly, and went on before Linwood could make any answer:

"I could not remain in Livonia. Oh, you do not know how desolate, how dreary is that castle! To be shut up there all the long, long winter, I should indeed have died. In Paris—what will you?" with a shrug and uplifted brows; "there I have so many friends; there society will not suffer me to be quiet, to choose my own way of living. In Paris one must be gay and well, otherwise life becomes insupportable. The Parisians do not understand that one cannot always laugh."

"In London," said Linwood with a smile, "one does not understand how one ever laughs."

"Oh, that I will not hear. Have we not laughed in the old days—the happy days we lived in Bruton-street? *Helas!* those—will they ever come again!"

"Why should they not?" said Linwood.

"That *salon* is broken up," answered the princess, shaking her head; "the merry evenings, the light laughter and jest, those charming reunions, that were only possible where such a spirit as Vera's reigned—these are passed, my friend. That dreadful tragedy, ill changed all. How very strange it was! I was too it at the time to be told much about it, and when I met Vera—it is now a few weeks—she could speak but a little of it. But I am curious to know more. Tell me, then, of it, I entreat you."

"Dear princess," Linwood said half deprecatingly, "it is a painful theme, and would only distress you. You are sensitive and nervous, and if I was the cause of bringing bad dreams to you, I should never forgive myself."

The princess leaned back in her chair and laughed.

"You men amuse me," she said; "you are so wonderfully careful for us. My dear friend, we are not made of sugar."

"No; but of such delicate texture," returned Linwood, "that we dare not put too great a strain on it. Would you have us less careful for the fair and beautiful women who are all the world to us?"

"All the world, plus cards, plus horses, plus wine!" said the princess dryly. "My friend, do not try and be a humbug to me; you see I serve myself with your good downright English word! Now tell me about this murder. I will be amused in my own way."

She stooped forward as she said this, and took up the kitten, laying her soft cheek against the silky fur of the little creature.

Linwood laughed.

"There it is," he said, willing, as she saw, to try and shelve the sublect of the murder; "women are enigmas! Here you are dying with curiosity to hear about horrors that were ruin to your best friend, while you fondle a kitten and smother it with caresses."

"My friend," answered the princess, looking at her visitor with the quizzical, half-mocking glance that he knew of old, "we are no better than our lords and masters; but never mind that, we will not become metaphysical, and therefore dull. I have the wish to know of this murder—while I fondle my pretty Zu—that is her name, Zuleika."

"There is really nothing to tell, princess," said Linwood with a touch of brusquerie; "it was all in the papers at the time."

"And I, as I have told you, did not see papers. I was lying ill, and was almost dying, and knew nothing which befell my friend," said the princess with a little pathetic quiver in her voice; "now I am anxious—and you will not ease me; you like rather that I shall be amusing; but it matters not! I see that you care no longer to please me one little bit!"

With that the offended princess almost hid her face in Zu's fur, and began chattering to her in Russian—a language of which Linwood understood not one word; and who knows what she might be saying to that pampered little animal about him?

Linwood was a vain man, he could not bear that his brusquerie should be held up to the reprehension of even a Persian cat. The princess's ebullition of temper took him rather by surprise, but his vanity caused him to think he discerned more in it than anger, merely because her whim was not at once gratified; surely she was also piqued at his reluctance to speak of what was painfully connected with Vera, who, she had always heard, he had aspired to win? But to put a woman in a temper with you, and then have the delightful task of getting her back into a good humour again, was exactly to Linwood's mind; a flirtation to be a flirtation at all must not run on wheels too well oiled.

He paused a moment, and then bent forward, saying half deprecatingly:

"But, princess——"

She went on talking to her kitten, looking the while so charming that Linwood began to wish that she would transfer some of those wasted caresses to him.

"Dear princess," he said softly, "will you not even listen to me?"

"Oh yes; I will listen to you, if you find that amusing," said the Russian, just giving him a glance from out her dark eyes. "Zu, my pretty one, my pet!" in her own tongue, "my dear little friend!"

"But you talk all the time to to your kittten," said Linwood reproachfully.

" And why shall I not? She cares for me!" said the princess with a touch of pathos. "She will do for me anything—not, my Zu—?"

As a matter of fact the Persian partook of the usual characteristics of all her race, and was about as selfish a little animal as any other cat.

"And don't you think I care more for your lightest words," said Linwood gently, "than Zu can for all you give her? Ah, princess, do not be cruel!"

"But it is not I who am cruel; it is you who will not do what I ask, because—ah, *mon cher*," and now she looked up with the most arch and bewitching of smiles, "think you I do not know why you have reluctance to speak of this murder? That beautiful Vera! Ah, but she turned the heads of all you men quite—quite round. There was the little Dalton, and there was my Lord Devereux. Well, what have you——" for Linwood had started and flushed, and something like an oath had risen to his lips. "And there was you, and a great many others. And who do you think she liked of you all? You poor men, of whom only one can be the possessor!"

Linwood laughed, a hard laugh.

"Who can answer for a girl's fancy, princess? Any man was a fool that took hope from her smiles!"

"Well, my friend, it was necessary that she should smile on everyone, in her position. Ah, M. Linwood," said the princess, laughing softly, "I fear you were one of the fools—in those days."

"If so," returned Linwood, bending a little towards her, and with a glance that lent meaning to the words, "I am so no longer."

The princess met his look with one that was half coquettish, half mocking.

"That is what they all say," said she; "but now you shall prove it in telling me what I have prayed you! I am a woman, *cher* M. Linwood, and I come back always therefore to my point. Now if you are no more one of the foolish ones, you can prove it to me—you understand? Who was the suspected one?"

"No one was suspected," said Linwood rather shortly. "Why should you think that? Who was there to suspect?"

"How shall I know that? I am a stranger to the affair, but one knows that in a house like our friend's, there shall be many who shall be glad to silence the host. Is it not so?"

"I don't know. I only know that it was supposed to be the work of burglars—money was stolen. I should fancy the police have given up looking any more now."

"Your police are not very clever," said the princess; "in Russia that is different, we should find the murderer."

"That I doubt," said Linwood with a covert sneer that did not pass unheeded by the fair Russian. "The man, whoever it was, must have laid his plans well and surely. It was, as is usual in London, a nine days' wonder, and though some profess to remember and regret the fair *diva* of the *salon*, naturally, by the majority of the London world the whole thing is forgotten."

"But you," said the princess archly, "have you not a soft place of memory left for the fair *diva*?"

"Can you ask that—now?"

"Oh yes, I can ask it—now," answered the princess, mimicking exactly and with pretty mockery his tender manner. "Why not? You will protest that in my presence of course any good constituted man must forget other women, for you see I know all you will say. Not? But I believe you not all the same."

I remember you were ever a sceptic as regards our constancy," returned Linwood with a laugh that he strove to render careless; "but do not think I could so easily forget you, princess."

"Ah, well, I suppose that I must take it for granted that you mean a little what you say," said the princess lightly, "else you had not come to devote a half-hour to an old acquaintance."

"Acquaintance! May I dare claim to be more than that?" said Linwood, bending forward.

"Oh, we will not quarrel about a word," answered the Russian with that brilliant smile which had made many a man's heart beat higher. "What, you will go? It becomes late, I suppose, but," as she rose with a half-checked sigh, and bent a little away as though to arrange a fold of her dress, "one notices not the flight of time when one is content."

Then, as if she had not meant to say so much, she looked up and laughed. "You understand, I have been so long a time away in my old *chateau*, that I rejoice to meet again my friends."

"Then I may come again?" Linwood asked eagerly.

"Assuredly. It will give me always pleasure to receive you at this time; earlier I am never visible, my health is yet not good."

"I can live then on that promise?" said Linwood. "Now I must tear myself away."

He held the beautiful hand she gave him longer than was necessary, and then bent and touched his lips to it with great devotion.

"*Au revoir* then," he said, "I shall live in the hope of being soon admitted again to your presence."

She smiled as she touched the bell, but when the door closed on him, her face changed, the smile died away, and an expression of bitter contempt passed over her features.

"So," she said within herself, "that will do; he is quite ready to be fooled by me, though he loved Vera so passionately. Love! He will just keep his hand in by making love to the Princess Glinka." She glanced down at her hand, and gave the back of it a little impatient rub. "Ugh!" she said, "I must go and wash it!"

CHAPTER XXX.

THE TALK OF THE " WORLD."

IF the Princess Glinka had wished to become the fashion, she could have taken no surer means to this end than the course she was now pursuing.

Conjecture was rife in the circles where she had formerly moved, as to the why and wherefore of her present determination to live a perfectly retired life.

It was in vain that Lucius Linwood gave out, with the air of one who knows, and is admitted to the confidence of the person in question, that the health of the princess had suffered, and that, besides this, she wished to pass some period of her widowhood in retirement.

People smiled at the idea that the Princess Glinka had been so very devoted to the late prince; others suggested that she was remorseful, and was doing penance for her neglect of that worthy man during his life.

These things, however, troubled the princess but little. She laughed when Linwood recounted to her all the surmises that were made in the clubs concerning her, and gave him to understand, without saying it in so many words, that she was much happier in the society to which she had chosen to limit herself, than ever she had been in the world.

"And I," said Linwood, with a smile that meant a great deal, "am the last man surely to wish you to mingle in the crowd of idle worshippers."

"Why?" she asked him, toying with her fan.

"Can you ask it, princess? Should I not be one of many then?"

She looked at him with a peculiar smile.

"You are very modest, M. Linwood," said she.

He flushed suddenly, and with a suppressed eagerness said :

" I do not understand.   Do you mean——"

The princess interrupted his words by rising abruptly.

" Bah !   You are dull," she said, with the impatience of a woman who has permitted herself to say too much to a lover unskilled in interpreting hints. " All Englishmen are dull.   Or no—some are not.   But you are not one of these."

And she turned away and began petting her canary.

She always had some creature or other on which to lavish caresses when her human adorers were either dull or tiresome.

From these few words it will be seen that Linwood had made some progress in his suit, of whatever nature it was, of the princess, who showed herself, after the manner of her sex, now gracious, now wilful and *difficile,* and a lady not to be counted on to drop like a ripe cherry into the mouth first opened to receive her.

She knew almost to a word how to enslave Linwood, who valued nothing that was easy to conquer ; and she would often lift him up with some such hint as she had just given of regarding him with special favour, only the next minute to madden him with a jealous fear that she found Lord Devereux more brilliant or more devoted than Linwood.

Hitherto, the two men had never met at the villa in Brompton.   Linwood heard from the princess that Devereux sometimes came, and she was a past mistress of the art of playing one lover against another; but she had no particular desire that they should meet; nor was there anything to be gained by it.

Vera shrank, on the contrary, from the thought of playing the part of enchantress to Linwood before the man to whom her heart and her life were given.   It was hard enough as it was ; she had to fortify herself hourly with the talisman, " It is for his sake"; only that thought enabled her to go through her task.

There were times when Devereux broke through the restraint he had imposed on himself—when it seemed impossible to stand by and see his darling suffer as he knew she must, although she never willingly let him see her pain, when he told her he was degraded in his own eyes to allow her to bear so much for him; and then, though the girl trembled inwardly to think that he knew not even now all that she had done, she would not suffer herself to be moved. But it was rarely that Devereux broke from his habitual self-control; he had said he would not make her task more difficult to her, and by that he abided.

Meanwhile Devereux's cousin Alise was on the tip-toe of curiosity to be introduced to the Princess Glinka, and petitioned Ernest, as she had preferred the same request with regard to Vera, to introduce her to the Glinka.

"If only because she is a friend of my dear Vera," said she. "I have not forgotten her, sir, if you have."

"I am glad you have such a long memory, dear coz," laughed her cousin in answer; "you would not get much more information out of the Glinka about Miss Vera than is contained in those thin foreign sheets you get from time to time; and as to introducing you to the princess—that, my child, is out of the question."

"Why? Is she so very grand and exclusive?"

"Not the least in the world," returned Devereux, unable to forbear a smile at the idea of the princess's grandeur and exclusiveness. "Another time, no doubt, she would be delighted to make your acquaintance, but she wishes to remain out of society at present, and if she opens her doors to new friends she must do it to a great many."

"Yet she receives you and Mr. Linwood?" said Alise. "He is for ever boasting about his footing at the villa. Odious man!"

"We are old friends," Devereux answered, passing over the last part of her speech.

And Alise looked at him, as she thought, covertly; but, nevertheless, Devereux was quite aware of the glance, and its meaning, which said plainly enough: "What, are you beginning to forget Vera?"

But Alise never ventured to question her cousin about Vera, for she remembered his words to her when they had parted in the summer; nor did she really think that Devereux was likely to forget her.

"People are saying," she remarked after a minute, "that the princess is likely, perhaps, to make a second marriage before very long. What do you say?"

"Who do they assign to her for the bridegroom?" asked Devereux, laughing. "Your dear friend Linwood? I should say that the Glinka had had enough of the married state."

"Well, isn't she supposed to be mourning for the late prince?"

"She has never given that out; all the same, how can I tell?"

"Oh, I thought you might be in her confidence," said Alise, with some archness.

"Not to that extent, my child," returned Devereux, smiling. "She would scarcely entertain me with fond reminiscences of the late prince."

"Why should she not?" asked Alise, rather sharply.

"Wouldn't interest me, dear."

And with this reply, Alise was obliged to make herself content.

From the Earl of Evringham, Devereux underwent some questioning with regard to the fair Russian—questions which he answered with imperturbable good humour, but without committing himself to anything. The poor earl was not best pleased to hear of another fascinating foreigner coming up for the suffrages of the gilded youth.

"You young men," he grumbled, "are always running after a new sensation, instead of quietly settling down to a useful life, marrying respectably as we used to do in my time, and being a credit to society. There is a charming young lady in every way cut out for you; but no, you prefer to flirt with all the rackety foreigners who come over to make their fortunes, and what can it all come to? You can't marry these people."

"Not all of them, certainly," answered the young man, who had listened to this harangue with so grave a face as to suggest the idea of much inward amusement.

"Nor any one of them, I should hope," rejoined the old gentleman, tartly. "Who is this Glinka, as you call her? As if any man who had for her the respect a lady ought to inspire would speak of her as though she were some opera-dancer."

"My dear father, she is a Russian princess."

"She may be a Russian empress for all I care. Is she well born? But I suppose she has money, and that does as well nowadays."

"She is of high birth, and I believe has money, but that has nothing to do with me; I am not going to marry her," said Devereux, which statement was true enough. "Do you suppose that I wish to marry every woman who is agreeable?"

"It is to be hoped not," said the earl, grimly, "for it seems to me that you find every woman agreeable; and one wife is as much as most men can manage; but you are likely, I think, to fritter away the best part of your life in dangling after these Russians and Poles, and the Lord knows what besides. If you would make up your mind to marry——"

"The aforesaid charming girl," said Devereux, smiling. "My dear father, she will not have me. She prefers to endow Jack Crawford with her revenues, as you know already."

"For him to run through!" said the earl, angrily. "I have told your aunt that they will never have my consent; if they like to do without it, let them! I can't prevent them; between you all, you have set me at defiance and utterly disregarded my wishes."

A slight flush crossed the young man's cheek; he rose and made a half movement as if to go, but paused, giving way to the softer impulse that compelled him to speak, although he might be misunderstood:

"It has been pain more bitter than I can say, father," he said earnestly, "to have so to cross your dearest wishes, though you may not believe me; but one cannot command one's heart or give love to order, and Alise had no love to give me, nor I to give her; for us to marry would have been to condemn us both to misery."

"Hem! I don't know so much about the misery on her side," said the earl rather dryly; he was softened, but did not choose to show it. "It must be an odd woman who could be downright miserable with you; for though you are a disobedient son enough, all the women profess to find you charming."

Devereux could not but laugh.

"But that is very well in society," he said, "and then, if there exists no other lover."

"Well—well, you have settled it all amongst yourselves, and I cannot force you or that silly girl to be sensible, and young folk always think they decide for the best, in spite of what everyone may say! Go your own ways. But don't bring your Glinka home to me as your wife."

"I have no intention of doing so," said Devereux, meekly; and the earl saying no more the conversation dropped, and Devereux straightway went to call on the Princess Glinka, it being about the time that lady received.

"MY LORD DEVEREUX DOUBTS THAT IT IS OF YOU THAT I HAVE RECEIVED THESE NOTES," SAID VERA.

No. 10.

CHAPTER XXXI.

"CAT AND MOUSE."

 "SO I hear that everyone is talking about poor me!" said the princess, looking with a half smile into her husband's face as she stood beside him in the little inner boudoir; "everyone is dying to visit me, and cudgelling their brains to find out why I see nobody."

"You manage, then, to know something of what passes in the world, sweetheart?" said Devereux.

"Oh yes! Mr. Linwood keeps me well informed; it all goes to prove what an exceedingly fascinating creature he must be to have the *entree* here."

"Alise is one of those who are 'dying' to be introduced to you," Devereux said; "but I told her that you wished to live out of society, and see no one save a few old friends."

"Alise!" said the girl, softly; "dear little girl! She writes me such loving letters abroad. Janet sends them over to me as she sends back also my answers. I should like to see Alise, but I dare not; with Linwood I am secure, but I could not feel the same with a woman. How does Mr. Crawford's suit prosper?"

"Excellently, so far as Mamma Mainwaring is concerned, but not so with the head of the family, who declares that the headstrong young people shall never have his consent, but that they must do as they will. He has not forgiven me either for not marrying as he had planned."

A deeper shade came over the girl's face, and she half sighed:

"Will he ever forgive you, Ernest, when he knows all? Ah! I was wrong to yield to you——"

But Devereux interrupted her quickly:

"Hush, Vera! You must never reproach yourself; do you think I would have the past undone, save in this that I would to God I had nothing with which to reproach myself—that I had given you at once before all the world the protection of my name."

For a moment the girl made no answer, but stood looking down into the fire, quite still; then she said low and steadily:

"And I thank God from my heart, Ernest, that you did not; for the path I am treading now would have been a simply impossible one to follow had I borne your name before the world."

"I would it had, Vera! I wish to heaven it had!" said Devereux strongly. "It were better for me to suffer to the utmost than you."

"Nay," Vera said, looking up for a brief second into his face, and speaking with an unconscious pathos; "I am used to suffering; and then, you would not take away from me the only reparation I can make you!"

"Reparation, Vera! What is the wrong you have done me?"

Vera did not immediately answer; she seemed as though balancing in her mind whether to give a serious one or not, and finally broke into a soft laugh, and laid her face against his shoulder.

"I will not tell you," she said; "you will only dispute, and you know we must not begin to quarrel until we see more of each other."

"You and I will never quarrel, sweetheart, if we live a lifetime together," said Devereux, tenderly stroking back the curling rings from her forehead.

"Ah, we cannot tell," the girl returned archly. "Others have been just as confident, and behold! they have not stood the test of even one little year."

"I am quite willing to run the chance, Vera."

She smiled, but again made no answer; words seemed difficult to her this evening, and something either in tone or in touch of his, both so infinitely tender, straitened her heart and brought the rare tears too near the surface; so she took refuge in silence, and he, divining what her mood was, did not speak; it was sweet enough to both simply to be together for this brief space of time, to forget, at least actively, the shadows lying so close over their lives; and the moments went by only too quickly. Vera knew that probably Linwood would come this evening, and so Devereux left her early.

But Vera was not long alone; fain as she would have had solitude if she might not have her husband's presence, she was not allowed to enjoy it, for Linwood was announced before Devereux had been five minutes absent; so quickly, in fact, that Vera thought they must have met, and this impression was made into a certainty when she saw the expression of Linwood's countenance, and heard his first word.

"So Lord Devereux has been here!" he said; "I met him just without. By heaven! he shall not cross me again!"

The princess turned and looked at him, arching her fine brows in the prettiest surprise, not unmixed with amusement.

"What do you mean? Of course Lord Devereux has been to see me; why shall he not?"

"Why shall he not?" returned Linwood, unconsciously repeating the foreignism of her answer. "Rather, why shall he? Has he not come across me once too often?" He paused, biting his lip, aware that he had permitted his passion to betray him into saying more than was politic, seeing that he was addressing a woman.

"I really understand you not, *cher* M. Linwood," said the princess, shrugging her shoulders with nonchalance. "You are—pardon—putting yourself out of temper for nothing worth. If Milord Devereux has been in times past more fortunate with some lady whom you both adored, what shall that say to me?"

How sweetly, how innocently she planted her sting! And yet the very sting gave him to understand that she was, perhaps, ever so little piqued at the idea of his having carried his devotion, in other times, to another shrine; so that, while he was stung, he should also be soothed.

"You do not understand," he began; but the princess interrupted him, without anger, but with that kind of good humour which a man generally considers rather worse than anger.

"Oh, but yes; I understand quite well. There is not anything so very hard to comprehend. M. Linwood is, perhaps, just a little jealous of Milord Devereux, as once he was before when both worshipped. Ah, *cher* M. Linwood, you see I know ever so much—so much more than you thought!" And the princess laughed her little soft inward laugh. "Poor M. Linwood, who has no coronet, and no title!"

"You mistake, princess," cried Linwood, making a half-spring forwards. "Nay, but you must hear me!"

She waved him back with the same half-imperious, wholly bewitching good-humour.

"What shall I hear? I want not to listen to the recounting of your affairs of the heart, my friend; they will have, for me, no interest—oh, none whatever! You were—what you call in love with *la belle* Vera. Well, it was nothing to me. But then you affirmed that you never cared for her. *Fi donc*, M. Linwood! And Milord Devereux was more favoured than you; and so that is why you would not speak of the murder!" and the princess began to laugh still more, as though the whole thing were intensely amusing.

It perplexed and disconcerted Linwood all at once, and made him angry too; and yet he seemed to have an impression that this laughter was dangerously near to tears on her part, and the soothing idea would keep pace with his annoyance and jealousy that the princess was angry and disappointed because he had cared for another woman.

He stood silent, not knowing exactly what to say, or how to take the singular merriment of his fair friend. At last he said sullenly:

"I fail to see, madame, what you find so very amusing. Is it not natural that I should fear when I have so much at stake?"

The princess looked at him for a moment with a half-arch glance in the eyes that yet seemed soft with tears.

She tried to smooth her lips to gravity, but smiles still lurked about the mouth.

"Poor M. Linwood!" said she; "he does not like it to be laughed at! And I, who have so little in my life to make me merry—he grudges me one little laugh at his expense. Well, forgive me, I will remember how you English are touchy;" and she held out her hand with a smile so bewitching that all Linwood's anger melted, and he seized the fair white hand and covered it with kisses.

"It is of you I should ask forgiveness," he said rapidly and with passion. "I will grudge you nothing that gives you a moment's pleasure. I would devote my whole life to make you happy, my princess. Olga, hear me!" For she, evidently startled, tried to free her hand from his clasp. "I love you. Is that so wonderful?"

"Oh, hush! hush!" the princess murmured, turning aside. "You must not speak to me such language! I —a widow but a few months!"

The man's heart leapt within him. She did not chide him, then, for loving, but only that he spoke too soon!

"Ah, forgive me!" he said, but there was little of true humility in his tone. "Can you wonder that my control broke down? But you do not spurn me? You do not"—he spoke quite softly now, and would have drawn her to him — "say that you cannot love me?"

But the princess was evidently not prepared to so early outrage the memory of the late prince, for with a sudden movement she withdrew her hand from Linwood's clasp, and stepped back, a haughty flash in her eyes.

The fair Princess Glinka had as many moods as her capricious kitten.

The sudden change in her manner had taken Linwood by surprise.

"You assume too much, M. Linwood," said she; yet she avoided his eyes as she spoke, as though unwilling to let him read too much in hers. "I have told you I should not listen to you. You will please me best if you say no more."

She paused half a second, and then added, with a softened voice, and lifting her eyes fleetingly to his face:

"Must I lose my friend—I who have so few?"

"Is it losing a friend to find a lover?" Linwood said, reproachfully.

"Oftentimes, yes," answered the princess, with a certain sadness. "And then, a friend I may have——"

She stopped again, and Linwood exclaimed passionately, taking advantage of what he deemed the half encouragement held out to him:

"A friend—a lover? Why may you, who are made only to be loved and worshipped, not listen to the language of love and homage? Is it possible to be with you day after day and not adore the very ground you walk on? And now you forbid me to speak of love. How can I obey?"

The princess listened to him with downcast eyes, and when he paused she only said, with the sweetest, softest voice, and something just a little mocking in the smile of her lips:

"And all these pretty and charming things that you say—you have said them already to the *diva* Vera. Ah yes, I know it. You have loved her first. And I," said the princess, with an indescribable little movement of her chin upwards—"I tolerate not a divided homage."

Linwood, who had not looked for such an answer, and who was bewildered by these changes of humour, fell back a step, flushing high.

Her mocking eyes maddened him.

"Why will you always throw that in my teeth?" he cried. "If I was caught like others by her beauty, it was no more than a passing fancy. I did not love her. I care for her no more. She is no rival to you. Oh, what shall I say to make you believe that it is you—you only that I love?"

"You shall say nothing—nothing at all," said the princess, laughing a little; "for if you no more love Vera, then are you fickle, and I will have none of you! And next year you shall relate in your club that you once did love the Princess Glinka——"

"Never—never!" interrupted Linwood, vehemently. "Hear me, Olga! Hear me, I implore——"

Whether it was that her patience was exhausted, or that she found this scene no more amusing, or resented the use of her christian-name, the variable Russian suddenly veered round from pretty mocking raillery to an unreasoning anger.

"Do you not see," she cried, suddenly turning to him, "that you trouble me? Or are you so dull? Leave me now. I will no more listen——"

"But——"

"Go! Leave me!" the princess fairly stamped her little foot—yet there were positively tears in her eyes. "If you loved me, you would obey me!"

Linwood made a half-step to the door, and then paused.

He saw that she must not be trifled with while in this mood.

"I may come again?" he said.

But the tone showed too much assurance; it was less a humble question than an assertion, which, no doubt, the princess was quick enough to perceive.

"I do not know—no. I care not," said she, incoherently.

And Linwood dared not disobey; but bowing his head, went out.

But there was a light of triumph in his eyes as he passed down the garden-walk.

"She loves me!" he muttered. "There is a struggle in her heart; I shall win her! Her anger will not last. She cannot do without me for long. She is torn with jealousy; but she loves me!"

Vain assurance! Could he have read the thoughts in the mind of the woman who was making him her tool!

"He will come back—the fool!" she said inwardly, with a bitter smile. "He is fairly in the toils now. But I must show him my power, and not yield too soon."

She broke off and leant her face down on the mantel-piece wearily. "Oh, Ernest—Ernest," she murmured, "for thy sake—ever for thy sake!"

And in that thought she was strong.

CHAPTER XXXII.

THE PRINCESS SHOWS HER POWER.

UT Mr. Lucius Linwood waited in vain for the summons from the princess which he had so confidently looked for, and he began to think that she was a woman who had not the feminine weakness of giving in directly it was too late, or almost too late, to repair the wrong done. He began also to think that he it was who should have to eat that humble-pie which he in his thoughts had already prepared and baked for his haughty mistress.

He had pictured to himself the scene—had arranged almost to a word or a caress what he should say and do; and instead of the little half-penitent note he had believed he would receive the next day, there was silence—silence total and defiant for days.

That Devereux in these days had called and been admitted he took care to ascertain, and he ground his teeth in rage, but dared speak no word to the viscount, of whom indeed at this time he saw little.

There had never existed anything but the slightest acquaintanceship between the two men, and since the *salon* in Bruton Street had broken up, the chances of their meeting were much reduced.

Naturally, neither sought the society of the other, and Linwood even shunned that of Lord Devereux.

He dared not permit himself the vulgar triumph of allowing the viscount to see that he, Linwood, held a power over him, for the terms of his agreement with Vera were stringent; and he knew that to break them was to forfeit the supplies which she sent to him and to render her reckless of consequences.

If Linwood had been wise, or could he have seen for one minute into the undiscovered land of the future, he would have taken the opportunity and broken off his friendship with the Princess Glinka; for it was **a** dangerous game that he was playing, and he knew it; but the knowledge only served to increase his eagerness in the pursuit.

It was hazardous, because he did not apprehend **very** clearly himself what was to be the outcome of it all.

Already legally married, as he believed, to Vera, he could not also legally be married to the princess.

If he went through the ceremony, concealing from her the true facts and presenting her to the world as his wife, he did not feel by any means certain what Vera might do; she had strange notions, notwithstanding her bringing up, and it was no more than probable that she might come forward and denounce him to the world.

"The last would hardly be to her interest," he muttered to himself; "let her do that, and she knows I hold her lover in the hollow of my hand. Repudiate her I would not if I could, nor get up a case for divorce against her, for it is to the last degree important that her mouth should be shut against me. As my wife she can give no evidence. Vera could be perhaps bribed or coerced into remaining silent, she is not likely to insist on being acknowledged by me. Still, by fair means or foul, Olga shall be mine! Her wealth alone, without other attractions, would be worth risking much for."

Every day that he was absent from the princess only served to rouse in him a fresh passion of jealousy against Lord Devereux. All this time, doubtless, the viscount was improving the time, free from any rival.

Linwood had also to run the gauntlet of a considerable amount of chaff from his club acquaintances, who managed to know—what is there that club-gossips do not contrive to know?—that he—Linwood—had not been so constant in his visits to the princess of late, and who noticed also his moody and irritable manner.

"Has the fair recluse thrown you over?" was the laughing remark of Lord Dalton.

"Of whom do you speak?" returned Linwood, coldly.

The remark was made at the club, and was particularly unpleasant, as at this moment Devereux happened to be in the room.

"Don't be a humbug, Lin!" laughed Dalton. "As if you didn't know the recluse of Brompton; you know her well enough."

"Oh, ah, the Princess Glinka!" Linwood answered, carelessly, suppressing, in Devereux's presence, as far as he could, any signs of irritation. "My dear fellow, I should think you were old enough to be aware that one cannot be always hanging about one woman and thinking it paradise to be only in her presence."

"Especially when she thinks it paradise to be in someone else's presence," chaffed Dalton, with a glance at Devereux, not lost upon Linwood, who flushed angrily, and gnawed his lip.

"The princess is indisposed," he said, shortly, perfectly aware that his remark was quite inadequate to the occasion.

"Ladies always are when they have had enough of us," retorted Dalton, cheerfully. "It's no use attending to all that, and letting other fellows make all the running."

"When I want your advice, I'll come to you for it," was Linwood's answer, spoken almost rudely, and Dalton stared, laughed, and turned on his heel with a shrug of his shoulder.

"When a fellow can't take chaff," said he, *sotto voce*, "it shows he's hard hit."

And the remark being a general one, not calling for an answer from anyone in particular, it was allowed to pass without challenge, and Linwood presently got up and left the room.

"Never saw Lin so touchy over anything before, and he hasn't an angelic temper," said Dalton, the moment he was gone. "Is he making up seriously to the princess, I wonder?"

"She's a potful of money," remarked Tom Fosby, who was supposed to know everything. "Old Glinka cut up for about four million roubles, and she has every penny, and no children"

"She is worth making up to, then," said Dalton laughing. "'Pon my word, I think I'll manage to get the *entrée* of that villa, and try my luck. What do you say, Devereux? Think I've any chance?"

"Try, dear boy, if you like; the field is open," answered Devereux, looking up with a smile.

"Humph! Very fine to talk of a fair field and no favour, when one can't even get into the field."

"Take my advice, Dalton," put in Fosby, "keep clear of these Russian beauties, with their millions of roubles. They're as slippery as eels. Find their castles are mortgaged up to the hilt to a lot of greasy old Jews. Never trust 'em. Marry some good honest English girl, and know what you're about."

"That's just like you, Fosby," said Dalton, laughing. "Don't go in for speculation, do you? Well, I daresay the Glinka has had enough of matrimony for the time, and it would be premature to try and tempt her yet. When she comes into the world again——"

"What a sensation she'll make!" remarked Tom; and Devereux said "Yes," rather absently.

He was thinking what would be the manner of her re-entrance into that world from which she had for a time disappeared.

Verily, stranger and more startling than ever he dreamed of.

CHAPTER XXXIII.

ENCOURAGEMENT.

S Linwood walked away from the club, the words spoken by Lord Dalton rang continually in his ear:

"You should not let other fellows make all the running."

They gave a fresh impetus to the jealousy that was already consuming him, and made him resolve then and there to call on the princess, to swallow his pride, and, on some pretext or other, to sue again for admittance to her house.

He looked at his watch. It was not yet luncheon-time, and he had been expressly told that the princess never received before five.

He determined, however, to try if she would relax this rule in his favour, and accordingly hailed a hansom, and had himself set down a little way from the road in which the villa was situated.

On ringing at the entrance-gate, the woman who dwelt in the tiny lodge came out, and, without opening the side-wicket, inquired his business.

"My business is with the princess," Linwood answered with some irritation. "Allow me to go up to the house."

"The princess sees no one, sir," returned the woman respectfully, but without offering to open the gate. "I have orders not to send anyone up to the house until madame gives permission."

"Pooh! nonsense!" said Linwood carelessly. "My good woman, Madame la Princesse does not mean that to apply to old friends like myself. Let me in, and I will ensure that you not only do not get blamed, but——"

He stopped significantly and smiled, but the woman was either not to be bribed, or she valued her place at more than a stray *douceur*.

She shook her head.

"I dare not, sir," she returned; "madame has such uncertain health. She is not even now risen. If you call in the afternoon, doubtless madame will then see you."

And as Linwood could extort nothing further from the inexorable personage, he was obliged to go away, cursing inwardly the stringency of madame's rules.

He came again late in the afternoon, and this time was admitted.

As the hall-door opened, he heard the sound of the piano, and the rich tones of madame's voice singing— not one of those strangely wild and melancholy Slavonic songs, to which she was so partial—but a saucy French *chanson!*

She had not taken his defection much to heart then!

"Madame is alone?" he asked quickly. And the servant replied, without allowing himself the luxury of a smile at the too evident feeling that prompted the question, "Madame is alone, monsieur," and ushered Linwood into the drawing-room, retiring noiselessly.

There was no other light in the room save that given by the flickering rays of the fire, and the greater part of the apartment was in gloom; so perhaps the princess did not immediately observe her visitor.

At any rate, she finished her song, of which there remained only one bar, before rising; and then she made him a profound bow, which had the effect of checking his quickly advancing step.

"Ah, good-evening, M. Linwood! I am charmed to see you. At last the poor prodigal, who has become to me almost a stranger!"

But the look from her dark arch eyes belied the action, which seemed calculated to keep him at a distance—that said, "You are not yet forgiven." The eyes added, "Take my hand if you like, and see what comes of it."

Linwood obeyed the latter naturally, and came to her and caught both her hands, bending forward to her.

"I tried to keep away, but I could not," he said under his breath; and the girl's eyes flashed at this admission of her power.

"So you tried to keep away, and you could not," she answered him, and laughed a little, but suffered her hands to rest lightly in his. "Why did you do something so foolish? I could have told you at once that you must return."

"And yet you professed to believe," Linwood said reproachfully, "that I love Vera Temple. Will you believe me now that it is you only that I love?"

She interrupted him, holding up her finger.

"And now," she said, "you will step again on to forbidden ground? Come, let us be seated; we will have no lamp yet. I love this light, and it is so agreeable to my eyes, which are no more so strong as once. It is because I have wept so much," with a short quick sigh.

"You have wept so much!" Linwood said softly, but with subdued earnestness. "You, who should be so happy! Why should you weep?"

The princess half turned aside, as though for a moment embarrassed, then laid her hand gently on his arm.

"Ah, my friend," she said quite softly, "that lets itself not be said"; and from under the long lashes there came again that swift glance that seemed to say so much more than she permitted to her lips, that sent a thrill through the man's every pulse; he threw himself at her feet on a low stool, and looked up into the beautiful face, now so soft with some tender emotion, that he scarcely dared interpret as he longed to do; but Olga, with a half laugh and a slightly heightened colour, drew back into the shadow a little. "Nay," she said, but without anger, "my friend, you embarrass me. I want to try and remember, and—and you make it for me too difficult."

Her voice gave a little as she said the last words, and she drew away the hand on which his rested to cover her eyes.

A swift flash of exultant triumph leapt up in Linwood's heart. She would fain remember the duty she fancied she owed the dead, but his love was irresistible; she was only a woman after all.

A man of a more noble nature would have seen in this apparent struggle between duty and an influence she felt to be mastering her, only cause for forbearance and a chivalrous abstention from pushing an advantage, but Vera knew exactly how to count on the nature with which she had to deal.

"You have wept!" he said in a voice that trembled, despite his effort to render it steady; "you, who have all that women prize—wealth, and beauty, and love——"

"Ah, stop there!" the princess interrupted, lifting her hand slightly, and speaking with deep pathos. "What do you know of all the needs a woman has? You men think so often that if one has wealth, and beauty, and homage, which you call love, one is happy. Believe me, my friend, a woman has deeper needs than these. Homage, adoration, this has been mine, but love——"

"Love!" Linwood cried passionately, "this you have now; this I lay at your feet—love true and without stint. Ah, do not be angry with me. Even at the risk of once more incurring your anger, I must speak this time. You have been unhappy. Oh, dare I think that——"

"Think nothing at all," the princess said hurriedly, and rising in great agitation. "I pray you—no—no. I am not again angry, but, whatever my heart may prompt, I must not listen yet, and I know not how to trust its voice. So many have offered me such homage; so often have I been deceived. Can love be true that is given to so many? You who kneel before me now and swear to me that it is I only that you love, so have you sworn to another that you love her. Are you faithful? Are you constant? What shall I think?"

She stopped, covering her face, her breast heaving. Linwood had never seen her so deeply moved. She who used generally only the weapons of mockery and coquetry. Here was the ring of passion, and it filled him with a triumph to which he dared not give rein. She had a thousand humours, this witching princess of his adoration, and who knows what she might do or say next?

He came to her side and drew both her hands into his.

"What shall you think?" he said. "That, I tell you, was but a dream; I have never loved till now; you alone have had the power to teach me what love really is! How can I prove it to you? There is no sacrifice that I would not gladly make for your dear sake; only give me one sweet word of assurance that you love me!"

She suffered her hands to remain in his clasp for a moment, her head drooping a little, her eyes not meeting his. Then she sighed and withdrew them gently.

"Be satisfied, my friend," she said, looking up into his eyes for one brief second. "Your friendship, your devotion, are very sweet to me. Will you not let it so rest? I think"—she paused and turned aside, and her next words were spoken very low—"I think—you need fear nothing."

"Olga!" cried Linwood with a passionate joy, and sprang forward; but she lifted her hand and smiled again, with the old half-mocking archness.

"No, my friend, I have said nothing. You are so terribly in earnest—all you English, and I am tired." She threw herself into the low fauteuil, and leaned back as though weary. "Cannot you do something to amuse me—you, who love me so much?" laughing. "Or—— Ah, there comes my Lord Devereux! Heard you not the ring of the bell! We play, shall we— ecarte? Whatever you will—yes!"

Linwood's brow grew black as night.

"Devereux!" he said. "Olga, is it not I who have cause to be jealous now?"

"Why? Because Lord Devereux comes? Can I prevent him? My friend, do not make yourself ridiculous! I have yet given you no right to be jealous!"

The door was at that moment thrown open, and the servant announced: "Lord Devereux!"

CHAPTER XXXIV.

THE TRAIN LAID.

HE princess received Lord Devereux with *empressement*; Linwood greeted him with a cold politeness, which, however, seemed to make no profoundly dispiriting impression on the viscount; he bore himself with his usual easy grace of manner, and evidently had not the least idea that he was interrupting an interesting *tete-a-tete*, or, at any rate, he took no outward cognisance of the fact; indeed, it seemed to Linwood's jealous fancy that Devereux had much the bearing of one who knows himself to be welcome, and has no need to apologise for an interruption which he pretty well knows to be quite apropos.

"You come to very good time," said the princess, ignoring Linwood's possible view of the case. "Mr. Linwood and I—we were at the point to bore ourselves with the society of each other."

"Allow me at least to protest against that assertion," interposed Linwood somewhat stiffly.

"And I," added Devereux, bowing to the fair Russian with a smile, "find it quite impossible to believe that anyone could be bored in your society."

"Ah, *méchants*," cried the princess, laughing; "these things you are obliged to say. You say them to every pretty woman; to Madame This and the Countess That. To—to the beautiful Vera," added she, with a swift glance of raillery at Linwood.

He flushed and bit his lip, yet felt quite elated that the woman he adored should be so consumed with jealousy against an earlier object of worship.

"Ah, she was truly beautiful," added the princess, meditatively.

"Madame la Princesse resembles her greatly," said Devereux. "I have heard it often remarked that you and she could well pass for sisters."

"Ah, flatterer! with these lines here, and here?" said the princess, passing a slender finger down by the laughing mouth and over the brow. "The Vera was young, and had all the grace of youth; but I—and if that is so, that I am like her, then it is to a reflection of her that you both pay devotion."

"Madame is a little severe," said Devereux, with a slight smile.

He did not disclaim the inference, or pay any compliment, and the princess glanced at him and lifted her brows ever so little, and then turned to Linwood.

"If Milord Devereux," said she with a half smile, "had the courage, he would say that I was jealous of our fair rival. But come, we waste time. Shall we play? It is long since I touched a card."

The card-table was drawn into the small drawing-room. The soft-stepping Ivan brought in the lamp with its deep shade, and the three players drew near and seated themselves.

"You do not find it too dark?" the princess said; "it makes me so much pain for the eyes—a glare of light."

"The shade throws the light down on the table," returned Linwood, "which is just what we want; the only drawback is that——"

"My face is in the shadow," interrupted the princess quickly, with a merry laugh. "You see I know always exactly what compliment you will make me! But you will, neither the one nor the other, want to look at my face; it is the cards to which you must look."

"'Business is business,' as we say, princess," said Devereux rather dryly, as he dealt the cards, and again the princess shot him a half-defiant glance from under her brows, but only returned laughing,

"Oh, yes, and I mean to do a great deal of business to-night. I am going to win a lot of money from you."

"To lose one's money to you, princess," said Devereux with a low bend, "were an honour and a pleasure."

"But the paying, count—the paying!" said she, archly.

"Lord Devereux, my dear princess," said Linwood, with a smile that was half a sneer, "manages his debts very neatly—to ladies; he pays them in dogs."

Devereux laughed, pulled his moustache, and, slightly lifting his brows, said with a decided drawl,

"Dear boy, haven't you forgiven me yet that little triumph? I suppose the *diva* liked St. Bernards, and didn't like pugs—that was all."

Linwood flushed high, and was about to make some hot rejoinder, when the princess broke in.

The *diva*, the *diva*," said she, tapping her little foot impatiently on the floor; "one hears only her name; one is tired always to listen to it. If she preferred to take the present of Lord Devereux, what can it signify to you, M. Linwood?—at this distance of time, too," she added with a look into his eyes that was half reproachful and half angry.

"I don't think, princess," said Linwood with a short laugh, "that there was much 'preference' about the matter; and if there were"—he shrugged his shoulders and looked straight across to Devereux—"the *diva's* preferences were not worth quarrelling over—lightly won, you know."

"And yet, I think, if my memory serves me rightly," Devereux answered very quietly, and smiling, "Mr. Linwood has altered his opinion on this matter since some time—I remember we came something near a quarrel the last night in Bruton-street. In fact the very night of the murder."

"The princess, who had been looking covertly at Linwood, saw him change colour, marked the swift flicker of the eyelids downward, and then a fierce gleam in the eyes that he lifted again as swiftly.

He leant forward and said slowly, and speaking like a man who is holding some strong passion in hand:

"And since you have such a good memory, you may perhaps recall something I said on that occasion."

Devereux laughed.

"Not I, faith," he said carelessly and leaning back. "In those days you were so fond of using melodramatic warnings and so forth, that your words have not dwelt in my memory."

The princess, who was now looking from one to the other with mingled surprise, curiosity, and some apprehension, interposed, laying her white hand on Linwood's arm.

"What is it you will be making a scene over, my friend? I entreat you not to recall any words that——"

But Linwood half rose, and the hand that lay on the table was quivering with suppressed passion.

"Don't be afraid, Princess Olga," he said rather slowly, and looking for a moment at her, "Lord Devereux will know best whether he would like to quarrel over the words I recall to him. What I said was this : 'I take up your challenge, my lord, but not now and not here. I can afford to wait.' Lord Devereux will know whether or not I have waited to some purpose."

Before Devereux could make any reply, if indeed he had intended to do so, the princess again interposed hastily, turning pale and then flushing, and with a quick movement pushing Linwood back into his seat.

"It is enough—it is enough," she said half imperiously, and yet with a sort of appeal in her voice. "What! you two will make a quarrel in my presence? My lord, I forbid you to answer. You also, M. Linwood. Come, let us address ourselves to cards, and remember no more that we have wrongs or rivalries."

Devereux shrugged his shoulders slightly, smiled, leaned over the table to take up the cards again, and said in the same nonchalant way as before :

"Have no fear, princess. The day is gone by for duelling; and as to rivalries, we have none; and as to wrongs—well there are some that one does not exactly forget."

"You will forget them now at least," returned the princess. "Do you know," smiling, "that you two men absolutely frighten me! M. Linwood talks like the villain in one of your melodramas, and one would think he possessed one secret, or power, or something so dreadful. But it is all nonsense—of course not. In my country one knows such things; but here, in your free country——"

"Here, in our free country," remarked Devereux, rather dryly, "strange things happen, princess."

"Ah," said she laughing, "but not so strange that one man in good society shall have another in his power. That belongs to us, where we have Nihilists, and one can bring who knows how many nobles to Siberia or to death."

"You don't believe that possible, then, princess, in this land?" said Linwood with his sneering smile.

The princess gave a little involuntary shudder, and answered hastily:

"We are not in Russia, M. Linwood. But come, let us play."

"Certainly, let us play!" said Linwood, with an undercurrent of eagerness in his tone that did not escape the fine ear of the princess, on the alert, as she ever was, to detect the slightest signs as to how he was affected by words or looks.

She had marked every change in his face as she spoke of one man having power to give another to death.

No more was said now. The three gave themselves up to the fascinations of play, and the princess grew eager and excited over the chances of the game.

They played, of course, for money, and the stakes were not at first high; but the princess, who was losing, insisted on having them now double, now treble, till Linwood drew in his breath and looked at her.

Devereux, however, neither looked nor said a word, but played in his usual easy, careless fashion, to all appearance hardly caring whether he lost or won, but winning always, till at last the princess rose up, throwing down her cards half in despair, half in anger.

"I will play no more," she said. "I am deeply in your debt, milord. Another night I will have my revenge."

"Whenever and wherever your highness will," answered the viscount, bowing low.

But he made no disclaimer about the debt, nor did he offer to let her pay it in some trifle of jewellery that she wore about her person.

On the contrary, he received quite calmly the notes she gave him, and bent over the pretty hand that held them out with some speech as pretty, but at which the lip of the princess, Linwood fancied, curled, and a thrill of triumph shot through his soul as she turned to him with a smile to say farewell.

He was permitted to hold her hand for a moment to linger after Devereux had gone, but only for a brief time; then he, too, was dismissed.

CHAPTER XXXV.

ANOTHER MOVE IN THE GAME.

LAY, thus introduced in the princess's *salon*, was soon fairly established as an almost habitual custom when either or both of her friends came to see her—at least it was supposed to be the custom when Lord Devereux came—it is needless, however, to say that when alone these two never touched a card; play for its own sake had no attraction for them, but play formed part of a plan which Vera had conceived —a random shot, as it were, and which was more than likely to fail, but which her bold spirit was determined upon.

She did not shrink from baccarat, a game in which the Princess Glinka had been always known as proficient, and in this she often won considerably, and as often lost very considerably; but nothing appeared to daunt her, and Linwood gave it one night as his opinion that she was a " plunger."

" But, then, I have plenty of money to pay," said she, with her habitual shrug of her shoulders; " at least, when I have not—I will borrow."

" Make me your banker," whispered Linwood, softly, and Olga replied with a half laugh:

" Beware, my friend; it is possible that I take you at your word."

And Linwood said that would make him the happiest of men.

" You have some plan in your head, Vera," Devereux said to her the first time they were alone. " The other night I followed your cue blindly; I knew that I was expected to win from you, and also to hold you to the debt, and I have, perhaps, an idea of what you wish to do."

"I am going to lose very considerably to you, Ernest," answered the girl; "and you will please not commute my debt; see, this is my idea. You remember that the notes which you paid to my father on the night of the murder were taken by Linwood; I have the numbers of them all—I think," she said, with a fleeting smile, "that I know them by heart; it is possible—nay, I think probable, that Linwood, afraid to trust these notes out of his immediate reach, carries them always on his person. I must get hold of them."

"Difficult, Vera—I had almost said impossible, if I did not know that you will not allow impossibilities to exist," said Devereux. "Under no circumstances, I imagine, would he be persuaded to part with one of those notes; they are to him, as to us, of the last importance."

"It will be difficult, as you say, but I will hope not absolutely impossible," returned Vera. "I have many weapons in my armoury, and there are few things to which a woman cannot persuade a man in love. I can pretty well twist Linwood round my finger. Of course, the attempt must be made some night when he has no other money upon him; my need must be urgent, because you require the debt to be paid; and if I am not mistaken in Lucius Linwood, he will do almost anything which shifts my obligation from you to him. He will not think that you know the numbers of the notes —you do not as a matter of fact?"

"No; I am careless in such things."

"It is but a random shot," said the girl gravely. "It may succeed, or it may fail, but it is worth trying; only," she added, with one of those bright flashes of her old spirit of fun, "it is making you play a very ungrateful part, my poor chivalrous Devereux, who would rather die than put pressure on one of our weak sex."

Devereux smiled.

"That is of no moment," he said, but the smile passed soon, and he turned away and began pacing the room.

He stopped after a few minutes opposite Vera, and put both hands on her shoulders, looking straight into her eyes.

"Are you quite keeping faith with me, Vera?" he said gently and gravely.

She flushed from cheek to brow, but her eyes never drooped.

"It is for you," she made answer steadily; "I am not compromising the name and honour you have bade me keep unsullied. Hereafter the world will know why I suffered Lucius Linwood to think he was my lover. It is a hard world enough, Ernest, but I do not think that many would be found to say that I had really compromised my name. I shall not be in his power, even if I owe him money—he will be in mine."

It was not possible to say any more then, for at that moment Linwood was announced, and the three were speedily absorbed in the fascinations of play."

Since that evening when Linwood had striven to force a quarrel with Lord Devereux, there had reigned a certain amount of peace between the rivals.

The relations were what diplomatists call strained, but there was no open warfare.

Devereux made not the slightest change in his manner towards the other, and continued to treat the princess with the sort of assured air which announces to the world that you know exactly your ground and the extent of your power.

Linwood constantly received the impression in a vague sort of way that Devereux viewed the princess from some standpoint of which he, Linwood, was ignorant, and that his mode of treating her suggested a thought of hidden power somewhere; and this suspicion filled Linwood with a fierce and bitter jealousy, creating a perpetual irritation against Devereux that he was unable to conceal, and leading him continually to more than hint at a power he could wield, if he chose, over his rival.

"You puzzle and quite bewilder me," the princess said to him; she looked, indeed, half vexed, half afraid, as she suffered him to kiss her hand in parting. "I imagine myself once more in my own country. Some day, *mechant*," playfully, "I shall make you explain to me what it all means."

"It will be then," returned Linwood with a frowning brow, "when I ask of you why you let that man treat you as if you belonged to him."

The princess drew back, flushing quickly.

"But you are mistaken," said Olga hastily, and Linwood thought with some confusion.

"I permit Devereux nothing. Ah, ungrateful! Do I allow him to keep my hand, as you do? Do I permit him all that I grant to you? How can I help it that my Lord Devereux feels himself to be an English viscount, and," the princess laughed, "so much better, therefore, than my poor little Russian self."

"It is more than that," persisted Linwood. "Devereux is haughty, but he has not that stiff English pride. I have thought at times——"

He paused, and seemed to hesitate; then, taking her hand once more in his, added:

"Forgive me, Olga—do not be angry, for I speak only out of my love to you—but it has come to me sometimes that perhaps you are under obligations to Devereux that you cannot shake off."

The princess glanced up quickly, perhaps apprehensively; but she shook her head, smiling.

"I am not angry," she said with more graciousness than Linwood had cared to hope for. "But these are fancies, my friend—only fancies. Listen!" looking inimitably arch and roguish, "and I will tell you a little secret. My Lord Devereux is ungracious to me because he is afraid that I shall make him in love with me."

And before Linwood could gather himself together to answer, Olga had swept him a curtsey and vanished into the inner room.

Nevertheless the impression remained, as she meant it should, that there lay something between her and Lord Devereux which rendered it expedient for her to put up with the lack of that homage the princess had always been accustomed to receive as her right.

"He plays into my hands," thought the girl with a smile, when Linwood was gone. "It is a convenient impression for him to have got, for it renders my task so much the easier."

It was only a few days after this that Linwood received a little note from the princess. It was brought to him at his club.

He tore the envelope hastily open, recognising the hand at once. It contained a gracious message enough:

"Come to me a little earlier than usual. I expect the viscount later. I would like so much to see you alone.—Your OLGA."

It may readily be conceived that Linwood was immensely elated with this summons.

Never before had the lady of his love written to him to come for a *tete-a-tete* like this. Plainly she permitted to him, as she had said, privileges that were denied to Devereux.

Being alone at the time in the room, Linwood pressed the note to his lips, and took great satisfaction from the signature—"your Olga," run on, instead of the Olga being below.

Did she not mean by this to say, "I am your Olga; it is no mere polite form?"

"It will all go as I wish," muttered Linwood, "if only nothing comes out from that cursed Vera! I wonder if they correspond, and if my princess, after the manner of ladies, makes Vera a *confidante* of all her love-conquests? If so, my obstinate wife must feel pleased that her sometime lover, Devereux, has transferred his homage to her dear friend, Olga. I must find out. But Vera will never tell a soul of her marriage—that I know well enough."

He lighted a fresh cigar, and strolled out of the room, pausing, however, on the steps.

"I must try and clinch matters soon," he said to himself. "Things are coming to a crisis with me. Money is tight, and I'm almost up to the hilt. Vera won't send more at present. I have deuced little ready money, unless it be some that I will part with almost anything sooner than touch."

He found the princess alone when he reached the villa that evening—alone, and seated in a chair by the fire.

The lamp was not yet brought in, and the uncertain light of the flickering flames was the only illumination in the room.

Yet even by this light Linwood perceived that there were traces of tears on the face that Olga lifted at his entrance, and his heart bounded as he marked the sudden flash of light that chased away for a moment the troubled expression the beautiful features had worn.

"It is you," she said, and rose, holding out her hands to him.

He clasped them both in his closely.

"Of course it is I," he returned, bending down to press his lips to them. "Did you think I should not obey you when you sent for me? You are glad to see me, Olga?"

"Come and sit down," was all the answer in words that he got, and she drew him forward to a seat near to hers; but he dropped on one knee beside her, and still keeping her hands in his, looking up into the face which she half averted from him.

"My darling," he murmured, "you are troubled— you are unhappy! Nay, do not shake your head. I can see the trace of tears. Ah, Olga dearest, you have been weeping, and I was not by to help you."

Her hands lay passive in his for a moment, then she drew one gently away, and placed it over her eyes.

"I think," she said very softly, and with an almost plaintive accent, which, coming from the Princess Glinka, had, for Linwood, all the charm of novelty—she had, hitherto, not given him much of the melting mood —"I think, my friend, that you could not help me a great deal. You must not be unhappy about me. It is nothing."

"Nothing which can make you weep, Olga—you who are so bright?"

"The brightest of us have troubles," said the princess evasively. "A smiling face, that often covers an aching heart!"

"Has Devereux anything to do with your aching heart?" Linwood said with a frown.

She detected the quick jealousy of his tone at once.

"How jealous you are, my friend!" said she with a faint smile. "Do you truly think that he is the cause of every pain I suffer?"

"It is because I love you so much, Olga, I am jealous of every thought you give him—every look, every word," said Linwood passionately.

The princess laughed a little, but looked at him very kindly.

"You must love me very much," she said, smiling, and Linwood's ear or his perception was not fine enough to detect the shade of irony in her tone. "Well, then, my friend, if you will save me thinking about your viscount who you hate so much, you can, it may be, assist me." She paused, apparently hesitating, and then added, laying her white hand in his: "You said once that you would be my banker; will you now fulfil that promise?"

For a minute Linwood was silent; the request came upon him rather like a thunder clap, for, although he had with a lover's rash tenderness made the promise—or the offer, as he preferred to regard it—of money at some indefinite date, it was in the full persuasion that the time would never come for any claim to be made on him.

The princess was rich—what should she want with money?

And yet the request gave him a swift and sudden thrill of sweetest triumph. Olga, this haughty Olga, who one moment smiled on him, in the next laughed at him or sent him away—she was asking him for money, which if given would be the means of putting her to some extent in his power; she would be under deep obligation to him. To be in debt is to lose part of one's freedom.

"You do not answer," said the princess, flushing slightly.

She spoke as if offended, and Linwood hastened to plead.

"Forgive, dearest," he said quickly, "if I seemed to hesitate; it is only that I am filled with despair—that you have made me a request that for the moment I do not see my way to granting."

"How? You have no money? You so rich and so powerful," Olga said reproachfully. "I have plenty of money—that is, I will have in a few weeks, but at this moment I cannot pay Lord Devereux a debt of honour. Think of that, my friend!"

As Linwood was not so infrequently in the same predicament, he did not share her apparent horror of the situation.

"Why have you put yourself under obligations to him?" cried Linwood quickly.

"What would you?" returned the princess, shrugging her shoulders. "One plays, one loses. Perhaps I shall win to-night, perhaps lose."

"It is the truth, Olga," Linwood cried in despair. "I have at this minute not a pound of ready money. I am myself hard pressed. Don't doubt me. Don't think I would not give you thousands if I had them; but I have nothing."

The princess rose, withdrawing her hand from his.

"Very well," said she carelessly, but Linwood felt with passion that there was no more kindness in her tones. "If you have no money, I cannot look to you for assistance; but I thought I might count upon you. To-night I must win. If not, I must throw myself on the mercy of Devereux. He will, perhaps, not fail. No more," for Linwood endeavoured to speak. "There is his ring at the bell."

But the princess lost again that night, and her farewell to Linwood was cold.

"Good," she said to herself; "he has no money—but that. When next I ask, he will give me that."

CHAPTER XXXVI.

A CONVERSATION AT THE REGINA.

HE more Lucius Linwood thought over the conversation of that evening, the more thoroughly dissatisfied and angry with himself, with the princess, and with Devereux did he become, for, look at it which way he would, he felt that he had made a false step, and one difficult to retrieve.

Relying on his friendship and professed devotion, the princess had sought aid of him in her need—aid which would have freed her from a humiliating obligation to the man who, above all men, Linwood hated, and he had been obliged to confess that at that moment he was unable to lay his hands on some few hundreds of pounds.

Certainly the princess had not appeared to believe that he was actually unable to give her the help she prayed of him, but that was scarcely a better aspect of affairs for Linwood.

For what, then, was his boasted love worth? His protestations became so many idle compliments.

If she did believe that he had no money, then he stood confessed either as a needy man who must seek a rich wife, or a man who, having means, had wasted them, and whose debts would probably exceed the amount of his income.

In either case her riches were what he sought, the princess would conclude, and would withdraw from him the light of her smiles.

How cold was her farewell to him that night! She had barely touched his hand. He must make his peace with her somehow, and explain that he was only unable to help her through temporary embarrassment.

He had meant to do this last night, but she was always so impetuous, and would not suffer him to speak, and then Devereux came, and, of course, nothing was possible.

"It is easier to manage an untrained colt than her," muttered Linwood, as he paced his room that night, far too restless and anxious to even seek sleep. "Just when I seem to have made some way with her, and she is gracious and kind, comes this check. Dare I risk parting with any of those notes? It were madness! And yet, what harm could come of it? She will pay them to Devereux—true. But he will not know the number of one of them. He said only the other night that he never took the number of any note or check he received. There would be little risk there, then. The notes cannot have been stopped at the bank, for the old man would have had no time to enter them; the space between my interview and Devereux's was too short, and Vera, of course, could not have seen them—there I am at least safe."

He paused and stood in deep thought for many moments.

"I must make an end of this," he began muttering again; "it's getting hot for me, and I have too much to think about. One never knows what may spring the whole concern in the air. No. I must bring Olga to the point, and get abroad and marry her there—if she insists on the form," as he spoke, the bitter sneering smile curled his lips, "and make terms with my charming wife. She will do anything to get her lover, and if I withdraw my claims on her and keep dark about the other, she will hold her tongue about her marriage, which she doesn't look on as much more than a legal ceremony as it is. Where she managed to pick up such fantastic notions, Heaven knows! But if they serve my turn I shan't complain; I shall still have the power over her and Devereux, and when I want money shall have two instead of one to count upon. But I must first clinch matters with my princess."

This clinching matters with the princess, however, was a harder task than he had chosen to imagine to himself. The next day when he called the princess was indisposed; the next he saw her, it is true, but not alone. Devereux was also there, and she was indifferent in manner to the verge of coldness. It was as though she did not care whether Linwood were present or not; she looked pre-occupied too.

Linwood was inwardly furious, but he dared not show anger. He indicated, however, pretty plainly, the lover's wounded heart, and the princess had to sustain the gentle fire of more reproachful glances than she thought had often fallen to her lot in either of her characters. His own affairs, meanwhile, were becoming more and more involved. He was deeply in debt, and not in a position to raise money, because his credit was at an end, his expectations were nothing, and his luck at play appeared to have almost deserted him.

In the hope of winning money, indeed, Linwood plunged deeper and deeper into debt, for he played for high stakes, and if he won, staked his winnings the next minute in the hope of getting more; sometimes he did win more, but it was only these winnings which kept him going. There was not the least margin for supplying the princess.

Yet he was more than ever resolved not to use the notes which he had stolen, though he kept telling himself that through these he could not possibly be betrayed.

He began to find that he grew nervous and anxiously watchful, without any cause that he could trace, except that he was so worried with money affairs and the situation with the princess; and a conversation that took place at this time at the Regina helped to revive fears and anxieties.

"Here's something about the Bruton-street murder in the paper," said Lord Dalton.

He spoke to no one in particular, the remark being a general one.

Linwood, standing smoking by the fireplace, seemed either not to have heard or to pay no attention.

But Devereux noted the watchful look that came into his eyes, and also that he sent a furtive glance over to where the viscount sat, as if to see how he took the remark. "The inattention was overdone," Devereux said to himself, because the murder was a subject which even at this date, months after the tragedy, had not lost its interest for anyone who had been a visitor in Bruton-street.

"What is it, Dalton?" asked Jack Crawford eagerly. "Any chance of clearing the mystery?"

"I am afraid not; it's rather the other way," answered Dalton: "the police have withdrawn the reward they offered—seem to have given up the job as hopeless."

"I imagine," Devereux said, "that it will be relegated to the list of undiscovered murders; the assassin, whoever he was, had plenty of time to get away."

"One can't conceive how the fellow got in," remarked Charlie Bolton. "None of those notes have ever been traced, have they?"

"Not likely. These people circulate them about for years sometimes before they turn up at the bank, and then they come through respectable hands."

"I understood," said Linwood, speaking for the first time, "that the numbers were not known; if I remember rightly, Miss Temple said so at the inquest."

"Did she?" Dalton said. "Oh, then, I suppose they may be circulating now—who knows?" said he, laughing. "One or other of us may have some of them about us!"

"Wish I had!" quoth Charlie. "By Jove! I'd like to find a bank-note on me just now, wherever it came from."

"What, cleaned out, Charlie?" said another.

"Clean as a whistle," returned that youth dolefully. "Your fault, too, Linwood. You had infernal luck last night."

Linwood smiled sardonically, and threw away the end of his cigar.

"You can have your revenge to-morrow," said he, glad to seize the opportunity of turning the conversation away from a subject that made him feel unaccountably nervous. "I am at your service."

"I generally find," observed Charlie sententiously, "that having one's revenge means losing another potful of money."

They all laughed.

"You're right there, my boy," said Dalton. "Moral: when you've lost everything don't play any more."

"The worst of it is," remarked Crawford, "that no one ever did allow himself to be influenced by the excellent moral you have pointed out."

"And no one ever will," finished Devereux.

"Morals are not in our line," said Jack, laughing. "Devereux, are you coming my way? I'm off for a stroll in the Park."

Linwood remained long alone, after all the others had dispersed to various pleasures or duties. The conversation left a disagreeable impression on his mind. When would people forget that murder? Well, it was satisfactory, at any rate, to know that the police had given up the search. Yet——

"I must put an end to all this quickly," Linwood said, rising abruptly. "I can't stand it much longer."

And that afternoon he betook himself down to the villa in Brompton.

"How will she receive me?" he mused. "One never knows how to take some women. But if Olga were not Olga, would she hold me as she does?"

Mr. Linwood forgot to include as a factor in the hold Olga possessed over him the fact that he never knew for two days together whether she would be his or not. With such men possession is the destroyer of love.

CHAPTER XXXVII.

THE PRINCESS PLAYS A WINNING CARD.

"MADAME LA PRINCESSE is not at home," said Ivan, who opened the door to Linwood.

He spoke with some hesitation, and loooked a trifle scared.

"Not at home!" repeated Lucius in surprise, and a heavy cloud gathered on his brow. "There must be a mistake; madame never refuses me at this hour."

He made a step forward as he spoke, emboldened thereto by the servant's manner.

He did not oppose a bold front to the enemy, but seemed to waver, as though uncertain.

Linwood understood that he might be open to golden influences, so he, in quite a casual way, drew forth a piece of gold.

Ivan's hand was not long in hesitating over its acceptance.

"But I dare not admit you, sir," said he in his broken English. "My lady would send me away. She say to me, 'Ivan, I will never see M. Linwood again! When he come, you shall send him from my door!' Madame was angry—yes, she was very angry when she say that," concluded Ivan reflectively.

"Can you think, Ivan, of anything that had made her so?" asked Linwood.

Getting "primed" as to the humours of ladies through the agency of their servants was nothing new to him.

Ivan shrugged his shoulders.

"How can I tell? Something has happened. It is, perhaps, that monsieur did not come yesterday, or——"

"I don't want your opinion and perhaps," said Linwood impatiently. "Can't you tell me, if you know, as I am sure you do—that is if a Russian can give a straight answer?"

Ivan grinned; he felt the remark a tribute to his genius for shuffling.

"Well, if monsieur asks me," said he, "it may be that a letter made madame angry. How shall I know?"

"A letter!" said Linwood eagerly. "What kind of letter? What sort of writing?"

"That I cannot tell," replied the man. "It shall, perhaps, have come from a gentleman—perhaps from a lady. The letter was a thin one."

"A foreign letter?"

"Such thin paper as English ladies write upon to the Continent," pursued Ivan, as though no interruption had occurred. "It was then madame sent for me, and said, with great agitation, 'I must not admit monsieur,'" Ivan finished with a deprecatory bow.

"Now, look here, Ivan," said Linwood resolutely squaring his shoulders, "I am going to see madame. You had better not try and stop me. I will make your peace with your mistress. Let me pass!"

He pushed the man aside as he spoke, Ivan loudly protesting, but not, if Linwood had been careful to notice, opposing any very real bar to his movement, and reached the door of the drawing-room.

He opened it and entered, Ivan following.

The princess, who was pacing with quick steps up and down, turned and faced the intruders, and looked from one to the other, her beautiful eyes flashing.

"Ivan," she said—and the unfortunate domestic appeared to shrink together under the wrath of his mistress—"did I not forbid you to admit this gentleman?"

Linwood interposed, gathering the sense of her speech, although the words were unknown to him.

"The man is not in fault," he said; "I forced my way in——"

"Do not speak," she said, turning to him with anger. "You dare to enter my presence when I have forbidden it! Go, Ivan! I trust you no more! No answer! Go!"

And Ivan, with many bows and protestations in Russian, withdrew. He descended to his own regions, however, with a smile upon his lips.

"Olga," cried Linwood as soon as they were alone, and he sprang forward to her side, "what have I done to merit this? To find myself spurned from your door —denied your presence!"

The princess turned from him with a gesture of passionate resentment; she was evidently deeply agitated. Her hands were clenched, and her lips quivered convulsively; but she did not speak.

"Are you so angry," Linwood said with an almost despairing entreaty, "because I have dared to venture into your presence? If so, oh, believe me! it was only my love for you that led me to brave your just anger. Olga, I have been miserable! I have been despairing! Something—I know not what—has come between us, and has changed you towards me. I could bear it no more. I must come, and, face to face, beseech you for more kindness! Your servant refused me admission, but I could not obey the sentence of exclusion. Olga, can you not forgive me?"

He stopped, his voice breaking.

Then the princess spoke; but instead of the torrents of reproach and angry words which her aspect had led Linwood to expect, she answered with a bitter irony; but the working of her lips, the movement of her hands, expressed the passion which she was holding back.

"Oh, very well, M. Linwood; your speech is quite a nice little dramatic effort. I make you my compliments! You will play the innocent lover; but I—shall I play the soft and believing heroine? No, no, the part will suit me not at all!—I doubt not you can enact the same scene to every woman you have passionately loved— only making a change of name."

"I swear I do not understand you!" cried Linwood. "Who has been poisoning your mind against me? I have prayed you to pardon my intrusion. What more can I say to soften you?"

"There is nothing—nothing," cried the princess, dropping the ironical tone, which the rush of her anger no longer permitted her to retain. "Can you suppose that for so little a cause my whole being is shaken—that the ground of my heart is moved? This I could forgive! but not this perfidy—this lie! Was I not right when I said, 'You have breathed such vows to another?' Oh, you think that you—you, because you are man and have success with women—that you can come to me and make me second to anyone! I, who have been and shall yet once again be the queen of courts, the adored of princes and nobles! I have once told you, I shall be first! In the heart of the man who will love me, I alone shall reign!"

"In my heart you are first—you alone reign," said Linwood. "You speak of perfidy, of lies—and you speak in riddles! I beseech you, Olga, tell me what I have done? It was my misfortune, not my fault, that I could not give you that aid you needed—had I thousands, how willingly would I lay them all at your feet!"

"In your heart I am first!" the princess interrupted him with quivering lips. "Insult me no more with such false words!" She snatched from her dress a letter, and flung it down before him. "To-day I received this from my friend—from Vera! Ah, you start, M. Linwood!"

For Linwood had indeed started violently, and a sudden pallor overspread his features.

He stepped quickly forward and picked up the letter, coming close under the lamplight to see the writing.

"What do you give this to me for?" with the impatient anger that is born of fear. "It is in German —I cannot read it."

"But you can read the signature—the name," said the princess. "Here it stands — Vera Temple. It needs not that you read it; I will tell you what it holds for you."

She marked the fierce impatience of the man with a stern satisfaction.

He strove indeed to control the terror of appre hension that he feared must be too manifest to her, but in vain.

"Of what does she accuse me?" he said huskily. "Whatever it be, you have no right to believe her without hearing me; that is neither just nor merci- ful——"

"Just! merciful!" cried Olga, pressing her hand to her forehead. "Is it just or merciful that you have been to me? While you have breathed to me of love that shall be eternal—while you kneel at my feet and swear that I am the only woman you love—see, you are no more free! You have made a promise to another woman. She gives to understand that she holds you still in chains—that you love her. Oh," cried the princess in a transport of grief and passion clasping her hands before her eyes, "your language is too cold, too calm to speak to you the scorn I have. Ingrate! per- fidious—— And oh, this man—this man has broken for me the heart!"

She sank down by the table in the very abandonment of anguish, and bowed her face on her arms. It was a splendid piece of acting. The sudden change from fierce reproach to those heart-breaking sobs, would have brought down the curtain, had she been on the stage, amid thunders of applause; but it was no acting to Linwood; it was real; and while her accusations awoke in him a very agony of fear, the last touch that revealed the womanly nature filled him with a triumph that was not all made up of gratified vanity or of success in a selfish passion.

"Olga, for God's sake!" he muttered hoarsely, and for a second covered his eyes with his hand; but almost even in that second the flash of true feeling had passed; he dropped his hand and bent over her, saying gently but with reproach: "I scarcely seem to understand you Olga; you are the victim of, and we are both the sufferers by, some strange mistake. I have never made any promise to Vera;" he paused a minute, and then added through his teeth: "at least not any that could cause you one pang of jealousy."

Olga lifted her head, dashing the tears from her eyes with a kind of self-contempt.

"You do say, then," she s , "that you have made to her some promise? Ther can be no mistake. You have deceived me, and I will never look upon your face again!" And once more the princess hid her face from him. "Go!" she said, with a gesture of her hand; "it is all you can do for me now."

But Linwood caught her hand in his own.

"Olga!" he cried passionately, "hear me! you must hear me! I am bewildered, startled by this sudden accusation. It is false that I have striven to win you when I was not free to offer you my name. Oh, Olga! you whom I love better than life—than all, save honour, can you think this treachery of me? One hour of calmer thought must make you see how impossible it is that I should do you this wrong!"

He stopped, his voice stifled with emotion, and bent his forehead against the hand that she had only feebly tried to withdraw from his clasp.

The princess seemed touched almost against her will; impulsive, and easily moved to anger, she was as easily influenced to softer emotions.

"Vera would not tell to me what was not true," she said uncertainly; and Linwood took fresh hope from the tone—he was not, then, irretrievably ruined.

"Ah, Olga," he murmured; "Vera is but your friend—I am your lover! Will you not believe your lover, when he swears that he had no thought to wrong you—that heart and hand were alike free when this lover dared to woo you?"

"What, then, is her meaning?" said the princess in the same half-uncertain way, as though she were willing to be convinced, but was too proud to yield her position without a struggle.

"Will you not tell me exactly what she does say?" said Linwood gently. "Give me the chance of explaining or denying. Is that too much to ask of your——"

"No. Stop there!" the princess interrupted rapidly. "If this be true, my love is dead to you for ever!"

She rose to her feet, as if she wished to throw off, by some action, the influence she felt overcoming her, and took up the letter.

"I will read to you what Vera says," she said in a voice that sounded dry and hard from the suppression of feeling. "Listen: 'So you relate to me that Lucius Linwood has told you he loves you. Have no faith in his vows. He is not any more free to make them. He has made to me a promise; dearly have I paid for it.' That is all; is it not enough?"

"It is not enough," said Linwood, lifting his head—his face was ashen grey, and he gnawed his under-lip as he paused after that abrupt protest.

The princess folded her hands, and, looking at him, said:

"Doubtless you can, then, explain."

There seemed a desperate struggle in the man's soul. Nor was it all acting. He quailed in very truth before the clear gaze of those dark eyes.

He knew not for the moment in what way it would be safest to explain the words which went so near to severing the hope he had of making the princess and her fortune his own; yet his uncertainty and agitation could only serve to deepen her impression of his want of good faith.

He turned away and began walking up and down the room for some seconds.

"Well," said the princess, "the explanation seems a little difficult to make—not?"

Once more he turned to her, stretching his hands towards her, his lips working convulsively. Then, seeing no relenting in her face, but rather a growing sternness, he bent his forehead on his clasped hands.

"Oh, Olga—Olga," he said in a sort of agony, "if you could know all, surely—surely you would not be so hard—you would pity me!" There was a pause, during which the man in such throes of anguish was thinking, "If she is anything of the woman I take her for, this must touch her."

And, indeed, it seemed to have an effect on the princess; the lines of her face softened strangely.

You would hardly have thought this the same woman who had poured out reproaches to her lover a few moments ago; her lip quivered, her eyes drooped.

"But shall I pity the man I love?" she murmured, with that musical cadence in her voice the power of which she knew so well.

Linwood sprang to her and fell at her feet.

"You love me—you love me still!" he cried in passionate joy. "Oh, say those words again. You are too true, too noble to suffer a few words from one who deems herself your rival to kill love. Have faith in me still, Olga, I beseech you!"

"Why did you say, 'I shall pity you,'" the princess said, turning aside.

He paused a minute before answering.

"If I were to tell you," he said then, in a low voice, "I should be breaking that promise which Vera says, so far truly, I have made to her! Tell me, Olga—you shall decide: shall I break faith with Vera, and tell you what I swore should never pass my lips, or shall I——" He stopped, bowing his face on her hands. "No, no," he said; "I cannot—oh, I cannot risk the loss of all that makes life for me. Do not bid me keep this promise that should never have been made—that I made in a moment of weakness, and have ever reproached myself with having made."

"What is this promise—this terrible secret?" the girl half whispered, with her eyes growing wide and fearful. "You owe it to me to explain. Why shall this promise make you no more free to—to love me?"

"Ah," Linwood murmured, still averting his face, as though in self-abasement; "it is always so difficult for a man to clear himself from suspicion, when, to do so, he must throw doubt on a woman. Dearest, you yourself are so true that you will not understand how jealousy can turn a woman's heart against her best friend. This promise has no concern with the question of love and constancy. It binds me in no sense to Vera as a lover."

"Tell me—quick!" interrupted the princess, with a half-feverish yet half-pleading impatience. "You keep me in suspense; you make me frightened!"

"Forgive me! it is such pain to go back to that terrible time, to recall that crime——"

"Crime!" Olga grew white and made a movement to draw back, speaking under her breath. "That dreadful murder! What will you say? It is not possible." She shivered from head to foot and bent forward. Then, with a sudden movement, "Lucius," she whispered hoarsely, "the promise was not to shield —yourself?"

As if struck with an electric shock, Linwood sprang to his feet.

"Girl," he said through his set teeth, "what could make you say that? Great God! what have I said to give you such an idea? No one has ever hinted it. There was no tittle of evidence to support such a charge."

His face was livid, the drops stood on his brow; he seemed for the moment utterly unmanned. It was the passionate anger of fear that shook him, not the just indignation he might well have felt at the lightest breath of suspicion coming from the woman who had said she loved him.

Olga shrank back with a look almost of terror, but quickly recovered herself.

" Ah, it is I now who must pray for pardon," she said a little hurriedly. "No, no; of course I did not mean that. Will you not believe? I do not know what I say. You have made me quite nervous." She laughed, indeed, with a little nervous movement of her hands together, and drew nearer to him. "Forgive me. And now you will tell me this promise that has concern with the murder?"

Linwood passed his hand over his brow, striving with an effort to recover his calmness.

"I was too violent," he muttered, laying his hand on hers. Ah, how internally every fibre of her seemed to shrink from that touch! "But the bare thought was too horrible. No, Olga," and now he spoke low but steadily, "my promise was to shield Vera's lover

—who, mark you, is her lover still — Ernest Devereux."

The princess fell back a step, gazing at him with dilated eyes—horror, amazement, incredulity, all mingled in that glance.

"Devereux! Oh, but it is impossible!"

"Anything is possible where there is sufficient motive," returned Linwood, "and here there is motive enough. Devereux was deeply in Temple's debt; he loved Vera, but could not make her his wife; and the old man, from whatever reason, would listen to nothing else. I, fortunately or unfortunately—I know not which—found irrefragable proofs of Devereux's guilt. Vera frantically implored me to save him. What could I do? It was wrong to, in a manner, compound with crime, but who could act otherwise when a woman pleads? So I have kept this secret, and met Devereux as though no crime was on his soul. Tell me, have I done wrong?"

The princess covered her eyes with her hands, shuddering strongly.

"Oh," she said in a low voice of infinite pain, "and this man I have received as a friend—you have allowed that I touch his hand—you have allowed that I stand in his power! He who has shed the blood of my friend's father!"

"Forgive me, Olga," Linwood pleaded. "I had passed my word, but my very soul revolted against the part which I, in a moment of weakness, had consented to play. Do you not understand now my apparently causeless anger and seeming jealousy when you only gave a kind word or thought to Devereux? And yet I was forced to be silent. I have suffered, heaven knows, in this knowledge! May not that atone to you, Olga?"

He came to her side, and took her hand.

She half drew it away. At his touch a shiver shook her through and through.

In this moment, had her will, her high courage, been one second allowed to lapse, she had perhaps hazarded the loss of all for which she played her desperate game by betraying the fierce horror his lightest clasp brought to her; but nature is sometimes stronger than will, and her exaction was that one shiver away from the contact that seemed to pollute the wife of Devereux.

Olga suffered Linwood to draw her hand into both his own, and to clasp them closely, and then she murmured brokenly :

"I have been hard, and have misjudged you. Forgive me, But, oh,"—with a sudden movement she turned and threw herself on his breast, and burst into passionate weeping—"you will not let me now stand in this man's power? If you love me—if you love me, save me from this humiliation!"

Was this his Princess Olga, whom he had known as proud, as gracious, as coquettish, but who, even in her most gracious moods, had kept him at such a distance—had never allowed aught but the lightest caresses, had never offered one herself.

"My darling," he whispered, and strained her closer to him, "give me only one promise—give me only the right to protect you against all and any humiliation, and I will compass heaven and earth to free you from his debt—only one word, Olga——"

"But it must be now—now," she said with feverish haste, checking her sobs, and lifting her face to his, the tears yet wet on the long lashes. "He may—nay, will come this evening. It can be; and I cannot—oh, I cannot—be one hour in his presence, and still not free! You have—you must have money on you. Ah," with soft music in her voice, and laying her head now against his heart, "you love me—you will not say no to this one little thing! And I," she stopped a brief second and drooped her eyes, "I will promise all!"

"To-morrow, dearest—to-morrow," Linwood said; "it is impossible to-night."

"Ah, no—no!" Olga looked up again with eyes half pleading, half arch—a look irresistible to the man who held her in his arms, who feared lest one word of his should make her start away, and turn this sweet loving pleading into anger again. "To love, you know, nothing is impossible; and I—oh, I am so wretched! And I think you will save me. In a few days all I have will be yours, and I—I shall be yours also."

"But if I have not the money, dearest?" said Linwood. He wavered, he would try and struggle against the fascination that he felt was scattering all his senses and making him her obedient slave, until the novelty wore off.

"Now, that is but an excuse! *Fi donc!* let me see." The little hand stole softly to his vest-pocket, but he caught it and held it in his.

"Stay, Olga," he said gravely. "My darling, I would give you anything you want, but this I cannot. See, I will appeal to your generosity. I have money upon me; but it is money I cannot part with; it is not mine."

"Then it will be for gambling debts or—or for some woman," said the princess. She flushed and her eyes flashed. "Oh, you can protest of love, like all men; but you can make no sacrifice! I thought you were not so! To save me from misery and humiliation before another man, you will not give up one thing—not one!"

"No—no, Olga; indeed you are not just," cried the unfortunate lover, distracted, and resolved to humour her at whatever cost. "You shall see that I will risk much for your sake. I will make you free, you shall owe me this; it is my joy!"

He drew from an inner pocket a small pocket-book quickly, as though he almost feared his own resolution.

The girl gave him one swift grateful glance, and just laid her soft lips against his hand. Her heart was beating fast; for a second her brain seemed to reel; she was almost at the consummation of those hopes she had staked her all to realise; she almost held her breath while Lucius Linwood opened the pocket-book, gave one look into her face as though to read there some sign of relenting, and then put it quickly into her hands.

CHAPTER XXXVIII.

A FOOL'S PARADISE.

S the princess took the pocket-book and her fingers closed round it, she flashed Linwood a glance that seemed to him a reward almost enough for the risk he ran, if indeed risk there were any. He forgot in that moment all but that this woman owed him now a deep debt; the obligation was shifted from Devereux to him, and he would know how to use his power.

He watched her with an eager glance while she quickly opened the book and drew out the notes, one after the other, holding them in her pretty delicate fingers and looking at each; afterwards he remembered that she had never once let them go out of her hand, not even just to lay them on the table.

"How good you are!" she said caressingly, and lifting her eyes to his face. "Oh, you have made me free—free." She drew a long breath and for a second pressed her hand over her brow. "I will never forget that—no, never."

He would have caught her in his arms again, but she seemed to sway aside, and with uplifted finger and laughing eyes, stayed him. "No, no," she said, "you have still something to do for me. These notes, they are not signed."

"Signed," repeated Linwood with a smile; "but they are not cheques, Olga."

"I know that, but they shall still be signed, or what does one say?" said the princess with a pretty impatience that suited her charmingly, "Here on the back, you shall write your name."

"Oh, you mean endorsed," said Linwood, laughing. "My sweet princess, that is not necessary."

"But yes," persisted the sweet princess; I like to have it so, and you will do what I wish. All the English notes that I have had, they were always so, endorsed—is that right?"

"But this is only a fancy, Olga."

"And if it were," the princess shrugged her shoulders and looked more bewitching than ever, "have I not a right to my whims! Afterwards you will want that I give way to your whims, monsieur! But now—here is ink and pen."

"You don't seem to mind if Devereux knows where the money comes from, *cherie*," said Linwood with a half smile, yet gnawing his under-lip. But Olga clapped her hands softly together.

"That is quite famous," she said laughing like a gleeful child. "He will be so jealous; he will say, looking so stern, 'Why does he give you money? What right has he?' for oh, he hates you, *mon cher*, very much. And I shall make him a pretty curtsy and I shall say, 'Monsieur, in England may one not receive benefit from one's *fiancee?*' Shall not that be a triumph for you —and for me?" she added with that thrill of pathos in her tone which she knew Linwood could never resist.

He hesitated, wavered for a moment, and then took the pen she held towards him, and dashed down his name on the back of each note. There were four in all, each for five hundred pounds.

"And you shall come," said she archly, "and hear me tell milord. To-night, perhaps he will not come, and if he does I will not see him, for I am too tired. I have suffered, oh, so much to-day!" She paused, pressing her hand to her forehead, then went on: "Come to-morrow at this time, and you shall hear without being seen."

"Be sure I shall not fail when the command is to come and see you," said Linwood.

"That I know," returned the princess, taking up the notes, and putting them in her dress. "And now I think I must be alone, *mon ami*, for I truly feel quite ill with all I have to-day suffered."

"What, you will send me away so soon?" said Linwood reproachfully.

"Yes, really. Indeed, I am too stupid to be entertaining!" returned the princess, who had, in truth, invented no excuse when she said she felt tired. "To-morrow you will come again, and hear what I shall say to Milord Devereux, not——"

"If I could only be sure, Olga," Linwood said, lingering as he took the hand she stretched towards him, "that you cared as much for me to come as I care to come."

"It is good for men that they be not certain of everything," she said. "Be sure only of one thing—that a woman does not express all she feels."

And with this Linwood had to be satisfied, and to appear delighted therewith. It is questionable, however, if he appreciated this womanly delicacy in his adored princess. He took his leave, nevertheless, promising himself a repetition of to-day's happiness on the morrow.

He was in a state of high satisfaction with the success of his account of the murder and its effect on the princess. His winning card had procured for him all that he wished.

She was secured to him. A few days more would see her entirely his own; and he cast off his mind the lingering uneasiness that made itself felt when he thought of his giving up those notes.

He wished now he had not yielded to her persuasiveness. He could have gained her, he flattered himself, without parting with them. The woman was not born yet who could long stand out against him. But, after all, what did it signify? No harm could come of it—no one could identify the notes. And, with this comforting reflection, Lucius Linwood jumped into a hansom, lit up a cigar, and gave himself up to pleasing day-dreams.

If he had been gifted with second-sight, and could have seen some few hours into the future, he had not bowled along quite so comfortably, satisfied with himself, the princess, and the world in general—a satisfaction which induced him to give the driver sixpence over his fare—a piece of generosity which testified to a very happy frame of mind in the donor.

CHAPTER XXXIX.

VERA MAKES CONFESSION.

OR a minute or two after Linwood had left her, the princess stood quite still, listening intently. Her lips were parted, her eyes had an almost feverish brilliancy in them; she had said she was tired and "ill." And indeed the terrible strain of the scene she had just passed through had tried her more than she knew yet; but not now could the reaction come to her.

And though for one moment as she heard the man's step grow fainter and fainter on the gravel-path without, she was unable to master the tremor of nervous excitement that ran through every limb, it was quickly subdued, and with a swift movement of her hands over her forehead she pulled herself together and shook off the weakness, as she called it. There was yet much to be done.

She stepped to the bell and rang it. Ivan appeared, bowing low to his lady, who did not seem to have kept the slightest anger against her refractory servant.

"Ivan," she said, the while writing quickly a short note in Italian—a language he did not understand, "it is yet early, take this to the address I have written on it, and give the letter yourself to Lord Devereux; do not allow it to pass out of your hands. If he should not be at home, then go to the Opera, Covent Garden, and to Mrs. Mainwaring's box—you know it?—and you will find him there."

Ivan simply bowed in silence and left the room; he knew his business to perfection—to do as he was bid without asking a question or showing by so much as a look that he thought any proceeding strange.

When he had quitted the house on his errand, the princess rose and went upstairs to her own room, where she unlocked a cabinet, and touching a spring, disclosed a secret drawer. From this she took out the little book in which Berkeley Temple had entered the numbers of the notes received from Devereux; she compared them with the notes in her hand and found them correspond.

It was with strangely conflicting feelings that she awaited the coming of her husband.

Now, standing at the very threshold of discovery, able, perhaps, in a few weeks to point out to the world the assassin of her father, and so to free the man she loved from the hateful bondage that had been borne only for her sake, able to come to him with freedom in her hand, longing for the dear presence that alone could win her from the thought of all she had endured in this last hour, for the kiss that alone could purify her from the pollution of Linwood's touch, Vera yet trembled before the thought of that presence, trembled to think of the confession she must make him to-night. Would it give his love a shock to know that she had deceived him in concealing from him the whole truth, even though it were done for his sake?

"Ah, no, no!" she murmured again and again to herself, as she paced the room, too restless to keep still. "Surely he will not be angry or wounded; that would be so hard to bear. He loves me so much, and I"— she paused with uplifted face, a half smile on her lips, a look of infinite tenderness in the dark eyes—"from henceforth I will be so obedient; a look, a touch shall lead me; I will teach myself to be—but no, I shall have no need to teach myself, for I love him. Hark!" she started and flushed, and her eyes grew brighter, and then fell; "that was his step without on the gravel. Ivan must have found him at home, and he would have come on at once."

One moment more, and Vera, with a half-smothered cry, had flung herself into her husband's arms and clung to him, not weeping, but trembling, and for perhaps the first time since entering on the part she had set herself to play, utterly unnerved, unstrung.

Devereux held her close clasped to his breast, without speaking; he was deeply anxious, even alarmed for her; never before had he seen her so abandon herself, seemingly unable to rely on her strong will, to such almost wild emotion. Yet he was silent; not even his deadly anxiety, his fears of he knew not what, should make him question her when she was like this.

But his soft touch soothed her, the clasp of his hands, instinct with strength and sympathy, quieted the overwrought nerves, and the long-drawn shivering breath came less and less, and she seemed to rest like a tired child against him. Then he drew her down on to the sofa, and still keeping his arm about her pressed his lips to hers in a long tender kiss.

"Oh, Ernest," she whispered, "it is so good to feel the touch of your hand—to know that you hold me! You will forgive me? These hours—oh, they have been one long agony!"

"My darling, if I could have spared you!"

"No one could do that," the girl answered. "Well, it was the plan I set for myself, and I have carried it through; aye, even unto the very end." She sat upright as she spoke, and drew in a long breath. "I have got the notes from him, Ernest; they lie now in the bosom of my dress."

She felt how the clasp of his hand tightened on hers, felt the electric thrill that shook him for one moment— understood to the full the conflict of feeling that made him unable to say a word or to ask a question as to how she had gained her object. He turned aside, covering his face with one hand, setting his teeth.

"They are the very notes you paid to my father," Vera continued in a quiet tone. "The numbers correspond, and I have made him endorse them. He did not wish to do so; I suppose some fear made him shrink from doing that which renders it impossible to repudiate the notes as being once in his possession. I could have laughed" the girl said with a kind of bitter mirth, "if the whole interview had not been on such tragic lines, at the comedy which I was playing him—how I was fooling him to the top of his bent, while he was relating Vera's sins to Vera herself, and playing the self-sacrificing friend, shielding you from the consequences of your crime. Oh, I could have struck him where he stood! And I was forced to take sides against you. Oh, Ernest, that went through my very soul, but still, it was for you!"

"That does not make it light for you, Vera," said Devereux, in a suppressed voice.

"But yes," she answered him, smiling; "always I have said that to myself, and then—but I do not want to talk about that; it is nothing that I have done—'women and wives,' you know," with a half smile, though her lip was trembling, "'are only created to serve their lords and masters.' You won't have it so? Well, then, will it please you to know that I have promised Mr. Lucius Linwood to go away with him in a few days? That is not being a very meek wife to you, is it?"

"Child, you are jesting!" said Devereux, almost sternly, the blood leaping to his brow. But Vera put her hand on his.

"It is the last promise of the sort that I shall make to him," she said, with a half smile, "and that, of course, I shall not keep. But I was obliged to seem to yield everything in order to gain my object."

She then shortly related the ruse by which she had obtained possession of the notes, Devereux listening in silence.

"I felt sure," she said, "that he had the notes still, and would carry them always on his person. It needed a strong pressure put upon him to make him give them up at all; but the old motives which have been found to sway the world as long as it has existed did not fail to exercise their influence. Love, or what passes current as such, and jealousy are tolerably omnipotent. To gain the Princess Glinka, and with her fortune, for his wife, and to place it out of your power to aspire to her favour, Linwood would do and has done much."

"He trusts to my not knowing the numbers of the notes paid to Temple," said Devereux.

"He is coming to-morrow," Vera continued, "for the pleasure of hearing me announce to you that he has generously freed me from owing anything to you. To-morrow," she drew a long breath and said slowly, "the last act of the drama must be played out."

"He will be arrested," Devereux said, shortly.

"Yes; and he must not know yet that the arrest comes really through me," returned Vera. "He will probably think that you have retained the number of the notes, and had him arrested on suspicion. He must not identify me yet; it is not needful, and will make so much unnecessary public talk. It is foolish of me," she said, half deprecatingly, and for a moment hiding her face against her husband's shoulder, "but I shrink from that; it must come, I know."

She was trembling now, and her voice faltered.

Devereux, with the quick intuition his love alone would have given him, divined that there was some deeper feeling in her than the mere shrinking from public discussion over her disguise, and the thought struck a sudden cold chill to his heart; but he drew her closer to him, and gently lifted her drooping head, looking straight into the eyes that met his with that clear loyal gaze.

"You have something to tell me, my child," he said, very tenderly and gravely; "I knew it when I came in and you sprang to meet me. I know it even more certainly now. You are not afraid of me, my Vera?"

"Afraid? Ah no!" she answered him, with a look full of such trust as made his heart leap; "yet, you might well be angry when you know how far I have gone, for I claimed your blind faith for permission to do what you would never have allowed if I had told you then what I will tell you now."

"Vera!"

"Ah! wait—wait!" she pleaded, almost hurriedly, her breath coming quick and short, "I know I did not tell you all the truth—I in a manner deceived you, who trusted me so blindly; but there was no other way. Would you ever have consented to let me go through a form of marriage with Lucius Linwood?"

Devereux sprang to his feet with a passionate exclamation,

"By heaven—no!" he said, the red blood flushing to his brow. "For your sake, I have yielded more, it may well be, than it beseems a man to give!" He stopped abruptly, and turning aside bent his head down on the mantelpiece, clasping his hands over his forehead. "Oh," he said, speaking out of the bitter soreness of shame in his heart, "will a woman in her blind devotion ever fathom that there may be one thing dearer to a man than his life?"

The words were almost cruel; unjust they certainly were, and he knew it, and felt it almost ere the last had passed his lips; but though the girl shrank a moment, and shivered as if a knife had cut into her flesh, she made no answer, nor even gave passing place to a thought that her self-sacrifice surely merited not such bitter words. She knew he spoke on the impulse of the moment, and had she not indeed stretched the cord of honour almost to breaking?

He had indeed only spoken on impulse, and felt directly, with a flash of most bitter self-reproach, how unjust his pain had made him towards the woman who had sacrificed so much, and had counted it as nothing. He turned to her and wrapped her to his breast, with broken words.

"Forgive me—forgive me, Vera. Forget that cruel reproach. It was not thought nor meant. But, oh, child, this crushes me to the dust—it crushes me to the dust! Have patience with me yet a little."

She made at first no answer in words, only lifted her face to his, and with caressing hand swept back the hair from his brow.

It hurt her more to hear him reproach himself than to bear the fleeting pain of a few words uttered without thought. She comprehended so well all that "crushed him to the dust," and that it was the suppressed pain of all these months of endurance that was finding expression now.

"Listen, Ernest," she said presently, very softly. "I can have nothing either to forgive or to forget. If I have been able to sacrifice a little for your sake, do you think I have taken no count of that which you have made for me? Have you not laid down your pride—that high and noble pride that suffers humiliation in accepting sacrifice? You, of your own free will, would have chanced all risks sooner than allow me to act as I have done. But you knew what that would be to me; and do I not know all you have endured so patiently?"

But he shook his head and smiled—a smile half sad, half bright.

"Sweet sophistry, my child," he said, tenderly; "comfort that I cannot take to my own heart. We will not try to measure sacrifices. In the presence of your deep self-devotion I tread as on holy ground. To your pure soul it must have been agony, that a man may not more than dimly apprehend, to go through all you have done. And it was more than my life, Vera, that you have striven to save."

Her hand was laid quickly on his arm; her pleading eyes looked up to his.

"Hush!" she said. "Let us speak no more of that, if you love me. Did you not say 'we shall not measure sacrifices'? Let me rather make my confession to you; and," now she smiled with her old bewitching archness, "I promise amendment in the future, if you will only give me absolution—only I want the absolution first—it is the last call I will make on your faith, Ernest."

He could only press his quivering lips to hers again and again; he had no words in which to utter the forgiveness she craved, and none were needed; and in the deep joy of those precious moments Vera could forget all the suffering of the past and the ordeal she must yet brave before the clouds would quite roll away, and her husband stand free and without suspicion in the sight of the world.

CHAPTER XL.

"WHOSE HAND WAS IT?"

PUNCTUALLY as the clock struck five the next evening, Linwood mounted the low steps that led up to the princess's door, and rang. He said "Good evening" cheerfully to Ivan, who replied to the summons, and smiled as that functionary preceded him through the hall.

He was in excellent spirits; the consummation of all his hopes seemed very near; and was he not about to taste the sweetness of revenge—that revenge only in part fulfilled? Would it not be sweet indeed to know that he had crossed his enemy's path again here—again deprived him of the satisfaction of winning the woman he loved?

And yet there was a certain nervousness running like an under-current through Linwood's heart. What if, after all, things should somehow turn out a little differently from what he expected? If Devereux, for instance, should by chance have retained a memory that he had seen the number of one of those notes before?

Bah! What nonsense! What was the use of disquieting himself like this? Linwood involuntarily straightened himself as he went into the drawing-room, where the princess awaited him.

He would have met her effusively, claiming all the privileges of a betrothed, but she gave him her hand to kiss, very graciously, with a very coquettish glance, but with something in her manner which checked his ardour, but did not damp it.

"I have counted the moments to this hour," he said, rapturously.

"That is what they all say," she said. "I suppose you also have paced your room all night?"

"Don't you believe in love, Olga?" said her lover half reproachfully.

"Oh yes, I believe in love," returned the princess. "Can you doubt it, my friend? What an unbeliever I should be if I doubted the existence of that of which I am always hearing! But come, you shall now go into this little room and hear me tell Milord Devereux that I can pay him his debt. Ah, happy moment when I am no more in his power! I do not forget all I owe to you."

If Linwood could have divined the meaning lying under the sweetness of her words, he certainly had not given her such an adoring look as he passed her and went into the inner apartment.

She drew the *portiere* across the doorway, but left the door itself slightly ajar, so that Linwood could hear every word that passed. Neither had long to wait before Lord Devereux was announced.

"I am indeed glad that you have come," said the princess, advancing to meet him with outstretched hands.

And Lord Devereux, thus welcomed, bent low over the hand, answering:

"It is but rarely that the Princess Glinka deigns to extend to me such gracious words. I value them, believe me."

"You are ironical, count," the princess rejoined, drawing back with some hauteur, and Devereux smiled slightly and shrugged his shoulders.

"You are pleased to think so?" he said. "Well, I cannot help it; I suppose you will never give me the credit of speaking in good faith. And I must think I have forfeited your—what shall I say?—your favour for good because of that wretched money?"

"We need not speak of that," said the princess. "I am able now this minute to free myself from the bondage. I have the money here."

"Whenever it pleases you, princess," he said. "It grieves me that you look upon so simple a matter in such a tragic light."

"It is you who have made it so," she interrupted him, half under her breath; "but let us be silent over that. Thank heaven, I am able at last to be free!"

"You have got this money very suddenly," said the viscount; and the princess only smiled and drew forth the notes, laying them down on the table.

Devereux took them up in silence and glanced at the endorsement, and his face changed.

"Lucius Linwood!" he said quickly, almost sharply. "How do you come to be possessed of these?"

"I could ask you," returned the princess, "what right have you to put me that question? That is your debt, and the rest is my affair. But I will answer you. Lucius Linwood has given me these notes."

"And by what right does he give you money to discharge your debts?" said Devereux; "or do you mean that the notes have merely passed through his hands? Yet his is the first endorsement."

"He will tell you himself," answered the girl, "if you have doubt. Lucius!"

Linwood came quickly from the next apartment in answer to her call, glancing furtively at Devereux. Inwardly he had been dreading this ordeal. What if the viscount had recollected the number of some of those notes!

"So you have prepared a comedy, fair princess," said Devereux with a touch of irony as he bowed to Linwood, but the princess spoke quickly:

"My Lord Devereux doubts that it is of you that I have received these notes, and will know why I permit myself to accept from you so much money."

"That is easily said," returned Linwood with an assumption of carelessness he was far from feeling. "It has been my happiness to be able to accommodate the princess, who may surely receive from her affianced husband the loan of a few hundred pounds."

Devereux only bowed in acknowledgment of this explanation, and Linwood was unable to divine from face or manner how the announcement of a rival's success affected him.

"In that case," said the viscount, "it only remains for me to offer you my congratulations, and to thank you, princess, for the honour you have just done me. I will no longer detain you—adieu."

The princess did not seek to detain him, but only bent her head in answer to his farewell, and Devereux left the room.

He did not, however, as Linwood supposed, also quit the house, but waited in another apartment until the princess's lover should have been dismissed. He would not willingly leave Vera alone with Linwood.

As soon as the door had closed on Devereux the princess drew a long breath as of relief.

"That is well over," she said, "I feared he would make me a scene, but he is proud, as all you English are, and if he is disappointed, he will not show it. Now, my friend, I shall also send you away, for I am tired, and also, if I must go away from here, I have much to do."

And Vera held out her hand with charming grace.

"What, you will not let me stay with you?" exclaimed Linwood reproachfully, and with a cloud, too, on his brow that she did not fail to mark. "You are very cruel, Olga."

"Ah, I cannot help it," said the girl a little wearily. "*Mon cher*, you will have quite as much of me as is good for you in a few days."

The answer to which was naturally a still more reproachful glance and a protestation that that was an impossibility.

"Well, we shall see," said the princess, with a smile that Linwood afterwards remembered; "now you may kiss my hand, and say me farewell."

Linwood obeyed. The princess was not one with whose moods one could trifle with impunity, and he judged it best to yield. After all, he thought with triumph, in a few days at most she would be his, and he would know how to tame her haughty spirit.

So he took his leave and threw himself into a passing hansom, reflecting that he would have time to dress and dine with a friend at whose rooms some very high play was indulged in.

He was altogether in a much more contented frame of mind than he had of late enjoyed; he began to breathe freely once more. There was evidently no fear of danger arising from Devereux's possession of the notes. He had not given the remotest sign of knowing them.

"I won't worry myself any more over the matter," thought Linwood; "from to-day I mean to enjoy myself."

It was not quite half-past six when he entered his own rooms, and, looking at his watch, found that he should have plenty of time to read some letters that had arrived by the afternoon's post. He threw himself into his favourite armchair therefore, and had just torn open a delicate-tinted envelope, doubtless an invitation to some fashionable gathering, he thought with a smile, when he should be hundreds of miles away, when his servant entered and informed him that two gentlemen desired to see him on business.

"Rather late," said Linwood with a slight frown. "Do you know them, Hudson? Are they people I don't wish to see?" for Hudson knew all his master's duns, probably better than his master did.

"I don't know the gentlemen, sir," the man replied.

"Well, I will see them," said Linwood. "Deuced inconvenient, but I shall cut 'em short. I'm going to dine with Fortescue to-night."

Hudson withdrew, and in a few minutes ushered in a quiet-looking personage, remarking in a kind of tentative tone:

"The other gentleman said he would wait in the ante-room, sir."

Linwood looked a little surprised, and a sort of vague uneasiness sent a chill through his veins, but he only said, "Very well, Hudson," and Hudson once more retired, decidedly puzzled, and more than vaguely uneasy, though of course his thoughts only flew to arrest for debt.

"You call on business, my servant said," said Linwood rather curtly. "I have not the pleasure of knowing you."

Linwood's visitor walked quietly up to Linwood, and just lightly touched him on the shoulder.

"I am a police-officer, sir, and I arrest you on this warrant for the murder of Mr. Berkeley Temple, late of Bruton-street."

For perhaps one second after the officer ceased speaking Linwood sat like one paralysed, bereft of every power of movement, literally thunderstruck with the sudden blow dealt him, he knew not whence; he went so ghastly white that the man almost thought he was about to faint; then all at once the full meaning of the words he had just heard rushed upon him and he sprang to his feet with a fierce oath.

"It is false—monstrous!" he cried. "Great heaven! there must be some fearful mistake. I arrested for—for——" his lip writhed, he could not bring the word "murder" over them in connection with himself.

"I will read the warrant over to you, sir, if you please," said the officer, with that deadly official calm to which nothing is terrible. "You will find there is no mistake."

And Linwood listened while the warrant was read over to him, glad of the moment to try and gather himself together, and strive to meet the charge as an innocent man would do. His thoughts flew to the notes, those fatal notes. A thousand times he cursed his folly in letting them pass from his hands. Yet it was not an hour since he had quitted the Brompton villa, how could they be at the bottom of this arrest? As he heard that the warrant was issued on the information of Ernest Algernon Devereux, he set his teeth and a look of intense hatred leapt into his eyes. All sorts of wild surmises swept through his brain, but no flash of the truth, no suspicion how he had been fooled by the woman who in a few days was to have been his wife.

"So my Lord Devereux is plucking up courage to throw his guilt on an innocent man," he said when the officer had concluded. "Well, of course I must go with you, but I suppose I may give some directions to my servant?"

"Certainly, sir, if you don't wish to see him alone."

"What! you don't trust me?" said Linwood, with a half sneer.

"I must do my duty, sir," replied the official without a change of countenance.

Linwood laughed, he would try another tack—anything to get a minute to himself.

"Of course you must, my good fellow," he said, more good-humoredly; "but your duty needn't prevent you having a glass of wine, need it?—and something with it, eh? It's only in the next room."

"No thank you, sir," the man replied, keeping a quiet watch on Linwood's movements; "and I must caution you, sir, that anything you say here may be used against you."

"Pooh, man! I've said nothing you might not repeat," said Linwood carelessly, though he bit his lip with baffled anger at the failure of his attempt to bribe the official out of a few moments to himself. "I suppose you will be turning my things topsy-turvy?"

"We shall not disturb anything unnecessarily, sir."

Linwood made no further remark, but rang for Hudson, to whom he gave a message for his friend Fortescue, and then desired him to call a cab, a four-wheeler.

And in another quarter of an hour Lucius Linwood sat cursing his fate in a prison-cell, and striving, with the drops of agony on his brow, to trace out, amidst the mystery that enveloped his arrest, every possible and impossible clue that Devereux could have got hold of. Had Vera Temple's hand guided the blow?

CHAPTER XLI.

MANY-TONGUED RUMOUR.

HERE was food enough for gossip and conjecture the day after Linwood's arrest; the morning papers—it was Sunday—contained sufficiently startling news, although the announcement was restricted to a very few lines, and one paper had only "Rumoured arrest of a gentleman well known in society," but one journal made up in the size of its headline for the paucity of information, and made as much out of it as possible by recapitulating the half-forgotten details of the Bruton-street murder, and speedily that murder again became the theme of every tongue.

"It is said," concluded one statement, "that Viscount Devereux will be one of the principal witnesses."

"Is it true, I wonder?" said Lord Dalton, laying down the paper with a rather bewildered air. "Charlie," to that young gentleman who now rushed into the Regina, breathless and excited; "ah, I see you've got the news too. Odd, isn't it?"

"Odd! Why, I never heard anything so extraordinary in my life," cried Charlie Bolton, sinking into a chair. "Linwood arrested on a charge of murder, and that murder, too! Why, he was dead sweet on the *diva!*"

"It's a mystery," said Dalton; "I've always thought there was something more in that affair than met the eye, you know. What can Devereux have to do with it?"

"Do you think it's the police have found out anything?"

"Can't tell, dear boy, but should think not," laughed Dalton. "I suppose we shall know more to-morrow. Linwood will be brought before the magistrate. Poor

Lin! I'm deuced sorry, though, as you know, I never was great friends with him."

"Still, a cell's a deuce of a place to pass Sunday in," remarked Charlie, "or, indeed, any day. Wonder what are the grounds of the accusation."

"I wish Devereux would come in," said his lordship.

But Devereux did not come in, nor did he make his appearance in any club that day, for he knew that he would be assailed by a hundred questions, and he hated to hear the thing talked over and Vera's name brought in.

But it was impossible for him quite to avoid all intercourse with friends and acquaintances, and indeed almost the first thing in the morning Jack Crawford came to his rooms.

"You've seen the news this morning, Devereux?" he asked, as the viscount shook hands with him, and pushed his cigar-case over to him. "Do you suppose it's true?"

"Do I suppose what is true?" answered Devereux, smiling; "that Linwood is arrested?"

"No, no, of course not; but whether he is guilty or not. It's very queer."

"Well, happily it is not often that a man in a good class of life is brought up for murder."

"How strange you are, Dev," said Jack, curiously; "and what in the name of heaven have you got to do with the affair? Or is that a stretch of the reporter's imagination, saying that you will be a witness in the case?"

"No, it's quite true," answered Devereux quietly.

"But what—what the deuce do you know about the murder?" said Jack, looking bewildered as Lord Dalton had done. "I shall begin to think that it was through you Linwood was arrested."

"Which conclusion has caused you to arrive at the exact truth of the case, my son," replied the viscount, and for a moment Jack sat and stared.

"But what do you know about it?" he said at last; "and if you could have said anything to clear the mystery, why didn't you do so at the inquest?"

"Simply because such evidence as I could give was entirely uncorroborated, and would have served to cast suspicion on myself," answered Devereux. "I tell you so much, Jack, because I know I can trust you not to chatter; but the why and the wherefore of all this will all come out before the magistrate to-morrow—the public will make enough chatter over it, heaven knows."

"Well, it beats me!" said Jack. "I was never more astonished in my life. Tell me one thing, Devereux; will Miss Vera be called into this?"

"Yes, Jack, she will."

That was all, and Jack felt he could ask no more, though he was longing to know what her share was in this extraordinary affair.

"How will our fair unknown, the Princess Glinka, take all this, I wonder?" said he as he rose. "She was awfully interested in poor Linwood—or at any rate Linwood used to say she was. Does she know it yet?"

"I should think she sees the morning paper," returned Devereux. "Shall you see Alise to-day, Jack?"

"Of course, I go to lunch there," answered Crawford. "Shall I see you?"

"No, I shall be invisible," replied the viscount, laughing. "I am not brave enough to stand under the fire of questions, and I have so much to do."

"Well, good-bye then. I shall come down to the court, of course."

The two men shook hands, and Jack went off to Eaton-square, while Devereux turned back into the room. He felt indeed in no mood to meet the questions and answer the conjectures that would be put to him; he was anxious enough, more so than he would have thought possible, now that the crisis was so very near. There was a possibility that everything might after all break down, but on that he would not suffer his mind to dwell, and indeed that day there was little time for anything but active work, and in the evening he went down to Brompton.

And so passed the weary day of interval; and even Linwood, shrinking with an inexpressible dread from the terrible morrow, welcomed the first streak of dawn that must end to some extent the agony of uncertainty.

CHAPTER XLII.

COMMITTED FOR TRIAL.

HE morning broke fine and mild; the first promise of spring seemed to breathe in the air—such a day as sometimes comes in early February to cheat us into the belief that warm weather is really to be with us; it was indeed to the man who perhaps had tasted his last of freedom under a pure sunshine a kind of mockery, this bright genial day; he cursed the sunshine that made it tolerable for that gaping crowd to come and look at him going into a felon's dock—cursed it with a kind of sullen ferocity.

For him was not even the scant consolation of a clear conscience, and the wildest hope would not allow him to suppose but what he would be at least committed for trial; and for the issue of that trial he had not much real hope, however he might try to buoy himself up.

The court was already full when the magistrate took his seat, although it was probable the crowd would have to wait some time before the case of all-absorbing interest was heard; the night charges had to be disposed of first, but this did not daunt the courage though it tried the patience of the denizens of St. James's. They occupied the time easily with wondering how the accused would look and how he would meet the charge, and whether the *diva* would be a witness, and whether there was anything between her and Devereux, &c., &c.

Alise had come with her mother, escorted by Jack Crawford; she looked anxiously about to try and see her cousin, and there was a sensation when he did come in with a lady closely veiled, who everyone said must be the *diva*, and Alise wanted to go and speak to her, but was advised not to by Jack.

"She won't want a lot of fuss and bother," said he, "and the more people speak to her the more she will attract attention.   Here is Linwood!"

"What a fearful position to be in," said Alise with a shudder ; " he must feel it a thousand times more than those men we have just seen."

Linwood bore himself calmly enough whatever he felt. As he stood in the dock he lifted his eyes a moment and scanned the well-known faces that surrounded him, people familiar enough to him in that world to which he was now perhaps taking his farewell; and then his glance travelled to where Devereux stood, and he gnawed his lip. From him to the tall slender form near, and then a sudden swift change swept over his face ; for a second he flushed and then grew deadly pale ; for surely that was Vera Temple come to accuse him ! But Vera Temple was abroad ; only a few days before a letter from her had reached him dated from Florence ; how could she have heard of this and got over in time ?

A fearful, a wild thought rushed across his bewildered brain—an impossible suspicion that made all things reel about him, so that for a minute he could not realise anything, where he was, or who was speaking, till a touch on the arm from his solicitor recalled him to himself, and with a violent effort he gained some mastery over the fear that shook him, and a sinister light came into his eyes.

What if they brought Vera? She could give no evidence against him—the law closed her lips; she was his wife!

He bent and whispered something to his solicitor, and then stood erect, attentive to every word that was to be said.

Mr. Grant was shortly stating the facts of the murder with which the prisoner was charged, and he proposed only, he said, calling sufficient evidence to enable the magistrate to send the case for trial.

"The circumstances of the murder," he said, "would be fresh in the recollection of everyone—how Mr. Temple was found dead in his study by his daughter.

There was then apparently no trace of a weapon with which the deed had been committed, nor could any clue to the mystery be found. A large sum of money—notes for two thousand pounds, which had been paid to Mr. Temple only that evening by Lord Devereux, were missing. It was supposed, therefore, that the murder had been committed for the sake of robbery, and a verdict in accordance with this theory was recorded at the inquest. Thus the matter rested. But at the inquest not a tithe of the truth came out; and one witness, whose evidence to-day was of the highest importance when taken in conjunction with that of others, was not called. The real facts of the case were these:

"On the night before the murder there was a party of Mr. Temple's friends gathered, and to these friends Lord Devereux showed a very curiously-wrought antique dagger, which he had promised to bring one evening. This dagger he slipped into the pocket of his wrap-coat on taking leave, and throwing the coat over his arm, as the night was warm, accompanied some friends to his club, the Regina. He then returned to Bruton-street, as he wished to have a private interview with Mr. Temple, in order to pay him a debt of two thousand pounds, and also to speak on affairs of a private nature, to which I will not more particularly allude now.

"Lord Devereux let himself in with a latch-key, which he had previously borrowed of Miss Temple, as he knew that at the late hour he must see Mr. Temple the servants would not be up. I am obliged," said Mr. Grant "to enter into these details, as they will make it abundantly clear the motive the witness had in not coming forward at the inquest. Unsupported then without that link which has since been obtained, he would have become subject to the darkest suspicion himself.

"Lord Devereux saw Mr. Temple, paid him the money, and left; but he left behind him, forgotten under the influence of deep agitation, the coat and dagger he had brought with him. Going out hastily, he passed on the step of the house a man apparently about to enter. This man, there is the strongest circumstantial evidence to show, was the prisoner.

He was a suitor for Miss Temple's hand, but she had refused him.

"It is supposed that the prisoner went with the intention of intimidating the old man alone, at the dead of night, in order to force him to use his authority with his daughter. The books of the murdered man, as well as those of the prisoner, will also prove that he was deeply in Mr. Temple's debt for money lent, and that he had not the means to pay these liabilities.

"We now come to the discovery of the deed, and this really took place at an early hour in the morning. Miss Temple entering the room about eight found the body of her father stabbed to the heart; beside him lay the dagger stained with blood; the overcoat lay as if tossed there on a chair; the table-drawers were in disorder. At this juncture the prisoner came into the room, and seeing the coat and dagger, at once accused Lord Devereux of the murder, saying that as he was passing the night before he had seen him emerge from the house obviously in a most agitated state, so much so that he scarcely appeared to notice him; but the rest of this singular and diabolical plot to transfer guilt to an innocent man, and to secure for himself the hand of the woman who had refused to wed him, will be best told by the witness herself, Miss Temple, whom I shall shortly call."

And after the formal evidence of the constable who arrested the prisoner, and took possession of the dagger and coat found in Linwood's rooms, Vera was called.

There was a distinct sensation, a visible stir as the tall slender girl stepped forward.

She had removed her veil, and all bent eagerly forward to see again that rare beauty which had turned the heads of half the gilded youth of London.

Linwood leaned over the rail of the dock, scanning, with that fear anew clutching at his heart, every feature, every line, noting the bronze-gold hair, the satin smoothness of the skin—and yet—and yet—seen in the full light of day—how very like that woman who had enslaved something more than his fancy!

But before even the clerk had opened his lips to ask her name, quickly Mr. Ray rose.

"I object to this lady being called as a witness; her evidence is inadmissible," he said, and there was a barely suppressed murmur in court, a sudden look of bewilderment on every face. Almost involuntary, too, Devereux moved a step nearer his wife.

"On what grounds is your objection made?" the magistrate asked, and the answer sent a thrill to the hearts of those who had known Vera.

Vera stood like a statue.

"This lady is the prisoner's wife," replied Mr. Ray, with a certain ring of triumph in his voice, and Linwood smiled—a sinister smile, and breathed more freely; Mr. Ray continued: "The marriage is easily proved, in assurance of which I will hand up the certificate given by the registrar, whose books will also prove the marriage."

"Oh," whispered Alise in despair, while Mr. Plant, the magistrate, examined carefully the document submitted to him; "why doesn't she deny it? It must be a wicked, wicked falsehood!"

"Hush! old Grant is speaking," returned Jack; "there's some mystery to come out here."

"Allow me, sir," he was saying, "to give a little explanation. It is true that the witness went through a ceremony of marriage with the prisoner; we do not dispute the genuineness of the certificate; but there existed a bar to that marriage, as Miss Temple was already the wife of Viscount Devereux. That marriage was performed by the Rev. Dr. Poyntz, at the parish church of Greenleaf, in Wiltshire, in proof of which," said Mr. Grant with a quiet look of humour at his opponent, "I beg to hand up this certificate, and also to add that Dr. Poyntz is in court."

A kind of hushed murmur, instantly subdued, from the audience, as though everyone, till now on the strain of interest and expectation, relieved his or her self by drawing a long breath.

Linwood's face was a study; he was ghastly pale, and he gnawed his lip till the blood came; in that moment he could have slain Vera as she stood there so calm, so apparently unmoved.

"Outwitted—undone!" he muttered, for a moment forgetting the surrounding crowd. "Ten thousand curses on her! The very devil's in the girl."

"The date of this certificate," said Mr. Plant, after examining the fresh document, "is prior to that of the registrar's; but that no doubt may exist as to identity, or a possible mistake in the date, I think it will be advisable to call the clergyman who performed the marriage."

Dr. Poyntz was accordingly sworn, and said that he perfectly recollected the marriage, and would have known the parties to it anywhere; they were not easily mistaken. Everything was done in a strictly legal way.

"In that case," said the magistrate, addressing Mr. Ray, as the witness retired, "this lady is undoubtedly entitled to give whatever evidence she can for or against the prisoner. The first marriage is fully proved; the second ceremony is of no value."

Mr. Ray bowed and professed himself satisfied.

"The fact of a previous marriage, which, of course, renders Lady Devereux liable to a charge of bigamy, was quite unknown to me and to the accused, but I now withdraw my objection."

It was with strangely-mingled feelings that Vera for the first time spoke that name as her own rightful one to bear. Steadily, clear as a bell, that sweet soft voice fell on the listener's ear, and Linwood ground his teeth as he heard the hated name—"Vera Marie Devereux."

Vera Marie Devereux, when the sacred book was given to her, kissed it reverently and then clasped her hands lightly on the rail before her, and in obedience to the request to relate what happened on the morning of the murder, bowed her head slightly.

"On that morning," she said, and there was a breathless silence, "I came down, as I often did, early to practise; as, near breakfast-time, my father did not appear, I went to his study. He frequently rose quite early and wrote letters before breakfast. When I entered I saw my father lying on the floor between his table and the door. There was blood on the carpet, and he was still bleeding from a wound in the breast. A dagger lay beside him, which I instantly recognised as that belonging to Lord Devereux, and which he had shown us the night previous. On further examination I found an overcoat also belonging to him. I was startled, not because I thought Lord Devereux had done this deed, but because I knew he must have been with my father after all the guests had left, and must have forgotten his coat and dagger, and might be involved."

"What made you think he had been with your father?" asked Mr. Grant.

"He had told me that he should come in order to pay two thousand pounds he owed, and to tell him of our marriage."

"What did you do on making this discovery?"

"My first thought was to let no one see the weapon. I knew the prisoner would be at the house early—he had said he should call; I did not want him to see them."

"Why particularly the prisoner?"

"Because he and Lord Devereux were not on friendly terms, and only the evening before some hostile words had passed between them. From what the prisoner had said I feared he might seize any opportunity of injuring Lord Devereux."

"Was the prisoner a suitor for your hand, Lady Devereux?"

"Yes; but I had refused him."

"Was your father favourable to his suit?"

"No."

"What did you do with the dagger and coat?"

"The prisoner came in at that moment and saw them; he prevented me concealing them, taking them into his own possession. He then told me he had seen Lord Devereux leaving the house very early in the morning, before it was light even, and that he thought something had occurred as he appeared so much agitated; he added that these things of Lord Devereux's having been found beside the body with stains of blood upon them, coupled with the fact of his also being seen to quit the house under such suspicious circumstances, would go very far to condemn him as the guilty man. He, the prisoner, however, would keep silence as to all that he knew on condition that I should become his wife. I refused at first; then a plan came into my head by which I hoped to trace the real criminal and save my husband from a wrongful accusation. I said I would marry the prisoner before a registrar, but that we should immediately part and he should leave me perfectly free for one year. I undertook to pay his most pressing debts and also send him money. He bound himself to silence, and I had at least gained time."

"Was this compact carried out?" asked Mr. Grant, as for a second the girl paused and drew her breath a little quicker.

"It was," she answered him, speaking in the same steady, passionless tones; "we went through the ceremony, to which my servant, Janet, was witness. I left immediately for the Continent, only telling my husband where I had gone."

"Did you think at this time that the prisoner was the guilty party?"

"I suspected him the moment he came into the study and saw the body of my father. He did not seem surprised, but rather as if he expected to see a dreadful spectacle; he had no air of being startled."

"Was that all on which you founded your suspicion?"

"The strange behaviour of my dog, Gellert, further roused suspicion; he had followed me into the room and when the prisoner entered I could scarcely keep the dog from flying at him; he had never testified any active dislike to Mr. Linwood before this time, though he had no affection for him."

"Was the dog always loose at night?"

"Yes; but on this morning he was found shut up behind the door at the top of the kitchen-stairs."

"Who found him?"

" My maid, Janet."

" Did you call anyone when you discovered the body of your father? "

" Not till after the prisoner had left me; I let him out and then went back to the study; then I called Janet and Andrew, the man-servant; I led them to suppose that I had only just made the discovery."

" Was there anything to lead you to suppose that robbery had been committed? "

" The writing-table drawer was half open, and the papers were in great confusion. When Andrew had gone for a doctor and a constable, I sent Janet away, and searched for the money Lord Devereux had told me he should pay my father; it was nowhere to be found."

" Might it not have been that Lord Devereux did not pay the money? "

" He had paid it; for afterwards I took from a secret drawer the book in which my father entered the particulars of all such payments; the numbers of the notes were plainly marked, and the date and hour of payment."

A smothered exclamation broke from Linwood.

It came upon him now in a flash how he had been duped—how miserably he had played into the hands of the girl who had set herself to track him down like a sleuth-hound; and all the control which it was, above all things, so necessary that he should maintain, could not quite stifle that cry of baffled rage.

For a moment Vera's eyes rested on Linwood's face, and the half-mocking light he had learned to dread in the Princess Glinka sprang to them; then she turned them again from him, answering Mr. Grant, who handed her a small book.

" This is the note-book. That is my father's handwriting. It was in my possession up to last Saturday, when I gave it to the solicitor who has charge of this case."

The numbers of the notes entered as payment of Lord Devereux's debt were read out, and found to correspond exactly with those alleged to have been in Linwood's possession; then Mr. Grant asked Vera:

"When did you obtain these notes, Lady Devereux?"

"Last Thursday. The prisoner gave them to me himself."

"Was anyone else present at the time?"

"No, not then. The next evening, Lord Devereux came, and seemed astonished at my receiving money from Mr. Linwood. He pretended not to believe it, though I showed him the endorsement. The prisoner was, by arrangement, in an inner room, and heard all that was said, and came in. He told Lord Devereux that the notes were his, and that he had given them to me."

"You were, then, going under the name and identity of someone else, were you not?"

"Yes; I had taken the identity of the Princess Glinka, who really died last year. I, Vera Temple, was supposed by the world to be abroad. I wrote to the prisoner from the continent—various places; that is, the letters were posted abroad by my servant."

"Why were you going under a false name?"

"Because I meant to find out the truth about the murder of my father. I knew that I could do that if I got a power over the prisoner, and as the princess I could easily influence him."

"Did you know that the prisoner kept these notes about him?"

"I did not know it; I only supposed he would do so, as he would probably be afraid to have them out of his sight."

"Where they endorsed when he gave them to you?"

"No. I asked him to endorse them, and he did so, after some persuasion."

"Thank you, Lady Devereux; I think that will do."

Mr. Ray intimating that he had no questions to put to the witness, Vera bowed slightly, and stepped down; and, as she did so, there was an attempt at some applause, which was instantly suppressed.

Devereux was the next witness called, and he identified the dagger and coat as his property.

"When was the last time you had the dagger in your possession?" he was asked.

"On the night of the —th of June," he answered; "I showed it to some friends at Mr. Temple's house, then went on to the Regina, and returned to Bruton-street later, still having the coat over my arm; the dagger was in the coat-pocket."

"Well, tell us what happened then."

"I let myself in with the latchkey, and found Mr. Temple in the study. I paid him two thousand pounds in notes——"

"Pardon me a moment—were you in debt to Mr. Temple?"

"Not beyond that sum; that was borrowed to settle a debt of honour with the prisoner."

"You had an acknowledgment, I suppose, from Mr. Temple?"

"Yes, here it is," handing over a receipt; "it is quite informal, as the money was borrowed in a friendly manner."

"All this time, while you were talking with the deceased, where was the dagger?"

"I threw the coat, with the dagger yet in the pocket, on a chair."

"Were you long with the deceased?"

"I should say not more than twenty minutes. I told him that his daughter, Miss Temple, was now my wife, and that I meant to take her away from his roof the next day."

"Was he angry?"

"He was," Devereux answered briefly, but without hesitation.

"And I dare say some high words passed between you?"

"Yes; but I cut the interview very short, and left the house."

"Now, Lord Devereux, on your oath, during any time of this interview was the dagger ever in your hand?"

"Before God—no!" Devereux said, steadily; "it was never in my hands."

"Did you take it up as you left the room?"

"No; I never remembered it or the coat, and left them behind me."

"Did you ever see either coat or dagger again?"

"Never till this moment."

"Did you know that the prisoner had got them?"

"Not of my own knowledge; my wife told me he had."

"Did you notice anything when you went out of the house on the night of the murder?"

"As I was on the step I brushed quickly past the form of a man also on the step; he was coming up as though to enter the house."

"Did you speak to him?"

"No; I was not in a very calm state of mind at the minute, and saw without noticing very particularly."

"Did you not notice enough to recognise who it was?"

"I had a very strong impression that it was the prisoner."

"Will you swear that it was the prisoner?"

"I will not swear it," came the answer, free and steady, as though he had been able to answer without a doubt. "In my own mind I am certain, yet as I was not calm, it is within the bounds of possibility that I might have been mistaken."

"Was that the reason you did not come forward at the inquest?"

"In a great measure—yes; I had no evidence to give that would have brought the murder home to anyone."

"At the time both you and the prisoner were visiting in Bruton Street were you on amicable terms?"

Devereux half smiled.

"We met as men meet in society," he said; "but we were not friends."

"Do you know of any reason there might exist on the prisoner's part for ill-will against yourself?"

"He might have looked upon me as a rival," answered Devereux, and at that, most people, looking at the two men, smiled.

"Was there ever any quarrel between you?"

"Hardly an open quarrel——"

"Did the prisoner ever use any threat towards you?"

"One occasion I remember. On the night I brought the dagger to Bruton Street, the prisoner made some remarks which I resented on behalf of Lady Devereux —who then was known only as Miss Temple; in answer to something I said, he answered, 'I take up your challenge, my lord, but not here, and not now—I can afford to wait.'"

"We now come to a more recent period. Were you present when the prisoner gave the notes to Lady Devereux — then passing as the Princess Glinka?"

"I was not; I came about an hour afterwards, in answer to a note Lady Devereux sent me, and she showed me the notes, the numbers of which were identical with those entered in Mr. Temple's note-book— the notes were endorsed with the prisoner's name."

"Do you know of your own knowledge that the prisoner gave these notes to the Princess Glinka?"

"Inasmuch as he himself asserted that he did so— yes," answered the viscount. "When I affected to be doubtful as to her having received so much money from him, he came from an inner room and said that he had had the honour to accommodate the princess."

This closed all the evidence which the prosecution intended to bring forward at the preliminary examination, and on Linwood being asked if he had anything to say, he merely replied that, with the advice of his counsel, he meant to reserve his defence.

He was then formally committed for trial, and there was a general stir after that, and many of the commoner sort of onlookers pressed forward to stare at an honourable committed for murder.

"It is most dreadful," said Mrs. Mainwaring, shuddering; "I never thought it would be so distressing to be present at such an inquiry. Will he be found guilty do you think, Mr. Crawford?"

"Can't tell, I'm sure," answered that individual; "looks ugly for him if he doesn't bring very strong witnesses. But, come, we must try and get down. I want to catch the *diva* and be the first to offer my congratulations to Lady Devereux."

"Oh yes—do, Jack," whispered Alise, eagerly; "and tell Dev to wait for us. I must see him."

Devereux and his young wife were already surrounded by a group of friends, and it was rather difficult to get at them. But Jack succeeded before long, and Vera turned and gave him her hand with the old bright smile that had made Jack, as well as every other man, her bond-slave, in the Bruton Street days.

"So I'm not the first after all to congratulate you," said he, rather ruefully.

"Am I to be the first to congratulate you?" said the girl archly, and Jack laughed.

"Alise is in a fever to come and talk with you, and gave me strict orders to keep Devereux," he said, irrelevantly.

A slight shade crossed Vera's face.

"But I think," she said, hurriedly, "we must get away."

Even as she spoke a kind and gentle hand was laid on her shoulder, and turning, the girl saw Mrs. Mainwaring by her side.

"I think," the lady said, and her manner touched Vera to the heart and set every doubt at rest, "that you and Devereux must drive home with us to luncheon, unless you have any other wish."

"You are very kind," Vera answered, in a low voice.

And so it was settled, and then they got away to the carriage through the private entrance, and were driven to Eaton Square.

But though the burden might be lightened, it was not yet lifted. Many days, perhaps weeks, must pass before there could be a real rest for the wife who had braved so much for her husband, for who could predict the outcome of the trial? And who could say if the Earl of Evringham would receive a daughter who had been erst the *diva* of a gambling-saloon?

CHAPTER XLIII.

THE EARL IS RECONCILED TO THE DIVA.

"AND to think," cried Alise, as soon as she got Vera into the privacy of her own apartment, where she embraced her friend with warm affection, "to think that you were the Princess Glinka! And I teased Dev to introduce me, and he never would, till I thought her highness must be something dreadful."

"And she was only the *diva* after all," Vera said, a little wistfully, and smoothing back the young girl's hair from her forehead.

"Only," answered Alise, "the dearest and best; you must be, you know, or Devereux wouldn't have cared for you as he does! Do you know," said the young lady, wisely, "I knew a great while ago that he was in love with you, and he wasn't happy then, dear fellow. And oh!" cried she, laughing, "I ought to hate you—you are my rival!"

"Am I?" said Vera, innocently. "My dear, I never thought Jack Crawford cared seriously for me."

"Oh, you naughty girl—you know that's not what I mean; that was Dev's doing," she added, rather irrelevantly. "When Uncle Evringham found that it was no use, and that Devereux wouldn't have me, he no longer actively opposed Jack, and mamma was always inclined to be kind."

"I am very glad of that," said Vera, earnestly; "it is quite settled, then?"

"Well, I suppose so; we must have Uncle Evringham's formal consent, and I suspect when he finds that Devereux is irrevocably out of the running, as Jack would say, he will give in with a good grace."

"Perhaps," returned Vera, a little absently; in truth, however, her heart was fearful as to the reception the head of the family would accord to his son's wife. Would he ever be able to forget that she had been once the *diva* of what was almost a gambling-saloon?

She was not long, however, to be left in suspense, for Devereux determined to lose no time in seeing his father, who was in town, but confined to the house with an attack of the gout. Devereux only feared that he would have seen the evening papers, and be highly incensed that he was allowed to discover first from the newspaper that his son was married.

"My father is still up, Mason?" the viscount asked of the valet.

"Yes, my lord, he is. His lordship has just sent me for the evening paper," returned Mason with the ghost of a well-bred smile on his decorous countenance.

"Which you can give to me, Mason," said Devereux. "I will take it up."

He took the paper from the man as he spoke, and sprang lightly up the stairs.

The earl was seated in his easy-chair, quite alone, when his son entered.

He looked tired and weary, but lifted his head, and brightened up visibly as he saw Devereux instead of his valet, and clasped the hand Devereux laid in his warmly.

"Glad to see you, my dear boy. I am boring myself with this confounded confinement to the house. Haven't even seen the paper yet. Well, what's the news? Is it true that Linwood was arrested on Saturday?"

"Quite true; and was committed to-day. I was in court."

"Good heavens! you don't say so? Is it possible? To think that no one ever suspected him! But how should they?"

"There were at least two people," said Devereux quietly, and, as he spoke, he moved to the mantel-piece, and stood there, leaning one arm lightly on the shelf, "who did something more than suspect Lucius Linwood. I was one."

The earl sat straight up in his chair, and looked at his son.

"What, in heaven's name, had you to do with it?" he said, puzzled and uneasy. "And who was the other?"

"The other was Mr. Temple's daughter," answered Devereux. "If you can give me half-an-hour, father, I will explain all which seems to you extraordinary in this affair. I would not trouble you now, as there is much that may anger you, but that you must see it all in the evening papers; and it is right that you should hear it from my lips."

"Speak, in God's name!" said the earl, with trembling voice. "I never dreamed of your being mixed up with that murder. What have you to tell me? Whether it anger me or not I can bear it."

He listened without interruption while his son told him the circumstances of the murder, and how he, Devereux, had become implicated, so that Linwood could have thrown suspicion on him. He spoke then of Vera's noble self-devotion, and how she had extorted terms from Linwood; how, afterwards, returning to London as the Russian princess, she had once more got Linwood in her power and succeeded in obtaining the notes, the possession of which was so necessary to complete the evidence of his guilt.

"It is an extraordinary romance," said the earl, looking up as Devereux paused for a second. "This girl must be a heroine. The whole thing is tragic, for, of course, she has done all this, not alone for her father's sake, but for yours. Is it not so, Ernest?"

He said the last words softly—it was rare indeed that he used his son's Christian-name—and stretched out his hand; and, deeply touched, Devereux came, and, bending down, clasped his father's hand in his own.

"Father," he said, and his voice was low and unsteady, "forgive me! You know now, if you have not before, why I could not fulfil your hopes—all my love was given to Vera. To no other could I give my hand, and she is of all most worthy to bear an ancient and noble name; and to her I have given my——"

"Have given!" interrupted the earl. "Devereux, I had not thought this of you."

"Bear with me, father. I could not see her alone in that house. I knew I could not get your consent."

"So you thought the best way out of the difficulty was to do altogether without it?" said the earl, rather grimly. "And when my consent is no longer of any value, you tell me you are married—secretly married to a woman who, whatever her title to homage and respect, is scarcely the wife a Devereux should have chosen. I thought you had pride enough at least not to marry out of your class; but I am bitterly disappointed, Devereux."

There was a moment's silence. Devereux had raised himself, and stood motionless, with folded arms and compressed lips.

It cut him to the heart to have to give such pain to his father, and that sorrow for the old man's shattered hopes kept him from making the haughty answer that rose to his lips.

And he had, too, all the while a half conviction that the earl was saying more what he thought he ought to say than speaking the real feelings of his heart.

He did not break the silence, and presently the earl moved a little uneasily and passed his hand over his eyes.

"She must be a very noble woman," he said, half to himself. "She must have suffered much for your sake."

"Suffered!" repeated Devereux, with a kind of suppressed passion in his voice; "God knows it! Such suffering as is only known to a woman who loves and is a wife, and yet is forced to act as though she were still free to be won."

"It is a terrible story," said the earl, shuddering. "The thought of your labouring under such a suspicion —a Devereux!"

"A suspicion," said Devereux, quickly, "from which I could never have freed myself, and from which her act has saved me and so saved the honour of our house. Father, you will—you must take her to your heart;

love her first for my sake—it will not be long ere you love her for her own sweet sake. From her childhood up, she has never known a home, a father's love. She is a daughter of our house now. Nothing can change that. Make her also the welcomed daughter of your heart."

The earl was deeply touched. He found it, in truth, difficult to be as angry as he thought he ought to be with this only son who had certainly disobeyed him, and chosen to marry without the consent of the head of his house, but who pleaded his love with such fire and passion.

He was unconsciously pleased, too, that Devereux had not demanded as justice the recognition of his wife, but had rather appealed to his love for his son; and though Devereux had not done this with the view of working on the softer side of his father's nature, having spoken rather on impulse than of deliberate purpose, the effect was the same.

And Devereux was his only son—the only heir to his ancient name! And he, the earl, was getting old; and after all a man must, within due bounds, marry to please himself, not his father.

"Well, well," he said at last, and took once more his son's hand in his own feebler clasp, "you plead your cause well, my boy; and if a girl is ready to do so much for lover or husband as—as your wife has done, why she must be worthy to be even a Devereux's wife. And if," said the old man, and his voice gave a little as he spoke more softly, "if she will give me a daughter's love, and forget that I have perhaps been proud and hard towards you, she shall receive the honour and the welcome that we have ever given to the women who have allied themselves with us."

"Dear father!" Devereux said, greatly moved.

It was all he could say, and all that was needed. In that moment they were nearer to each other than they had been for years—the misunderstandings wrought on the one hand by the young man's too reckless extravagance, on the other by the father's failure to loosen the reins of authority, seemed tacitly to be arranged, and the restraint that had been felt in their intercourse was broken through.

Though the Earl of Evringham was now only anxious to see his new daughter, as he called her, and to have her installed as Viscountess Devereux, it was too late when Devereux rose to leave him to bring her that night.

The earl, far from well, had been too much excited and over-strained by this interview to be able to bear more just now, and the presentation was therefore deferred until the following day.

He retired to rest happier than he had been for very long. And Lord Devereux went back to Eaton Square and passed the evening very quietly at his aunt's house, with his young wife.

Vera was strangely quiet; there was a half-dreamy look in the dark eyes, a sort of wondering gaze in their depths, as though she only half comprehended where she was, and how she came here, welcomed and loved by these two women, whose lives had lain hitherto so utterly apart from those dangerous paths in which she had walked.

Devereux had whispered softly to her once:

"Darling are you happy?"

And she answered him with that dreamy look and smile that gave him at once such exquisite joy and pain.

"Happy! oh, so happy! too happy! I think it cannot last, Ernest; only—you will not leave me—that I know, but all else is so strange. I have been happy before, in the old days, when you came, but this is rest!"

And then he would softly kiss the sweet lips that so answered him, and whisper a thousand words of love and tenderness, or they sat silent, and only heart spoke unto heart in that wondrous language that only love comprehends.

*   *   *   *   *

The newspapers were, it may well be imagined, full of the extraordinary revelations made in the course of Linwood's examination at Bow Street; the whole of the romantic story was in everybody's mouth, and for days nothing else was talked about. The villa in Brompton acquired an interest which it had not previously enjoyed, and throngs of people came to stare at the garden-gates, for the house was invisible from this point, and it became necessary to station policemen in the grounds in order to prevent people from obtaining ingress in unlawful ways.

Meanwhile the Earl of Evringham, having once given in to the inevitable with regard to his son's marriage, lost no time in according Vera her true position, and the whole family, following the lead of the head, received her with open arms. Vera, however, went out but little in these days; she was weary of society, she said, she wanted only to be quiet till the trial was over.

"People seem to look upon me," she said to Devereux, "as a kind of show; everyone stares at me, and I can't move hand or foot without being observed; and do you know," said she, half laughing, "the other day a reporter called and wanted to 'interview' me. I had half a mind to see him for the fun of the thing, and tell him all sorts of nonsense. But I thought that wouldn't do now! there is quite enough notoriety without that."

Gellert, too, the great St. Bernard, came in for a large share of attention, and when one of the grooms took him out for exercise in the park, he had almost always some story to tell of how a little crowd gathered round the stately animal, and how Gellert, in his dignified way, enjoyed this notoriety much more than his mistress.

Gellert, on first meeting his mistress after the long parting, had been nearly frantic with delight, and for many days had refused to budge from Vera's side, and when Devereux took his wife abroad, Gellert, of course, went with them.

Vera stood sorely in need of rest, for the events of the past year, the perpetual strain under which she had lived, had told upon her somewhat; and so, as the trial of Lucius Linwood was not to come on before the end of March, there was plenty of time to take that rest.

For Lucius Linwood, these long slow weeks preceding the trial were indeed like a foretaste of death.

Outwitted, duped by the woman he had thought to make his tool; going over and over again the scenes in which he had believed she was the most unhappy creature on earth, and that he alone could save her from the hand of his hated rival.

Linwood cursed the day he had ever seen the Princess Glinka; his solicitor warned him that he had very little to hope from any defence he could set up, the evidence on the other side was too strong.

His only chance, he said, was to admit that in a moment of madness he struck the old man with Devereux's dagger, which lay close at hand, and had not intended to kill Temple, and that he then stole the notes in order to make the affair look like a burglary.

"This is the only possible tenable line of defence," he said, "and then I will not deny that your having concealed the dagger and held possession of it as a sort of power over Lord Devereux looks very ugly."

"I'll not admit anything that I have not done," said Linwood doggedly; "the dagger and coat I concealed in order to save that wretched girl's lover. This is the reward I get for it! The notes old Temple gave me in discharge of a debt."

"Have you any proof of that?"

"Worse luck, no!" returned Linwood.

The solicitor shrugged his shoulders.

"Unfortunate indeed," he said as he made a note of the assertion. "I am afraid we shall hardly get a jury to believe that when there is documentary proof that you were deeply in Temple's debt. Of course we shall do the best we can for you. Our greatest chance is to pick holes in the prosecution."

"It's one of the most hopeless cases we've had for long," said he confidentially to the junior counsel afterwards. "We really haven't a leg to stand upon worth calling a leg; but he swears he didn't touch the old man, and we're not bound to know anything that he doesn't tell us."

In the meanwhile as the day of the trial approached, public feeling became more and more excited, and every scrap of gossip that could be obtained with regard to the chief actors in the drama, was eagerly retailed by the " societies "—by society, and filtered down to that large and comprehensive body known as "the general public."

On the day of the trial the court and all its approaches were simply crammed; most who were not provided with the *entree* to the bench had come as early as eight o'clock in the morning, and many who came even a little later were unable to obtain standing-room.

By nine o'clock the approaches to the court were cleared and no one further was permitted to pass in, there being no more room; and the crowd without contented itself, therefore, with looking on while favoured occupants of the bench passed in, and cheering such witnesses as were favoured by the majority.

Inside the court the interest was breathless as the prisoner was brought in. He moved with quiet step and somewhat haughty mien, and as he entered the dock, lifted his eyes and scanned for a moment attentively the faces of judge and jury.

And as the latter were being sworn in, he watched each but challenged none; then his eye went to the bench, and it might have been a row of the Grand Stand at Ascot, that he saw before him—so many well-known faces!

All these were people that he knew and had met in society, with whom he had mixed as equals.

With this man he had played at the *diva's*; with that girl he had danced and flirted, and now they had all come to look on while he went through his death-agony —he, Lucius Linwood, the sometime man of fashion, the assassin.

A cynical smile curled his lip, and then he dropped his eyes and folded his arms, and in answer to the usual question, said steadily, but to fine ears with some effort:

" Not guilty."

No word of Sir Charles Hinton's opening speech escaped him, and his heart grew sick and his hopes sank to the lowest as he saw the array of facts marshalled against him, and knew that every one of these would presently be proved.

One by one the witnesses against him were examined, and not one did the prisoner's counsel venture to cross-examine; it would do more harm than good he had said before.

The court adjourned for luncheon before the case for the defence was opened, and everyone began to talk, of course, and discuss what could possibly be brought that would clear Linwood from the charge against him.

"He has no defence," said the Earl of Evringham to his son; "the verdict is a foregone conclusion."

The defence was indeed no defence at all, but simply a picking holes in the prosecution, challenging the worth of evidence given by Vera, "whose own statements," said Mr. Garstin, "proved her to be a young lady, to say the least of it, utterly unscrupulous as to the means by which she attained her ends, who was capable of using any deception, or saying or doing anything to work the downfall of the unfortunate man who possibly knew too much for the lady's advancement in life. The prisoner is, I affirm, solely the victim of a conspiracy, and the very acts dictated by a generous desire to shield the man who was preferred to him by the woman he loved, have been used as weapons against him. Unfortunately the prisoner stood alone, with nothing but his bare word to assert his innocence, as against the array of witnesses for the prosecution."

Mr. Garstin went on in the same style for some time longer, but everyone felt, as he knew himself—no man better—that he was like a man fighting the air.

He was producing not the slightest effect on either judge or jury, and the fine peroration with which he confidently left the prisoner to that sense of justice which was rightly the praise and the boast of every Englishman, made no impression; it was even felt to be ridiculous.

The summing-up was dead against the prisoner, as indeed, it must be, reviewing the facts, and the judge took occasion strongly to comment on the line of defence. There was no evidence whatever to support the theory more than hinted at for the defence, and nothing whatever to show that Viscountess Devereux had any cause to fear any revelations the prisoner might make concerning her.

There was a breathless silence when the jury, having retired for not more than ten minutes, returned, and the foreman announced that they found the prisoner guilty of the murder of Berkeley Temple.

"No; he had nothing to say, since the law of England shut a man's lips until anything he might say could have no import."

So the last act of that terrible drama was played out; and Lucius Linwood, once the admired of ladies of fashion, welcomed in *salons*, and at least liked, if not loved, by most men, left that felon's dock to die a felon's death, nevermore to come forth to that world which had known him—nevermore to breathe the fresh, free air of heaven, till he stood on the scaffold to expiate his crime by a shameful death.

CHAPTER XLIV.

PEACE AT LAST.

F anyone had ever had the faintest doubt as to the sort of reception which Vera would meet with in the London world when she appeared before it as Viscountess Devereux, all such doubts were speedily set at rest. The earl having once accepted the inevitable with a good grace, found quickly that he had gained a daughter indeed, and he wondered how it were possible that he had once thought so hardly of the beautiful girl who had shrunk from nothing in order to clear her husband's name before the world, and to track the real assassin of her father.

Society would fain have made a lion of Vera, but she shrank from all such homage, and a very short time after the trial of Linwood was over Devereux took her abroad—to "rest and recruit," he said.

"I should like," she said, "to go quite away from everybody, where no one knows me or anything about me."

"But that would be very difficult," said Devereux, smiling.

"Yes," Vera answered rather sombrely; "I am known in so many places."

Devereux laid his hand gently on hers.

"You must not let that be a shadow on your life," he said, and the girl dropped her eyes.

"I will try to forget it," she said.

So Lord Devereux took his young wife abroad, not travelling by any well known tracks, were they were likely to meet faces they knew in Piccadilly and the Park; and in the fresh mountain air, and with such perfect happiness as the girl now had, her elastic spirits soon recovered its tone, and the sort of depression that had followed naturally enough after all the tension of the last year, vanished.

At an out-of-the-way village in the south of Spain came a letter to them from Alise.

"I do not know," she said, "whether you will be most shocked, or perhaps relieved, to hear that the last penalty of the law will not be suffered by Linwood; he was found dead one morning—only a day ago, in fact—in his cell; at first it was thought to be suicide, but examination proved that he had died from heart disease, from which it appeared, he had for some time been suffering; of course he would well have deserved his fate, but somehow I cannot help being glad that it is taken out of our hands. I wonder if you will think the same? To come to our own affairs, Jack is very anxious that our wedding shall take place in the early spring—so is Uncle Evringham; now that he has reconciled himself, thanks to you, to the marriage, he is all anxiety until the knot is really tied; but I have said I will not be married until you come home and can be present; so you see, Vera, how much depends on your return—you must come. Don't you see?"

Vera could not forbear laughing.

"She is such an affectionate little thing," she said; "we must return then for her sake. I am quite myself again, Ernest, I am indeed."

They returned therefore very speedily, and, shortly after, Alise's marriage took place at Evringham, the earl giving her away. Devereux and his young wife were, of course, present, and there were great rejoicings on the estate, for Jack was a general favourite, and Alise was an old pet of the earl's people.

And so Vera, the *diva* of society still, though in a somewhat altered sense, had entered on her new life of almost unclouded happiness; she had trodden those dangerous paths, and had overcome the perils and difficulties with which her steps were set about.

"I feel afraid, Ernest," she said once, wistfully, "I am so perfectly happy! It cannot last, I fear."

And that was the only shadow that ever even passingly disturbed her peace; the old life seemed like a dream that had faded, the new way so full of the sunshine of love and happiness, that they made a kind of dazzling mist between her and those dangerous paths she trod no more.

THE END.

www.ingramcontent.com/pod-product-compliance
Lightning Source LLC
Chambersburg PA
CBHW080820020726
47501CB00009B/2352